He took her hands and drew her to her feet. As his arms slid around her waist, she came unresistingly to rest against him as he continued, his words hypnotically tender. "We haven't been married long, and I know that trust is not built overnight; but I hope you know you can trust me, for I have pledged to protect you until I die."

He kissed her then, a warm, melting kiss that left her breathless and caused her knees to tremble. When he released her, she sat down abruptly on the bed as he turned away and retraced his steps to the door.

"Good night, Katherine. Sleep well."

Katherine blew out her candle and crawled under the quilts, but it was a long time before she slept. . . .

IN THE SHADOW OF ARABELLA

Lois Menzel

FAWCETT CREST • NEW YORK

A Fawcett Crest Book
Published by Ballantine Books
Copyright © 1993 by Lois Menzel

All rights reserved under International and Pan-American Copyright Conventions. Published in the United States of America by Ballantine Books, a division of Random House, Inc., New York, and simultaneously in Canada by Random House of Canada Limited, Toronto.

Library of Congress Catalog Card Number: 93-90089

ISBN 0-449-22228-4

Manufactured in the United States of America

First Edition: July 1993

For my parents, Ruth and Richard

Let me not to the marriage of true minds
Admit impediments; love is not love
Which alters when it alteration finds,
Or bends with the remover to remove.
O, no, it is an ever-fixèd mark
That looks on tempests and is never shaken. . . .

Sonnet 116,
—WILLIAM SHAKESPEARE

Chapter 1

As THE OUTSIDE door slammed with enough force to echo through the house, Katherine Stillwell looked up from the household budget she was struggling to balance. She glanced at the ormolu clock on the mantel and a puzzled frown crossed her face. Only her stepfather was wont to slam doors and he was never home for dinner.

Soon she heard the muffled voice of one of the servants in the hall, then the angry response from Sir Humphrey Corey. "Get out of my way, you babbling idiot! Where is my stepdaughter?"

Now the voice of Martin, the butler, was closer. "I believe she is in the salon, Sir Humphrey, but it is nearly the dinner hour. Would you perhaps like to change?"

Katherine suspected her stepfather had been drinking; spirits evoked his worst behavior. She also realized that Martin was trying to shield her from Sir Humphrey's vile mood. She closed her ledger and rose from the desk as the door opened and her stepparent bowled into the room. His hunting clothes were wrinkled and soiled, his boots scuffed. She was accustomed to Sir Humphrey's outbursts—they occurred often. She was also prepared for his request—it never varied.

"I find myself a bit short, Katy. No doubt you can lend me a fiver till quarter day."

It was less than one month into the quarter, yet Katherine regarded him with a face schooled to display as little emotion as possible. In the past she had made the mistake of allowing her disapproval to show. If she voiced her shock at the price of a new stallion he had purchased, if she expressed her concern over the maintenance cost of his extensive stables, if she showed her disappointment at his inability to manage funds or her disgust of his drinking and gambling habits—all these actions on her part were met with blazing anger on his.

"I have a guinea or two in my reticule upstairs," she replied. "I'll go and fetch them for you."

"No need," he answered. "I'll go myself and perhaps have a glance through the rest of your room. You must keep the ready there, for I know it's not in that desk of yours. I've searched it often enough and never found a penny."

He was already moving away as he uttered these last words, and Katherine followed him numbly down the hall. Surely he hadn't meant what he said; he wouldn't actually search her room. Yet he climbed unsteadily up the main staircase, leaning heavily on the carved oak banister. When he stumbled and a footman quickly reached out a helping hand, Sir Humphrey shook the man off angrily. "Keep your hands off me, you fool!"

When Sir Humphrey arrived at the door of Katherine's bedchamber, the butler, who had followed, intervened again. "Sir Humphrey, perhaps—"

Red-faced and fuming, Sir Humphrey rounded on him. "Say one more word and you will find yourself out the door! I should have dismissed you years ago, but my wife insisted on surrounding herself with servants who don't know their place. Go away! I don't want to see your face again today."

He turned the door latch and stepped into Katherine's room while she laid a restraining hand on the butler's arm and whispered, "Martin, please, I can handle him. I don't know what I would do without you if he sent you away."

"Very well, miss. I'll be downstairs. If you should need me, please ring."

He left reluctantly while Katherine followed her stepfather into the bedchamber. She found him standing in the middle of the room, his bloodshot eyes sweeping over the numerous chests, cupboards, and wardrobes that lined the walls of the chamber. He walked to the nearest chest and pulled open the drawers one after another, spilling their contents onto the floor.

With a shriek of dismay, Katherine hurried to him. "Please, you will find no money among my things." She lifted her reticule from the mirrored dressing table and fumbled inside, producing the money she had promised earlier. "Here, take this. Truly, it is all I have."

He snatched it from her, demanding, "And what of the money you receive each quarter day? I know you don't spend it. Where is it?"

"I don't have it sent to me. My solicitor invests it in the Funds, to build a dowry for Serena."

"A dowry for Serena!" He snorted. "Not for yourself? You're not an antidote, though you are growing a little long in the tooth. If you don't marry soon, none will want you. Which reminds me . . . I spoke to Archie Postlethwaite day before yesterday about your sister. All is arranged there."

"What is arranged?"

"Her betrothal. We agreed on settlements. Even set a date for the wedding—September."

"Wedding!" Katherine exclaimed. "Archie Postlethwaite and Serena? Don't be absurd! He's over fifty while she's not yet eighteen!"

"Just what the chit needs, a man capable of controlling her headstrong ways."

"But what about her Season? You promised you would bring her out next year."

"Why waste the blunt? We have a perfect husband to hand, wealthy and eager to have her to wife."

"But surely she deserves some say in the matter," Katherine persisted. "With a Season she would meet other eligible men. She could choose for herself—"

"Choose for herself? As you did, I suppose. Three Seasons you had! Three opportunities to do the choosing you speak of. And how many paragons did you meet in all those months, at all those fancy parties? None that I ever heard of! You found not one man to your liking. Or if you did, you couldn't bring him up to scratch—which amounts to the same thing.''

"I met Viscount Parnaby," she said quietly, trying to defend herself.

"Parnaby doesn't count; he's a neighbor. And you didn't meet him in London, you met him hunting at Rolly Beecham's. He'll never marry you, girl, mark my words. He may have a list of titles as long as winter, but he's also got a purse as empty as a Gypsy's promise. He has to marry money, and lots of it. Which leaves you sucking hind teat.''

Obviously bored by this discussion of Katherine's marital prospects, Sir Humphrey proceeded to the next furnishing, which happened to be a wardrobe, opened the doors, and began stripping its contents into a heap on the floor.

Katherine's clothes weren't fancy or fashionable, but they were all she had. "You will find nothing there!" she protested. "Why won't you believe me?"

He turned suddenly to face her, and she shrank from the fury in his eyes. "I don't believe you because you are a lying minx just as your mother was. She pinched every penny, denied me the smallest pleasures, harangued me about my horses every day of our married life. I have some of the best heavy hunters in the county, but could she accept that? Could she be proud of it? No. She doled money out to me as if I were a child. Even doled out her favors toward the end, denied me her bed when she thought I'd had too much to drink.''

Katherine's eyes widened in shock at the indelicacy of his remarks.

He noticed her deepening blush. "You didn't know that, did you?"

She moved toward the open door and took the handle in her fingers. Striving for a normal tone, she said, "You must believe me when I tell you that the money I gave you is all I have.''

He crossed toward the door, saying nothing. She suspected he was already eager to convert the guineas he had dropped into his pocket into a pint with his cronies at the local tavern. He would even have enough for an evening of cards if the stakes were low.

She stood her ground as he advanced on her, her hand still on the door holding it wide for him to pass. He stopped inches from her, close enough for her to see black horsehair on the red cloth of his jacket and to detect the unmistakable odor of horse that the morning's hunt had left on his clothing.

Reaching above her shoulder, he gripped the edge of the door, easily pulled it from her hold, and slammed it firmly home. "I have no intention of leaving this room until you give me the money you have hidden here. You have exactly ten seconds to tell me where it is."

The shabby gig rattled noisily over the frozen rutted road. The gray cob that pulled it had been handsome once, but advanced years and a meager diet had eroded his former glory. Sparing no expense when it came to his hunters, Sir Humphrey saw no need to waste money on the horses provided for the use of his stepdaughters.

With his head drooping low and his ears splayed wide, the old gelding paid scant attention to the roadway beneath his hooves. He moved at a tedious walk, but even though Katherine held a buggy whip in one gloved hand, she did not employ it.

Tightly wrapped in a warm cloak, her brown hair carefully tucked into her bonnet, she sat straight on the seat, holding the reins with confidence. On the floorboards near her feet were two small, much-worn packing cases. She had taken her best dresses, but beyond that she had gathered only the necessities, collecting them almost at random from the scattered clothing her stepfather had strewn about the floor. She'd had no time to pack properly, and she knew most of her things would be too shabby for London anyway. She fixed her gaze steadily on the road ahead, her regular, aristocratic features bleak: the dark brows slightly furrowed, the bottom lip occasionally pulled between the teeth, the large gray eyes shining with unshed tears.

Sir Humphrey had been bullying her for years; she was

accustomed to it. But today he had finally gone too far. Her sister was a sweet child, as innocent in Katherine's eyes as she had been the day their mother died, leaving them in Sir Humphrey's care. Serena had only been eleven then, while Katherine had turned seventeen.

Suffering with grief herself, Katherine had found her younger sister devastated by the loss of their cherished parent. The child had wept uncontrollably until she was physically exhausted. Afterward, she had maintained an eerie silence, speaking to no one while awake, subject to horrifying nightmares when she slept.

Through the weeks and months of Serena's indisposition, Katherine had seldom left her side. During that time their relationship had changed from that of sisters to one more profound. Katherine now looked upon her sister with a mother's pride, cherished her with a mother's love. She would defend her now, if necessary, with a mother's sacrifice. She raised her chin with determination and brushed away her tears.

It was already after six and the sky was unusually dark with dense, forbidding clouds streaming overhead. As Katherine raised her face to examine them, she clucked to her horse, then added, "Looks like snow, Blue. Perhaps we should hurry." The gelding swiveled his ears at the sound of her voice but offered no noticeable increase in his gait.

Another mile brought them to the well-maintained drive that gave access to Harrington Manor. This Katherine turned onto, following its curving, raked surface between a double row of chestnut trees, their bare branches buffeted by the high wind.

When she stopped her carriage outside the house, a servant hurried to help her down and take charge of the horse. At her request he placed the cases at the top of a shallow flight of stairs. Just inside the massive front door the familiar face of the Harringtons' butler appeared. "Miss Stillwell," he remarked. "We did not expect to see you again so soon."

"I know, Jamison," she answered. "Is Miss Charity at home? I must speak with her."

6

"Indeed she is, miss. She is in the salon with Lord Harrington. Shall we bring your bags inside?"

These were quickly moved into the hall while the butler accepted Katherine's cloak and bonnet. He passed them into the waiting hands of a footman before he led her down a wide, darkly paneled hallway.

It was a relief to be out of the wind. Katherine patted her hair, tucking in a few strands as she followed Jamison to the salon.

When the butler announced Katherine from the doorway, both Charity Harrington and her father looked up in surprise, for Katherine had visited to say good-bye to them earlier the same day.

"Katherine! We didn't expect to see you again until summer," Charity exclaimed.

As Lord Harrington rose to his feet and extended a hand to greet their visitor, he immediately noticed Katherine's swollen and bloodshot eyes. "Katherine! You've been crying. What's wrong?"

Looking into his concerned face, his hands gripping hers with a loving, compassionate squeeze, Katherine knew it would have been the simplest thing in the world to accept his sympathy, allow the tears to come, indulge her distress. But instead she lifted her chin bravely and forged ahead.

"Oh, my lord, everything's wrong. I've had a horrible row with my stepfather."

Charity Harrington came slowly across the room to join them, her progress impeded by her lame leg. She encouraged her friend to sit on the sofa. "Tell us what happened. Was he drinking again?"

"Yes. He often starts before noon, but he's seldom home for dinner. Today he came home early. He had run out of money and wanted me to give him more. When I told him I had only a little, he wouldn't believe me. He stormed up to my room and began rifling through my things, emptying every drawer. When he found nothing, he took me by the arms and began shaking me, demanding that I tell him where I hide my allowance."

"Damn," Lord Harrington muttered, "this is too much! Stepfather or no, he has no right. I will speak to him, make it clear—"

"Please," Katherine interrupted, "there is no need. I gave him all the money I had, and he finally took himself off to the Red Lion. The instant the door closed behind him I packed my things. Charity, you asked me earlier if I would accompany you to London. If the invitation still stands, I should like to go."

"Of course you're welcome," Charity responded. "My aunt and uncle specifically invited you, knowing how long it's been since you've been to town. But what about Serena?"

Before Katherine could answer, Lord Harrington stood, and Katherine regarded him with suspicion. "You will not confront my stepfather, sir?"

"I should like to, but I will not go against your wishes. To know you are safe with us must content me, at least for the present. I need to speak with the coachman about tomorrow's journey," he added. "I'll leave you two to talk."

When he was gone, Katherine took the opportunity to confide more to her friend. "There's more, Charity, things I couldn't say before your father. You must never tell him."

Charity's pale blue eyes regarded her friend with interest. "What is it?"

"Do you remember I once told you that whenever my stepfather was in his cups, he would grow disgustingly familiar?"

"Yes, I remember. You said it was the way he looked at you and the things he said."

"Yes, well, it has become rather worse in recent months."

"Worse? How?"

"The arguments have become more frequent and more violent. When he shook me today I was truly frightened. I have given him all the money I have, and there are two months before he receives funds again. What will I do the next time he asks? I have nothing more to give him. I never told you this, but when I sent Serena away to that young ladies' seminary in the fall, my reason for insisting she go was that I didn't want her exposed to Sir Humphrey's outbursts. She is only seventeen and so naïve. She was overset for days after she heard us arguing once.''

"But you can't stay in London forever, and Serena's term will end in the spring. What will you do then?''

"I have thought this through carefully and I have a plan, but I will need your help.''

Charity shifted closer to the edge of the sofa, eager to hear how she could aid her friend.

"My stepfather will be angry, but he cannot keep me from leaving. The house is his, but the income that supports us is mine and Serena's.'' Charity's eyes widened, but she said nothing.

"When my mother died,'' Katherine continued, "her property—much of it inherited from my father—was settled in equal parts on Serena and me. As Serena's guardian my stepfather still controls her half, most of which he spends on his horses soon after it arrives. Control of mine came to me when I turned twenty-one. I have been saving much of it the past several years and I believe I have enough. I am going to London with only one purpose—to find a husband.''

Charity regarded her friend in some amusement for a moment and then suddenly sobered. "You're serious!''

"Absolutely serious.''

"But I have no intention of doing the Season,'' Charity retorted. "I hate London. You know that. Mama is forcing me to go.''

"Well, you will do me a great favor if you will attend functions with me.''

"But, Katy, what about Viscount Parnaby? Have you given up hope that things might work out for you?''

"I still love James. I hope to see him when I'm in town. When he understands my situation, surely he will help me.'' She paused a moment, then continued grimly. "Sir Humphrey says James will never marry me, that he must marry an heiress.''

"What if Sir Humphrey is right?''

"Then I shall be forced to look elsewhere. I've been considering the matter and I believe I should be able to find someone respectable who is willing to marry me. My family is good, if you discount my stepfather, and I have some money—"

"But what if you can't find anyone? You had three Seasons—"

"And I had offers, too, you'll remember. I'll just have to be less choosy, that's all."

"I can't believe I'm hearing you say this!" Charity exclaimed. "You who have always said that if you cannot marry for love, you would prefer not to marry at all."

"That was before Sir Humphrey arranged a marriage between Serena and Archibald Postlethwaite."

"He did what? That's ludicrous! I mean, I knew Archie was interested, he even dangled after me once, but he's too old for Serena!"

"Sir Humphrey doesn't think so. He told me today that all is settled. They even chose a date in the fall."

"Katy, you can't allow that child to marry such an old man. She would be wretched."

"I know. I also realize that I cannot remain in my present situation, never knowing what Sir Humphrey may do next. Of the limited options available to me, I choose marriage. With a husband I will have a home of my own, free of my stepfather's control, and a safe place to take Serena. For I swear to you, Charity, she will never marry Archie Postlethwaite or any other man she doesn't choose for herself."

Chapter 2

LORD AND LADY Brent and their youngest daughter gathered in the green salon of their town house in Berkeley Square to await the arrival of their young relative from Lincolnshire. The *Gazette* absorbed Lord Brent, while his wife busied herself with a piece of fine embroidery. Eighteen-year-old Marie, an attractive brunette with soft brown eyes and a small, upturned nose, eagerly paged through the latest issue of her favorite fashion magazine.

Sophia Brent was a kindhearted matron who had managed to retain her youthful figure through the births of seven children. Her husband, Marcus, having raised five daughters, had achieved a level of female tolerance unknown to many of his sex. He had grown accustomed to the atmosphere created by a house full of people. He always enjoyed the visits of his niece and had been pleased to hear that she was coming for an extended stay.

The journey had exhausted Katherine and Charity. As their coach finally approached the outskirts of London, Charity said sleepily, "Thank goodness, we're almost there."

"It has been a long day," Katherine agreed.

In order to arrive in town early enough to avoid inconveniencing their host and hostess, they had left the inn where they spent their one night on the road at a very early hour. Twelve hours in the jolting coach with only one short stop for a meal at midday had left them tired and hungry. Charity's maid, Molly, slept peacefully in the corner and the young ladies marveled at her ability to do so. The coach was well-

11

sprung, but the roadway had become rougher as they progressed into the town, yet the bouncing and bumping had not awakened her.

"I had forgotten how noisy the city is," Katherine commented, as carriages clattered by and people shouted to one another along the streets.

"And how it smells!" Charity added. "There is always so much smoke."

"As the weather warms, there will be less." Katherine studied her friend's frowning face. "Charity, we are going to have a wonderful time, I promise you. Your mother was right; you *have* been rusticating too long. When was the last time you shopped in London or went to the theater? You used to love the theater."

Charity responded with little enthusiasm. "I do love it. But you know how I hate hobbling about city streets, Katy. I feel as if everyone is watching me."

"If they are, it is only because you are so lovely."

"Oh, Katy."

"Truly, Charity, I lose all patience with you! So you limp a little! I would be willing to wager that there are at least a dozen plain, well-bred girls in London who would trade places with you in an instant. I envy you myself, you know—your hair, those eyes . . ."

"Katy, you are such a liar! You know you would never willingly trade with me. Only look how you love to ride."

"I have always insisted *you* could ride as well," Katherine said. "It is your father who discourages you. Personally, I think riding is the perfect exercise for you. The horse does all the walking while you sit and relax."

"I am never relaxed on a horse," Charity objected. "They are so big, so unpredictable."

"You feel that way because you are unaccustomed to them," Katherine persisted. "You would soon change your mind if you rode more often."

This conversation was interrupted by their arrival at Brent House. They were warmly welcomed by Lord and Lady Brent, who were delighted that Katherine had decided to accept their invitation after all. When she apologized for giving them no warning, they made little of it, saying the house echoed with empty rooms now that most of their children were married and gone.

The weary travelers were shown upstairs to tidy themselves, and within the hour dinner was served. Sophia Brent's warm good nature, Marie's bright-eyed admiration of her older cousin and her friend, and Marcus Brent's congenial manners did much to restore their spirits. By the time the girls retired to bed soon after dinner, they agreed that coming to London might be an exhilarating experience after all.

The following morning Lady Brent took her young female guests to the morning room, announcing that they had much news to share. Her questions to Charity concerning their trip south were generously interspersed with tales of her four married daughters and her plans for Marie's come-out this year.

Katherine sat with Lord Brent and in no time they were sharing stories of the year's best hunts—horses and hunting being a subject dear to them both.

They had enjoyed perhaps thirty minutes of uninterrupted conversation when the butler opened the door to announce some morning visitors. "The Earl of Rudley, my lady, and Mr. Oliver Seaton."

Any casual observer would have judged that the two gentlemen now entering the room were related. Both were tall and much the same height, and although the earl was dark and his brother fair, there was a strong resemblance between them. Each possessed dark blue eyes under prominent brows and a marked similarity of feature in the lines of the cheek, nose, and chin. Both were immaculately dressed in proper morning attire: tight-fitting cutaway coats of superfine, skin-tight pantaloons molded to muscular legs, and gleaming Hessian boots. It would have been hard to choose which was the elder and in fact only two years separated Edward Seaton, fifth Earl of Rudley, from his brother, Oliver. Both men had served under Lord Brent in the army and had remained good friends in peacetime.

Lord Brent rose with a smile and stepped forward to greet his visitors. "Ned, and Oliver, too! How good to see you. When did you arrive in town?"

"Only yesterday," the earl replied. "But you are engaged. Perhaps we should call another time."

Lord Brent cut him short. "Nonsense! I should like you to meet my niece and her friend. They arrived last evening from Lincolnshire."

Katherine looked up in surprise when the visitors were announced. She recognized the earl immediately, for they had met the previous year at a hunt ball in Leicestershire. She glanced quickly at Charity and found her friend blushing slightly, but beautiful as always, even after two grueling days of travel. Charity's bright golden hair was gathered in a knot on the crown of her head, leaving two luxuriant curls to fall over her shoulder. Soft wisps had escaped to frame her delicate face, while her striking blue eyes sparkled as she smiled at the gentlemen. She was breathtaking, and Oliver Seaton was startled into staring, as were most men when they first met her. He recovered himself quickly, however, and stepped forward to be introduced by Lady Brent.

As the earl took Katherine's hand in his, she said, "We have met before, Lord Rudley, but you may not recall."

"On the contrary, Miss Stillwell, I remember the meeting well. You, Miss Harrington, and, I believe, her parents were the guests of Lord Beecham. It was one of the best hunts of the season."

"Indeed it was, my lord." She smiled and nodded as he moved on to greet Charity. Katherine was not surprised that the earl remembered them, for Charity's was not a face to be quickly forgotten.

Rudley and his brother stayed twenty minutes only, then, amid protests, rose to leave.

"If you are planning to stay in town for the Season, we are sure to meet again," Mr. Seaton said. He stood beside Charity's chair, his own fair head bent over hers and a pleasant smile on his handsome face.

"My aunt is planning a musical evening late next week," the earl added. "Perhaps you would all join us?"

Lady Brent beamed upon him, accepting his invitation graciously, but after the gentlemen had departed Charity was moved to object. "Are you sure you should have accepted such an invitation for me, Aunt Sophia? The earl's party is certain to be very grand, and I had not intended—"

"I know what you intended," Lady Brent interjected. "Each time you come to visit it is the same. You buy a few tawdry dresses; you go to the lending library; you visit those dusty museums. Well, this time things will be different! Marie's come-out will be at ton parties and balls, and where we go you girls shall go as well."

"I'm hardly a girl, Aunt Sophia," Charity objected. "I will be six and twenty in the fall."

Lady Brent continued as if Charity had not spoken. "Your father has agreed to stand the nonsense, and we shall begin our shopping this very morning. There seems to be an overabundance of silly, empty-headed females on the town this year. It will be refreshing for everyone to have two older, more sensible young ladies to converse with. As for your infirmity, Charity, I will not listen to any nonsense. The Marquess of Strickland's eldest daughter is coming out this Season. She is blind in one eye, and no one thinks a thing of it. We will go to Rudley's party, and we will all enjoy ourselves."

Since no one seemed inclined to dispute this startling decree, Charity said innocuously, "They seem to be pleasant gentlemen, Lord Rudley and his brother."

"You will seldom find two finer, my dears," her aunt agreed. "Both quite devastatingly handsome, both with position and fortune. Oliver, of course, has not Rudley's wealth or title, but I believe that their father, the fourth earl, provided generously for all his children."

"My friend Sally Drayon calls them the 'eligible widowers,'" Marie put in.

"Which is no reason for you to do so, miss," her father replied dampeningly. "They have both lost their wives, it is true, but I find it most unfortunate for men so young to have their lives disrupted by tragedy.''

Seeing that Charity's and Katherine's interests had been captured, Lady Brent continued, ''Oliver lost his wife—it must be more than six years ago—in childbed. They had been married only a few years. She was a fair, gentle thing, seeming not at all frail. It surprised everyone when she had trouble with the birth, and she lived only a few hours after the child was born. The babe was quite strong and healthy, however, and I hear he is the image of his mother.''

''And Lord Rudley's wife?'' Charity asked.

''Ah, the lovely Lady Arabella,'' Lady Brent went on. ''She contracted some malady three or four years ago. I don't believe the doctors ever knew exactly what it was. She and Rudley also had a child, a daughter born early in the marriage. She must be nine or ten years old by now, for Rudley was quite young when he wed. I have wondered why they never had other children. I should have thought Rudley would have wanted sons.''

''He is a young man, Sophy, and can easily marry again,'' her husband remarked. ''But even if he don't choose to, there is no lack of heirs to the title. There is Oliver and his young son Nicholas, as well as Rudley's youngest brother John and his sons.''

''As to Rudley's marrying again,'' Lady Brent countered, ''he certainly has shown no inclination to do so, though I have lost count of the matchmaking mamas who have cherished hopes in that direction.''

''What about Lady Milicent Battle, Mama?'' Marie asked.

''Yes,'' Lady Brent mused, ''I was beginning to wonder about her. He has escorted her several evenings lately, and I saw him driving her in the park. She's a beauty, no question, but her tongue is too sharp for my taste. Even so, he does not act like a man who is eager to settle down. Why, only last week Beatrice Weatherby was telling me that she saw him with yet another of those actresses—'' She stopped suddenly in some confusion when her husband cleared his throat noisily.

Into the rather awkward silence that followed this interruption Katherine interjected a question. "Does Lord Rudley's daughter live in London?"

Pleased to be back on a safe subject, Lady Brent answered readily. "No, my dear, Rudley's daughter and Oliver's young son both live at his lordship's country home in Hampshire. I must agree that the country is the only place to raise children, even if they must be separated from their parents for long periods of time. Although, I must say, most parents see more of their offspring than do either the earl or his brother. Both gentlemen reside at Rudley House and live much of the year in town."

At this point she interrupted herself. "Oh, dear, just look at the time! I promised Beatrice Weatherby we would call on her this morning, and we must not delay our visit to the shops. We have little enough time before your first party." Rising from her chair, she lost no time in sweeping her daughter and houseguests from the room.

Lord Brent watched them out of sight, then settled back into his chair and opened the *Times*. He was certain that with three young ladies in the house it promised to be an interesting and busy Season.

In an imposing mansion in Cavendish Square, the Earl of Rudley lounged in his favorite armchair, a glass of brandy in his hand. His feet toasted near the hearth where a lively fire crackled.

During dinner he had endured a full twenty minutes of his brother's superlatives concerning the person of Miss Charity Harrington. They agreed that it had been many years since such a beauty had descended upon the London scene. More than a few mamas with plain daughters would find their precious ones looking plainer still once Miss Harrington had entered the room.

Oliver had eventually gone on to his club, but Rudley declined to accompany him, preferring, he said, to spend the evening reading. And, indeed, he intended to do so, but the volume he had chosen lay unopened on the table beside him.

It would have surprised Katherine considerably had she known it was she, and not Charity, whom Lord Rudley most remembered from their meeting last winter in Leicestershire. Even now, as he stared into the fire, he could see the great bay horse she had ridden taking each jump of a difficult course with the heart of a giant.

It was not unusual to see such a fine animal, nor was it unusual to find a woman who rode well. Few women, however, cared to exhibit their skill on an animal as strong and spirited as the one Miss Stillwell rode that day. Her riding was superb. He could still recall the stunning picture she made: her cheeks flushed in the cool air, her eyes dancing with excitement. Later that same day Rudley had asked his host, Lord Beecham, who she was.

"On the bay gelding, you say . . . Oh, you must mean Katy Stillwell. Her father was a particular crony of mine—taken in his prime by the influenza. Katy has been coming here for my hunt since she turned fourteen. No better seat in the North Country in my opinion. She has no decent beast of her own, so I mount her each year on the best I have, and she shows us all the way. Take that bay—loves to jump, jumps anything but hates people. He threw two of my grooms last week; one of them broke his arm. Katy started with the horse Tuesday. It took her only three days to convince him to accept the sidesaddle, and she assured me he was ready to go today. And, by Jove, she was right! He went for her like a lamb, and I've seldom seen a better run."

At the ball that evening Rudley sought an introduction. When he complimented Katherine on her riding, she thanked him, then introduced him to her friends, the Harringtons. Katherine soon joined the dancing with Viscount Parnaby and Rudley moved away.

He found his attention attracted to Miss Stillwell several times during the ball. She spent most of the evening near her dazzling blond friend, who was lame and did not dance.

Miss Stillwell herself was no beauty, her features being more pleasing than handsome. He judged her to be about five foot six, too tall to be modish. Though she was past the first bloom of youth, he admired the way her simple gown flattered an excellent figure. She had an abundance of richly colored chestnut hair, and if her features in general were unremarkable, her eyes were not. They were smoky gray in color, large and widely spaced, and framed by sweeping dark lashes. Deep dimples appeared whenever she smiled, which was often.

Rudley found himself wondering what sort of person she was. Curious, he thought, how one person could observe another indefinitely and be able to discover little. Yet given the opportunity of ten minutes uninterrupted conversation, one could normally gather enough information to form a relatively valid judgment. His casual observation told him only that Miss Stillwell was a graceful dancer and that she had more than a passing interest in young Parnaby. Rudley hadn't asked Katherine to dance that evening, however, and he had left the house party two days later without speaking to her again.

The earl slowly finished his brandy and set the glass aside. If Miss Stillwell and Miss Harrington were to stay in town, he would undoubtedly meet them often. He found himself looking forward to the dinner party at his home the following week. If he was given the opportunity to advance his acquaintance with Miss Stillwell, perhaps he would discover what had brought such soberness to her fine gray eyes, which had once sparkled with humor.

That same evening, while the Earl of Rudley was remembering the first time he met Miss Stillwell, she was sitting at a small writing desk in the handsome bedchamber allotted her by her hostess. She carefully opened the journal she had purchased earlier in the day. On the top of the first page, in neat spidery writing, she inscribed "James Haygarth, Viscount Parnaby." She turned to the next page, running her finger down the crease to make the sheet lie flat. Then, dipping her quill again, she wrote "Mr. Oliver Seaton" at the top of the second page. At the top of the next she hesitated, glancing across the room to the sofa where Charity sat reading.

"What is the Earl of Rudley's given name, Charity, do you remember?"

"I believe my uncle called him Ned."

"Ah, yes. I'm sure you're right." She then entered "Edward Seaton, Earl of Rudley" across the top of the third page. "Well, that makes three."

"Three what?"

"Three prospective husbands."

"You're writing down their names?" Charity asked, crossing the room to look at the journal.

"Not only their names but everything I discover about them."

"That's a big blank page," Charity observed. "Will you fill it?"

"I should be able to. I have several months, and I intend to be observant, listen carefully, and collect all the information I can."

Charity looked doubtful. "I can't help thinking this is not the proper way to go about finding a husband, Katy. It seems so . . . calculating."

"Perhaps—but practical, too. I'm under no illusion that an earl might fancy me for a wife, but he *is* single and therefore eligible. I intend to list all possibilities, however unlikely. If I discover later that a particular candidate either drinks or gambles to excess, I will simply strike him off, for I am determined not to involve myself with any man cast in the same mold as my stepfather."

"I should think not," Charity responded with feeling.

When Charity returned to her book, Katherine made some notes on the pages bearing the names of the Seaton brothers. Then she turned back to the page where she had lovingly written Viscount Parnaby's name. She had once believed she would be his wife, that his name would be hers. But the death of his father the previous year, followed by the discovery that his inheritance had been depleted, made him shy away from a commitment to her. He still insisted he loved her, but he never mentioned marriage. Leaving his page blank, she closed the journal and tucked it away in the bottom drawer of her desk. She didn't need to keep notes on James.

Chapter 3

LADY BRENT KNEW the earl to be as good as his word and was therefore not surprised to receive, the very next day, an invitation to Rudley House the following week. "Dear me," she exclaimed over breakfast, "that gives us only six days to provide you with proper gowns."

"We brought our best gowns with us, Aunt Sophy," Charity offered. "Surely they will do for his lordship's party."

"My dear child," her aunt pronounced emphatically, "this is a party at Rudley House! The invitation mentions a 'small gathering of intimate friends.' That could mean as many as thirty guests, perhaps more. And you may be sure they will be only the cream of London society, for Rudley, you must know, moves in the first circles. If you attend such a gathering in last year's styles, believe me, it will be nothing short of disastrous. You will be stamped dowdies from the moment you set foot within the door!"

The vehemence of Lady Brent's reply convinced the girls that she was determined to rig them out in the latest style. Immediately after breakfast they began their second exhausting shopping expedition. They needed morning dresses and evening gowns, walking dresses and ball gowns, each with shoes or slippers, bonnets, gloves, and wraps to match. They chose fabrics and patterns and were assured by the dressmaker that the gowns they ordered for his lordship's party would be ready in plenty of time. For that evening Charity chose a gown of pale blue crêpe over a slip of white satin, while Katherine settled on India mull-muslin and Brussels lace.

Katherine and Charity did manage to purchase much less than Lady Brent intended. Though Lord Harrington had placed no limit on his daughter's expenditures, Charity was, nevertheless, modest in her purchases. Katherine, in her turn, was conscious of her limited budget and intended to spend each shilling to the best advantage. Elegant but not extravagant, she told herself, quality, not quantity. She must do nothing to endanger her plans.

When Lady Brent urged Charity to order a lavish ball gown, she protested. "Need I go to balls? I have no intention of attending every function to which we are invited."

"I should think not!" her aunt replied, clearly shocked at such a thought. "Once it is seen that you have been guests to the Earl of Rudley, you will receive invitations of every sort. You may rely upon me to choose only the best and most proper ones for you to accept."

"Of course we shall depend upon you, Aunt, to guide us in such matters." Charity spoke meekly, but Katherine knew that she found the situation as amusing and absurd as Katherine did.

To Katherine the London world had always seemed preposterous, quixotic. She had come three times for the Season: when she was eighteen, nineteen, and twenty. She had stayed each time with a maiden aunt of her mother's who had hovered just on the fringes of polite society. Katherine had been invited to a great many social engagements and had enjoyed herself, but as far as her stepfather was concerned, she had been a social failure. She had failed to find a husband—Sir Humphrey's only reason for permitting her to go in the first place. When the old aunt died before Katherine's twenty-first birthday, the visits to London ceased.

Now she had come again, discovering it was still the dramatic change it had been for her the first time she visited. In the country she was often occupied with housekeeping duties, but now the biggest decision of her day was whether to have the blue silk or the French muslin! She found herself in the midst of a society of leisure where people seemed to think of nothing but dressing, dancing, eating, and making polite, jejune conversation. She was distracted by the absurdity of it all but determined not to lose sight of her goal.

The following morning Charity and Katherine set off for Bond Street, where Charity had a fitting scheduled. The day was fair, cool but sunny, so they decided to walk, taking Charity's maid with them.

When the fitting dragged on, Katherine grew restless. "Would you mind if I stepped to the milliner's across the street?" she asked. "I could look for a bonnet to match my blue cloak."

"I don't mind in the least," Charity responded. "How boring for you to sit and wait. Take Molly."

With the unobtrusive maid at her side, Katherine left the dressmaker's shop and carefully made her way across the street. The milliner's had nothing to please her, or at least nothing she felt she could afford. On the street again, she looked in the window of the next shop and was drawn inside. The window exhibited delicate silk fans, skillfully painted in multicolored Eastern florals. Just inside the door a display case held all manner of jewel-encrusted trinkets. There were ladies' snuffboxes set with diamonds; brush and comb sets of finest ivory; jewel boxes in every size and shape carved from fine wood and decorated with jade, rubies, and sapphires. Katherine allowed her eyes to feast on this lavish finery, then resolutely turned away.

As she emerged once more onto the street, she hesitated, wondering if Charity would have finished by now. Glancing across the roadway, she noticed a young man and woman emerge from a jeweler's shop several doors to her right. She had been prepared to cross back to the dressmaker's but now froze where she stood, for the fashionable gentleman across the way was none other than Viscount Parnaby, her beloved James.

Her eyes grew soft at the sight of him. Surely no man was so handsome. He was tall; the young lady on his arm barely reached his shoulder. His shiny beaver sat at a jaunty angle over light brown locks, while his lips offered the lady a tantalizing smile.

Katherine had shifted her gaze to the brunette in a pink pelisse at the viscount's side when a voice near her said, "Good day, Miss Stillwell."

She turned, startled, to gaze up into the face of the Earl of Rudley. She returned his greeting pleasantly but could not resist glancing across the street again.

"You know Lord Parnaby well, I believe," the earl said. It was more a statement than a question.

"Fairly well, yes. He lives near us in Lincolnshire. I first met him several years ago at Lord Beecham's. We both enjoy the hunt."

"Ah, yes. Parnaby does sit a horse to perfection. Are you alone, Miss Stillwell?"

"No," she replied, wishing the earl would take his questions elsewhere and leave her alone. "Miss Harrington is with the *couturière* across the way. I am waiting for her."

Parnaby and the young lady were walking toward a point directly across from Katherine and Rudley. If he looks across now, he will see me, Katherine thought. She willed Parnaby to do so, but he did not. He was speaking earnestly to the young lady, who had her arm tucked through his. She was petite and stylish, Katherine noted, but not particularly handsome. Another woman, with the sober look of a companion, walked a few paces behind the couple.

"Allow me to give you my arm across the roadway," the earl said. "It's slippery from last night's rain."

As Viscount Parnaby and the lady in pink disappeared around a corner, Katherine accepted the earl's offer and soon found herself at the dressmaker's door.

"Thank you, my lord. You are most kind."

"Not at all. I believe Lady Brent accepted my invitation for Friday night. Will you be coming as well?"

"Yes, I plan to be there."

"Then I will see you Friday," he said as he took a step back, bowed slightly, and turned to walk away.

Katherine entered the shop to find that Charity had finished. Charity chatted amiably on the way home, while Katherine listened with half an ear, her mind busy searching for a way whereby she might speak privately with James.

This opportunity presented itself much sooner than she expected, for the next day while Katherine and Charity sat sewing in the morning room the butler announced Viscount Parnaby.

He entered the room with a quick step, his emerald velvet riding coat contrasting sharply with the splendid cascade of white lace at his throat.

Charity spoke first. "Lord Parnaby, how nice to see you again."

He smiled briefly at Katherine, then spoke to Charity. "I just met your uncle, Miss Harrington, at White's. When he said you were in town, I came straightaway. I had no idea you were coming down this year. How delightful! I am told Lady Brent is not at home this morning."

"No, she's not," Katherine replied. "She and Miss Brent have gone out."

"I'm sorry to have missed her. You must give her my regards."

"We will certainly do so," Charity answered.

As the door closed behind the butler, the viscount immediately abandoned his formal speech and behavior and came to Katherine's side, taking both her hands in his. "Why didn't you let me know you were coming?"

"I decided at the last moment. We have been in town only three days."

His next words were softer. "I've missed you. It's been more than a month, do you realize that?"

As Katherine and Parnaby stood close together, still holding hands, Charity spoke. "I think I will play a bit, if you don't mind. I'm growing sadly out of practice." She walked to the pianoforte in the far corner of the room and began to play softly.

Katherine smiled at her friend's discretion as she invited the viscount to be seated near her on the sofa. "Charity is too conscious of the proprieties to leave us alone together, so she has discovered a way to stay in the room and still allow us some privacy," she said.

"She can't even see us from where she is sitting, for the music board blocks her view," he replied as he leaned forward and kissed Katherine gently on the cheek.

She blushed and turned her hands within his, her hopes soaring at his warm greeting. "I came to town for a specific purpose, James, and since we could be interrupted at any moment by Lady Brent, I must speak quickly. My stepfather has become unbearable and I have decided I can no longer live with him."

His brow clouded as he regarded her. "I don't understand. If not with him, where else would you live?"

Her courage failed under his direct gaze and her eyes fell. "I was hoping you might have an idea where I might go."

"Me?" he asked, sounding quite shocked. "Why would I—"

"James," she interrupted, "my situation is grave. We've meant—we mean . . . a great deal to each other." Her voice dropped to an intimate whisper. "We have admitted we love each other. I thought—I mean, couldn't we . . ."

She finally stopped in confusion, almost angry that he was making this so difficult. When he said nothing, she raised her eyes to see a look of shocked dismay distorting his handsome features.

"Katy, I've told you how my father left things. My lands are mortgaged to the point where I am struggling to hold them. I have nothing to offer you."

"There's my income," she argued. "I know it's not much, but we could be together."

He let go her hands and stood suddenly. "We can't live on love, Katy. I know it sounds romantic, but, believe me, it wouldn't be."

"But we wouldn't be paupers. We would have enough—"

"And what about my property, my home?" he asked. "There have been Haygarths in Norfolk for three hundred years. Am I to simply let it go without a fight?"

Into the silence that followed this passionate outburst

Katherine said slowly, "Let me be certain that I understand you. Are you saying I should not expect a proposal from you?"

"Not now," he affirmed. "Perhaps in time, when I have somehow managed to put my affairs in order—"

"Time is something I can no longer offer you, James. I am four and twenty. I have decided I will not go back to Sir Humphrey when the Season ends. If it's in any way possible, I plan to marry this year. I love you, James, but I cannot wait forever for you to put your house in order."

Before Parnaby could respond, the door burst open and Lady Brent entered with Marie in her wake. "My butler said you were here, my lord Parnaby. What a pleasant surprise!"

Lady Helen Manville, youngest sister of the previous Earl of Rudley, resided with her nephews in Cavendish Square and managed Rudley's household in an efficient and unobtrusive manner. Lady Helen had been married in her youth to a dashing naval officer who was lost at sea during his first voyage. Declaring herself to be one who would love only once in her life, she had settled down quietly with her former governess in a cottage near Greenwich. When the present Lord Rudley's wife died in the spring of 1814 and Lady Helen offered to help her nephew with his young daughter, Rudley said she could best serve him by taking over the reins of his residence in London. This, Lady Helen had done with an aptitude that made invitations to her nephew's entertainments among the most sought after in London.

The earl's intimate party included some forty guests, all, as Lady Brent had predicted, from the beau monde. Standing at Rudley's side, his aunt greeted the guests as they ascended the grand staircase.

Among the first to arrive was Rudley's only sister, Margaret, Countess of Finley. She was a charming matron of thirty-two. Her brother Edward was one year her senior, while Oliver was one year her junior. With Oliver she shared a fair complexion, golden hair, and an open, friendly smile; with both brothers she shared intense dark blue eyes. Lady

Margaret had been an instant success at her come-out and had married the Earl of Finley in her second Season. She had two young daughters still in the schoolroom.

The Countess Finley remained standing at her brother's side as her husband passed into the salon. When Lord and Lady Brent's party was announced, Rudley himself introduced Miss Harrington, Miss Stillwell, and Miss Brent to his aunt and sister. As the young ladies moved away, Lady Finley turned to her brother and exclaimed in an undertone, "My dearest Ned, you describe her as a very handsome young woman? She is incomparable!"

"Miss Harrington, you mean?" he asked.

She rapped him with her fan. "Of course I mean Miss Harrington. What a stir she will cause! I suppose the limp is permanent? It's a great pity, of course, but one can hardly spare a thought for it when presented with such a delicate figure, and I don't believe I have ever seen a more perfect face."

Her brother's dark eyes rested on the retreating figure of Miss Harrington as he nodded in agreement. "I believe you will find her manner as pleasing as her appearance. But tell me, Meg, what is your impression of Miss Stillwell?"

"She has not her friend's beauty, certainly, but she seems presentable. She has a fine figure and carries herself well. Her manner didn't strike me as particularly warm; her greeting seemed rather stiff."

"Yes, I agree," her brother said thoughtfully. "But she was not always so."

"You have met her before?" she queried.

"More than a year ago at Rolly Beecham's hunt. She was quite different then, I assure you."

His reminiscent tone caused his sister to look searchingly at him. There was unquestionably a frown on his face as he remembered the Miss Stillwell of that earlier meeting. Lady Finley wished to pursue this conversation but was distracted by the arrival of her youngest brother John and his wife, Fanny.

The Honorable John Seaton, youngest of the late earl's four

children, greeted his aunt and sister briefly and began a hurried apology to his brother.

"Sorry to intrude in this way, Ned. I know we weren't invited tonight. Hope you don't mind."

"My dear John, there is no need to apologize. You and Fanny are always welcome. Believe me, if Aunt Helen and I had thought there was the slightest chance of your accepting, we would surely have issued you an invitation."

It was true that Mr. John Seaton, M.P., was not often to be seen at social functions of this sort, for his seat in the Commons and his growing family kept him well occupied. He was possessed of a sober, scholarly nature and felt that the majority of London's social gatherings were a shameful waste of time.

Rudley guessed that John's presence tonight was due largely to a curiosity about Miss Harrington. Their brother Oliver had shown little interest in any woman since the death of his wife, Lydia, but during the past week he had mentioned Charity Harrington several times—more than enough to make his family take notice. Rudley was certain Fanny had convinced her husband to come tonight in order to make the acquaintance of the incomparable Miss Harrington.

The musicians tuned their instruments as several couples prepared for the first dance. The ladies of Lord Brent's party seated themselves at the far end of the large drawing room, a room well suited for the size of the party and the dancing. Its high walls were painted blue-gray, the wide floorboards so highly polished that they reflected the light of the chandeliers overhead. Tall paneled windows hung with dark coral brocade covered one entire side of the room and opened onto a balcony overlooking the garden below. The sofas and chairs lining the walls were Louis Quinze, delicate and exquisite. Huge vases of fresh-cut flowers in charming arrangements had been placed between each set of windows. The scent of blossoms carried softly through the air; the effect was that of a summer garden brought indoors.

"What a lovely house this is!" Charity exclaimed. "This room is so tastefully decorated."

"I like it very much," Katherine replied. "It is simple and at the same time grand." She turned to Miss Brent and asked quietly, "Who is the beautiful woman with Lord Rudley?"

"Lady Milicent Battle," Marie answered.

"The young woman Lady Brent said Lord Rudley was spending time with? Do you know her?"

"Mm . . . a little. Her father is the Earl of Carstairs. That relates her closely to royalty."

Katherine openly observed Lady Milicent as she stood in conversation with the earl. She was tall and slender, remarkably elegant in a gown of deep-sea blue. Her jewelry consisted only of diamonds but those were in abundant supply. Above the low neckline of her gown a priceless pendant lay against her white breast while a diamond tiara nestled in her high coiffure and diamonds dangled from her earlobes and encircled her slender, shapely wrists. Her face was arresting, for without being classically beautiful she had a presence that was commanding. She had hair as dark and shiny as mahogany and large, widely spaced eyes. High, arched brows were raised at something his lordship said to her, and her sensual mouth curved in a half smile.

"She's . . . unusual," Katherine said, for lack of a better word.

"I know what you mean," Marie responded. "There's something about her . . . a magnetism, an aura. She attracts men by the score but isn't particularly popular among the women. She seldom speaks to me. We don't have much in common."

"I think any woman who is a favorite among the gentlemen tends to be unpopular with her own sex," Charity added. "Jealousy is part of human nature, however despicable."

"Well, I'm not jealous of her," Marie continued, but broke off as their hostess, Lady Helen Manville, approached with a young man at her side who she introduced as Lord Peter Everett. When he asked Katherine if she would care to dance, she hesitated.

"Go on, Katy, enjoy yourself," Charity urged. "Marie will keep me company."

Charity loathed these first moments at a party, when men who did not realize that she could not dance would ask her and she would decline one after another until they ceased to ask. At home everyone understood her infirmity, but here in London she knew it would be difficult at first, and she dreaded it. Two gentlemen, one quite young and one rather older, approached her for the first dance. When she declined both, the younger asked Marie to join him. Lady Brent gave her daughter a nod of consent and Marie went off happily on the young man's arm.

Oliver Seaton did not make an appearance until the end of the second set, an example of tardiness that won him a disapproving glance from his aunt. He offered her one of his most disarming smiles, then moved into the drawing room to search out one of his brother's guests.

"Good evening, Miss Harrington."

"Good evening, Mr. Seaton," Charity answered, smiling warmly at a familiar face.

"May I have the honor of the next dance, ma'am?"

"Thank you, sir, but I do not dance," she replied quietly.

Most men would have excused themselves after such a rebuff, but Oliver had intended for the past week to ask the enchanting Miss Harrington to stand up with him. Certainly he could coax this shy country girl onto the floor.

"But, Miss Harrington, I have requested the next piece of music especially for us."

She smiled again. "I am sure you did no such thing, Mr. Seaton, and indeed I must decline your invitation."

"If you don't know the steps, I will be happy to teach you," he offered, taking her hand and drawing her to her feet.

Watching this exchange from across the room, Katherine spoke to her partner for the next set. "Pray excuse me, sir," she apologized, "I see that my friend has need of me." He nodded as she turned away and hurried to Charity's side.

Charity was blushing, clearly confused by the gentleman's

persistence. She turned to Katherine with relief. "Mr. Seaton will not believe me when I say I do not dance."

"I will not take no for an answer," he affirmed.

Katherine could see instantly that the gentleman was being particularly stubborn. Well, then, only a direct blow would put him off. "Miss Harrington is lame, Mr. Seaton, and does not dance. I am sure you will excuse her."

Chapter 4

STARTLED BY KATHERINE'S blunt remark, Charity sat down quickly, staring at her folded hands in confusion.

Katherine's eyes met Oliver's squarely. No man could have been more embarrassed than he was at that moment. She expected him to mumble an apology and retreat. She was therefore considerably astonished, and more than a little impressed by his courage when he hesitated only briefly before addressing Charity again. "May I have the pleasure of your company for the length of the dance, Miss Harrington?"

Good manners allowed only one answer to this question. Therefore, Charity raised her eyes to his as she replied quietly, "Certainly, sir, if it would please you." Eager to end the awkward moment, Charity caught Katherine's eye. "Your partner is waiting for you, Katy."

As Katherine moved away, Oliver Seaton took the chair beside Charity. "You must allow me to apologize, Miss Harrington."

"Please, Mr. Seaton, there is no need."

"On the contrary, ma'am. Any gentleman would have desisted after your first refusal. I am genuinely sorry to have distressed you."

"Truly, Mr. Seaton, you have not . . . it is only . . . my friend was rather direct."

"And rightly so, for I was being an insistent bore!"

"No, sir, indeed you were not. You are in high spirits for a party, and you had no way of knowing. Please, enough has been said. Could we not change the subject?" She glanced up at him, a tentative smile hovering on her lips.

There was a pronounced twinkle in his eyes as he replied, "We are having fine weather for this time of year, are we not, Miss Harrington?"

Later that evening Oliver Seaton danced with Katherine and took the opportunity to apologize for his earlier behavior.

It was quite some time, however, before Lord Rudley invited Katherine to stand up with him. He had been a model host all evening: circulating among his guests, dancing equally with all the ladies, conversing amicably with the gentlemen.

As he swept Katherine into the waltz, she was impressed by the firm grip of his large gloved hand on her smaller one. Her last partner had seemed hesitant to touch her, barely brushing her fingertips as they danced. The earl's hand at her waist was strong and warm, guiding her expertly about the room.

He was dressed immaculately in knee breeches and a black silk evening coat that fitted across his broad shoulders without a wrinkle. Deep in the folds of his elaborately tied cravat a single diamond sparkled. He wore no other jewelry save a heavy gold signet ring bearing what Katherine assumed to be the Seaton family crest. His hair, styled à la Brutus, was very dark, nearly black. Katherine glanced up to meet piercing blue eyes gazing soberly down at her.

At that moment, with her fingers resting lightly on his powerful shoulder and his hand at her waist, she had an odd sensation of *déjà vu*. She felt as if she had lived this moment not only once before but many times. Such a notion was silly, for she had never before danced with the earl. She didn't know him well, had only heard him converse in Lady Brent's morning room for less than twenty minutes, yet he seemed a man of dimension—imperturbable and shrewd. She wondered briefly if he were given to excess.

As she continued to hold his eyes, wondering what he was thinking, he shattered her illusion of his worth by voicing the single most common and unoriginal question she had heard in town.

"How are you enjoying your stay in London, Miss Stillwell?"

She sighed inwardly, prepared to respond with an equally common and unoriginal answer, when suddenly she decided she would not play the game by society's rules. "Would you like to hear the proper, polite answer to your question, my lord, or the truthful one?"

If she thought to startle him with her question, she was only half successful. He cocked his head and raised an eyebrow at her challenging remark. "The truthful one, by all means."

"Well, then," she considered, "I must admit I have always felt rather like a duck out of water here. London society is all frivolity and pleasure-seeking."

"My brother John would agree with you. Yet you certainly have entertainments in the country," he said.

"We have our pleasures and pastimes, Lord Rudley, but we also have a busy, worthwhile, and practical side to our lives, one that seems to be lacking in town. I find all my days here filled with shopping, visiting, and strolling in the park. Our evenings in the weeks to come are replete with parties, routs, and balls. I don't believe there to be a single day in the next two weeks when we are not engaged to attend some function or another."

"The Season doesn't last forever," he replied. "Surely there is time within the year to both visit the metropolis and fulfill our obligations."

"Perhaps you're right," she conceded, "and no doubt we shall enjoy the entertainments. I am only saying it is a one-dimensional sort of life. I, for one, could not pursue it for long."

The dance ended and no more was said on the subject of the carefree London life. Katherine never regretted the instinct that caused her to be honest with Lord Rudley that evening, even though she learned in the weeks to come that his lordship was one of the most active participants in the very life-style she had deprecated.

Later that same evening after Rudley had bid his guests

good night, he thought again of Miss Stillwell's comment. It was true, as his youngest brother John often remarked, that the large majority of London entertainments were self-serving. Rudley rode and boxed to keep his body in condition; he drove and fenced to keep these skills finely honed; he sat in the House of Lords to do his part, as his father and grandfather had done, to give and receive views on the present state and future prospects for the well-being of the country. A great deal of the remainder of his time, however, was spent in the pursuit of idle pleasure. Countless balls, endless dinners, hours of meaningless flirtation—Miss Stillwell was correct—much of it could be considered a waste of time.

He recalled the question he had put to her earlier: "How are you enjoying your stay in London?" He had been making polite, simplistic, inane conversation for so long that he did it now without thinking. He was conditioned to thoughtless chatter and he was honest enough to admit that it served quite well for most of his acquaintance. He felt very much as if Miss Stillwell had plucked the rug from beneath his complacent society manners. Before he retired to bed that night he decided never to put another question to her that might be considered the slightest bit trite.

Katherine twirled round the room in the capable arms of Lord Peter Everett, her aquamarine gown skimming softly over the polished floor. Tall, shy, and clever, his lordship had been humming along with the orchestra, pointing out their shortcomings to his partner.

"The brilliant composer who penned this music never expected it to be hacked about by louts like these."

"I have always been impressed by people who can play the violin, even poorly," Katherine replied. "It seems an incomprehensible instrument to me."

"The instrument may require skill," he said, "but one would suppose that having conquered the instrument, the musician could at least manage to count to three. It is, after all, all that is demanded in a waltz."

Katherine finished the dance with a smile on her face, for

Lord Peter was always a congenial partner. She was claimed for the following set by Arthur Witford. Following Lord Witford's name on her card was Viscount Parnaby's. He had approached her moments after she arrived at the evening's festivities and insisted that she allow him a waltz.

Now, as she sat at the edge of the room chatting with Charity, she wondered if he intended to collect her or if he would allow her to sit the dance out. She glanced about casually. Most of the couples had already taken the floor, waiting for the music to recommence.

Suddenly he was there, bowing over her hand and drawing her to the edge of the dance floor. When he spoke to her earlier, he had been all smiles. Now his face held a stern expression.

"What has gotten into you, Katy? In all the years I have known you, I have never seen you behave like this."

Taken aback by this seeming attack, she countered with, "Behave like what?"

"All this dancing and smiling. You've danced twice with Witford and at least twice with Everett. Every time I look you're with a different man."

"They asked me to dance, James. I have always loved to dance."

"Yes, but not each dance, and not with every man who asked. You would often sit out a dance with Charity. I can remember when you were more particular—"

"I don't see what concern this is of yours," she interrupted.

He held her a little away and looked down at her. "You were serious the other day, weren't you? When you said you were determined to marry?"

"Do you think I would be likely to jest about such a matter? Of course I was serious."

"I'm starting to believe you are. It's unfortunate that we were interrupted by Lady Brent, for there was more I needed to tell you. I want you to wait for me, Katy. I love you, and I will not lose you now."

These last words were whispered so softly and with such

passion that she felt again the same thrill she had known when she first realized he cared for her . . . when he first held her . . . when he first kissed her.

"If you truly love me," he continued, "you will wait for me, wait until I can offer you the kind of situation you deserve."

"The other day you said we couldn't live on love, James. If love is not strong enough to see us through your present difficulties, what makes you think it strong enough to see us through this waiting period you seek? How long would we need to wait? Can you tell me that?"

"Two years, three at the most."

She was shaking her head before he even finished speaking. "If it were only myself I had to worry about, maybe I could wait that long. But I'm not the only one that matters anymore. Sir Humphrey plans to marry Serena to a very old man in September, and I have sworn I won't let it happen."

"Perhaps I could speak to him," he suggested, "convince him that such a marriage is not in her best interest."

"You know my stepfather," Katherine replied. "Once he has decided something, he never changes his mind. But I promise you: I intend to see that that marriage never takes place."

Before going to sleep that evening, Katherine added some comments to the growing list of names in her journal. She now had eleven men entered on the pages as matrimonial possibilities. She scanned the names with approval. It seemed there were more available men than she had at first suspected. Most on her list were congenial; several were wealthy; all could give her the secure home she needed in order to rescue her sister from Sir Humphrey's unfeeling plans.

James had been jealous of her popularity tonight, of that she was certain. Katherine did not believe in manipulating men, and she certainly refused to play the teasing games she saw other women employ; yet she realized that if her quest

39

for a husband caused James to be jealous and brought him to his senses, perhaps he would offer for her after all.

She smiled as she thought, What a heavenly moment that would be! James declaring his love, admitting that any hardships they must share would be worth it so long as they could spend the rest of their lives together. They would announce their engagement and Sir Humphrey would see that he was wrong about James. Together she and James would be more than a match for her stepfather. Sir Humphrey would never insist on Serena's marrying a nobody like Archie Postlethwaite once she was the sister-in-law of a viscount. With connections to the Haygarth family, Serena could look much higher than a mere country squire.

With this best-of-all-possible-worlds scenario running through her mind, Katherine tucked her journal away in the desk and blew out her candle. Slipping a hand under her cheek, she drifted off to sleep, dreaming of her future as the Viscountess Parnaby.

Chapter 5

"YOU CANNOT BE serious, Oliver! The lady is lame!" The earl and his brother were enjoying a leisurely repast in the oak-paneled breakfast parlor. Beyond the opened draperies a dense morning fog evaporated from the streets as the sun climbed over the rooftops. Oliver had just suggested they call in Berkeley Square and invite Lord Brent's houseguests to ride with them.

"Miss Stillwell assured me that Miss Harrington does ride, but she insists upon an extremely mild animal. I have found the most docile gelding you can imagine."

"Not in my stable you haven't!"

"No, certainly not. I heard of him yesterday from Hower, and I intend to take Marcus Brent to see him today. He is accustomed to carrying elderly ladies and small children; I was assured he has not a single evil or fractious bone in his entire body."

"I hope Marcus does not intend an equally docile mount for Miss Stillwell," Rudley interjected, "for, I can assure you, she is a bruising rider." He considered for a moment and then continued, "Tell him to put her on Karma—*there* is a horse to suit her skill."

"Very well," Oliver said, "she shall have Karma if Marcus agrees." He regarded his brother thoughtfully for a moment before he added, "She interests you, doesn't she?"

"Who? Miss Stillwell? Why do you think so?"

"Something you said the other day about how changed she was from your previous meeting. And you danced with Milicent only once the other night—that's a deviation from the norm for you. Also, after your dance with Miss Stillwell, I addressed no less than two comments to you that you never heard. Your mind was elsewhere. I assumed it was on her.''

"Your powers of deduction are uncanny," Rudley returned. "You should offer your services to Bow Street."

"No. My powers only work well on you, and you're not likely to be on their list of dangerous criminals."

"Nevertheless," Rudley insisted, "my thoughts may as well be written on my forehead, you read them as easily."

"Milicent will not be best pleased if you transfer your affections to another," Oliver warned.

"Let's not get the cart before the horse, dear brother. A passing interest is a far cry from affection. Besides, I have made no promises to Milicent."

"You have done enough to make the tabbies sit up and take notice," Oliver persisted. "Lady Carstairs has been walking about lately with a perpetually smug look on her face, much like a cat at the cream bowl. It is clear that she, at least, expects an announcement soon."

"Lady Carstairs's expectations are not a matter of great import to me."

"You will remember I warned you about Milicent. Spending time with her is rather like playing with a poisonous snake—provocative and stimulating, but deadly dangerous."

Never during his acquaintance with Lady Milicent had Rudley considered her as a possible mate. Even though she was an enchanting, enticing creature with many good attributes, she had two outstanding qualities that he knew would cause disharmony between them: she was exceedingly proud and she was excessively self-centered. She was always on her best behavior with him, yet he was shrewd enough to recognize that life with her would be stressful.

Unlike some of his friends, who viewed marriage as a necessary inconvenience, something to be pushed as far into their future as the pressures of family and society would allow, Rudley had always considered it a desirable state. His parents had shared a long and happy marriage, and his sense of family was strong.

As a young man Rudley had always assumed he would marry and that his life would follow, more or less, the pattern set by his parents. He had entered into his early marriage with the blind enthusiasm of extreme youth, and when that union ended in disaster, he had accepted full responsibility. While not abandoning the idea of marriage, he had resolved to make his next choice with cool deliberation. His first wife he had chosen neither wisely nor well; if he ever married again he was determined to do better.

When Lord Rudley and Mr. Seaton arrived in Berkeley Square two days later, they were informed that her ladyship and Miss Marie were out but Miss Harrington and Miss Stillwell were at home. The purpose of their visit was soon revealed and Charity, not unexpectedly, tried to refuse the invitation. However, with Katherine supporting Oliver in his entreaties, she finally yielded, and the following morning was set for a short excursion to Hyde Park.

The day proved fine, the gelding was everything Oliver had promised, and Charity actually enjoyed herself. Katherine was equally delighted with the bay mare Karma. As Oliver rode beside Charity, reining in his black gelding to match her horse's plodding pace, Rudley and Katherine rode ahead.

She reached forward to run a gloved hand down her mare's sleek neck. "Lord Brent tells me that Karma is only a three year old, my lord. He also said you personally vouched for my ability to handle her."

"You mustn't forget, Miss Stillwell, I have seen you with one of Rolly Beecham's Thoroughbred hunters in hand. Believe me, I have no concern that you will spoil that filly." It was unquestionably a compliment, but before she could respond he continued, "Were you at Beecham's for the hunting this year?"

"Yes. We had a wonderful time. But you weren't there."

"No, I couldn't go. I had personal business that kept me in town."

"You missed some excellent weather and many marvelous runs."

"I don't doubt it. But tell me, did Rolly have some unmanageable horse all picked out for you to gentle for him?"

She turned to regard him. "Why do you ask?"

"I was so impressed with the bay gelding you rode last year that I asked about him. Rolly told me that you were responsible for his fine performance that day."

She smiled, allowing him a glimpse of the easy humor he remembered. "He was being rather unpleasant with the stable lads," she said, "but I was most anxious to try him. He tested the limits of my skill, though. He nearly threw me twice."

"Rolly didn't tell me that."

"I didn't tell him! I was afraid he wouldn't let me hunt Wizard, and I wanted to, desperately. He went splendidly!"

"He certainly did; I won't ever forget him. Nor will I soon forget your riding. I've seldom seen a better seat."

She flushed with pleasure. "Why, thank you, my lord. Coming from such a noted horseman I consider that rare praise, indeed. The horse you rode that day—he was impressive, too. What was his name?"

"Tortuga. He is a steadier horse than your Wizard but not nearly so bold a jumper. He seldom refuses, however, and has wonderful stamina."

"I would be terribly disappointed if I had to miss Lord Beecham's hunt," she continued, "I so look forward to it."

"Do you keep any hunters of your own?" he asked, knowing the answer but not wanting her to know that Beecham had shared such personal details with him.

"No. My parents are both dead. There is only my younger sister and I, and I'm afraid our budget doesn't allow for a stable."

"How old is your sister?"

"Seventeen, almost eighteen. She attends Westleigh Academy in Lincoln."

They suspended their conversation as heavy traffic forced them to ride single file, the earl checking his horse while

Katherine went ahead. Once inside the park they rode abreast again and Katherine was the first to speak.

"I had a hunter of my own once." She half smiled again, remembering. "His name was Jeremy, I can't imagine why. It was the name he had when my father bought him, and we never changed it because he knew it well and answered to it." The tone of her voice changed subtly. "He had to be sold when my father died."

"How long ago was that?"

"More than ten years."

"Ten years! You were very young to have a hunter of your own, surely?"

"I was young, but nevertheless he was all mine," she said proudly. "He was just over sixteen hands. I had to climb a fence to mount him, but we had some grand times together."

Rudley was pleased with the direction their conversation had taken. "Did you live in Lincolnshire as a child?"

"No, my father's home was in Devon, situated in rather indifferent hunting country. But Jeremy and I managed to find some obstacles worthy of us."

"Such as?"

"I really shouldn't tell you. I was out of favor for weeks as a result of the course we chose."

"Now I must know, for you have piqued my interest unfairly."

"Very well, I will tell you, but you must remember I was only eleven at the time and I had a horse that loved to jump. There were a few hedges and fences about the countryside, but the most tempting obstacle in the entire neighborhood was the lovely stone wall surrounding the church cemetery. It was only a short gallop through the woods behind our house and then over the wall we would fly. Once inside there were all those marvelous tombstones, spaced just far enough apart. I went early in the morning when no one was about the church and I was never seen . . . until one unfortunate day."

"What happened?"

"One of the village children had told me how she occasionally avoided going to church by feigning illness. If you knew how boring our minister's sermons were you would understand why it sounded like a marvelous suggestion.

"So one Sunday morning I tried it on my mother and it worked. She tucked me up snugly in bed and went off to morning services with my father. No sooner were they gone than I dressed and ran down to the stables to ride Jeremy. We rode far afield, avoiding the church and all the roads leading to it.

"When it neared time for the service to be over, I turned toward home. I had a few minutes remaining so I decided on a quick gallop through the woods. Before I came too close to the church I started to pull Jeremy up, but he wouldn't stop! He had galloped that way so often and enjoyed it so much that he was determined to finish our regular course. I was not strong enough to hold him, and I was too much of a coward to jump off. Over the wall we sailed and over the tombstones in full view of half the congregation flowing out of the church onto the lawn outside. Jeremy never slackened his pace. He galloped through the cemetery, over the wall again, and home through the woods to the stables.

"The scene when my parents arrived home was as unpleasant as you can imagine. I was forbidden to see or ride Jeremy for a month, and I had to apologize to the minister."

As she finished her story, Rudley laughed aloud, and she continued, "You may well laugh, my lord, but my favorite ride ceased on that day. When I was permitted to ride again, I had to promise to go nowhere near the cemetery and, in fact, never went there again. At least not until my father . . . until the funeral."

His laughter dissipated as he asked gently, "How did he die?"

"It was the influenza. Mama had a miscarriage, and she wasn't strong. She caught it first, then Papa took it while he was nursing her. The servants wouldn't let me go near them. . . . Mama slowly recovered, but I never saw my father alive again. I was angry . . ."

Katherine had been unconsciously gathering the reins and

now Karma tossed her head in protest. The mare bumped the earl's stallion with her hindquarters as Katherine brought her under control again. She quickly apologized. "I'm sorry, my lord, I should pay more attention when I'm on a strange horse."

"You're doing well with her. I'm sorry about your father. I didn't mean to distress you."

"You didn't. It's only that I seldom talk about my parents." She turned to look at him then, wondering why she was talking to *him* about them. He was almost a stranger.

The conversation stalled. In an effort to turn it away from herself, Katherine said, "Lady Brent mentioned that you have a daughter, my lord. How old is she?"

"Pamela turned ten last December."

"Does she ride?"

"She has a pony."

"Does she enjoy horses?"

"I really couldn't say. I have never discussed it with her."

"I see."

Her tone indicated most clearly that she didn't see at all and he felt obliged to add, "I don't see my daughter often, Miss Stillwell. She lives at my country seat in Hampshire." As an uneasy silence fell between them, Rudley realized that although he had been intrigued by Miss Stillwell's disclosures about her personal life, he felt acute discomfort when led to share his.

Katherine remembered Lady Brent saying that Lord Rudley did not seem a fond parent—it appeared her ladyship was correct. Katherine was momentarily at a loss for words. Hoping to return to a safe subject, she admired the earl's horse. "That is a handsome fellow you have there, my lord, and well-mannered, too. He didn't even object when Karma jostled him."

"This is Navigator. He is one of my favorite mounts in town. I make an effort to ride him every day."

Having reestablished an easy topic between them, they continued the ride enjoyably. Katherine rode part of the time beside Charity, but when they were nearly home, Oliver brought his black up beside them. "Have you enjoyed the ride, Miss Harrington?"

"Yes, very much," Charity replied. Her cheeks were flushed from the cool air and Katherine thought she looked more beautiful than ever.

"Will you come out with us again?" he asked. "You must agree your uncle has supplied a wonderfully quiet horse for you."

"He is everything Uncle Marcus promised, and yes, I should like to ride again."

"And you, Miss Stillwell, can I convince you to come?"

Charity laughed. "That will take little effort, sir, for Katy is never happier, I think, than when she is on a horse."

"I shall be delighted, Mr. Seaton," Katherine confirmed.

"It's settled, then. Shall we say Thursday at the same time?"

"We do not wish to monopolize your time, sir," Charity offered.

"Ned and I ride often," he said. "It will be a great pleasure to have amiable company."

Several days each week from that day on, Oliver arrived before breakfast in Berkeley Square, sometimes with the earl as his companion, more often with his friend, Lord Peter Everett. Charity and Katherine rode the same two horses, and Marie sometimes joined them mounted on her own chestnut. Each day she rode, Charity gained confidence. She soon had complete trust in her gelding and turned her attention to learning the finer points of good horsemanship.

Katherine had previously found no opportunity to ride in London. Now, thanks to Oliver Seaton, she rode often and found the exercise exhilarating. She was immeasurably delighted with the mare Lord Brent allowed her to use and pleased to see that Mr. Seaton had taken more than a passing interest in her friend Charity.

Katherine met Lord Rudley nearly every day either at a party or during a morning ride. She enjoyed his company, for she had discovered she could speak her mind on nearly any subject without the least fear that her frankness would be misinterpreted. Sometimes Katherine had the feeling that her remarks unsettled him; at other times she laughed at herself for supposing that anything an inconsequential girl from the country could say on any subject would leave an impression upon the influential and powerful Earl of Rudley.

Katherine finished dressing early for the Marquess of Strickland's ball. She took a few moments to add some notes to her journal, then went to Charity's room. Charity was fidgeting impatiently before the mirror while her maid worked to fasten the intricate arrangement of curls that comprised her coiffure.

"I don't like it," Charity complained. "It's too full on the left, too flat on the right. You'll have to start again." The young maid threw Katherine a frustrated glance as she began to remove hairpins.

"Let me do it," Katherine offered. "I know just how it should be, especially for tonight."

When Charity offered no objection to this proposal, the maid gratefully stepped aside. "I don't think we'll need you further, Molly. You may meet us downstairs with our cloaks."

"Yes, miss. Thank you, miss."

As the door closed quietly and Katherine plied the hairbrush, she asked, "How many times did you make her redo this? It looked fine to me."

"She has no knack with hair, Katy. She could learn much from you."

"Do I detect a note of anxiety in you tonight, my love? Could your annoyance with Molly have anything to do with our escort for the evening?"

Charity regarded herself in the mirror, took a deep breath, then let it out suddenly. "You're right. I'm being a perfect shrew, and I *am* nervous."

"Well, you need not be. Your dress is stunning; you look, as always, radiant. Mr. Seaton will not be disappointed." Katherine twisted a curl expertly about her finger, then fastened it securely with a hairpin. "I have taken him off my list of husband candidates," she offered.

"Who?"

"Mr. Oliver Seaton."

Charity turned so quickly that Katherine dropped the next curl. "Why?"

"It's as clear as the way to the parish church that he admires you."

"He is attentive, it's true. But simply because a man is a gallant escort it does not necessarily follow that he has serious intentions."

"I won't argue with you, Charity, but I know what I know, and in the end we'll see who's right. There, your hair is now perfect, and if you say it is not so, I will know there is no pleasing you tonight."

Two hours later, Katherine's partner returned her to her place at Charity's side. Katherine sat gratefully, arranging her skirt with care. She unfurled her fan in an attempt to cool her dance-flushed face.

She glanced at her friend—calm, pale, eternally composed. "I swear you are glowing, Charity, and have been since the moment Mr. Seaton collected us this evening. You never dance, yet you enjoy yourself at a ball more than anyone I know. How hot it is in here! It feels like an oven."

Marie, who was seated on Katherine's other side, leaned over to speak to both of them. "Have you heard the news? The marquess has just announced his daughter's engagement and you'll never guess who her intended husband is. Your friend, Katherine, Viscount Parnaby!"

For Katherine, the heat in the room suddenly intensified; it became insufferable, unbearable. Lord Rudley, who had walked up to claim Katherine as his partner for the next dance, arrived in time to hear Miss Brent's announcement and to catch Katherine as she slumped in her chair then slid to the floor.

When Katherine came to her senses a few minutes later, she found herself lying upon a sofa in a small salon. The ballroom music continued beyond closed doors. Lady Brent's face swam into view. Charity and Marie were there as well.

Katherine was disconcerted to discover that Lord Rudley was chafing one of her wrists. She pulled her hand away as she asked, "What happened?"

Charity answered her. "You fainted, Katy. It was the heat, no doubt, and perhaps too much exertion on the dance floor."

As memory flooded back, Katherine closed her eyes against the pain. *James has asked another woman to be his wife! A wealthy woman. A woman of no particular beauty, blind in one eye. . . . Sir Humphrey said James would never marry me. Sir Humphrey insisted James would marry money. Sir Humphrey was right.*

Hands were helping Katherine to sit upright. Along with a splitting pain in her head she fought to overcome nausea. "I need to go home," she managed.

"Of course you do, my dear," Lady Brent responded. "Mr. Seaton has gone to call for the carriage. As soon as you feel you can walk—"

Just then Oliver Seaton appeared in the doorway. "I've had the coach come to the side entrance, Miss Stillwell. You need not go out through that great crowd of people."

"How considerate of you, sir," Charity said. "Do you think you can walk as far as the coach, Katy?"

"She need not do so, Miss Harrington," Rudley replied. "I will carry her." With seemingly no effort he collected Katherine in his arms and followed his brother from the room, down a series of halls and corridors and eventually to a street entrance to the marquess's mansion. The rest of the party followed quietly behind.

Katherine's initial impulse to protest was overruled by her weakened condition. She felt childish being carried so but had no strength to resist. She managed to mumble, "I'm sorry, my lord. You must think me foolish."

"I think you are ill. There is no need to apologize." When she began a reply, he said, "Please don't speak. It is not necessary, I assure you."

She said nothing as he placed her carefully inside the coach beside Charity and together they tucked a carriage rug close around her. "Shall I come with you?" he asked.

Charity smiled as she replied, "I'm sure that won't be necessary, Lord Rudley. My aunt and I can help her, and we'll have the footmen if we need them. Thank you. You have been most kind."

Oliver took Charity's hand briefly as he said, "Good night. We will call tomorrow to see how you go on." He slammed the door as the carriage rolled off into the lamp-lit streets.

As Rudley stood at the curb watching the coach disappear around a corner, Oliver asked, "Do you think it was the heat that caused her collapse?"

"Not at all."

"What then?"

"Miss Stillwell has suffered a wound to the heart, and we both know, don't we, how crippling that can be."

"A wound to the heart? How so?"

Rudley turned and slung one arm over his brother's shoulders, turning him back toward the house. "Come, let's make our excuses and go home, then I shall tell you all about it."

Chapter 6

EARLY THE FOLLOWING morning Charity entered Katherine's room without knocking and approached the bed. With the draperies closed the room was dark. She whispered, "Are you awake, Katy?"

Katherine's voice answered from a sofa near the windows. "I'm here, Charity, and I appreciate your concern, but I would rather be alone."

Charity pulled the draw cord and the heavy brocade slid aside, allowing the slanting rays of the sun to penetrate. "You have been alone long enough. We need to talk." She moved to the couch and sat beside Katherine.

"If Marie had known how you feet about Lord Parnaby, she would never have told you in such a way. She did not intend to hurt you."

"I know she didn't, and I don't blame her. What does she think? What does your aunt think?"

"Only that you danced too long and were overcome by the heat. I even added for good measure that you had complained of a slight headache earlier in the evening. I don't think they suspect."

Katherine smiled weakly and patted Charity's hand. "You're a good friend, but you didn't need to lie for me."

"I didn't mind. It was only a tiny white lie, anyway."

"How did I get into the salon?"

"Lord Rudley carried you. He was there just as you slipped from the chair. I barely realized what was happening and he had already caught you."

"Did people stare?"

"There was such a press I don't think many even noticed what was happening. My aunt mumbled something about the heat to those nearby and someone directed us toward the private room."

"I have never fainted in my entire life. It is so humiliating."

"Viscount Parnaby has acted with great dishonor," Charity said.

"Has he? He has done what most men facing bankruptcy would do. He has decided to marry a fortune."

"But, Katy, he should have told you himself. He should never have allowed you to find out in such a way. He owed you that, at least."

"Did he? Did he owe me? I thought about it a good deal during the night. He made no promises to me, and although he did ask me to wait for him, I suppose he has a right to change his mind."

"What do you intend to do now?"

"I intend to do what I started out to do. I shall cross James off my list and continue to court the other candidates." Her voice wavered and her eyes filled with tears. As Charity reached to envelop her friend in a consoling hug, Katherine whispered confidingly into her shoulder, "I love him, Charity, I truly love him."

The Earl of Rudley arrived late to the grand ball held by the Duke of Stowe to launch his youngest daughter into society. The duke's massive mansion in Park Lane was bursting with over three hundred guests. The earl, dressed impeccably in strict evening attire, made his way steadily through the throng, hardly realizing he was looking for Lord Brent's party until he noticed Charity and her aunt a little distance away. When he inquired if Miss Stillwell had accompanied them, he was informed that Katherine was indeed present but that she had gone to dance with Lord Witford. This information did little to please his lordship and a deep frown settled over his handsome face.

Although on the wrong side of forty-five, Arthur Witford

was a moderately wealthy and considerably charming peer. During the past several weeks he had shown an inordinate interest in Katherine. Rudley had never cared for Witford and had recently discovered he cared for him even less when he appeared in company with Miss Stillwell. Yet despite his age and reputation, Witford would be considered a good catch for a modestly dowered woman.

Rudley spent nearly half an hour circulating through the ballroom looking among the dancers for Katherine. He finally saw her coming in from the balcony on the arm of Lord Witford. He realized, almost with a sense of shock, that she must have been with the man the entire time he'd been searching for her.

He moved immediately in their direction, keeping his eyes on the pale blue of Katherine's dress. Her gown was trimmed at the sleeves and hem in velvet ribbon of midnight blue, with the narrow skirt falling from yet another dark blue ribbon caught up under the breast. It was a lovely gown, but Rudley was not in a mood to admire it, for his brain was in sudden and somewhat surprising turmoil. None of his thoughts, however, sounded in his voice or showed in his expression as he greeted them.

"Good evening, Miss Stillwell." With a nod to his lordship he added, "Witford." Returning his gaze to Katherine, he asked, "May I have the honor of this dance, ma'am?"

"Of course, my lord." She inclined her head toward Lord Witford, who nodded in return, then laid her hand on the earl's arm and moved away with him toward the center of the ballroom floor.

They executed the early part of the dance in silence until Katherine remarked, "You are quite late this evening, Lord Rudley."

"Actually, I have been here for some time, but you were, of course, engaged with Witford." His tone was brusque and Katherine looked up in surprise as he added, "Any young lady who truly values her reputation would not spend half an hour in the company of a rake such as Witford."

"Come now, my lord," she objected. "Surely if my reputation can survive an hour of riding in your company, it will withstand thirty minutes of conversation on a rather crowded and well-lighted balcony with Lord Witford."

"*Touché!*" the earl replied as the steps of the dance separated them. When they came together again, Katherine found that Rudley was not ready to quit the subject. "Heed me," he continued. "The man is no fit companion for you."

"I hesitate to disagree with you, my lord," she protested, "but Lord Witford has done nothing improper. Quite the contrary, in fact. He has made me a most 'proper' offer of marriage."

This communication so startled the earl that he missed his step. "The devil he has!"

"Indeed he has, my lord," she insisted, "and for the second time in four days!"

His frown intensified as he asked, "And have you accepted him?" The dance was ending, and now it was Rudley's turn to draw Katherine away. They walked through the hall and he led her down a narrow passageway toward the conservatory. As the crowd around them thinned, he repeated his question impatiently. "Have you accepted him?"

"No, my lord, I have not," she replied testily.

"Will you?"

"I don't know. Perhaps. At first I didn't believe him to be sincere, although he assures me that he is. He is also most persistent."

"I believe I know why," the earl replied. "Witford has buried two wives already and has no sons. No doubt he has perused the eligible young ladies and chosen you as the best brood mare of the lot."

This comment stopped Katherine in her tracks, and she turned disbelieving, angry eyes to him. "You are insulting, Lord Rudley," she said.

"I am truthful, Katherine," he replied, using her Christian name, "and *that* I thought you, of all people, would appreciate. How can you even consider an alliance with a notorious womanizer, a man old enough to be your father? You can't possibly think to find happiness there!''

"My happiness is not the issue here, my lord," she replied tartly. "Rather, it is my opportunity to have position and independence, to be able to provide a proper home for my sister. I would be foolish indeed if I did not at least consider such a chance to establish myself. Ask any of your friends here tonight," she challenged. "You will not find one in ten who would not think me fortunate to receive such an offer."

"I daresay you are right," he agreed ruefully. "But I did not think you the person to accept a man like Witford only because society in general would approve it."

"Nor did I ever think to do so," she agreed, "but I am beginning to change my mind."

"Why?" They had been walking slowly through the narrow aisles of the conservatory. The air was humid and heavy with the combined odor of fragrant blossoms and warm earth.

"I am learning, my lord, that people in society are more realistic than I, and that if I intend to make my way in this world I must learn to accept the facts of life."

"Which are?"

"Which are, that if a woman wishes to find security, she had best put aside all notions of love, destiny, and other such nonsense and make the best bargain she can with whatever assets she has at her disposal."

"Sell yourself to the highest bidder, in fact?"

She met his eyes defiantly. "Yes. Why not? If I cannot have the life of my dreams, I can at least have the security that wealth and position offer." As she finished speaking she dropped her eyes to the handkerchief she had been ruthlessly twisting between her hands. A long silence followed.

Finally Rudley put his hand beneath her chin and lifted her face until her eyes met his once again. He spoke gently. "I cannot bear to think of you wed to Witford. You are much too young to do such a desperate thing."

She trembled at his touch but managed to answer him quite steadily. "I am four and twenty, my lord."

An indulgent smile crossed his face. "You are a babe,"

he insisted. "You deserve a chance to have at least some of your dreams come true."

Confused by the tenderness in his voice, she turned away and without speaking again they retraced their steps to the ballroom.

Nothing is so detrimental to a good night's sleep as a mind that will not be quiet. Katherine lay awake long into the night, her eyes open, staring into the blackness above her, pondering questions that had no answers. More now than at any other time in her life she wished for a confidant, someone who could share her burden. She was stuck with one set of thoughts and feelings—her own—and by themselves they had no depth. She had decisions to make that would affect her future, and she found herself incapable of making them. The weight was too heavy, the answers obscure.

Katherine believed those things she had said to Rudley: that Lord Witford's offer was a flattering one, and that she should take what she could get in terms of security for her future and Serena's. Yet she was not ready to give up her dreams. She didn't wish to marry Lord Witford, but she was determined to end her dependency on Sir Humphrey. The earl was right in saying that Lord Witford was no bargain, but then neither was she. She was not well-connected; she had no particular beauty; her income was modest.

The knowledge that she wasn't likely to receive a better offer had kept Katherine from refusing Lord Witford. But neither had she accepted him. He was becoming impatient, pressuring her for an answer, while she was confused, weighing her options and finding no easy road.

When Rudley had taken her face in his hand and called her a babe, she had denied it, yet that was exactly how she felt. She wanted more than anything to cry like a child, admit that she was confused and alone, and beg him to tell her what she should do. But she had not been able to admit it, and she could not ask for his help. She had to keep her fears and misgivings about the future to herself, just as she had to bear the pain of James's rejection, just as she had kept inside, all these years, the anger she felt when her father had died and her mother soon followed him, leaving her alone.

The following morning Katherine was seated before her dressing table in a close-fitting riding habit of forest green when Charity poked her head in the door. "I saw you disappear with Lord Rudley last night, Katy. Where did you go?"

"He showed me the duke's conservatory," Katherine answered. "It was lovely. There were many blooms, marvelous colors. I'm surprised you noticed us though," she teased. "You seem to have eyes only for Mr. Seaton."

"I do admire him a great deal," Charity admitted, "but I'm not letting myself hope for too much."

There was so much sadness in her voice that Katherine asked, "Can it be that you have fallen in love at last? I couldn't be more happy for you!"

"It may be too soon for joy, Katy. Marie says Mr. Seaton was devoted to his first wife. I don't think he is particularly eager to marry again."

"Then you must see to it that you change his mind," Katherine persisted. "How wonderful it would be if you could marry the man you love! I don't know anyone who ever did that. Even my own parents' marriage was arranged, though my mother admitted that she fell in love with my father afterward."

"Well, whatever the future holds," Charity said practically, "Mr. Seaton and I enjoy being friends. I can't wait to see the expression on Papa's face when he sees that I'm riding. I haven't written to him about it. I intend to surprise him with a demonstration."

As they left the room together, Katherine remembered her conversation with Rudley the previous evening and considered that it might be uncomfortable to meet him this morning. But then, she reasoned, it was quite likely he would not ride with them today.

She was not prepared, therefore, when she and Charity descended the steps some moments later, to find that Oliver was indeed accompanied by his brother. Oliver was, as usual, at Charity's stirrup, so Katherine accepted Rudley's assistance in mounting. They rode through the streets in silence and entered Hyde Park by the Stanhope Gate. There were seldom many people about during these early-morning rides, for late afternoon was the fashionable time to be seen there. Most of the riders taking exercise at this hour were men, either alone or in pairs.

The silence between them was becoming oppressive when the earl finally broke it. "I would like to apologize for my behavior last night," he began. "I should not presume to tell you how to conduct yourself. It is, after all, none of my affair. I was merely surprised to learn that you are so eager to marry."

"I am not particularly *eager*, my lord, but the offer is tempting. I believe I am not unlike most women in wanting a husband, a home, and children. I am no longer a young girl. I cannot expect such opportunities to last forever. I am only here for the Season because the Brents were kind enough to invite me."

"Are you still considering Witford's offer?"

"Yes, my lord, I am."

"Will you then be pleased to consider mine as well?"

"*Yours,* my lord?"

"I would deem it a great honor, Katherine, if you would consent to become my wife."

Nothing he could have said would have shocked her more. She turned to stare at him in utter astonishment and then struggled to find her voice. "You wish to marry *me*, my lord? I can believe you might wish to marry again, but I understood that Lady Milicent Battle was your choice for a bride."

"Indeed? What makes you think that?"

"I have heard several people speak of it."

"Saying precisely what?"

"The usual things: that you make a handsome couple, that you are well suited both in rank and fortune."

"And what do you think, Katherine? Do you think Lady Milicent and I are well suited?"

"I don't know her well, but yes, I suppose I do."

"So, as a friend, you would advise me to offer for her?"

"If you wish to marry again, yes, I suppose I would."

"I'm sorry to hear that my happiness isn't important to you."

"What?" she asked, startled.

"You know as well as I do that Lady Milicent would make me the worst possible wife," he replied bluntly. "She talks incessantly of herself and has more pride than an entire regiment of Hussars."

"Well, if not Lady Milicent," Katherine persisted, "then some other young lady. There must be any number of them, most more attractive than I, some with fortune or rank to match your own."

"You are quick to criticize yourself, Katherine. You do not then consider yourself a suitable bride for me?"

"No, my lord, I do not!" she answered baldly. "I think it would be a very uneven match."

"You have frankly admitted yourself to be lacking in beauty, fortune, and rank," he continued. "Are you willing to give an honest appraisal of your feelings for me as well?"

She answered unhesitatingly. "You surely know that I have a great regard for you, my lord. I consider you my friend, and I admire and respect you, but I am not in love with you."

These things were indeed true, although as Katherine answered she realized she had not been aware of how strong her attachment for Rudley had grown over the past weeks. She did enjoy his company, more than that of any other gentleman of her acquaintance. She never had to guard her tongue with him but could say exactly what she was thinking and be sure of a fair and sensible response. What had initially been admiration for his pleasing manner and address had become a preference for his company from this companionship, trust and affection had quickly sprung. To say she was not in love with him was simply a matter of form. After weeks of brooding over James, she was more than willing to admit that any clear understanding of *that* emotion was beyond her comprehension.

Charity and Oliver had trotted ahead, and the earl saw that

they had stopped to rest. He brought his horse to a standstill, and as Katherine did likewise, he turned to her.

"Katherine, you know I have been married before. Arabella was the daughter of a duke, endowed with a handsome marriage portion. She was young and beautiful, and we were in love. You have cited all these things as desirable in a marriage. My marriage had them all, yet it was not a success. You have said you respect me, that I am your friend. These things, unbelievably, were lacking in my marriage." He paused briefly, then continued, "There is something I should like to tell you about myself before you make any decision concerning my offer. Could we walk for a space?"

"Yes, of course." She tried to keep her voice casual, but the conversation was causing her mind to reel. One part of her brain warned her that she should instantly refuse his offer and decline to hear his confidences, yet another part was intrigued. She hadn't known that his marriage was less than perfect.

He helped her to dismount, then led both horses as they walked on across the damp grass. Just ahead, Charity and Oliver were enjoying their privacy yet taking care to remain properly within sight of their companions.

"What I am about to relate is extremely personal," he began, "and something I have never spoken of to anyone save Oliver. I was eighteen when my father died and I succeeded to the title. I was only twenty-two when I met the Lady Arabella Holt. I fell head over heels. I had never seen such a lovely creature. She was beautiful, witty, and charming beyond belief. We were married as soon as arrangements could be made, but it was a disastrous mistake. Within a few months the marriage was over. The immediate family realized, of course, but for the rest of the world we made some attempt at normalcy."

Katherine knew she shouldn't interrupt but found herself asking, "What happened?"

He looked at her strangely, as though he had momentarily forgotten she was there. "We were totally unsuited. The passion between us soon died, and we found we had little in common. Our tastes in almost all things were dissimilar. We were not friends. We could not communicate, or share even the simplest feelings. And, perhaps most shocking of all, there was little honesty between us.

"The first four years of my marriage were a prison sentence for me. I hated living a lie—a mockery of marriage—but there was no escape. Then, when Oliver's wife Lydia died in 1811, we both joined the army in the Peninsula. We found plenty there to occupy us, but in the autumn of 1813 I was wounded and sent home. Oliver stayed on until the peace was signed the following spring.

"It seemed that during my absence my wife had developed the habit of riding out to meet her lover. One day about six months after my return she was caught in a cloudburst and took cold. The congestion settled in her chest. Other complications led to a fever that the doctors couldn't break. She died three days later without ever once asking to see me or our daughter, Pamela. I will never forget the relief I felt when she was dead."

Katherine halted suddenly and turned to stare at him.

"Yes." He returned her look steadily. "Relief. I could not leave Rudley Court quickly enough. I came to town and have spent most of my time here since. I try not to dwell on the past, but, speaking of it now, I realize that time has done little to heal the pain."

As he paused to take a slow, deep breath, she could think of nothing to say. A short distance ahead Charity and Oliver had begun walking their horses again.

Katherine knew he was waiting for a response and she began hesitantly. "My lord, I must beg you to understand that all this has come as a great shock to me. I never expected to receive an offer from Lord Witford, and now this from you . . ."

"I know I have surprised you. I had not intended to speak so soon. I had hoped we could become better acquainted first. But when you said last night that you were considering Witford's offer, I could wait no longer. Do you remember our conversation the first night we danced together?"

"I remember it quite well, my lord." She blushed, knowing her words that evening had been blatant disapproval of his life-style and that of many of his friends.

"You said you found London society to be frivolous and pleasure-seeking."

"I was perhaps too critical, my lord."

"No. You were not. Your appraisal was accurate. And I, more than most, have been guilty of wasteful, decadent behavior. I made an unfortunate marriage, but it is time that I put it behind me. I have duties and responsibilities to my family and my tenants that have been too long left in the hands of others. Lately I have felt that I would like to live on my estate again. I would be pleased and proud if you would accompany me to Hampshire as my wife."

He stopped walking and, turning to face her, took one of her hands in his. "I am very fond of you, Katherine. We have mutual respect for each other rooted in a strong friendship. We have the beginnings of an honest relationship that cannot help but grow with time." He smiled ruefully. "If you are seriously considering a marriage to Arthur Witford, you would have a much better bargain in me."

Katherine smiled, too, for she had been thinking the same thing herself. "Your offer is tempting, sir."

"Then why do you hesitate?"

"I like you too well, my lord, and I fear to be the cause of making you unhappy again if you find you have made a bad bargain."

He took her other hand and held them both together between his. "I have asked you to marry me, Katherine, because I feel that together we will be able to bring some meaning and purpose to our lives."

"Don't you think, Lord Rudley, that you should take more time to consider? You haven't known me long . . . you know very little about me."

"It may surprise you to learn this," he countered, "but I have given a great deal of consideration to this proposal. I feel that marriage should provide contentment and companionship. I want a wife who is intelligent and informed, industrious and diligent. You have all these qualities and many more admirable ones as well. As you have said, there are many women from whom I may choose, but I know my own mind, and I have chosen you.''

She stood gazing up at him. His eyes were tender and sincere. His hands were warm, his clasp vital, and somehow, in that moment, she felt she could trust his instincts. Perhaps with him she could realize some of those earlier dreams she had cherished. She would have a handsome and attentive husband, a man reputed to be wealthier than she could even imagine. She did not love him, and yet, she reasoned, loving James had brought her no happiness. Perhaps the fondness she and the earl felt for each other would be enough.

Even as she considered accepting him, her thoughts swung back the other way. She knew so little about him. What would his daughter think about such a marriage? She was old enough to have an opinion. And others of his family—perhaps they would object. Finally, and most important, she knew she was not all she seemed to be. She was certain that Rudley would not want her if he knew she was in love with another man. He had told her plainly that there had been little honesty in his first marriage. She could not accept him with such deceit between them.

''My lord,'' she began quietly, ''I cannot accept your flattering proposal.'' Her hands fell from his and she extended one to take the reins he held.

She looked up to meet his eyes as he asked, ''Can you tell me why?''

''There is so much you don't know about me—''

''I am not interested in history,'' he interrupted.

''But I am,'' she insisted. ''And there are other things, things I don't know about you and your family.''

''When you have told me what you think I should know, and when you have learned what you would of me, then will you reconsider my offer?'' he asked.

''Perhaps.''

''And will you promise not to accept Witford meanwhile?''

"Yes, sir, I can safely promise that."

"Good. My brother and Miss Harrington are coming to join us, so I fear your questions must wait. If you are to be at the Martinsons' this evening, perhaps we will find the time to continue this conversation."

When Katherine returned from her ride, she found a letter from her sister Serena awaiting her. Its tone could only be described as frantic.

Westleigh Academy
Lincoln

Dearest Katy,

I am sending this to the address you gave me in London and hoping you will answer immediately, for I am in dire distress! Angela Longstreet has written me that she heard her father tell her mother that he overheard Archibald Postlethwaite boasting at the Red Lion that he had struck a deal with Sir Humphrey for my hand in marriage! I am praying that her ears deceived her or that Mr. Postlethwaite was in his cups, for if this should be the truth, I could not bear it! Can you confirm or deny this rumor? Of all the males of my acquaintance, Archibald Postlethwaite is the most odious. His teeth are rotten and his breath always reeks of garlic. He is also ancient beyond belief. What can Sir Humphrey be thinking? I would sooner die a thousand deaths than be wed to that revolting, repulsive, loathsome man. Please answer soon.

Your loving sister, Rena

Katherine realized that she should have guessed that some word of Sir Humphrey's plans might reach Serena. They lived in a relatively small village where such an arrangement would be startling news. She answered her sister's letter immediately.

Brent House
Berkeley Square
London

Dear Serena,

I am sorry to say that the news Miss Longstreet conveyed to you is indeed genuine. Sir Humphrey and Archie Postlethwaite have come to some such agreement. But please, I beg you, do not let it concern you, for I promise (and you know I have never broken a promise to you) you will *never* marry Archie. I wrote you earlier that I had gone to London with Charity for the Season. I did not mention that I have plans to marry soon myself.

Here Katherine hesitated, wishing she could truthfully say she was engaged to be wed. Instead she wrote:

When I am established, I am convinced Sir Humphrey will relinquish your guardianship to me. If not, I am prepared, with my husband's help, to seek your guardianship through legal means. There is, after all, no blood relation between you and Sir Humphrey. Please trust me to do as I say. I love you dearly and will take care of you always.

Your devoted sister, Katherine

Chapter 7

SOME PEOPLE HAVE minds so quick that they have a retort at their command the moment their companion stops speaking. Others, no less intelligent, need more time to formulate a reply. Katherine belonged to the latter group. She liked to consider her words, at least for a few seconds, before she spoke. But even with an entire afternoon to consider how she would tell Lord Rudley about her stepfather and her involvement with Viscount Parnaby, she had discovered no satisfactory approach. By the time she finished dressing for the evening, she realized she was no more prepared to speak with him than she had been that morning. She was determined to be honest about James, but although she practiced several ways to introduce the topic, she finally decided there was no graceful way to broach such a subject.

Rudley greeted her soon after their party arrived at the Martinsons' soiree. During their first dance together she asked him about his daughter.

"Pamela is one of my responsibilities that I have left too long in the hands of others," he said. "I admit I am not a good parent. I spent little time with the child while my wife was alive, and have spent even less since Arabella's death. My sister misses no opportunity to inform me that Pamela needs a mother, but please don't think my offer puts any obligation upon you in that regard. Oliver's son Nicholas also makes his home at Rudley Court, but both children are provided with worthy and capable persons to care for them. I would not have you think that if we wed, you will become a mother overnight, with all the duties and responsibilities of such a position.''

''Would your daughter object to your marrying again? Do you think she would resent another woman taking her mother's place?''

''I really couldn't say. I'm not certain what sort of memories she has of her mother. In any case, I don't intend to allow a ten-year-old child to dictate my future.''

This comment, along with others the earl had made about his daughter, led Katherine to suspect that all was not right in their relationship. Remembering vividly how her own world had crumbled at the age of thirteen, she sympathized with this child who had, like her, lost a parent. Katherine knew it was hard for some men to show the tenderer emotions, particularly to children. But in Rudley's case she sensed there was something more than that. Did he resent Pamela because she was not the male heir every man wants, or did it have something to do with Pamela's mother and his bitterness over his failed marriage?

Katherine had little time to ponder these questions, for as the earl turned her in the waltz, her eyes alighted on Viscount Parnaby standing not ten feet away. She stumbled, and as Rudley's arm tightened to steady her, she quickly apologized. But he had seen Parnaby as well and said clearly, ''It has become oppressively warm in here, Miss Stillwell. Perhaps a turn on the balcony?''

Katherine followed his lead gratefully as he guided her out of the brightly lit ballroom toward a deserted portion of the dim balcony. As the earl had suspected, Parnaby followed them almost immediately and was the first to speak. ''Miss Stillwell, I must beg a word with you.''

Rudley gazed at the frozen couple before him, from Katherine's face, white with shock, to the viscount's flushed handsome one. Only seconds passed, but it seemed longer before Rudley said, ''Excuse me,'' then turned and walked away.

Parnaby stepped toward Katherine, leaving an arm's length between them. ''Katherine, I'm sorry. I know the news of my engagement must have been a shock. I wanted to tell you myself, but the marquess announced it without warning only minutes after all was settled between us."

His words piled up one after another, but they made no sense to Katherine. During the time that had passed since the announcement of his engagement, she had not taken the time to consider what she would say if she spoke to him. He gestured with his hands and her eyes were drawn to them. As she recalled how he had once held her, she grew angry.

"I don't know why you feel it necessary to speak with me, James. Your actions have shown your wishes plainly."

"I have *not* done as I wished. I have done what I had to do to preserve my family name and my honor—"

"Your honor! Only a few weeks ago you asked me to wait for you, while all along you were planning to ask another woman to be your wife."

"It didn't happen that way. I had no intention of asking for her. It was her father's idea. He offered huge settlements, enough to pay all my debts and restore my lands to the prosperity they once enjoyed. It was the opportunity I had prayed for. You must understand why I had to accept it, why I had no choice."

"I don't see that you had no choice, only that your choice did not include me."

He took an impulsive step closer. "Katherine, I love you, that will never change—"

"Please don't speak of love," she interrupted in a bitter undertone. "You do not understand what love is. Whatever was between us, James, is over. Please don't come near me again."

He suddenly closed the space between them, taking her shoulders in his hands. She recoiled from his touch and moved quickly from the balcony into the lighted ballroom. Rudley had been watching for her and moved to her side. He noted her heightened color and her quickened breath as she said quietly, "I am not well, my lord. I must go home."

A few steps brought them to Lady Brent and Charity. "Miss Stillwell is feeling tired, ma'am," he began, addressing Lady Brent.

"With your permission, my lady," Katherine added, "I should like to go home."

"Well, of course, my dear. My, my, you *are* looking quite pale."

"But, Mama," Marie objected, "we have only just arrived."

"Marie is right," Katherine said. "There is no need for you to accompany me. I do not wish to spoil your evening."

"If you will permit me, Lady Brent," Rudley said unexpectedly, "I would be more than happy to see Miss Stillwell home."

As Katherine opened her mouth to protest, Lady Brent accepted his lordship's offer with a gracious smile. "So kind of you, my lord."

Charity looked her concern. "Shall I come with you?"

"No, please. It's only the headache again."

"You have not fully recovered from your previous episode, my love," Lady Brent said. "You are doing too much—staying out late each night, then riding at the crack of dawn. Have Cook mix you one of her draughts for the headache and go straight to bed. You will feel much more the thing in the morning."

Within a few minutes Katherine and Rudley were seated in his coach, moving toward Berkeley Square. "It was not necessary for you to escort me, Lord Rudley," she said. "It is only a short distance."

"I thought you might like some company. I know you don't have the headache, nor did you suffer from it the evening of the Marquess of Strickland's ball."

"How could you know that?"

"Because I have suspected for some time that you had formed an attachment to Parnaby. It follows, therefore, that his engagement would not please you."

"I warned you this morning in the park that there are things about me you don't know," she said.

He looked at her searchingly as he asked gently, "Do you love him?"

Her eyes flew open. "Love him? Never! I hate him!"

"I have found that sometimes it is hard to distinguish between the two."

She put both hands on his arm closer to her and gripped it tightly, crushing the fine velvet beneath her fingers. "You don't understand."

"Perhaps not. But I assure you I would like to."

She withdrew her hands and folded them tightly in her lap. "Do you remember the night in the conservatory when I said that childish dreams were too far removed from reality to have any worth?"

"Yes, I remember."

"I said it, but I don't think I believed it even then. Somehow I was hoping that a foolish dream I had, unlikely though it seemed, still had a chance to come true. Now I know it never will. In my heart I must have always known."

She turned on the carriage seat to face him. "I am sure you must find my behavior shocking, my lord. To tell you that I would consider your offer when I so recently hoped . . ."

"I appreciate your honesty in telling me this," he replied. "But it has not made me change my mind about wanting you for my wife."

"How can you say that now that you know the truth?"

"The truth is that Parnaby has chosen the road his life will take henceforth, and it is now time for you to do the same. Take whatever time you need to decide but be assured my offer is genuine and will not be withdrawn."

She remained silent as the minutes stretched on, until finally he asked, "What are you thinking now?"

"I was thinking how wonderful it feels to be wanted and how easy it would be to say yes."

"Then do it. Marry me."

"I would be saying yes for all the wrong reasons."

"Which are?"

"Financial security, a home of my own, a confidant, a friend and ally whom I know I can depend on."

"I see nothing wrong with those reasons," he said. "They seem perfectly legitimate to me."

"They are selfish reasons. They benefit only me."

"How can you say so? I would also benefit from a confidant, and from a friend and ally."

"You will think this foolish," she said, "but I am drawn to you because you seem a perfect person to depend upon, and I haven't enjoyed that luxury since I was thirteen. Again, a selfish reason."

"And if I told you I welcomed such dependency? What then?" He reached to take one of her hands between his large warm ones. "Lean on me, Katherine. I'm strong. Marry me."

She met his eyes unflinchingly, her own swimming with unshed tears. "Very well."

"Very well?" His eyes brightened. "Does that mean yes?"

"Yes. It means yes."

"Is there someone I may ask for your hand? An uncle or perhaps a grandparent?"

"No. There is no one."

A smile lit his eyes, and she could not help but respond in kind. He leaned forward then and kissed her lightly, the smile still on his lips.

It could not be said that Lady Finley was pleased when her maid informed her while she was still abed that his lordship, her brother, was belowstairs and wishful to see her on a matter of some importance. Trying to shake off drowsiness, she slipped her arms into the green silk dressing gown the maid held for her and tucked her tumbled yellow curls under a matronly cap before ordering that her brother be shown up to her boudoir. Her ladyship's earlier displeasure was quickly replaced by shock when Rudley's announcement fell upon her unsuspecting ears.

"You plan to marry Katherine Stillwell in six weeks' time!" she exclaimed. "You cannot be serious!"

When a heavy frown from her brother was all she received in response to this outburst, she tried again.

"Have you taken leave of your senses? Katherine Stillwell is practically penniless! Worse than that . . . she's a no-body . . . she's—"

"Enough, Meg!" The earl's voice cut through her protests, and her mouth snapped shut in midsentence. "You are speaking of the woman who is to become my wife. I will caution you, therefore, to guard your tongue." His voice was icy as he continued. "I realize it is rather short notice, but I would appreciate your help with the arrangements."

"Short notice? It's indecently short! It's impossible! You can't book St. George's—"

"We don't need St. George's, Meg. Any church will do."

"Are you telling me you truly intend to marry this woman?"

"Have I not just said so? I have not asked for your blessing or approval, Margaret, only for your assistance."

"Please, Ned, I'm sorry. I don't wish to provoke you, but are you sure you have thought this through carefully? I have seen your interest in Miss Stillwell, but is it really necessary for you to *marry* her?"

He rose irritably to his feet. "I *wish* to marry her, Meg! If you do not intend to give me the aid I seek, I will apply to Sophia Brent. I am certain she will be more than happy—"

"No, Ned, that will not be necessary. I am beginning to believe you are in earnest, and no one knows better than I that once you have made up your mind, there will be no changing it."

Later in the afternoon Oliver Seaton tracked his elder brother down at his club. "I've just spent half an hour with Meg," Oliver said. "She is convinced we need to talk. Do we?"

Rudley put his newspaper aside and motioned his brother into a black hide armchair near his. Muffled voices mingled with the soft rustle of newspaper pages being turned. A pale blue haze of cigar smoke hung in the air.

"Do you agree with her that I'm marrying beneath my station?" Rudley asked.

"Of course not. But I must admit your haste does concern me. Are you certain? You've known her barely two months."

"Let me ask you this, Oliver. How does your relationship stand with Miss Harrington?"

"It prospers. And I think—I hope—that we may have a future together. But I have not spoken, nor will I, for it's much too soon."

"But you see," Rudley countered, "our suits differ in one respect. You have the time you need to court your lady properly. I, on the other hand, had not that opportunity. Miss Stillwell feels she has waited long enough to wed. She hinted that this would most likely be her last opportunity to come to town, and I am convinced she intended to accept an offer before the Season ended. I had hoped to bide my time, but when I learned she was seriously considering another offer, I had no choice but to speak."

"Why had you no choice?"

"Because I felt that if she married someone else, I would suffer a great loss—a painful loss."

"And if you're wrong?"

"Like I was about Arabella? Should I spend the rest of my life alone because I fear making another poor choice?"

"No, I'm not suggesting that. I only wish it weren't happening so quickly."

"I am no longer the callow youth of two and twenty who became infatuated with Arabella. Call it a sixth sense, call it instinct if you like, but I'm telling you, Oliver, this match is right for me."

"Then allow me to be the first to wish you happy."

Rudley accepted his brother's outstretched hand with goodwill and shortly thereafter the two left the club together. As they strolled down the street speaking of other things, Rudley wondered if his brother would have acquiesced so readily if he had told him that his chosen bride was in love with another man.

Katherine contracted a cold that kept her at home for four days. Hence, when the announcement of her engagement appeared in the papers, she was not privileged to hear any of society's initial reaction firsthand. This varied greatly, from those shocked at what they considered the greatest mésalliance of the Season, to those friends of the earl who were pleased and happy for him.

On Katherine's first day out of the house she had a fitting at the dressmaker's. Upon her return she found Rudley awaiting her in the drawing room. He had been reading the paper, but when she entered he cast it aside and stood.

"I have missed you. Are you feeling better?"

"Yes, much better, thank you."

"You look tired. You mustn't do too much too soon."

"I only had a fitting; it wasn't too much. Charity tells me that you had an uncomfortable scene with Lady Milicent."

"*Uncomfortable* is a more temperate word than I would use. She gave me a rare dressing-down."

"Not in public, surely?"

"Not exactly," he said. "Only in front of Oliver. I was not embarrassed for myself, only for her. She sounded much like a small child deprived of a favorite toy. Then, not more than an hour ago, I received the cut direct from her mother in Bond Street. She stopped, looked at me as if I were a slug from the garden, then brushed by without so much as a 'Good day.' "

"I feel rather sorry for Lady Milicent," Katherine said. "You did pay special attention to her; I noticed it myself. It must be disappointing for her to have her hopes crushed."

"What you saw was no more attention than I have shown to any number of women over the past several years. If I offered marriage to every woman I have danced with more than once in an evening and taken up a few times in my curricle, I should have a harem at home!"

She opened her eyes wide in mock reproof. "You are assuming they all would have you, my lord! Such conceit! I had no idea you had such a fatal flaw. Who knows how many more I may discover as I come to know you better?'' At that moment she noticed a handsome arrangement of flowers placed on the table nearby. She moved close, touching one delicate blossom with a fingertip. "If, as I suspect, these are from you, we should add extravagance to the list."

When he didn't answer, she turned to find that his smile had vanished. Her own faded as he said, "I know I have a great many faults. Is this your way of saying that you have doubts about us, Katherine, or doubts about me?''

She was genuinely shocked at the serious turn the conversation had taken. "No! Certainly not," she denied, "I was only teasing you. You're not conceited, not in the least. But you *are* extravagant," she added judiciously.

At her smile he relaxed again and crossed the room to stand before her. "I am relieved to hear it, but I fear you will find this extravagant of me, too." He held a tiny jeweler's case on his open palm.

After staring at it for a moment and then glancing up at him, she opened it carefully and drew in her breath in surprise. Nestled on the dark brown velvet was the most stunning sapphire she had ever seen. It was a perfect stone, surrounded by tiny diamonds. He lifted it from the box as she offered her finger to receive it.

"Miss Harrington told me the size; it should fit." The ring slid snugly over the knuckle and glowed on her hand as if it were lit from within.

She looked from the ring to his face, her pleasure reflected in her eyes. "I don't know what to say. It's breathtaking."

"And extravagant."

She laughed. "Yes, extravagant. But so lovely."

"There are a great many rings in the family collection," he explained, "but I wanted to get a new one, symbolic of our new beginning together. I remember you once said you admired sapphires and this particular one took my fancy. I now consider us officially engaged."

He raised her hand to his lips, and when he released it

she threw both arms about his neck in an impulsive embrace. His arms closed around her back as he held her tightly against his chest and felt her lips brush his cheek. "Thank you," she breathed near his ear. "I will cherish it always."

Having given herself into his embrace, she could do little until he released her. He did so reluctantly, discovering it was pleasant to hold her so, her body molded to his. He realized the hug she had given him was little more than a sisterly embrace; nevertheless, it was the first physical overture she had made to him, and he was pleased by it. It had been spontaneous; it was a beginning.

"I have just spent several hours with my solicitor," Rudley said, "finalizing the marriage settlements. There are several details you and I must discuss."

"I know nothing of such things, my lord," she said as he led her to a sofa and sat beside her.

"I understand, and under normal circumstances I would consult your father or guardian. But since that's impossible, I'm afraid I must impose upon you."

Now is the time to tell him, Katherine thought, tell him everything, let him deal with Sir Humphrey in his own way. But before her lips could form even the first word, Rudley was speaking again, asking her a question.

"Do you own any property that I should be aware of?"

"The house in which we lived in Lincolnshire did not belong to us," she said. "When my mother died her income was divided equally between Serena and me. We receive it quarterly from a solicitor's firm in Exeter. I have some jewelry from my mother but no dowry, nothing to bring to my marriage."

She had begun this discourse looking at him, but as the inadequacies of her fortune were verbalized and she realized anew how uneven a match Rudley had chosen for himself, her gaze fell.

He startled her when he took her chin and lifted her face to his. "I don't require a dowry from you," he said. "If you had one, I would assign it to your sister or perhaps to the daughters you may someday have. Your mother's income you may also keep, to do with as you please. There is something else I should like you to know for your own peace of mind. I have, as part of the settlements, provided a dowry for Serena. It's handsome, but if you wish to discourage fortune hunters you need only say it's modest.''

Providing for Serena had been Katherine's dream for so long that her smile was spontaneous and her sense of gratitude overwhelming. ''How generous you are, sir, and to a girl you have never even met!''

''She's your sister, and that's enough. There is one other matter we must discuss: our honeymoon,'' he continued. ''Where should you like to go? The Continent? Greece?''

Her face immediately clouded. ''I thought you intended to return to Hampshire. Surely you said you wished to do so?''

''Yes, I do. And I would have gone soon if you had refused me, but you have accepted and every bride deserves a honeymoon. Shouldn't you like it?''

''Yes, I should, very much. But you would miss the spring planting if we went now, and you said you were eager to be home for that.''

''True.''

''And I must admit I am curious about my new home and eager to meet Pamela. Besides, you said that spring in Hampshire is more beautiful than anywhere else in England.''

''Also true, but I'm biased. Well, there is a simple enough solution. We shall repair to Rudley Court after the ceremony and postpone the wedding trip to another time, perhaps the winter, when a warmer clime and sunny skies will be most appealing.''

Less than an hour after the earl left Katherine, one of the Brent footmen brought her a letter just arrived with the morning post. She regarded it with interest, for it was directed in the unmistakable hand of her stepfather, Sir Humphrey Corey. She knew he disliked correspondence and, indeed, had heard nothing from him since her precipitate departure several months earlier.

She broke the seal and spread the single sheet.

Briarwood Place
Lincolnshire

Katherine,

No doubt it will surprise you to hear from me, yet I was obliged to write when I heard (one of my acquaintance seeing an announcement in the London paper) of your recent engagement. I must say, girl, that you have shown me to be wrong. I never thought you had it in you to land a fish the weight of Rudley. For all they say his pockets are deep, his manners can't be so grand, for I had no proper request for your hand—neither in person nor through the post. I know you'll say you're of age, but custom would require the man speak with me all the same. In any case, you've done well for yourself and should want for nothing. I, on the other hand, having not your good fortune, find myself short at the moment and would appreciate whatever you could spare me. If you find yourself unable to accommodate me, perhaps I should take the time to come visit your fiancé—a discussion of marriage settlements not being out of the question.

Your stepfather, Sir Humphrey

Katherine folded the sheet with a sigh. She knew Sir Humphrey seldom read more than the sporting news and had hoped he would not learn of her wedding until after it had taken place. She certainly didn't need to read between the lines to understand his thinly veiled threat. She drew a sheet of stationery from Lady Brent's secretaire and folded it, carefully enclosing a twenty-pound note from her reticule.

She could not bear the thought of Rudley asking Sir Humphrey for her hand. The very idea was ludicrous. She tried to imagine Sir Humphrey at her wedding, paying lavish, unwelcome compliments to all the ladies, then regaling them with slightly off-color stories, drinking too much—how he loved free wine—and talking too loudly. She carefully opened the sheet and added another twenty pounds before refolding it and applying the sealing wax. It was little enough to keep Sir Humphrey out of London and far away from her wedding ceremony.

Chapter 8

LADY FINLEY promised her brother she would help with
his wedding plans, but the results of their combined efforts
exceeded even her expectations. No one attending would have
imagined such a fine and well-managed affair had been arranged in a mere forty days. Every detail, from the magnificent flowers to the delectable food, had been seen to
personally by her ladyship. Only the best would do for her
brother's marriage; she accepted nothing less. The number
of guests was small—just over one hundred—and this fact
alone made Lady Finley's job considerably easier. The earl
had insisted on inviting only family and intimate friends. His
first wedding had been one of the major social events of the
Season; he intended for this ceremony to be quite different.

During the weeks preceding the wedding, Rudley was neither unaware nor unappreciative of his sister's efforts on his
behalf. "Katherine told me you called on her yesterday, Meg,
to take her shopping."

"Yes, of course," his sister replied. "I suggested Ma-
dame Boutou to make Katherine's gowns. She will need to
take on extra help to do so much so quickly, but the result, I
assure you, will be unexceptionable."

"I don't doubt it," he agreed. "I am obliged to you for
taking the time to advise her."

"My dear Ned, as much as I care for Sophia Brent, you
cannot think I would allow her to help Katherine choose the
fabric and pattern for a wedding gown! You know I don't
entirely approve of this hasty marriage, but if you *will* be

married now, then your bride must be dressed in the finest London can offer.''

The wedding ceremony itself progressed without incident; Oliver supported his brother as groomsman while Charity attended Katherine. Katherine's fear that someone would connect her with Sir Humphrey was never realized. She had been determined to tell Rudley about her stepfather, but the opportunity never presented itself. In the weeks preceding the wedding she seldom found herself alone with him, and when she, she found she couldn't bring herself to mention Sir Humphrey.

Just two days before the wedding Katherine had received a letter from the headmistress of her sister's school. Miss Styles reported that Serena had taken to her bed with a mild stomach complaint; regretfully, she would be unable to make the trip south. At first disappointed by this turn of events, Katherine decided that perhaps it was for the best. She would have found it difficult to explain to her sister why she had not discussed their stepfather with her future husband.

As Lady Finley had promised, Katherine's gown was stunning. Crêpe over white satin, it was high at the neck with long, full sleeves and buttoned cuffs. The bodice, full skirt, and train were lavishly trimmed with lace and seed pearls. A veil of spider gauze fell from a tiara of diamonds and pearls set skillfully into Katherine's elaborately braided hair.

The earl, always a meticulous dresser, was more splendid than usual and those few who knew him best noticed a subtle light in his eyes that kindled when he first saw his bride and lasted throughout the day.

"He has made an excellent choice, Meg," Oliver said as he joined his sister in a glass of champagne. He watched Rudley and Katherine across the room where they stood speaking with Charity and Lord Everett.

"I hope you may be right, Oliver. If he would only take time to consider. I cannot help but remember the haste of his first marriage and the tragedy—"

Oliver interrupted her. "Katherine is nothing like Arabella. She is a sensible woman, mature. She will make the best possible wife for Ned.''

''Yes, perhaps, but does she love him? And, even more important, can she make him happy?''

''Ned seems to think so. And you and I, dear sister, will pray he is right.''

Several hours later, when the newly married couple had left their guests behind and begun their journey south, Katherine found herself alone with her thoughts for the first time in many days. Her schedule had been so busy, so crammed with preparation that she had simply allowed herself to be swept along. As the spring countryside on the outskirts of London rolled by her window, she took time to reflect on the enormity of what she had done.

In the weeks before the wedding she had no doubts at all. It was only during the service, when she was making her vows, that the reality struck her. She had known Viscount Parnaby for years, had thought for several of those years that she would be his wife. Now, in a few short weeks, she had thrown that dream to the wind and accepted Lord Rudley instead. A sickening doubt overcame her as she realized she had promised the remainder of her life to a man she hadn't known long—didn't know well. She didn't even know him well enough to know if he intended to keep the vows he had made to her. It was, after all, commonplace for married men to have mistresses. Clearly, for many of them, their marriage vows were meaningless.

''You are very quiet,'' Rudley said, interrupting her thoughts. ''Are you tired?''

''No. I was thinking how unprepared I was for the ceremony. I had no idea how solemn . . . how profound it would be to take an oath before God . . . before all those people. It's almost frightening to think how permanent, how final it is.''

''Are you feeling regret that you married me?''

''No. Not regret, more like . . . more like fear.''

''Fear of what?''

"Of the things I don't know—the *many* things I don't know about you."

"Why must these be things to fear?"

"They needn't be, of course," she agreed. "No doubt I'm being silly."

"Not in the least. Don't you know I have the same insecurities you have? None of us can ever be certain that the decisions we make are the proper ones, that the road we choose is best. We do as well as we can and must be satisfied with that."

Emboldened by this confidence, Katherine asked, "Did you truly mean the vows you spoke to me today?" He drew breath to speak, but she continued quickly. "Do you feel that a marriage should be as the church decrees, a union of two, with mutual honor and respect . . . and faithfulness?"

"I meant—literally—every word I spoke to you today," he affirmed. "I believe that the best, the truest marriage, is the one we vowed today to make."

"But your first marriage," she said, "you intended it to last a lifetime."

"Yes, I did. And I was faithful to Arabella until she broke faith with me. She lied to me, deceived me, and in the process destroyed the love I had for her. A marriage must be held sacred by both partners, Katherine; one cannot do it alone."

Succumbing to a fatigue she had earlier denied, Katherine rested her head against Rudley's shoulder. Weary from weeks of preparation and the wedding day itself, she soon slept and woke only when the coach slowed to make the turn onto the drive leading to Rudley Court.

"Where are we, my lord?" she asked.

"We have arrived at Rudley. It has grown dark, but there is nearly a full moon and you can see the lake."

Hearing the warmth in his voice, Katherine knew he was happy to be home and she was relieved. She had feared that the events that had driven him away had given him a permanent dislike of the place.

She looked where he directed. The road skirted the side

of a gently sloping hill; below them to the left was the lake. In the calm night air the smooth surface of the water reflected the moon in a silvery glow. She could see the outline of a bridge ahead, silhouetted against the gray sky.

"The bridge spans the stream that feeds the lake," Rudley said. "When my great-grandfather came into the title, he had the stream dammed to form the lake. He was an avid fisherman and knew no greater joy than having his own well-stocked fishing haven no more than a stone's throw from the door."

The horses' hooves clattered over the bridge, and the house soon appeared on the right. As the coach drew up, the great front doors were thrown open and yellow light streamed out onto the wide stone steps and spilled into the graveled drive.

Not waiting for the footman, Rudley leaped down from the coach, offering Katherine his hand. She stepped down carefully, stiff from the long drive.

"Welcome to Rudley, Katherine," he said quietly. "May you always be happy here."

She smiled warmly at him. "I am sure I shall be, my lord."

"Come then," he said. "My household is eagerly waiting to meet their new mistress."

Indeed, there was a long line of his lordship's retainers awaiting them in the hall. They were greeted first by his secretary, Mr. Kendall, then by his butler, his housekeeper, his daughter's governess, his nephew's nurse, and so on down to the lowliest kitchen maid who blushed as she curtsied to her new mistress.

Unprepared for the size of Rudley's household staff, Katherine was overcome by this welcome, but she hid her surprise well, greeting each of the servants in turn and accepting their congratulations and welcome.

"I was expecting to see Lady Pamela and Master Nicholas," Katherine said when she noticed the children were not present.

Miss Shaw, Lady Pamela's governess, stepped forward. "Excuse me, my lady, Master Nicholas is visiting with his mother's family in Sussex, and Lady Pamela has a bad cold and has stayed in her room. She was most anxious to see you both tonight to welcome you home, but I explained to her that you would perhaps be fatigued after your journey."

Katherine turned to her husband. "I would like to meet Pamela tonight."

"Very well," he said, "we will look in on her as soon as we've changed."

Instructing his butler to have dinner served in one hour, Rudley gave Katherine his arm and together they ascended the massive oak staircase, which rose from the center of the hall and divided into halves, one half serving each wing of the rambling Tudor building. They followed the branch to the right and walked some distance along the corridor.

"The original building ended here," Rudley said. "My grandfather added the part we are now entering. I have always loved this house. I hope you will find it comfortable."

He finally stopped at a door to the left of the passageway. "These are your rooms. The baggage coach preceded us by several hours, so most of your trunks should be unpacked by now. If you need anything you have only to ask the housekeeper, Mrs. Windom."

He opened the door and they entered the large bedchamber together. "These were once my mother's apartments—and later Arabella's," he said. "Arabella had them done in blue, which she felt suited her complexion. I had them redone after her death, and you see them now much as they were in my mother's time. You are, of course, free to change anything you like to suit yourself. If you see any pieces about the house that you admire, simply inform Reeves and he will have them carried here."

They had advanced to the middle of the room and Katherine looked about in admiration. Walls of pale yellow harmonized with window and bed hangings of deep gold. The furnishings were tasteful and elegant. Double doors stood wide to reveal an adjoining sitting room with vases and bowls of red and yellow flowers on every table. "This is a charming room," she said, "and it pleases me just as it is. I begin to think your mother and I would have had a great deal in common.''

When she turned to Rudley, she surprised a troubled frown on his face. Stepping close, he put his hands on her shoulders. ''Katherine, you must know these rooms hold many memories for me—happy ones, and unhappy ones as well.''

For the first time since she had known him, she heard apprehension in his voice and suddenly realized how vulnerable he could be, how easily hurt by those he trusted. Arabella had hurt him in that way, and Katherine knew it had to be difficult for him to be here again . . . remembering.

Instinctively she reached out to lay her hand on his cheek. ''Our future begins today,'' she said. ''The past cannot be forgotten, for it has already become a part of us. But if we keep it in perspective we will manage well enough.''

He covered her hand with his own and, turning his head, gently kissed her fingers. ''I am sure you are right. If you should want me, my apartments are through this door. I'll collect you in thirty minutes. Will that be sufficient time?''

She nodded and smiled as he disappeared through the connecting door. No sooner had the door closed than a young maid appeared with hot water, which she poured into Katherine's basin. As soon as her task was accomplished, she curtsied and introduced herself. ''My name is Bess, m'lady. If you should like to tell me which dress you wish for dinner, I shall fetch it for you.''

''Thank you, Bess. There is a burgundy evening gown with black lace. Did you see it?''

''Yes, m'lady, I did. I'll find it straightaway.''

After she washed, Katherine brushed and rearranged her hair, then changed her gown. She was ready when Rudley returned at the appointed time.

They walked only a short distance down the hall before he stopped at Pamela's apartments. He knocked briefly, and when a quiet voice answered ''Come in,'' he opened the door and swung it wide for Katherine to precede him.

The room was brightly decorated in rose and white. A large four-poster bed hung with dark rose silk stood against the far wall. In it, propped up against half a dozen pillows, was Katherine's stepdaughter. At the sight of her father and his new wife, the child scrambled to the edge of the bed, slid onto the carpet in her bare feet, and dropped a creditable curtsy.

"Katherine, allow me to introduce my daughter, Lady Pamela. Pamela, this is Lady Katherine."

"How do you do, ma'am?" Pamela replied politely, then added shyly, "Welcome home, Papa." She was clearly pleased to see them, but once she had finished her greeting an awkward silence fell. Since Rudley did not seem disposed to bridge the gap, Katherine stepped forward and smiled at her.

"I am delighted to meet you, Lady Pamela, but please do climb back into bed before you take another chill." Pamela glanced self-consciously at her toes and then did as she was bid. Katherine approached the bed. "Do you mind if I sit here?" Pamela shook her head mutely as Katherine helped to tuck in the comforter, then seated herself on the edge of the bed. "Your father and I are sorry to hear you are not feeling well."

She glanced up at the earl, who had advanced with her and stood at the bedside. "Since you couldn't come down to greet us," he added, "we decided to come up to you."

"Miss Shaw wouldn't let me come down, though I wanted to," Pamela said. "It will be wonderful having you home to stay!"

This one artless comment made it clear to Katherine that Pamela regretted her father's absence from her life. Katherine could not conceive of such an arrangement. She had been only three years older than Pamela when her father died; she would remember the pain of his loss all her life. If Katherine, at Pamela's age, had endured months of separation from her father, she would have been instantly into his arms for a hug and a kiss. Yet here were Rudley and his daughter, speaking to each other civilly like two acquaintances meeting casually on the street.

Indeed, by his own admission, Rudley barely knew his

daughter. Katherine suspected it was hard for him to separate the child from the mother, a woman who had been a source of great pain and disillusionment.

Katherine saw at once that Pamela had inherited her father's eyes: deep-set and dark blue. Her hair, however, was pale yellow and hung in thick curls nearly to her waist. She did not think Pamela would ever be the great beauty her mother was said to have been, but she had no doubt the attractive child would grow to be a handsome young lady. Katherine quit Pamela's room with a promise to visit again on the morrow. Pamela, in her turn, promised to rest in order to speed her recovery.

The earl and his new countess retraced their steps to the main house, descended the stairway, and turned toward the dining room. As they crossed the hall, the dark mahogany doors of a drawing room stood wide directly before them. Katherine could not resist stepping inside.

"What a lovely room!" she exclaimed. The room was wainscoted and hung with pale blue figured paper. The far wall embraced a massive fireplace, finely wrought in stone. A cheerful fire burned in the grate, and despite its generous size the room was warm and inviting. Draperies of dark blue velvet provided the dominant color, while the furnishings had obviously been chosen with a discriminating eye. Many were rare and beautiful.

"This was my mother's favorite room," the earl remarked. "She chose the colors and materials used on most of the pieces here." He walked toward the fireplace, drawing Katherine's attention to the large full-length portrait that hung over the mantel. "This was my mother. She was Miss Rosalind Ashley before she married. This portrait was painted in the first year of her marriage. Her family were our neighbors to the west. A distant cousin has inherited Weiring and lives there now."

"She was beautiful," Katherine said simply.

"There were many who thought so, even though her dark coloring is considered more fashionable now than at the time of her debut."

"I see now where you and your brother John inherited your dark hair."

"Yes," he agreed. "And Oliver and Meg are fair, like my father. There is a fine portrait of him hanging in the picture gallery. You must remind me to show it to you."

Katherine's attention was drawn to a petit-point chair standing to one side of the fireplace. It seemed out of place in such an immaculate room, for it was worn and shabby, much in need of repair.

Rudley read her thoughts. "You are thinking that chair could do with some refurbishing. My housekeeper will agree with you, but I will not permit it. The scene depicted there is this house and the lake in the foreground. Every stitch was placed with great skill and care by my mother, who was a notable needlewoman. It is a comfortable chair and often used, so it has become worn, but it is one of a kind and therefore irreplaceable. I think I was younger than Pamela when my mother finished it, which means it is older than you are, Katherine."

Katherine, no mean needlewoman herself, could see that endless hours had been expended on the elaborate design. It showed great attention to detail and perspective; she could easily understand why Rudley would not wish to part with it.

"Well, I cannot speak for you, madam wife," the earl said, "but I am nearly perished with hunger."

"I'm so sorry!" she apologized. "I'm keeping you from your dinner. But there is so much to see!"

"And you shall see it all," he promised. "But not tonight. We will have our dinner and then get some well-deserved sleep. This has been a tiring day for both of us, and I have no doubt you will want to be up with the sun to go riding."

"Could we?" Katherine asked excitedly.

He smiled. "Certainly. If you wish it. I prefer to ride before breakfast, but if you intend to do a great deal of sight-seeing, we had best eat first."

They ate their dinner together at one end of a dining table that could easily seat twenty. Too excited to eat much, Katherine helped herself to a bowl of hearty chowder, a portion of delicately spiced partridge, and a tempting apple pastry.

When they had finished, Katherine asked, "Shall I retire to the drawing room, my lord, and leave you to your port?"

"You shall not," he responded. "Unless you wish to incur my displeasure."

"But it is customary, sir."

Rudley frowned. "First 'my lord' and now 'sir,' " he said. "It is entirely proper, Katherine, now that we are wed, for you to address me by my Christian name."

"Of course it is. I shall try to remember."

Rudley rose from the table. "I don't wish for any port tonight. I have ordered a hot bath for you. I thought you should like one."

"It sounds wonderful! The perfect way to relax after a momentous day."

Once again they climbed the staircase to the floor above. When they paused outside her door, Rudley took her hand and raised it gallantly to his lips. "Enjoy your bath" was all he said before he continued down the hall to his own apartments.

Katherine found Bess waiting for her, and though she cooperated in the mechanics of bathing and preparing for bed, her mind was elsewhere. Rudley had not said good night. That could mean only one thing. Clearly he did not consider the evening to be over.

Katherine had, like most women, she supposed, pondered what it might be like to be with a man. Unfortunately, her imaginings had never yielded much worthwhile information. In the past year or so she had thought about being with James. This was easier to imagine, for she loved him and could envision herself kissing him, holding him close.

In the weeks before her wedding she had tried not to think about this part of her marriage. Most marriages were arranged, and many women married men they didn't love, yet they all seemed to survive. They lived their lives and raised their children. Why could she not do as well as they?

Bess helped Katherine into a soft white nightgown and

matching wrapper, then brushed her waist-length hair until it shone in the candlelight.

As she stood behind Katherine and regarded her reflection in the mirror, Bess said, "You look so lovely, m'lady. You must have been the most beautiful bride. It's right proud I am to wait on you."

"Thank you, Bess."

"I'll be leaving you now, m'lady, if there's nothing else you need. Would you like tea or chocolate in the morning?"

"Chocolate would be wonderful, thank you."

"Very good, m'lady. Good night, m'lady."

"Good night, Bess."

The maid closed the door quietly while Katherine continued to sit before the mirror. Her face seemed pale in the candlelight, her eyes unusually large. Somehow she didn't like her hair worn loose about her face as if she were a young girl. She carefully divided it into sections and began braiding it into a heavy rope. She had finished and was securing the end of the braid when the door to Rudley's apartments opened.

Katherine watched his approach in the mirror. He wore an ornate dressing gown of green and gold brocade, belted at the waist. He advanced to stand behind her, taking the thick braid in his fingers. "How was your bath?" he asked.

"Extravagant."

"You are easily pleased, Katherine. You may have a bath every day if you wish it."

"That, my lord, would be *sinfully* extravagant."

"Stand up and turn around," he said. "Let me see this nightgown that Meg insists is all the rage in Paris."

Katherine did as he asked while he inspected her attire from head to foot.

"It is lovely, my dear, there is no denying that. But not nearly so lovely as you." He reached to take her by the waist and pulled her close, his lips meeting hers with a warm, rich kiss.

Katherine fought to overcome her instinct to stiffen in his arms. She willed herself to return his kiss. She forced her arms to close about him. With her eyes closed she concentrated her entire will on submitting to her husband, and though she succeeded fairly well in controlling the responses of her body, she found she could not adequately control her emotions. Try though she might, she could not stop the tears from forming in her eyes.

When the kiss ended, she lowered her head so he wouldn't see the telltale tears on her cheeks, but Rudley's hand beneath her chin gently lifted her face into the light.

She thought he might be angry, but could read only compassion in his face as he brushed a tear away. "It's too soon," he said. "I understand."

"But you have a right—"

"No," he interrupted. "I have no right that supersedes your wishes." Allowing her no time to comment on this pronouncement, he said, "Go to sleep. We ride early tomorrow, remember?"

He released her then and walked to the door, where he paused only briefly to say, "Good night, Katherine."

"Good night, Edward."

He smiled at her use of his name, then passed through to his own rooms. Katherine remained standing in the softly scented golden room and found herself thinking how little she understood the man who had become her husband.

Chapter 9

KATHERINE'S MAID WOKE her promptly at eight o'clock when she drew back the heavy gold hangings of the bed and fastened them to the bedposts. She had already opened the draperies over the windows and bright morning light filled the room. It was the same young girl, Bess, who had attended Katherine the previous night.

"Good morning, m'lady," she said. "I hope you slept well. I brought your chocolate, and I've laid out your riding things."

"Thank you, Bess. I meant to ask you last night if you had seen a small leather case with brass studs."

"Yes, ma'am. It's here in the bottom of the wardrobe. Mrs. Windom said it were personal belongings and I was not to unpack it. Shall I bring it to you?"

"No, thank you, Bess. I don't need it now; I only wondered where it was."

Katherine carried her chocolate to the open window. A stunning vista of blue and green met her gaze and she smiled with delight. From her northern-facing windows she saw spread before her those things the earl had described the previous evening in the gathering darkness. Directly beneath her was the wide graveled drive that led to the stables on the right and swept away to the left along the ridge they had traveled. The bridge was a masterpiece in fitted stone with two symmetrical arches rising gracefully above the racing water of the stream. Beyond the drive formal gardens descended in broad terraces to the lake, a placid, deep blue body that stretched across the valley and disappeared around a ridge to the east.

An absentee landlord the earl may have been, but his home showed no sign of neglect. The lawns vibrant with the new spring, were finely clipped to a short, uniform length. Shrubberies and flower beds proclaimed the husbandry of many busy hands. Everywhere early blossoms contributed wild splashes of color, vivid against the green. To the east of the lake an orchard hugged the shore line, its sprawling horizontal branches a mass of blossoms.

While Katherine's gaze was taking in the beauty of the Hampshire spring, her mind was dwelling once again on the unexpected consideration her husband had shown her the night before.

She had determined to put James entirely from her mind and fulfill the vows she made to her husband. Rudley had been an unfailing friend from her first days in London; he had reached far below his station in offering for her, thereby doing her a great honor; he had unknowingly delivered her from the power of Sir Humphrey and provided unselfishly for the future of her sister. For all these things she owed him an immense debt. To repay this debt in some small part she was prepared to submit to all he demanded. But no sooner had he kissed her than her traitorous mind returned to James and the love she had lost. She was furious at the tears that had undermined her resolution and betrayed her. Yet she was touched by Rudley's delicacy and forbearance.

When the maid gently reminded Katherine that his lordship awaited her belowstairs, she reluctantly left the window and hurried to dress. Some minutes later she entered the breakfast parlor to find that her husband had finished eating and was sipping coffee, a copy of the *Times* propped against a vase of oxeye daisies on the table before him. He came to his feet as a footman moved to hold a chair for her.

"You slept well, Katherine?" he asked.

"Yes, indeed!" she replied. "I am greatly refreshed—and hungry."

"There is plenty of time to eat. I have ordered the horses for ten o'clock."

She needed no further urging and helped herself from several dishes the footman offered. She ate her fill of poached eggs, broiled ham, delicious bread still warm from the oven, and fresh strawberries and cream. Since Rudley refrained from engaging her in conversation, offering instead to read several items from the paper to her while she ate, her meal was soon finished.

The morning was one of the brightest in recent weeks, and it was a good omen, Katherine thought, for her first ride at her new home. As they descended the steps to the horses, Katherine exclaimed with delight, "Karma! How does she come to be here?"

"Marcus agreed to sell her to me shortly after our engagement. I had her sent down last week, along with several others from my London stable. I have been wanting to make you a present of her; now that we are married, it is entirely proper for me to do so."

Katherine smiled warmly at him. "Thank you, my lord. What a generous gift!"

"You are welcome to try anything in the stables that takes your fancy," he continued, "but I thought for today, with your eyes on the scenery, you would prefer a familiar mount."

"Are you giving permission, my lord, for me to ride *any* horse I choose?" With the emphasis on *any* and her mischievous eyes on his bay stallion, she won an immediate response.

"None of my personal riding horses is accustomed to the sidesaddle, my girl."

"But didn't I tell you, sir, that I ride equally well astride?" she asked flippantly, a twinkle in her eye.

He cast her a withering glance. "That does not surprise me in the least." Then in a teasingly formal tone he added, "But come, Katherine, you are now a married woman. If such hoydenish behavior was acceptable in the wilds of Lincolnshire, believe me, it will not do for the Countess of Rudley."

She smiled in response. "I will try to remember, sir, to conduct myself with all due propriety."

"Which means you must refrain from jumping the cemetery fence," he said, "no matter how great the temptation."

"I believe I will be able to resist," she replied, smiling more broadly. "That is one lesson I learned well."

The morning air was crisp, the horses fresh, and the ride delightful. They started off toward the stables and continued along the far side of the lake, finally stopping at a spot directly opposite the bridge. Their path had taken them uphill, and as they turned to look back upon Rudley Court, Katherine could see why the earl had brought her here. There was a fine view of the house with no trees to mar it. The entire structure was light gray stone, weathered over the years to a soft, ageless beauty. They were high enough to see a portion of the park behind the house; the semiformal gardens there contained large areas of carefully groomed lawn contrasting with the darker hues of the shrubbery and trees. Beyond the park to the south stood several densely wooded areas, and in a small valley perhaps a mile distant she could see the steeple of a church and the roofs of several cottages.

"That is the village of Rudley," the earl said. "Several miles beyond and farther west is Weiring, the Ashley estate, where my mother was born. We will ride there one day. The property is considerably smaller than Rudley Court but much older; it has a special charm."

Later they visited with several of the earl's tenants, some of whom he had not seen for years. The news of his marriage had spread quickly. Everywhere they stopped, they met with warm wishes and congratulations.

When they returned from their ride, the earl showed Katherine through the house. In visiting the extensive kitchens they encountered Rudley's cook, Mrs. Simpson, who offered to meet with Katherine to review the menus and make any desired changes.

"That was good of her," Katherine commented when they

left the kitchens behind, "but I would not wish to interfere with her plans."

"You need do nothing regarding the menus, if you prefer," Rudley said. "It was her way of showing you she is pleased to have you here and that your comments would be welcome."

In the days ahead Katherine encountered the same cooperation in all of the servants at Rudley. It was obvious that their devotion to the earl and his family was exceedingly strong. They were willing to accept her simply because she was the earl's choice.

Before he retired that evening, Rudley considerably shocked his valet by asking him to search through the trunks in the attics. He wanted Wiggin to procure for him, if he could, a pair of his youngest brother John's riding breeches from when he had been perhaps fifteen years of age.

Katherine was awakened by a quiet tapping. She sat up, not certain from where the sound came. Her room was wrapped in intense blackness. The knock sounded again, and now, fully awake, she realized it came from the door connecting her apartments to her husband's. A pale light shimmered through the crack beneath the door. She slipped quickly from her bed and padded silently across the room.

"Yes. What is it?" she asked quietly.

The earl's voice answered. "May I see you for a moment, Katherine? I have something for you."

The door was not locked, and Katherine reached to open it. Then, just as her fingers touched the latch handle, she hesitated. She released the handle and took a step backward. "Surely it is very late, my lord?"

"Actually, it is quite early." She thought he sounded amused. "Open the door, Katherine, *please*."

His bantering tone made her hesitance seem silly, and she knew she had no right to refuse such a civil request. She took the handle firmly and swung the door wide. Her husband stood on the threshold, not in the nightshirt and dressing gown she had expected but fully dressed for riding in frock coat, buckskin breeches, and top boots. He carried a slim taper in one hand and what appeared to be a bundle of clothing in the other.

As the light from his candle fell upon his wife, Rudley was quick to take in the details of her appearance. She wore only her nightgown of fine white cotton, delicately embroidered over the bodice, falling to brush the carpet at her feet. Her hair, which he had never seen loose, hung in soft waves to her waist. It appeared thick and lustrous in the candlelight.

Rudley pushed the bundle of clothing into her arms and handed her the taper. "Here," he said, "put these on and meet me at the stables in twenty minutes." Then he turned and was gone, closing the door behind him.

Katherine stared at the bundle. It was a pair of men's riding breeches and a shirt and jacket to match!

She did as her husband asked. She used the taper to light several candles and then hurried into the shirt and breeches, finding the fit adequate. She quickly brushed her hair back from her face and secured it tightly at the nape of her neck with a broad ribbon, for she had no time and no one to help her put it up in the customary way. She pulled on her own fine leather riding boots and, taking up the jacket, made her way quietly through the passageway and down the stairs to the front door, which she found unbolted. Leaving her candle on the hall table, she slipped noiselessly outside.

She could see the dawn breaking in the east, and even though it was still rather dark she easily made her way to the stables. Upon entering, she saw a light burning to her right and turned toward it. Just ahead her husband was leading out Tortuga, the big bay he had ridden yesterday, already saddled.

"My lord!" she exclaimed. "Whatever are you doing?"

He turned to look at her, an appreciative gleam in his eyes as he regarded her slim figure in boy's attire. "Well, you were certainly quick, my dear. And may I say you look charming?"

"You may," she replied, blushing. "But you have not answered my question."

"Here, hold him for me, will you?" He thrust Tortuga's reins into her hands. "Take care he doesn't tread upon your feet. He is feeling rather fresh."

Katherine had no trouble holding the horse, but she did have some difficulty believing her eyes as she watched the earl step into the next loose box and proceed to saddle Navigator, the impressive chestnut he had often ridden in London.

She finally found her voice. "Do you seriously intend to let me ride one of these?"

"Yes, certainly," he answered. "The choice is yours."

"But I have never ridden a stallion before!" she exclaimed.

"You will find either of these as well behaved as any horse you have ridden," he said, "but there is a great difference in strength and stamina." He had finished saddling Navigator and, leaving him in the stall, returned to Katherine.

Her eyes were wide and shining. "I was only teasing you yesterday," she said. "It isn't necessary for you to share your favorite horses with me."

"Are you crying off then?" he challenged.

"No. No, I'm not! I would love to ride one of them!"

"Then make your choice, but quickly, for we must be on our way and back again before people are up and about. We can't risk having anyone see the new Lady Rudley in such scandalous attire."

"Navigator has not been out for several days," she reasoned aloud, "so I think I should be safest with Tortuga since you had him out only yesterday." Her decision made, Rudley led Tortuga into the stableyard. Taking Katherine's foot in his hand, he tossed her easily into the saddle. "My, but this feels strange," Katherine said, as she settled herself on the tall horse. "It has been a long time since I last rode astride."

Rudley maintained his grip on the bridle as she adjusted

the stirrups to the proper length. "How long has it been?" he asked. "Are you sure you care to try it?"

"I think I was fourteen when I last rode so," she said, "but I daresay one does not forget. I most assuredly wish to go. Such an opportunity cannot be expected every day!"

He allowed her to gather the reins and within a few moments he, too, was mounted. They trotted off down the tree-lined drive just as the sun broke over the horizon. Ninety minutes later they returned to the stableyard and ran directly into Henderson, his lordship's head groom.

"You are out early, m'lord," Henderson said. "Good morning, m'lady." His tone was formally polite and nothing in his manner suggested that he saw anything extraordinary either in his mistress being dressed in men's clothing or in her riding one of Lord Rudley's most spirited horses astride. He took hold of both bridles as the riders dismounted. "If you had told me last night, m'lord, that you wished to ride this morning, I would have had the horses brought round for you."

"It was a last-minute decision, Henderson, and I saw no reason to trouble you."

"It would have been no trouble, m'lord." He walked away leading the horses, and Katherine turned toward the house.

"We can get in through the side door in our wing," Rudley said. "I have a key," he added, as he produced it from his pocket.

Katherine was laughing. "You look like a guilty school-boy, my lord."

"Henderson has always affected me so," he replied, smiling. "He is never precisely critical but manages to be so disapproving that Oliver and I have always had the hardest time pleasing him. He has such definite notions of what is right and wrong, but he is the best man with horses I have ever known."

"He clearly disapproves of your saddling for yourself," Katherine commented, then added wickedly, "I must admit to a certain degree of astonishment myself that your lordship possesses such a skill."

He had turned the key in the lock, but as he swung the door open he paused to stare down at her, one eyebrow raised. "His lordship is also skilled in dealing with impertinent young ladies who are careless enough to tempt him too far."

If he had any intention of making good on this threat, Katherine chose not to wait to find out. When he turned to close the door behind them, she darted ahead of him up the back stairs, speaking over her shoulder. "Thank you for the ride. I had a marvelous time."

"So did I," he replied, watching until she disappeared at the top of the stairway. He gazed after her for a moment, then with a shake of his head strolled off down the passageway toward the breakfast parlor.

When her maid came to waken her, Katherine was back in bed, her infamous riding clothes hidden away. Alongside the chocolate on her breakfast tray lay a note. There were only a few lines.

Katherine,
   Kendall has informed me that there are some pressing estate matters that demand my immediate attention. I beg you will excuse me for the duration of the morning. I should be free by noon and will be at your disposal for the remainder of the day.

                                        Yours, Rudley

Left with a morning to herself, Katherine was eager to spend the time with Pamela. After breakfast she made her way to her stepdaughter's rooms and was pleased to see the child feeling better. She was not yet dressing, but she was out of bed, curled up in a large upholstered chair by the window, busy with some needlework.

"Your father insists that he must tend to business this morning, but I don't mind," Katherine said, "for it gives us a chance to enjoy a long visit."

"I would like that very much, Lady Katherine," Pamela replied.

Katherine leaned over to look at the embroidery the girl held. "Why, Pamela, this is lovely! You do beautiful work!"

"Thank you, ma'am." The child blushed at the praise. "I enjoy needlework."

"I have been thinking of starting a project myself," Katherine said.

"A needlework project?" Pamela asked.

Katherine nodded. "Let me go and find Mrs. Windom," she said, "and I will explain my idea to you both." Pamela's governess, Miss Shaw, had been sitting quietly nearby, but at Katherine's words she rose.

"Excuse me, my lady, I will tell Mrs. Windom you wish to speak with her."

"Thank you, Miss Shaw. Please do not take her from any important task. Tell her only that Lady Pamela and I should like to see her when it is convenient."

Barely five minutes had passed before Miss Shaw returned, accompanied by Mrs. Windom. The governess resumed her seat near the window and took up her embroidery, while the housekeeper asked Katherine how she could be of assistance.

"You are familiar with the chair in the blue drawing room," Katherine began, "the one his lordship's mother made, the one that is badly worn?" She glanced from Mrs. Windom to Pamela and saw that the child's face was troubled. "No, Pamela," she said quickly, "it's not what you're thinking. I don't wish to do away with it. I was wondering if you think I could copy it. As a surprise for your father!"

"Copy it, my lady?" Mrs. Windom asked.

"Yes," Katherine responded. "Make it over again. Buy wool instead of silk so the work will last longer. I could use the same colors and make a copy of the original design. We could then apply the new work to the old chair and in effect roll the calendar back twenty years. The original choice of color and design would still be the work of Lord Rudley's mother. I would simply be making it new again. What do you think, Pamela? Do you think your father would be pleased or displeased by such a change?''

"I don't know what Papa would think, but I think it would be wonderful to have all the colors bright again!''

"And what is your opinion, Mrs. Windom?'' Katherine asked. "Can it be done?''

"Well, my lady, it should be no problem to match the colors. And I suppose we could count the stitches and make a pattern for you to follow in the difficult places. It will take some considerable time, but I suppose it could be done. No one would be happier than I to have that worn chair out of the room, but I must tell your ladyship, I cannot be responsible for removing the old fabric without first consulting his lordship. He has made it very clear the chair is not to be tampered with.''

"I will take complete responsibility, Mrs. Windom,'' Katherine replied. "I have also considered that Lord Rudley might object to the change. We will have the old fabric removed carefully, and if he is opposed to the new chair, we can always have the old one back again.''

"Miss Shaw and I have discussed the scene on the chair, Lady Katherine,'' Pamela continued. "We think Grandmother must have made a sketch first and then done the needlework from that. The perspective is from the orchard.''

"Pamela has done a sketch of her own of that view,'' the governess added. "Should you like to see it, Lady Rudley? I think it is one of her best efforts.''

"Yes, please,'' Katherine said. "I would like to very much.''

Pamela's suite had an attached sitting room similar to Katherine's. As Mrs. Windom excused herself and went about her business, the other three moved into the adjoining room. It was not furnished as a traditional sitting room but was clearly used as a schoolroom instead. There were extensive bookcases taking up one entire wall. A large globe stood near two antique writing desks, while another corner was occupied by a pianoforte. The most striking aspect of the room by far was the large number of drawings, sketches, and paintings scattered about. Many were displayed on the walls; several sat on easels, some clearly finished and being exhibited thus, while others were still in the midst of the creative process.

Miss Shaw led Katherine to a group of watercolors on the near wall and indicated one. "It is the same scene as the chair, but in a different season, of course."

"I think I know the exact spot where Grandmother sat when she drew her sketch," Pamela said. "On the shore of the lake at the far side of the orchard; no other spot gives exactly that perspective."

Katherine studied the delicate sketch before her. While the scene on the chair depicted the vivid colors of high summer, this scene, though identical, stood in sharp contrast to it. The season was winter, the trees stark and barren, the gray house blending into the snow-covered ground yet standing out clearly from it. The lake, frozen and immobile, showed the palest tinge of blue in rare spots where the snow had blown clear of the thin ice. With little range in color available to her, Pamela had captured marvelous perspective in her painting. Even the sky, which an artist could have made believably blue at that season, Pamela had left dark and glooming—also gray. The evergreens held the only color worth mentioning. They were bold, their dark green seeming like the brightest scarlet when contrasted to the sullen grays of the scene. Katherine spent long moments staring at the watercolor. She didn't notice when Miss Shaw motioned Pamela to a nearby easel, where the child picked up her charcoal and continued a drawing she had started there.

Katherine's eyes were lured from the winter view of Rudley Court to the sketch next to it on the wall. It was an intricate rendering in charcoal of the gracious arched bridge over the stream. Above that was another watercolor, this time of a church—perhaps the one in the village. Next in line was a rich oil painting of a bay horse pacing in a grassy paddock. Katherine recognized Tortuga instantly. Beyond the oil was another charcoal, a portrait of the earl. Pamela had captured her father exactly, though Katherine felt his face appeared too harsh and uncompromising—perhaps Pamela saw him that way. Katherine turned to find herself alone and walked the few steps to where the girl was sketching.

"Pamela, your work is excellent! You have such a gift, and you use it so well!"

The child blushed with pride, but it was her teacher who spoke first. "Your ladyship is most kind to say so. I agree that Pamela has an excellent eye and a good memory for detail. She did the sketch of his lordship from memory."

Katherine glanced about at the easels and the array of works mounted on the far wall. "I should like to see the rest of your work, Pamela. Will you show them to me? Tell me what each is?"

"I have a great many drawings, Lady Katherine," Pamela explained. "The drawers of the desk are full of them."

Katherine's eyes brightened. "Good, I cannot wait to see them. I want to see them all!"

Chapter 10

THE MORNING FLEW by for Katherine. She had always appreciated amateur art, but the more she saw of Pamela's work, the more thoroughly convinced she became that the child had rare talent. She wondered why Rudley had never mentioned it. Surely it was uncommon to have so gifted a child; most parents would be outspoken about such an accomplishment. Yet Katherine knew her husband was not a typical parent. He had never willingly offered any information about Pamela. He seldom mentioned the child and in response to Katherine's questions supplied only the barest facts.

She met her husband at noon, determined to make Pamela one of their next topics of conversation. When Rudley asked how she had spent her morning, she found the perfect opportunity.

"I visited with Pamela. Why didn't you tell me she was so talented?"

"She is accomplished for her age," he replied, "but her governess tells me that she applies herself to her studies. That, of course, helps to explain her proficiency. Miss Shaw came with the highest recommendations I have ever seen for a woman of her profession."

"I was referring particularly to Pamela's skill in drawing and painting. I was impressed."

"Indeed?"

His question seemed to be a simple polite inquiry, but Katherine detected a note of disbelief in his tone. Was it her imagination? Perhaps he did not admire Pamela's style. Art was certainly a matter of individual taste.

She decided to be more specific. "Have you seen her latest charcoals depicting scenes of the stable and stableyards?"

"Miss Shaw delivers to me each month a report on Pamela's progress," he replied. "Her reports are very complete."

Katherine was not prepared for such overt disinterest; the subject was boring him. She felt deflated, and when she could think of no response to his last comment, she fell silent. She could hardly force him to discuss Pamela if he was disinclined to do so.

Later that afternoon Rudley and Katherine rode again, this time with Katherine properly mounted on Karma. In the weeks that followed they spent many pleasurable hours covering the miles of roads and lanes, fields and forests that were the earl's inheritance. Each day there was a new direction to explore, another tenant to visit, another memory for the earl to recount. They spent a great deal of time in the stables, with Katherine trying to learn the names of Rudley's horses as well as their bloodlines and the unique qualities that made each one special to him.

On rainy or windy days they stayed indoors where Rudley led Katherine on intricate tours of the house. Each room was full of beauty and history and memories. There were rare pieces of furniture and *objets d'art*, each with a story of its own. There were numerous portraits, many of them of the earl's ancestors. Some of these were lackluster individuals who had carried on rather humdrum existences, but others were much more colorful. There was Rudley's uncle Sidney, a dashing blond Adonis who was shot through the heart in a duel defending the honor of the woman he loved. There was the earl's great-grandmother who by the age of forty had not a tooth in her mouth but nevertheless grinned broadly for the artist who immortalized her. She was said to have sworn like a sailor and ruled her lord with an iron hand. There was Rudley's father, the fourth earl. In a full-length rendering by Sir Joshua Reynolds, he appeared to be an older version of Oliver—tall, fair, broad-shouldered, handsome—a renowned politician and leader of his party, a devoted husband and father, a lover of art who had filled his home with exquisite treasures.

As the days passed Katherine was permitted to see a side of her husband she had not seen before. In London he had behaved conventionally, and she had the impression that this behavior was an integral part of his personality. In the country, however, he seemed less rigid, more relaxed, even slightly reckless. If anyone had suggested to her in London that he would permit, even encourage, his wife to behave with impropriety, she would never have believed it. He had, however, done just that when he allowed her to ride his stallion astride. Nor had that adventure been a momentary lapse on his part, for they had since enjoyed two more secretive early-morning rides together. He was so attentive, so constant in his concern for her, that she would have been a fool indeed if she had not realized his feelings for her were stronger than those of mere friendship.

Rudley wanted more than anything for Katherine to return his regard, and without realizing it he was doing the one thing surest to attract her. He was not burying her with gifts, nor overpowering her with compliments. He was simply being himself and sharing himself with her. His time, except for that which he must give to the estate, was hers to command. He shared freely with her his home, which he clearly loved. He shared his thoughts, his memories, his plans for the future, his feelings—good and bad alike.

And his openness encouraged *her*. He wanted to know all about her life before they met, and she found herself recounting things she had thought long forgotten. He was the good listener she had suspected he would be, and as she had once confided in him about her horse Jeremy, she now related remembrances of her parents, sharing things she had never before spoken of to anyone.

For his part Rudley was pleased with the way their relationship was progressing. He had not been surprised by her need to postpone the intimacy of marriage. He knew she would not easily forget her attachment to Parnaby.

His times of temptation, however, were many and great. The morning he had taken her the riding clothes, he was thinking only of how surprised and excited she would be when he offered to let her ride one of his stallions. He wasn't prepared for her sleepy eyes, her tumbled hair in the candle-light, the allure of her intimate night apparel. He was sorely tempted to linger and talk with her, so he handed her the clothing and left quickly, shutting temptation away. During several of those long nights when he lay alone, knowing she was so close, he had almost gone to her, but then he, reminded himself that they had been married only a few weeks. He was determined not to rush his fences.

Late one rainy afternoon Rudley drew his curricle team up outside the house and handed the reins to Henderson. He had driven to Winchester on business and had time to regret taking an open carriage instead of a closed one. Inside the great hall he relinquished his wet hat and gloves to a footman.

He paused at the hall table where a pile of letters lay. Several were for Katherine. One he knew was from her sister—he recognized the handwriting—from the Lincoln boarding school; another was almost certainly from Charity Harrington, who corresponded regularly with Katherine. Also on the table was a letter for the outgoing post. It was addressed in Katherine's hand to a Sir Humphrey Corey, also of Lincolnshire. Assuming Katherine had left it there for him to frank, he uncovered the ink, selected a quill, and scribbled his name across the corner of the folded sheet. Then, taking his own letters with him, he went upstairs to change.

Later that evening during dinner he thought of the letters again. "You had a wealth of correspondence today," he said.

"Yes, I did," Katherine replied. "Actually, I need to talk to you about something. Lady Brent wrote last week to say that she is taking Marie to Bath for part of the summer and she offered to take Serena, too. There will be parties and informal dances, picnics, and so forth. Her ladyship thought Serena might enjoy it."

"I think it sounds like an excellent idea if Serena wishes it. When do they go?"

"They plan to leave in ten days' time."

"I thought you said Serena didn't finish school until the thirtieth."

"She doesn't, but I don't see why I couldn't take her out a few days early."

"How would you like her to travel? Shall I send a coach?"

"Actually, I was hoping to go myself."

"Yourself?"

"I thought I could leave the day after tomorrow, spend several days with Charity and her parents, then travel back to London with Serena and leave her in Lady Brent's capable hands. I'm almost certain Serena will wish to go to Bath. She has never had such an opportunity before."

"Are you sure you wish to undertake such a journey?"

"If Serena is to go with Lady Brent, I should like to see her first. I haven't been with her since just after Christmas. And Charity has been my closest friend for years."

"I'm sorry. I'm being selfish, aren't I?" he asked. "I can't expect you to desert your family and friends for me. I'll order the coach for early Monday morning. You will take Bess, of course, and Henderson, and Kendall."

"I can't take your secretary with me," she objected. "Not when you are so busy here."

"With you gone I will have nothing but time," he replied. "I can do his work as well as mine. You must take him. He will arrange accommodations, see to any problems that may arise, and keep impertinent travelers at a distance."

She smiled at the image this created. "You insist upon protecting me as if I were a rare piece of china. I'm not."

He reached to cover her hand where it lay on the linen tablecloth. "You are to me. Rare—and precious."

She had feared that Rudley would offer to accompany her, so she had included the visit to Charity, feeling relatively certain that he would not wish to intrude on such a reunion.

Now that he had acquiesced so readily, Katherine felt an overwhelming sense of relief. She would go north alone; she would confront Sir Humphrey, this time from a position of strength; she would rid her life of him once and for all.

This thought did much to lift her spirits. She returned the pressure of her husband's hand before withdrawing her own to lift her crystal wineglass, which had just been refilled to the rim by a hovering footman.

"Who is Sir Humphrey Corey?" Rudley asked, serving himself from a dish of braised fowl.

Katherine's delicate glass, held daintily between thumb and fingers, suddenly parted company with her hand. It fell directly onto a plate below, shattering into dozens of slivers and spewing red liquid over the white cloth and onto Katherine's dress. She jumped up, brushing the wine from her gown as a footman hurried to wipe up the spill.

"I'm . . . so . . . sorry," Katherine sputtered. "How clumsy of me."

Rudley, too, was instantly on his feet.

"I am afraid I have broken your beautiful crystal and spoiled this dress," she said. The front of her pale yellow gown was liberally splattered with wine stains. "If you will excuse me, my lord, I should like to change."

"Yes, of course."

As Katherine turned to leave the room, she paused and asked, "Would you mind very much if I retired for the night? I had a long day and I'm weary."

"I don't mind at all," Rudley answered. "I also had a tiring day."

After Katherine had bid him good night and left the room, Rudley reseated himself at the table. When one of the maids began to brush the shattered crystal from the tablecloth into a dustpan, he said, "Leave it. Bring me the brandy decanter."

For some time afterward he remained at the dining table, contemplating the brandy in his glass and the shattered wreckage of his wife's wineglass.

Once in her own room Katherine rang for Bess. While she waited, she struggled out of the spoiled dress as best she could on her own. She found that her hands were trembling as she fumbled with the buttons.

She didn't know how it was possible, but Rudley must have somehow seen the letter she had written today to Sir Humphrey.

When Bess appeared, Katherine asked peremptorily. "Did you post the letter I gave you earlier, Bess?"

"I took it down straightaway when you'd finished, m'lady, but the post from the village was early today. I left it on the table so Jim could take it tomorrow. Is there a problem?"

"No. I had thought it would go out today, that's all."

"I can have one of the footmen take it to the receiving office now if you like, m'lady, but the next mail coach isn't due till the morning."

"That won't be necessary, Bess. Tomorrow will be fine."

As Bess left to take the dress to the laundry to deal with the stain before it set, Katherine chided herself for her carelessness. She should have taken the letter to the village herself. What a fool she had been to react so violently when Rudley mentioned Sir Humphrey's name. What must he think of her? Yet if she hadn't shattered the glass, what would she have said to her husband? How would she have answered his question? Could she have lied to him? Would she have been forced to tell him the whole truth at last?

Katherine slipped her nightgown over her head and tied the delicate ribbons at the neck. She had escaped the earl's question for tonight, but what would she do if he required an answer tomorrow?

Katherine spent a restless night. The following morning she ordered breakfast in her room, then busied herself in writing to Serena, Charity, and Lady Brent. With her letters finished she supervised the packing for her trip. When she casually asked Bess if she knew what his lordship's plans for the day were, Bess replied that Lord Rudley had gone out with Mr. Kendall directly after breakfast.

"I expect with Mr. Kendall accompanying us, m'lady, they have many things to discuss before we leave."

"I'm sure you're right. What about shoes? Should I take these half boots or not?"

Katherine worried all day about dinner. She saw no way to avoid meeting her husband then and knew not what she would say if he repeated his question about Sir Humphrey. When she stopped in the late afternoon to say good-bye to Pamela, the child was unhappy to hear that Katherine was planning a trip.

Pamela's distress prompted Katherine to offer, "Why don't you and Miss Shaw come downstairs and join me and your father for dinner tonight? You have never done so. We would both enjoy your company."

Pamela accepted readily, flattered to be treated in so grown-up a fashion, and Katherine realized she had probably solved her problem with Rudley. He would be unlikely to mention her letter at dinner with both his daughter and her governess in attendance.

When the four gathered in the drawing room before dinner, Rudley welcomed Pamela and Miss Shaw genially. Although Katherine watched closely, she could detect no sign of annoyance in her husband. His manners throughout the meal were warm and gracious, even though the same emotional distance persisted between him and his daughter.

After the dessert had been served, Miss Shaw asked for permission to retire, taking her young charge with her. Katherine rose at the same time. "If you will excuse me, my lord, I believe I shall withdraw as well. Mr. Kendall informs me that we leave at dawn."

Rudley stood at the head of the table while all three ladies exited, then resumed his seat and motioned for a footman to pour his port.

Assuring herself that all was in order for the morning, Katherine was soon ready for bed. Into her small case she packed her writing implements and the journal in which she had written her list of husband candidates while she was in London. After she had accepted the earl, she continued to use the blank pages as a diary to record the events leading up to her marriage and her personal reflections during the weeks that had passed. Closing the case, she buckled it securely, then set it near the doorway before returning to sit on the edge of her bed. She was reaching to snuff out her candle when the passageway door opened and Rudley entered.

"I saw Bess in the hallway," he said. "She said you were ready for bed."

"Indeed I am. Was there something you wanted?"

"I'm sorry to have to tell you this, Katherine, but your diversionary plan for dinner will not save you from an interview with me. I know you have been avoiding me and I sense it is because you would rather not tell me who Sir Humphrey Corey is."

Katherine started to speak, but he held up a hand to stop her. "No, please let me finish. I know you didn't live the first twenty-four years of your life in a vacuum and that you must have ties in Lincolnshire. *My* past, I am certain, will also intrude upon us from time to time."

He took her hands and drew her to her feet, holding her fingers clasped between his own. "For now, while our alliance is so new, I will respect your reticence. But someday, when our marriage is whole, I will not allow any holding back. There will be no secrets, no shame, no past to put to rest, no phantoms to cast their shadows over the future."

As his arms slid around her waist, she came unresistingly to rest against him as he continued, his words hypnotically tender. "We haven't been married long, and I know that trust is not built overnight, but I hope you know you can trust me, for I have pledged to protect you until I die."

He kissed her then, a warm, melting kiss that left her breathless and caused her knees to tremble. When he released her, she sat down abruptly on the bed as he turned away and retraced his steps to the door.

"Good night, Katherine. Sleep well."

Katherine blew out her candle and crawled under the quilts, but it was a long time before she slept.

The following morning at dawn two coaches rolled away from Rudley Court, headed north. Mr. Kendall rode in the first with Katherine and her maid, while the baggage coach followed.

Rudley had joined his wife for breakfast in the predawn darkness, then walked with her to the coach waiting in the drive.

"Ned," she said, as they had descended the steps together. "I want you to know I appreciate all you said last night."

"Godspeed, Katherine. And hurry home. I will miss you. If you should discover that Serena cares not for the Bath scheme, bring her back with you. She will be most welcome here."

He took her hand, lightly brushing it with his lips before he helped her into the coach. Then he stood on the drive and watched until both vehicles disappeared from sight, wondering if he had been wise after all. Perhaps he should have followed his first instinct, which was to demand she tell him all there was to know about Sir Humphrey Corey.

Chapter 11

During the two days it took Katherine to travel to Harrington Manor in Lincolnshire, she had ample opportunity to understand why Rudley held his secretary in such high esteem. The smallest detail of Katherine's journey had been attended to with the greatest care. Nothing had been left to chance.

At each stop the change of horses was accomplished swiftly, but the women were nevertheless invited to step down either to exercise their limbs or to avail themselves of the facilities offered at the coaching inns. Wherever they were scheduled to dine, instructions had been sent ahead to reserve a private parlor and a tasty meal. First-rate rooms had been booked for overnight accommodations.

The hours in the coach passed pleasantly also, for Mr. Kendall could converse intelligently on many subjects. When Katherine asked how he had come to work for Lord Rudley, Kendall told her he had been recommended by his father, who was the village rector. He had held his position for five years; he was now twenty-six years of age.

Although Katherine had laughed at Rudley's suggestion that Kendall be her shield against importunate travelers, she discovered this to be his duty on more than one occasion. When an inn yard was crowded with men (as one was in a town where a prizefight was being held), he escorted her expertly through the throng, then attended her in the private parlor throughout her dinner, lest any drunken reveler enter her door by mischance. At the inn where they were to spend the night, he escorted Katherine and Bess to their room, then waited outside until he heard the bolt slide safely home.

Remembering dusty trips with Sir Humphrey—with few stops and the reward of a flea-infested bed at the end of a long day—Katherine decided she could easily be spoiled by such treatment.

When they arrived at Harrington Manor precisely on schedule, Katherine was not in the least surprised. "I must thank you, Mr. Kendall, for quite the most pleasant journey I have ever taken."

He bowed slightly as he acknowledged the compliment. "You're very kind, Lady Rudley. I'm pleased to know you were comfortable."

When urged to accept Lord Harrington's hospitality, Mr. Kendall declined, saying that he had been instructed to reserve lodgings for himself, the coachmen, and the footmen at the George Inn. They would be content there, he insisted, for as long as her ladyship desired to remain with her friends.

When all of Katherine's baggage had been unloaded, Mr. Kendall rose from the seat he had taken when Lady Harrington insisted he join them for tea. Katherine walked with him to the front door, where she said, "I have spent two entire days in your company, sir, and I don't even know your Christian name."

He smiled. "It's Peter, Lady Rudley. My father has six sons; all six are named after apostles."

"Peter is a fine name," she said. "Thank you, Peter, for all your care of me."

"I will take the coaches back with me to the George, my lady. If you should need transport or my services for any reason, you need only send a message to the inn."

"Thank you, Peter. I should like the coach tomorrow afternoon. I am going visiting. Shall we say two o'clock?"

As the coaches rumbled away down the drive, Katherine returned to her host and hostess.

"It is unfortunate your husband could not travel with you," Lord Harrington said. "He could deal with Sir Humphrey in the task before you now."

"He is busy with the spring planting, sir," Katherine replied, "and I asked to come alone. Serena is my responsibility and Sir Humphrey my problem. I wish to deal with him on my own."

"You have never been one to shirk your responsibilities, Katherine," his lordship responded. "Nevertheless, I would be happy to lend you my support when you speak with your stepfather."

"Thank you, my lord. But I truly believe I must go alone. Did you procure the documents I need?"

"Yes, I did. I had my solicitor set forth all the provisions you described."

"When will you go to see him, Katy?" Charity asked.

"Tomorrow morning. I see no reason to delay."

"We have less than an hour until dinner," Lady Harrington offered. "Let me show you to your room, Katherine, where you can refresh yourself and change from your traveling dress."

After Katherine had been shown upstairs, Lady Harrington excused herself, leaving her daughter behind. When the maid left the room, Charity asked, "Did you really wish to come alone? You *have* told Lord Rudley about Sir Humphrey, haven't you?"

Katherine faced her accuser guiltily. "I haven't. I intended to, but the longer I waited the harder it became, and somehow I just never found the right time."

"Katherine!"

"Charity, I know you're right, but you must understand. The man I married, the family I married into—family is everything to them. I know the Countess Finley wasn't pleased when her brother chose me. Can you imagine what she would have said if she'd known she was gaining Sir Humphrey as a relative—even as a steprelative? He is lewd, a drunkard, a reckless gambler. He's lazy. He lives off the income of his stepdaughters! How can I tell my husband that I lived for ten years in this man's house? What would he think of me?"

"He would think you had no choice, for in fact you had none."

"I could have gotten away sooner," Katherine argued. "I had offers, but I was selfish. I preferred to endure Sir Humphrey than spend all my days wed to a man I did not love. I don't see why my new family ever needs to know about Sir Humphrey. If he agrees to my terms tomorrow, he will be out of my life forever. I want to forget him."

"But, Katy, someday someone is bound to make the connection."

"Why should they? No one has so far. Sir Humphrey never goes to London, and no one who knew me in Lincolnshire moves in the same circles as the Seaton family. Even Lady Finley, who I am certain looked into my background, did not discover my mother's second marriage, for surely she would have told Ned if she had."

Katherine paused as she slipped a pale lilac dinner gown over her head and turned for Charity to fasten it for her.

"There is one problem that arose just before I left Rudley Court, but if all here goes as I planned, then I think I have a solution."

"What problem is that?" Charity asked.

"Ned saw some of my outgoing post, and before I left he asked me who Sir Humphrey Corey was."

"What!" Charity exclaimed. "How did you answer him?"

"I didn't. An interruption saved me, but I am certain that eventually he will ask again."

"What will you say?"

"I will say he is someone from my past whom I would prefer to forget."

"And you believe your husband will accept such an explanation?"

"I believe he will."

Charity finished with the dress and walked away, shaking her head in doubt. "I can't like any of this, Katy. A wife should tell her husband everything."

"Everything? I agree she should be honest about herself, but must she share the shame of her family?"

"I think so, yes."

"Tell me this, Charity. If you were so fortunate as to make

a match with Oliver Seaton, would you follow your own advice?''

"I would," Charity affirmed.

"You would tell all?"

"Yes."

"Would you tell him about the bastard your father sired in the village after his marriage to your mother?"

"But, Katherine, that was years ago—a youthful indiscretion! I am certain he has been a faithful husband since!"

"Would you tell Mr. Seaton about the time you disappeared with Henry Sprague and no one could find you for more than two hours?"

"But we were lost in the maze—and I thought I was in love with him."

"But would you tell Mr. Seaton about it? Would you tell him, as you say, everything?"

Unable to face Katherine's accusative stare, Charity turned away to the window. After several moments she replied quietly, "Perhaps not."

"Just so," Katherine replied. "I believe I have set the question to rest."

Early the following morning Katherine borrowed a horse from the Harringtons and, taking only a groom with her, rode to her old home. She avoided the main highway, following instead the farm roads and cart tracks. Along the roadside wild hyacinth bloomed in profusion, the drooping purple heads swaying gently in the breeze. One small meadow she rode across was a yellow sea of buttercups.

When she arrived at Sir Humphrey's house, Katherine left the groom and the horses at the stables and walked to the front door. She sounded the knocker and Martin's familiar face soon appeared. The butler's somber expression was replaced by a bright smile as he saw who waited on the doorstep.

"Miss Katherine!" he exclaimed, then corrected himself. "I should say Lady Rudley. How good it is to see you again. We did not expect you."

As he glanced behind her to discover the conveyance that had delivered her, she said, "I am staying with the Harringtons. I rode over to see my stepfather. I came early, because I know he is at his best at this time of day. Is he at home?"

"Please come in, my lady. Sir Humphrey has come down to breakfast. Should you like to join him?"

"Perhaps you had best take him my card, Martin, and ask if he will see me."

"Certainly, my lady."

As she handed him her visiting card she asked, "How are you getting on with him, Martin?"

"Much the same as always, my lady. Things have changed little since you left. He no longer has you to vent his anger on, and for that I am grateful. We were so pleased to hear of your marriage; your husband is said to be a fine man."

"He is, Martin, and I am content with him."

"Mrs. Green and the others will be pleased to hear it. Excuse me, Lady Rudley, I will take your card in to Sir Humphrey."

Martin returned in a few moments and led Katherine to the breakfast parlor, where he nodded to the servants to leave the room, then closed the door, leaving Katherine and her stepfather alone.

"And to what do I owe this honor?" Sir Humphrey asked, stuffing his mouth with a slice of beef.

"You must have known I would come," Katherine answered, seating herself at the table. "We cannot continue with things as they are. Serena finishes school in a week, and you don't want her here any more than I want her to be here with you."

"She won't stay long; she weds Postlethwaite in September."

"Serena doesn't wish for the match," Katherine replied, "nor do I. I will not permit it."

"*You* will not permit it? You have no say in the matter! It shall be as I have arranged."

"Why do you insist upon such an inferior match for her,

sir? If she comes to me now, she can do much better for herself. She can be brought out, meet eligible men—''

''Oh, yes, you are very well-connected now, aren't you, my lady,'' he said scornfully. ''A countess no less. Moving only in the best circles. The date is set, the settlements are arranged. Serena will marry Postlethwaite.''

''That is the heart of the matter,'' Katherine said. ''The settlements are all that concern you, not Serena's happiness nor the unsuitability of the match.''

Still chewing his last mouthful of breakfast, Sir Humphrey started to speak again, but Katherine forestalled him. ''Before you fly up into the boughs, I have a proposition to put before you,'' she said. ''Please hear me out. If you follow through on your plans with Archie, you will receive a fixed amount, which will in time be gone. The plan I am proposing will guarantee you an income for the rest of your life.'' She paused to see how this information would be received.

Sir Humphrey stopped eating for a moment, one eyebrow raised, before he said gruffly, ''Go on. I'm listening.''

Taking a deep breath, Katherine plunged into the speech she had prepared with great care. ''I should like you to resign your guardianship of Serena in favor of me.''

''Won't do it. Her income would come to you.''

''I realize that. Therefore, I, in return, will assign *my* total income to you *permanently*.'' He stopped chewing once again as the meaning of her offer became clear. ''In our present situation,'' she continued, ''you would have the benefit of Serena's income only three more years, until she turns twenty-one. If you accept my offer, you would have the same amount indefinitely.''

He took a long draught of ale, then asked, ''And what does your fine husband think about your tossing away the only income you brought to your marriage?''

As carefully as Katherine had prepared for this interview, she had failed to foresee this question. In the brief space before she answered, Sir Humphrey's eyes narrowed as he watched her carefully.

"He understands that I desire guardianship," Katherine said, "and he doesn't mind what I do with my own money."

"He doesn't know a thing about this little plan of yours, does he?"

"Of course he does."

"No, he doesn't, and there's no use lying to me, girl; I can see the truth in your eyes. That, of course, explains why your husband is not here with you. What business do women have dealing with money matters and issues of guardianship?"

"It is my money," Katherine returned angrily, "and it will be my guardianship. Who has more right to deal with it than I?"

"Don't get on your high ropes, girl," Sir Humphrey replied. "I haven't said no to your proposal now, have I? If I could trust you to keep your part of the bargain . . ."

"I have no intention of leaving anything to trust," Katherine said. "I've had a document drawn up by a solicitor. It states all the conditions I've mentioned. If we both sign it and have it witnessed, it will be a legal and binding agreement. I also have a document here that irrevocably assigns my income to you."

Katherine drew the papers from her reticule and handed them to her stepfather. He perused them for some minutes in silence, then rang the bell at his elbow. When the butler appeared, Sir Humphrey said, "Lady Rudley and I are about to sign some papers, Martin. We wish you to witness our signatures. Fetch quill and ink at once."

"Very good, sir."

When the butler left, Katherine asked, "You agree, then, to all the conditions stated there?"

"I would be a fool not to. I have nothing to lose and much to gain."

"You will break off the arrangement with Archie Postlethwaite?"

"I will."

"And I will receive no further communications from you asking for money?"

"Well, perhaps occasionally—"

"No," Katherine interrupted, "not occasionally, not ever. Once I have signed my income over to you, there will be nothing to send you."

"Surely your husband is generous—"

"I will not support you with my husband's money."

"You will have your sister's income."

"Which I will put aside for her. I will not bend on this point, sir. If you sign the agreement, you must manage on your own from now on. I can no longer help you."

By the time Martin returned with the writing implements, Sir Humphrey had made his decision. He set about signing the several copies of each document. Katherine signed after him, then Martin.

When all was done and Martin had left them alone again, Katherine said, "Lord Harrington has agreed to send the documents to both my solicitor and yours. He has assured me that once this is done, the Midsummer Day payments will be rendered according to the new agreement. Is this arrangement satisfactory with you?"

"I trust Harrington; I have no objection."

"Very well." After carefully returning the documents to her reticule, Katherine rose from the table and pulled on her riding gloves. "I appreciate your cooperation, sir. I think we have both profited from this morning's work."

As Katherine rode away from Briarwood Place, she prayed she would never see it again. The interview had gone much better than she had imagined it would. She knew she had been successful because she had found her stepfather sober. She wondered if Sir Humphrey would regret his decision the next time he was disguised.

When Katherine returned to Harrington Manor wreathed in smiles, her host and hostess and her dear friend knew her mission had fared well.

"Did he agree?" Charity asked.

"He did," Katherine answered. "To everything."

"I was certain he would," Lord Harrington added. "He

is much too shrewd to pass up such a good bargain, but I still think you were too generous, my dear."

"It was worth every penny to have Serena safely in my care at last."

He nodded approvingly. "That is true. His latest scheme to wed her to Postlethwaite was madness. I can't imagine what he was thinking."

"He was thinking of the money," Katherine said, "but he has agreed to call it off, and I will rely upon you, my lord, to make sure he follows through on his promise."

"I will certainly do so. You may depend upon it." Then changing the subject he added, "You young ladies had a busy Season. You, Katherine, married an earl. Charity actually learned to enjoy riding." Putting his arm around Katherine's shoulders and directing her to a comfortable sofa, he said, "You must tell me all about your new brother-in-law, who I understand was my daughter's riding instructor. Charity has been stingy with details about him."

Charity blushed becomingly but sat nearby and listened as Katherine gave Lord Harrington an all-encompassing description of Oliver's person and character.

At two o'clock Katherine's coach arrived to take her on her round of afternoon visits. Accompanied by Charity, she called on the vicar and his wife and several other acquaintances before she asked Charity, "How has Viscount Parnaby's mother been?"

"She is totally blind now and keeps to her room most of the time. I think it's a shame, especially on a day as glorious as this one."

"I should like to call on her," Katherine said. "Perhaps she will let us take her chair out into the garden."

She directed her coachman to the Parnaby estate, where they were welcomed warmly and taken to Lady Parnaby's rooms on the ground floor.

"My dear Katherine," she exclaimed, "and Charity! How thoughtful of you to come."

"I wouldn't travel all this way without stopping to see you," Katherine said, taking the older woman's hands and bending to kiss her cheek. "The day is beautiful and the sun is shining warmly. I imagine the aroma of the blossoms in your garden is heavenly. Will you come out with us?"

The viscountess smiled, her wide blue eyes staring vacantly into space. "I should love to."

A footman soon lifted the frail woman into her wheelchair. With a woven shawl over her shoulders and another across her knees, he pushed her through the house and out into the garden before relinquishing the task to Katherine. The chair rolled easily over the brick paths.

"I heard, of course, about your marriage, my dear," her ladyship said. "I am very happy for you, even though I had hoped . . ."

"I know, ma'am. I had hoped it, too, but it was not to be."

"Your garden is so lovely, Lady Parnaby," Charity said, skillfully changing the subject.

Her ladyship held out a hand and Charity laid her own in it. "And tell me, child, how you fared on this trip to London. Were there men writing sonnets to your beauty?"

When Charity blushed and failed to answer, Katherine supplied, "No sonnets, but there was a man who plied her with flowers and invitations."

"Indeed? And who was that, my dear?"

"My husband's brother, Mr. Oliver Seaton. He showed a marked preference for Charity's company."

"Then I suppose it won't be long before you shall wed as well. Then I shall lose both of my favorite young visitors."

Moved by the sadness in her voice, Charity offered, "But you will soon have a new daughter, Lady Parnaby, and perhaps grandchildren . . ."

Realizing too late how her words might hurt Katherine, Charity hesitated, casting an apologetic glance at her friend, who only shook her head and smiled as she added, "Charity is absolutely right. And in no time at all those grandchildren will be old enough to push your chair down these very paths, raising such a clamor that you will be wishing for your solitude again."

The smile on the viscountess's face told both girls that the picture they had drawn for her was a pleasant one.

When Lady Parnaby began to tire, Katherine and Charity took their leave, with Katherine promising to visit again on the morrow. "I am driving to Lincoln tomorrow afternoon to collect Serena, but I will ride over in the morning to see you, if you should like it."

"I would love it, child. You must tell me all about your husband and your new home."

The following morning Katherine visited with the viscountess for an hour. When it was time to leave, she walked round to the stables as was her custom. As the groom held her horse and she prepared to mount, she heard the clatter of hooves on the bricks behind her. She turned to encounter the startled gaze of Viscount Parnaby.

Chapter 12

"KATHERINE!"

"Lord Parnaby. Good morning. I have been with your mother. She didn't mention that you were here."

"She doesn't know. I arrived late last night."

After this burst of awkward speech they both fell silent until, conscious of the groom at her elbow, Parnaby asked, "Are you leaving? Allow me to escort you."

Unable to graciously refuse such a civil request with the groom listening to every word, Katherine said, "Thank you, sir, you are very kind." Turning to the Harringtons' groom, she added, "You may ride home, William. Lord Parnaby will see me back to the manor."

With only a nod the groom helped Katherine to mount, then collected his own horse and rode off, leaving Katherine and the viscount alone. Parnaby started his horse off at a slow walk and she followed suit.

"This is perhaps not wise, sir."

"Why not? You are a married woman. I am engaged. We are old friends. No one will think it strange if we choose to ride together."

"I thought you were in France," she said, searching for a harmless topic of conversation.

"I was. My intended wished to shop for her trousseau in Paris, so I escorted her there. It was actually quite entertaining."

"I have never been to Paris. I hope to go someday."

"I am certain Rudley will take you if you ask him. He knows the city well, I believe."

As they walked the horses along a highway they had ridden many times before, he said, "The horse chestnuts on the far side of Miller's Pond should be in full bloom. Shall we ride that way? It's a shortcut." He turned his horse right-handed onto a narrow lane, and Katherine followed.

The beauty of the spring countryside was undeniable. In a season often shrouded by clouds, mist, and rain, Mother Nature had offered two successive days of magnificent sunshine. The wood was fragrant with spring blossoms. Rabbits and hedgehogs scurried from sight as the horses trod the unfrequented road. Bees droned contentedly, seemingly overwhelmed by the sheer volume of flowers to choose from.

He paused near the pond where the trees were indeed robed in elegant white blossoms. "Shall we stop?"

She kicked her foot free of the stirrup and slid to the ground to stand near him. "This place is never lovelier than at this time of year."

"We had some grand times here, as I recall," he said, a twinkle in his eye.

She looked solemn. "Times we need not think of now—times past and gone forever."

"It was good of you to visit my mother," he said. "How did she seem to you?"

"Well. Hopeful. She is looking forward to grandchildren."

He looked out over the pond, where a cluster of ducks bobbed on the water's surface. "If my fiancée continues to be the cold, unresponsive creature I have found her to be so far, I think it's unlikely *that* dream will come true in the near future."

Katherine's voice revealed her shock as she replied, "James, you must not say such things."

"Why not? It's true. She has none of your passion, Katherine. When she looks at me, I feel none of what I felt with you." Then, rather bitterly, he added, "Does your husband content you? Can he satisfy you?"

Blushing painfully at this intimate remark, Katherine protested, "James, please. You must not speak so to me. Nor ask such questions."

"I've thought of you, you know, with *him*. Does he make you feel the way you felt when you were with me?" Without warning he took her into his arms. Taken by surprise, she instinctively raised her face to his as if no time had passed since the last time he had held her so.

His kiss was passionate, just as she remembered, but she was surprised to find that the embrace did not elicit the response from her that it always had in the past. She felt no quickening of the pulse, nor shortness of breath, but rather a sense of shock that he would so presume to trespass on her married state.

She pushed herself free from him as she said, "I will not discuss my husband with you, James, not now, nor ever. If you persist with this conversation or attempt to touch me, I will never speak to you again."

She turned away angrily, managed to mount her horse without assistance, and set off toward Harrington Manor. He caught her up after a space but maintained a prudent silence.

Absorbed in her own jumbled thoughts, Katherine hadn't considered that the road they were following would take them past the George Inn, where all of Rudley's servants were staying. Only when they were nearly upon the inn did she realize her blunder, but by then it was too late. Mr. Kendall was sitting on a bench outside the inn writing in a small book. He looked up and saw her and smiled. Her hope that she and her companion could ride by with a nod and a smile was dashed when Kendall put his book aside and stepped into the road to meet her.

Katherine drew her horse up beside him, striving for a normal tone.

"Mr. Kendall, allow me to introduce Viscount Parnaby, a neighbor and old friend." Then to Parnaby she explained, "Mr. Kendall is Lord Rudley's secretary. He arranged my journey and accompanied me."

The men nodded a mutual greeting before Kendall asked,

"I know you ordered the coach for three, Lady Rudley. Shall I come with you in the event the headmistress turns nasty?"

She smiled. "I should like that if you're sure you won't be terribly bored."

Glancing around at the remote inn, he replied rather ruefully, "This isn't exactly the hub of civilization. Three o'clock then."

As Katherine and Parnaby continued down the road he said, "You seem on intimate terms with your husband's employees."

"If you are trying to goad me into an argument, James, you will not succeed. My life and my friends are no longer your concern."

They managed to finish their ride without altercation and parted at Harrington Manor on relatively friendly terms. Parnaby declined to come in for refreshment. After a groom led Katherine's horse away, she climbed the steps alone then turned at the top to watch the viscount disappear around a bend in the drive.

Katherine's coach collected her promptly at three for the thirty-minute drive to Westleigh Academy where Serena was enrolled. Katherine had written to the headmistress of her intention to withdraw her sister from the school several days before the term ended.

Arriving at the square brick structure on the outskirts of Lincoln, Katherine laughingly assured Mr. Kendall that she could handle Miss Styles. She entered the building alone.

Her reception on this day varied greatly from the one that she had received when she first delivered Serena to the modest young ladies' academy. On that day she had been treated with polite deference. Today she felt more like royalty. She was shown immediately to what she was convinced was the handsomest salon in the building. Miss Styles was with her within seconds of her arrival, smiling excessively and seeing to Katherine's every wish. Would she care to sit? This chair was the most comfortable. Would she stay to tea? They would be so delighted.

Tea, for which Serena was invited to join them, was lavish. The headmistress chatted effusively, dropping so many "my ladys" into the conversation that Katherine began to feel as if she had strayed into Bedlam rather than a select school for young women. Miss Styles went on at length about how pleased she was to have Lady Rudley's sister grace her humble school. Certainly if Lady Rudley were to suggest Westleigh to her many elevated friends, Miss Styles would be eternally grateful.

Just as Katherine cast Serena a long-suffering look, wondering how they could tactfully extricate themselves from Miss Styles's presence, Mr. Kendall was shown into the room.

"Excuse me, my lady. Miss Serena's luggage is all loaded. If we are to arrive home in time for dinner, we must leave soon." He paused with an expectant look on his face.

Katherine rose instantly and extended her hand to Miss Styles. Serena curtsied demurely to the woman who had been her mentor for nearly nine months. Within minutes they were out the door and into the coach, the doors were closed, and they rolled away.

Only then did Katherine allow herself the laughter she had suppressed. "Peter, you were wonderful! How did you know I was desperate to get away from that woman?"

"It was simple," he replied. "Knowing you, and knowing the type of woman who operates such an establishment, elementary deduction was all that was necessary."

Controlling her mirth, Katherine said, "Allow me to introduce my sister Serena. Serena, this is Mr. Peter Kendall, my husband's multitalented personal secretary."

Kendall bowed from his seat opposite Serena as she extended her hand with a smile. "You were wonderful, sir. You quite silenced poor Miss Styles with your unexpected interruption and authoritarian manner. She is probably wondering, even now, who you are. It is so uncommon for gentlemen to be within the walls of Westleigh."

Kendall took the small hand offered and returned Serena's smile. He had noticed she was slightly shorter than her sister and her hair was a lighter brown. He suspected it was naturally curly, for the tendrils that had escaped from under her becoming bonnet curled tightly against her face. Her eyes, like Katherine's, were gray and lovely; her smile warmed her whole face.

The sisters hadn't seen each other for some months, so they chatted happily on the way back to Harrington Manor. Katherine had warned Serena in a letter not to mention Sir Humphrey. Faithful to her sister's request, Serena never mentioned his name until they were alone in the privacy of Katherine's room.

"Well, tell me," Serena demanded, the moment the door had closed behind them. "Did Sir Humphrey agree?"

Katherine took both her sister's hands, holding them in a warm clasp. "He did! You are no longer his ward but mine. You need not marry Archie Postlethwaite. You need not marry at all until you wish it."

Serena returned the pressure of Katherine's fingers. "But you gave up your income for me. How can I repay you?"

"You don't have to. I have all I need. Tell me what you think of my plans for your summer. Lady Brent is a sweet, good-natured woman and I know you will like Marie. Do you care for the Bath scheme?"

"Actually, I was rather relieved when you suggested it, for even though I don't know Lady Brent or her daughter, I had much rather go to them than foist myself upon you and your new husband. You deserve some time to yourself. You've only just married!"

"Don't be silly, Serena. We would love to have you with us. The last thing Ned said before I left was that if you didn't care to go to Bath, I should bring you home with me."

"I will accompany Lady Brent. Meghan Cavenaugh, one of my best friends from school, will also be in Bath this summer. Doubtless I will see her and perhaps others I know. I will come to you in August—when you're settled. Can you imagine how wonderful it will be to be together and away from Sir Humphrey!"

Katherine smiled. "It will be wonderful indeed. Do you

think, Rena, that you could manage to forget about Sir Humphrey? Ned doesn't know about him, and I would prefer it to stay that way.''

Serena frowned at this information, but since she was in the habit of abiding by her sister's wishes, she didn't question them now. "If you don't want me to talk about him, I won't, not ever. As far as I'm concerned he doesn't exist—never did.'' She hugged her sister then, more relieved than she could say to be free of the odious guardianship that had threatened her future.

Katherine and Serena spent several relaxing days with the Harringtons, then departed for London. There Katherine left Serena in the capable hands of Lady Brent before setting out on the final leg of her journey to Rudley Court.

As she drew ever closer to her new home, as landmarks and then roads became familiar, she realized she was eager to return.

She had suspected that her new status as the Countess of Rudley would give her influence. Her trip north had demonstrated to her just how much authority she had gained through her alliance with Rudley. Less than five months earlier she had been powerless against her stepfather, powerless to help her sister, dependent upon the charity and goodwill of the Harringtons and the Brents for her opportunity to go to London.

Her marriage had made it possible for her to rearrange her entire situation. She had Serena safely in her care; she had Sir Humphrey out of her life. She owed it all—a tremendous debt—to Rudley, and he didn't even know how greatly he had helped her.

From the time they had met he had given and given to her, and she had only taken. She remembered James's indelicate and improper comments about his fiancée's coldness and lack of passion. Rudley could fairly lay the same accusations against her. She had been no wife to him. She had talked with him, laughed with him, confided in him; but she had not given herself to him, not in the way a marriage intended, not in the way he wished.

Although there was much about her husband she did not understand, she had grown to respect him more than any man she had ever known. She admired the way he related to his friends and family—the depth of his loyalty to them and their fidelity to him.

She marveled at the way he was always in control, never ruffled, never at a loss. No doubt his power and position accounted for some of this, yet she believed that were he a man of no title and modest means he would command the same respect.

Most of all, she was touched by a vulnerability he displayed at the most unsuspecting times: he had carried a newborn lamb that had lost its mother from the field himself, putting it into the hands of his shepherd and making sure it was warm and cared for; there was a tenderness in his voice when he spoke of his mother and his determination to preserve the chair she had lovingly created; he displayed misgivings when Katherine teased him about his extravagance, or his experience, or his decadent youth; he had confided the pain of his first marriage, a disillusionment that still clouded his memory.

In these rare moments when he allowed her to see the chinks in his armor, she was permitted a glimpse of what she might bring to their marriage. She could play a crucial role in these small places: offering another perspective when hard decisions had to be made; repairing the trusting heart that had been left wounded by his first wife's betrayal; seeking a way to bridge the chasm that had opened between Rudley and his only child—this child who alone of all his family he held carefully at arm's length.

In this she knew she must take great care. If it were only the simple matter of cherishing Pamela there would be no problem, for the girl was a joy. But tied to Pamela was the specter of Arabella. Katherine was now convinced that Rudley was either unable or unwilling to separate them, either in his mind or in his heart.

The lake came into sight and the coach turned onto the curving drive. Would Ned be home when she arrived? she wondered. She imagined his tall form, his broad shoulders and dark hair. She could see his deep blue eyes, always tender and caring when they looked upon her. She realized she could hardly wait to see him, indeed, had missed him.

Then as the coach stopped and Mr. Kendall handed her down, she heard her name spoken and looked up to see Rudley descending the stairs two at a time.

"Katherine!" he exclaimed. "How I have missed you!"

Her glowing smile of greeting and outstretched hands were all the invitation he needed to envelop her in a fond embrace, very improper indeed before the interested eyes of more than half a dozen servants. In his enthusiasm, he lifted her off her feet momentarily, and she laughed as he set her down again, planting a chaste kiss on her mouth at the same time.

"We are shocking the servants, sir," she said quietly as she heard Kendall directing the footmen to unload the coach.

"It will do them no harm. They will have a subject of conversation for their dinner. You look wonderful. The trip went well?"

"It went superbly, mostly due to the skill of Mr. Kendall." As Kendall passed behind them, Katherine reached out to stop him.

"Yes, my lady?" he asked, smiling at her.

"Thank you again, Peter, for the ease of my journey and for all your help."

"You're very welcome, Lady Rudley." Then, noticing his employer's gaze fixed upon him, he asked, "Was there something you wanted, sir?"

"No, nothing," Rudley replied, offering Katherine his arm to escort her into the house. As they ascended the inside staircase alone he asked, "Peter?"

Katherine turned a questioning glance to him. "Peter is Mr. Kendall's given name. Surely you know that?"

"Of course I know it. I was just startled to hear you using it."

"Is it really so surprising? We spent days together in the coach."

"I knew you for months," he argued, "before I could even get you to utter my name, much less use it with the familiarity you showed with Kendall." By now they had reached the upstairs hall and stopped outside Katherine's bedchamber door.

She laid both hands gently against his chest as she said, "He is our employee. You were my suitor. A woman can't be too forward with a man who is courting her. She must be circumspect. Offer her favors sparingly, little by little."

"As an angler teases a fish onto the line, you mean?"

"If you like. Although I don't believe that fish enjoy being caught so much as men do."

"Oh, do we, indeed?"

"I think perhaps you do, yes." His arms moved around her and drew her close as her hands moved to his shoulders, then to caress his neck. "I missed you, too, Ned. I'm so happy to be home."

His kiss was gentle, hopeful, and she responded wholly, enjoying the sensation as much as he. He raised his head regretfully as approaching footsteps were heard down the hall. He opened her door and swung it wide. "I will see you at dinner. You must tell me all about your trip."

Chapter 13

THE CLOCK ON the mantelpiece in the blue drawing room showed five minutes past ten o'clock. Katherine was sitting near the fire with her needlework in her lap, occasionally glancing at the faded chair opposite. Rudley had once asked to see her work, but she had put him off easily, saying he must wait until the piece was finished in order to appreciate it fully. He was sitting on the other side of the room at a secretaire, writing. Pamela had been with them earlier but had gone to bed nearly an hour since.

Pamela was a shy, retiring child, totally different from what Katherine had been at the same age. By the time Katherine was ten, she had climbed every available tree, taken several nasty falls from her hunter, Jeremy, and even tumbled twelve feet off the balustrade of a bridge into the stream below. Pamela was a pattern-perfect young lady—always polite and proper, never speaking unless spoken to—a flawless product of the combined efforts of nurse and governess.

Katherine continued to be puzzled by the child and by her relationship with her father. Since Katherine's arrival at Rudley Court, she and Pamela had become friends. With Katherine Pamela put aside her formality and allowed her stepmother to see the natural inquisitiveness and youthful exuberance all children possess. But there seemed to be no sign of any improvement in Pamela's relationship with her father. In his presence she was unfailingly reserved.

"Pamela," Katherine had asked yesterday when they were walking alone in the garden, "are you afraid of your father?"

"No, ma'am," the child had answered readily. "Why should you think so?"

"You are so quiet in his presence; you never appear to relax with him. Why do you try so hard?"

"I want Papa to like me, Lady Katherine," Pamela had said innocently.

"Pamela! Don't be silly. Your father loves you! Surely you know that?"

"Mama didn't love me. She never said she did. She said I was in the way; she never wanted me with her."

"Oh, Pamela, I'm sure your mother loved you. Some people find it difficult to say they love you, but it doesn't mean they don't."

Katherine was shocked at the extent of the pain Arabella had inflicted. Not only had she destroyed Rudley's happiness for six years, she had evidently ignored the needs of her child as well. Katherine had found it appalling that Pamela had gone all these years feeling that neither of her parents bore any love for her! And then to have her mother die and her father desert her . . .

She had turned to Pamela and gone down on one knee to bring herself on a level with the child. She had looked into the wistful blue eyes and said firmly, "*I* love you, Pamela . . . very much. You know that, don't you?" Pamela had been in her arms instantly, and they had both wept.

"You have not set a single stitch in the last five minutes. Have you gone woolgathering?" Katherine's thoughts were dragged back to the present by Rudley's words. He had finished his letter and was watching her as she stared moodily into the fire. He crossed the room and stretched his long frame into his mother's handcrafted chair.

"I was thinking about Pamela," she replied.

"What about Pamela?"

"She thinks you don't love her."

His brows rose in surprise. "Did she say so?"

"Not exactly. She said she wanted you to like her."

"I have told you I do not consider myself a good father," he said.

"Did you know that Arabella never told Pamela she loved her?"

"No, I didn't know it," he replied, "but I'm not surprised."

"Pamela has suffered a great deal for one so young."

"Yes"—Rudley's voice showed some signs of irritation—"and no doubt you are about to put a large portion of the blame for that suffering in my basket."

"Didn't you realize that deserting her when her mother had just died would be a hard blow for a child of six?" Katherine asked.

"It wasn't a question of . . . ." He rose from his chair to pace the room and then began again. "I have already told you I seldom saw the child. I don't see that my staying or going should have affected her particularly."

"Well, it did," Katherine continued. "She was young, but old enough to understand you had both left her. And old enough to suspect that you didn't love her enough to stay with her or to take her with you . . . You resent the child because of her mother, don't you?"

He stopped pacing and turned to face her. He knew he shouldn't be surprised by such a question. Katherine was nothing if not direct. "Yes, I suppose I do resent her."

"But that is uncharacteristic of you, Ned. You are the fairest person I have ever known. I have seen examples of it time and time again in your dealings with people—with me. Can't you see that to blame the child for the faults of the mother is unreasonable, even cruel?"

This was hard criticism, and Katherine would not have been surprised to hear him respond with anger. But he did not. He said simply, "I don't think I can be reasonable in matters concerning my first wife."

"Couldn't you try to separate Pamela from your memories of her mother?" Katherine suggested. "She loves you so much, and she strives so hard to please you. If she felt you cared for her, I think it would go a long way toward easing her painful memories." She was silent then, giving him time to weigh her words. He came to her chair and, taking both her hands in his, drew her to her feet.

"It would please you if I made an effort with Pamela, wouldn't it?"

"You know it would."

"And you must know by now," he continued, "that I would do anything to please you. . . . I will try to be more considerate of Pamela's feelings in future."

"Not only for my sake," she objected.

"For your sake, for my own, and especially for Pamela's."

"And will you think, too, about engaging an art tutor for her?"

"Does she need one?"

"I believe she does, and Miss Shaw admits that she has taught Pamela all she knows. We both feel she would benefit from someone with more expertise."

"Has Pamela an interest? Will she apply herself?"

"Has she an interest?" Katherine asked in surprise. "You've seen her work. She loves it!"

He shook his head slowly as he answered, "I think I recall Miss Shaw reporting that Pamela drew well, but I can't remember ever seeing any examples of her work."

"But surely she must have shown you some of them?" Katherine asked in disbelief. "You said she gives you detailed reports."

"She does. Reports on Pamela's progress. I do not demand that she show me proof or example."

Katherine rose from her chair so suddenly that she startled him. "What is it?" he asked.

"Come with me. There is something you must see."

Katherine immediately led the way upstairs to Pamela's apartments while Rudley carried a branched candelabra to light their way. They entered the sitting room through its door to the outside corridor. Seeing that the connecting door to Pamela's bedchamber was closed, Katherine took a taper and proceeded to light all the candles in the room. As the level of light slowly increased, easels began to take shape from the shadows and the framed pieces on the walls came into view.

With the candelabra in his hand, Rudley moved to stand before the old globe of the world. How well he remembered spinning it when his tutor was absent from the room. He and Oliver had always preferred games to geography. Their youngest brother John was the bookish one, always telling them to apply themselves. How long ago it seemed.

He stepped around the globe to the table where they had partaken of their afternoon tea; it was being used now as a drawing desk. Sketched on a paper was a rough outline of the stableyard. Beyond the table, carefully pinned to a board, was a finished drawing of the main stable and its attached yard. It was minutely detailed, each brick of the building faithfully diagramed, not suggested. The perspective was excellent, the shadows fixing the time of day at midmorning. In one corner a young lad held a lady's horse while she mounted from the block. In the foreground several grooms harnessed a team to a curricle, while in the background any number of stable boys hurried about mucking out stalls. Some pitched fresh bedding and hay while others carried heavy buckets of water. Rudley noted that one bucket had even sloshed over, making a wet spot on the bricks.

"Pamela did this?" he asked without turning his head.

"Yes," Katherine returned. "They're all hers." She watched in silence as he moved from one work to another.

He made no comment until he came to the winter scene of the house and lake. "This is done from the same perspective as my mother's chair in the drawing room." He stood for long minutes before the portrait of himself but said nothing. When he had seen them all, he moved back to the table where Katherine stood. "She wants for discipline and technique, but the most important part, the instinctive talent, is there. How long has she been doing work like this?"

"Miss Shaw says she began to make copies of things she saw when she was barely six, but most of these she has done during the past year. You do think she is good then?"

"She has a God-given gift, and there is no question but

that it should be nurtured. I will hire a special tutor as you suggest. I am certain she could benefit from further instruction." He moved back to the far wall, once again studying the portrait of himself. "You must find it disgraceful that I know so little about those things that most closely concern Pamela."

"It is not what I am accustomed to. I was very close to my parents."

"And I to mine," he returned. "But it's not the same with Pamela. I've never felt any bond . . ."

"Because she reminds you of her mother."

"Partly. She . . ." He paused, then seemed unwilling to continue.

After a few moments she said, "You need not tell me. I do not wish to anger you by interfering."

He moved back toward her, placing his candelabra on the table nearby. "You are a part of the family now, Katherine. Any concerns you have cannot be considered interference. One of the many things I love about you is your perceptiveness. I would be a fool indeed if I did not allow you to exercise it! Besides, I am not easily angered, as you may have noticed."

"Yes, I have noticed," she answered, "and you have spoiled a very pretty compliment by mentioning it."

They stood close, and as she smiled at him in the candlelight, he brought his hands up to hold her arms above the elbows. His face was stern and her own smile faded. "Katherine, I hope you will be patient with me. I haven't been in the habit of noticing how people feel or caring what they think. Arabella gave me a distaste for wanting to know people that way. I have found it much simpler, and a lot less painful, to avoid such involvement."

"I think you are too hard on yourself," she argued. "You have been very sensitive with me."

"Perhaps. But then I am convinced you bring out the best in me. Thank you for bringing me here tonight. I have been at fault where Pamela is concerned. I will try to make amends, if it's not too late."

"I'm sure it's not." She raised herself on tiptoe and kissed him impulsively on the mouth, a shy smile skimming over her face. She was so quick that he had no time to respond, and when his hands tightened on her arms, she turned away. He released her, his eyes following her as she moved about the room extinguishing the candles. He glanced once again at the intricate stableyard charcoal before lifting the candelabra from the table. "I would like to see all these again with the benefit of daylight."

Katherine was pleased. "Come anytime. I know Pamela will be delighted to show them."

The following day Rudley had planned an expedition to a fine Thoroughbred stud. It was a two-hour drive, and since the morning was sunny with only a light breeze, he suggested that they travel in his curricle.

The sights and sounds of spring were everywhere, from the greening of the trees and the pink and white of the dog roses and honeysuckle, to the tiny cry of a newborn lamb separated from its mother. Katherine felt wonderful. She could never remember being happier or more at peace.

They made excellent time, arriving at Lord Gilborough's estate far sooner than Katherine expected they would. Rudley turned his team onto a long winding drive bordered on both sides by fenced pasture. A short distance ahead she could see a group of mares and suckling foals. As they came closer, the earl drew his team to a walk and then a standstill. He pointed to one particular mare.

"Do you see the bay on the left, the one with no markings? She is Karma's dam. I have been trying to buy her from Gilborough for years, but he won't part with her. Every one of her race-bred colts has been a winner, and even Karma, who was bred for hunting, has plenty of speed."

Katherine looked the mare over appreciatively. "What is she called?"

"Her real name is Thistledown," the earl replied, "but they call her Lady Halfmile. When she was a three year old, there wasn't another filly, or even a colt for that matter, that could touch her speed at the half-mile."

"Do you remember asking me the other day to decide what I should like for a wedding present," Katherine asked, "even though I told you I consider Karma a more than generous gift?"

"I bought Karma from Marcus because I knew how much you fancied her," he said. "I have a stable full of horses equally good. I want your wedding gift to be something special, unique."

"I think I have found the present I should like," she said, never taking her eyes from the stunning mare.

"Oh, no, you don't, Katherine! Never say you want Lady Halfmile! I have just told you that Gilborough will not sell her!"

"But, my lord!" she exclaimed in shocked tones. "As I recall your offer, you said you would give me anything I desired, so long as it was within your means. Are you telling me you cannot afford the mare?"

"You are a wicked girl, Katherine. If you continue to take literally every word I speak, I will make good my threat to beat you. And you may believe me when I say I shall enjoy it!"

They were still laughing as they pulled up in front of Lord Gilborough's home, and they remained in high spirits throughout the day. After a delicious luncheon, they enjoyed a tour of the entire stud. They viewed stall after stall and pastures full of magnificent Thoroughbreds.

When it came time to leave and Rudley was saying his farewells to Lady Gilborough, Lord Gilborough approached Katherine. He congratulated her once again on her marriage and handed her a small sealed note. "Lady Rudley, would you be so kind as to give this to your husband *after* you have arrived home again? It is something he can do for me, if he would."

"Certainly, my lord, I shall be happy to." She took the note curiously and tucked it safely away in her reticule. They drove home in a leisurely fashion, arriving in good time for dinner and declaring themselves very satisfied with the day's adventure.

Rudley found a letter from Oliver awaiting him. After dinner that evening he informed Katherine and Pamela that young Master Nicholas was coming home the next day—a prospect that delighted Pamela. Nicholas, turned six, was somewhat younger than she, but Katherine had gathered from conversations with Pamela that the two often shared adventures together. This was not surprising, considering how children were naturally drawn to one another. Katherine could remember how often as a child she had wished for companions near her own age. After Pamela retired, Katherine asked her husband how Nicholas came to be living at Rudley Court.

"When Oliver and Lydia were married, they took a house in Kensington," Rudley answered. "They had only two short years together. When she was so cruelly taken from him, he had no desire to stay on there. He sold the house after he and I decided to leave for Spain. That's when Nicholas was brought here."

"What is Nicholas like?"

"Do you remember the portrait of Lydia I showed you in the gallery?" Katherine nodded. "The boy is the living image of his mother. Even as a baby he had curly fair hair, as she did, and the same round face. Every year as he grows older he resembles her more closely."

"Does it trouble Oliver that Nicholas looks so like his mother?"

"I don't believe so. They are very close."

"But I thought Oliver seldom saw his son."

"On the contrary. They spend a great deal of time together. They have been together these past weeks in Sussex with Lydia's parents, and Oliver often comes here to see Nicholas. Lately, I suspect he has been thinking of marrying again, in which case Nick would go permanently to live with him."

"Did he say which lady has captured his interest?" Katherine asked, trying to sound nonchalant.

"I think it's plain to anyone with eyes to see that it's your friend Miss Harrington whom he admires." It was now Rudley's turn to go fishing for information. "Do you think she would welcome his suit?"

"I believe she would," Katherine said. "I know she admires him."

"I'm glad. I believe a relationship prospers best when there is mutual affection."

Then, in a sudden change of subject, he said, "It grows late. You must allow me to escort you upstairs. It has been a long day, and you must be well rested for your first meeting with young Nick."

"Heavens, my lord, you fill me with terror! Is he such a firebrand?"

"I must admit I find the activities of a normal six year old fatiguing in the extreme, but I have not the slightest doubt that you, dear Katherine, will find his antics very much to your liking."

He left her at her door, and with her maid's help she was soon ready for bed.

"Shall I blow out the candles, m' lady?"

"No, Bess, please leave them. I think I shall read for a bit, but you may go."

As the door closed quietly behind the maid, Katherine settled comfortably to enjoy a few pages of the novel she was reading. After a few minutes she discovered she couldn't concentrate. She was pleased to discover that Oliver was close to his son but was puzzled as to why Rudley spoke of Oliver's son with more warmth than he spared for his own daughter.

Chapter 14

KATHERINE AWOKE WITH a start. The candle at her bed-side was guttering, and she realized she had fallen asleep. She rose from her bed to extinguish the other candles in the room and saw that the clock on the mantel showed a quarter to midnight. She must have been more tired by the day's drive than she suspected.

Thinking of Lord Gilborough's lovely horses, she suddenly remembered the note he had given her for Ned. She had forgotten to give it to him! She took it from her reticule on the dressing table and stood, wondering what best to do with it. "I will give it to him first thing in the morning," she told herself aloud. Then she reconsidered. "But Lord Gilborough did ask me to give it to him tonight."

She turned decisively toward the communicating door, thinking that her husband might still be awake. She passed through the dressing room connecting Rudley's bedchamber with her own and saw light showing beneath his door. She knocked quietly, and when there was no reply, she knocked more loudly. Still there was no answer. Turning the handle, she found the door unlocked. She entered the room to find several candles lit and the fire still burning. There was, however, no sign of the earl. The bed had not been disturbed, and it was quite obvious that he was not in the room.

Katherine looked about with interest, for she had never been in the room before. She stepped inside, moving toward the warmth of the fire. The bank of windows to her right was shrouded by crimson velvet draperies. Directly before them sat an ornate low-profile writing desk. Clearly her husband enjoyed a view of the lake while occupied with his correspondence. Against the far wall a massive bed, also hung in crimson, displayed an intricately embroidered counterpane. Several framed paintings, indistinguishable in the shadows, adorned the dark-paneled walls. Katherine's feet sank into a plush Axminster carpet woven in an intricate floral pattern of blues and reds. Even as she was appreciating the softness of the carpet and realizing she had come away without her slippers, the hallway door opened and Rudley entered.

"Katherine!" His voice exhibited pleased surprise when he saw her standing there. "Did you want me? I decided I wanted some brandy and didn't care to drag Wiggin from his bed, so I went down to the library."

She held out the note to him. "This is for you. Lord Gilborough entrusted it to me this afternoon and asked me specifically to give it to you tonight, but I had forgotten it until now. I am glad I found you still awake."

He seemed to notice how lightly she was clad, for he stepped to the bed where a loose comforter lay and carried it to a small couch set near the fire.

"Sit here, Katherine, and wrap yourself in this." She traded him the note for the quilt and sat down as he suggested. She watched as he crossed to his desk to pick up a silver letter opener. Rudley had discarded the coat and waistcoat he had worn earlier in the evening; he was in his shirtsleeves with his neckcloth removed and his shirt open at the throat. His hair was slightly ruffled as if he had absentmindedly run a hand through it. As Katherine watched him, the firelight full upon his face, she tried to guess the contents of the note by reading his expression.

Rudley,

You have stolen a march on us all by capturing the most sensible woman in all of England. I can't imagine why she would have you, but, as they say, there was never any accounting for taste. For your lovely wife's sake you may have Lady Halfmile at the figure you offered me last summer. You may collect her anytime after her current-year colt is weaned. No doubt when you race the foal she is now carrying and beat me at the track, I will regret this generous impulse. I write this to you so that you may keep the mare as a surprise if you wish. Once more, my friend, you have my compliments on your marriage. May it be a long and joyful one.

Gil

Rudley was smiling, and Katherine was curious about the note. "What does his lordship say? He said something about a favor you could do for him."

Rudley laid the note aside and went to her. "Yes, there is something he would have me do."

"But why the note? Why did he not just ask?"

"It is rather a delicate matter," Rudley explained. "I imagine he did not wish to discuss it before you."

"I see," Katherine said. Actually, she didn't see at all, but Rudley's comment had effectively ended the conversation.

"Will you take some brandy, Katherine?"

"No, thank you. I should be getting back to bed."

"You shouldn't go about without slippers."

"Yes, I know. I forgot them."

He seated himself beside her on the couch. "And you shouldn't stand before firelight in only a thin nightgown, as you were when I came into the room." Her color rose as he continued, "There are some men who might be tempted to take advantage of you in such circumstances."

Putting both hands behind her head, he drew her slowly to him until his mouth closed over hers in a long, passionate kiss that sent icy shivers coursing through her. When he ran his hands down her back to her waist and pulled her close, she came willingly, and as she instinctively raised her arms about his neck, the comforter fell away.

He finally released her mouth, his lips trailing down her neck to her shoulders.

Her heart was pounding so violently that she found it difficult to breathe. She heard him whisper, "My God, Katherine, how I have longed to hold you." He was kissing her again, his hands caressing her back, when suddenly she brought her hands to his chest as if she would hold him away.

He released her instantly, his brows drawn together in concern. He clearly read the apprehension in her eyes.

"Katherine," he said earnestly, "surely you must know I love you . . . *have* loved you for weeks. I cannot bear to think you are afraid of me!" He looked searchingly at her, but she did not answer him. "You *are* afraid, aren't you?" he insisted.

"A little, yes." She spoke so quietly that he could barely hear the words.

He took her hands and held them gently. "As well as you know me now," he asked, "can you truly believe I would do anything to harm you? Surely you haven't allowed yourself to believe the old wives' tale, the one that claims husbands to be monsters who use their wives abominably, simply to satisfy their own desires? It's not true, Katherine!"

He was startled when his words elicited a spirited response from her. "There are most certainly men who treat women badly. I have known several!"

"Very well," he conceded, "there are some who do. I, however, do not number myself among them. Katherine . . . look at me." She obeyed him and he saw tears standing in her eyes. "You are my wife, not my possession. I cherish you, and I hope to God I shall never give you any reason to fear or mistrust me. Come," he said, rising to his feet. "You are shivering. I will take you back to your room."

Rudley led Katherine to her bedchamber and saw her into bed. He snuffed out her candles and, pausing only to say good night, returned to his own room. He poured himself some brandy, took it to a chair near the fire, and sat staring into the flames as if in them he would find some explanation for Katherine's unusual behavior.

When he had seen her in his room his heart had soared, for he felt this was her way of telling him that she was prepared for their relationship to progress. She had responded to his kiss with as much warmth as he could desire, but she had just as certainly pushed him away. He suspected he was still competing with the specter of Parnaby and knew instinctively that he couldn't force the issue. He was a patient man and he would be content to wait. As much as he wanted her—even more he wanted her to come to him willingly.

No sooner had the door closed behind Rudley than Katherine was out of bed again. This time she put on her slippers, pulled the golden counterpane from her bed, and dragged it with her to the window. She drew open the heavy draperies, gathered the coverlet about her, and curled up in the window seat. A crescent moon hung over the lake and was reflected in its black surface. She could see that it was setting and before long would fall behind the trees along the ridge.

She smiled. Ned said he loved her. She had wondered; now she knew. Yet she realized she hadn't needed the words to tell her what her heart had already guessed. For weeks past she had felt his love for her in the gentleness of his touch, heard it in the softness of his voice, seen it in the tenderness in his eyes. From the moment he began kissing her, she felt an awakening within herself—a desire and a need to return his embrace. She had not wanted to stop him, but some demon memory overpowered her, preying on the tiny doubt that remained.

Rudley's actions tonight had laid that last doubt to rest. He had placed her needs before his own without question and without hesitation. And wasn't that really what love was, after all? Putting the loved one first? For weeks he had been the most patient of husbands, while she had been less than an appreciative, dutiful wife. When next they were together, she was determined to be the wife he deserved.

Katherine slept late the following morning. When she finally went down to breakfast, she found a note from her husband awaiting her.

My dearest Katherine,

I have received by messenger this morning an urgent note
from my brother John. My presence is required in London
immediately to attend to some family matters. I am sorry
I could not wait to say good-bye. I did not intend to leave
you alone for Nick's homecoming, but I have every confidence you will handle all admirably. With any luck I
should be home again by tomorrow evening and shall look
forward to seeing you then.

Ned

Katherine was disappointed. She would miss him, but she
was determined he would have only good reports of how the
house had been run in his absence. She kept busy with her
needlework most of the morning and was happy for the di-
version when Master Nicholas arrived in the early afternoon.

Nicholas was exactly as Rudley had described him: a ver-
itable powerhouse of a boy, impish and blond, with the
brightest of temperaments. He was glad to be home but full
of news about his stay with his grandparents and the adventures he and his papa had had there. Pamela soaked up every
word, seeming to enjoy hearing about the exploits as much
as Nick had enjoyed participating in them.

Later that day the three of them rode together, Katherine
on Karma and the children on their ponies. One of the grooms
offered to take the children, but Katherine insisted she enjoyed their company. Their constant chatter distracted her
enough to keep her from being too lonely for her husband.

The following day was overcast and before midday it began to rain. The children were busy in the schoolroom, and
Katherine was restless. When the sky cleared somewhat in
the late afternoon, she decided to try a short ride. She would
take the lane toward London, and if she was lucky, perhaps
she would meet Ned coming home.

At the stables Henderson was hesitant when she ordered
Karma saddled. "Like as not you'll get a good soaking if

you go out now, m'lady. I doubt the rain has stopped for long.''

''I shall take my chances, Henderson. If I should get wet, believe me, it won't be the first time.'' It was not his place to argue with his mistress, so without further comment he had the mare saddled. Within a few moments, declining the company of a groom, Katherine trotted off down the drive.

To her displeasure Henderson's prophecy proved correct. She had gone something less than a mile when the rain began again. It was not heavy but steady, and in no time Katherine found herself quite soaked. Although she actually enjoyed riding in the rain, being wet and therefore chilled was not pleasant, for even though it was early June the day was not warm.

Reluctantly, she turned Karma toward home. Katherine may have been enjoying the weather, but Karma seemed not to share her enthusiasm, for no sooner had Katherine turned her about than the mare quickened her pace. A warm, dry loose box was undoubtedly her notion of the best place to spend a rainy June evening.

When Katherine trotted into the stable, she saw to her surprise that the earl's chestnuts were being unharnessed and rubbed down. ''Henderson, when did his lordship return?''

''He arrived almost fifteen minutes ago, m'lady, considerably wetter than you are, I would say.''

''I don't see how that could be possible''—Katherine laughed—''nor do I see how I missed him on the road.''

''Most likely he took a shorter way, m'lady, to save time.''

Gathering her hood close about her face, Katherine hurried across the lawns to the house. There was a young footman on duty at the front door, and she realized that the butler and most of the other servants were at dinner. As Katherine ascended the staircase, he said, ''I shall send Bess up directly, Lady Rudley.''

''No, please, Gordon, do not disturb her dinner. I don't need her.''

He shrugged his shoulders at this and returned to his post at the door.

Katherine entered her bedchamber to find Rudley toweling his hair before her fire. He had already changed into dry clothes, and he glanced up as the door opened. "Good God, Katherine!" he exclaimed at the sight of her. "Were you also caught in the rain?"

"No. I rode out in it purposely, hoping to meet you, but we missed each other."

"I hope you don't mind my using your fire," he apologized. "Mine was not lit."

"I don't mind in the least, but you should let me help with your hair. You are making a poor job of it. Where's your valet?"

"I came in by the side door. No one knows I'm here."

"Welcome home, my lord. We missed you."

"We?" he teased.

"All right, *I* missed you," she confessed.

"Turn around," he commanded. "I will help with your buttons." Her riding habit buttoned up the back, a detail she had forgotten when she so cavalierly rejected the services of her maid. She turned her back to the fire so he could see the small buttons; in no time at all he had them open for her.

"You are very quick, my lord. I wonder, have I discovered yet another hidden talent?" She cast a look of amused innocence at him and saw a slight smile curling his lips and a glint of appreciation in his eyes.

"I have a great many skills, Katherine, most of which you know nothing about." He picked up a wrapper from the foot of the bed. "Here, put this on, then we'll see if I can help you dry *your* hair." She took the wrapper from him and disappeared into the dressing room. She was gone only a few minutes. When she returned, she was struggling to pull the pins from her wet, tangled hair. Rudley sat in a chair near the fire. "Come," he said. "Sit on the floor at my feet and I will rub it dry."

"This reminds me of when I was a little girl," Katherine

said, complying with his request. "My mother had me sit like this to dry my hair."

"And in a few years' time, no doubt, you will be drying your daughter's hair in much the same way."

"I want children, Ned, very much!" she said impulsively.

He bent his head to place a kiss on her neck and felt her tremble at his touch. His lips were close to her ear as he spoke softly. "In order to have children, my love, we must first have a marriage in more than name only."

She rose to her knees and turned to face him. "I want that, too."

"Are you sure?"

"Yes, perfectly. I believe you love me . . . and I want you to make love to me. And I do trust you, Ned . . . completely."

After such a confession he could not resist kissing her. When he could pull himself away, he rose and crossed to the door, sliding the bolt home. He then did the same with the communicating door to his own rooms.

"What will the servants think?" she asked.

"They will think we do not wish to be disturbed."

Chapter 15

DETERMINED AS KATHERINE was to put her memories of James behind her, she was to find that such resolve was not completely possible. But if Rudley found his young wife shy and tense, she found in him nothing but infinite tenderness. He was gentle and patient, passionate but not demanding, and she found herself lulled by the security his love offered. By the end of a week her memory of James had been reduced to the status of a dream, and she was content to leave it so. She and Rudley spent their daytime hours much as before, but now their nights also were spent together, laughing, loving, and finally sleeping in each other's arms.

The final week of June offered a string of warm, sunny days. Katherine and Rudley had ridden far one morning and on their return stopped to visit with farmer Merchant.

"My best draft mare dropped a fine filly this mornin', m'lord. She come early so I'll be able to send back the geldin' Mr. Kendall has lent me to do the field work."

"Could we see the foal, Mr. Merchant?" Katherine asked.

"Why, for certain, m'lady, she's over here to the barn."

The new filly was tall and big-boned, so different from the spindly legged, fine-boned foals produced by Rudley's Thoroughbreds. But she was certainly beautiful and appeared strong and healthy.

"She is a fine-looking filly, Merchant," the earl said. "I can see why you are proud of her. We will hope she grows to be as willing a worker, with as fair a temperament, as her dam." He patted the huge mare as she stood calmly enjoying the attention. She was not in the least concerned to have three humans sharing the stall with her foal. The filly started nosing around for more milk, so they left her to her meal and walked back to where two of the Merchant boys were holding their horses.

On their ride home they enjoyed a conversation concerning the various breeds of draft horses being used by the farmers on the estate. When they arrived at the house, Katherine kicked her foot free of the stirrup and slid to the ground, but as she landed she was overcome by a wave of dizziness so strong that she had to clutch at Karma's saddle to keep from falling.

"Katherine, is something wrong?" Rudley's voice showed concern as he noticed her strange behavior and stepped toward her. As a groom led the horses away she took the earl's arm gratefully.

"I was suddenly dizzy," she explained. "I'm probably hungry. I had no appetite for breakfast and we are late for luncheon again, are we not?"

"Yes, I am afraid we are. Have you noticed that Mrs. Simpson is no longer preparing delicate perishable dishes for us at midday?"

"Yes, I have noticed. And we can hardly blame her, for we are never on time for the meal."

They had taken only a few steps toward the house when Katherine stopped again. After one look at her pale countenance Rudley lifted her in his arms and carried her into the hall. Reeves hurried forward.

"Her ladyship is feeling faint, Reeves. Have Mrs. Windom come upstairs and send one of the grooms for Dr. Bailey." Appearing outwardly calm, Rudley was nevertheless uneasy. He didn't actually believe that simple hunger could make a person faint. He carried Katherine to her bedchamber and laid her gently on the bed. After pouring water into the basin, he dampened a cloth and was bathing Katherine's forehead when Mrs. Windom hurried in.

"Mr. Reeves said her ladyship was feeling poorly, my lord. I have brought my smelling salts."

"She's not unconscious, Mrs. Windom. But I think if we could pull these boots off, she would be more comfortable." Together they removed the boots and then covered Katherine with a light blanket.

Taking Katherine's hand in his, Rudley asked, "How do you feel now?"

"Better, I think."

"Do you make a habit of fainting?"

"I've fainted only once before in my life. That night at the ball. You remember."

He nodded. "I have sent for the doctor and he should be here directly. It's probably nothing, but it will be best if he has a look at you, just to be safe." Bess came into the room then and Rudley excused himself, knowing the women would want to have Katherine undressed and properly between sheets so she could rest more comfortably.

Some time later Dr. Bailey opened Katherine's bedchamber door to find the earl restlessly pacing the corridor outside. Rudley turned anxious, questioning eyes to the doctor, a worried frown wrinkling his handsome brow.

"You may come in, my lord," the doctor said. "I have finished with my examination."

"And have you found anything amiss, Doctor?" the earl asked.

"Not precisely amiss, my lord, but I think I can tell you what has caused your wife to swoon." Katherine, dressed now in a demure white nightgown and wrapper, had been sitting on the window seat, but as the doctor spoke she rose and took a few steps toward him. "Congratulations, my lord," the doctor said, a bright smile on his friendly face. "I suspect you are about to become a father again!"

Several tense moments passed while all three stood in silence. Finally Rudley spoke, his voice incredulous. "Katherine is increasing?"

"It's very early still," the doctor replied, "but I am nearly certain it is what caused Lady Rudley to swoon."

Rudley's glance shifted to Katherine and he saw her staring at the doctor in puzzled disbelief.

"I suspect the fainting is only a temporary problem," Dr. Bailey said, "and should pass in a few days' time. Get plenty of rest, my lady, and regular meals, and I'm sure you understand you must not ride in your condition."

Rudley walked the doctor to the door, then returned to confront his still-silent wife. "Have you nothing to say?" he asked. "Aren't you pleased?"

"I . . . I just can't believe . . . How can it be so soon?"

"How do you mean?"

"Doesn't it take longer? My parents were married seven years before I was born. I assumed it would take more time."

Rudley led her back to the window seat and sat beside her, taking her limp hands in his. "It is true that in some marriages a deal of time passes before the couple has children, but other times it happens quickly, as it has with us. I believe that in each month there is a chance pregnancy will occur."

She listened to his words with interest, a look of wonder on her face. "Truly? I never imagined. It's so hard to believe. Just a few weeks ago I was saying I wanted children, and now I will soon be a mother."

A tentative smile lit her face and tears threatened. "What about you, Ned?" she asked, her hands finally finding life and returning the pressure of his. "Are *you* pleased?"

He smiled. "I would like a son, if you should be kind enough to give me one." Then, anticipating her next question, he added, "But should the child be a girl, she will be equally welcomed."

The summer months passed in a daze for Katherine. Her husband was more attentive than ever. The servants, already disposed to like their amiable, generous mistress, were pleased that she would be supplying the earldom with a child the following year. Secretly they all hoped for a boy but planned on a little wagering when the time drew nearer.

Pamela, who worshiped her new art tutor and immersed herself in learning all he could teach her, was delighted to learn that she was to have a little half brother or sister. Serena wrote regularly from Bath. She was enjoying her stay there but looked forward to joining Katherine in late August, especially now that a child was expected.

Katherine heard nothing from her stepfather (indeed she did not expect to) until one day in late July when a letter from him arrived with the penny post. She took it immediately to her room and opened it with shaking fingers. He had promised not to write. Why was he breaking his word?

Her mood changed from anxiety to anger as she read his casually worded request for funds. Surely she could spare him a bit from Serena's allotment. How could she and her sister possibly need the half of it with Rudley paying their way?

Katherine drew a piece of writing paper from her desk and answered briefly. She insisted she would not bend on this point. He had agreed to her terms and she had his promise in writing; he had no right to make demands on her. She added for good measure that this was the last time she would write, and if he wrote to her again, she would destroy his correspondence unopened. She folded the brief message and, without adding any funds (as she always had in the past), sealed it and had Bess hand-deliver it the following day to the receiving office.

Rudley had never repeated his request to know who Sir Humphrey Corey was. Katherine didn't think he had forgotten. Perhaps he had decided it wasn't important. Whatever his reason, she hoped he would never ask.

August was warm and blessed with abundant rainfall, so the crops flourished. Hay was being mowed on most of the farms. Since Katherine wasn't permitted to ride, Rudley had taken to driving her out most mornings in his curricle. One Thursday morning showers kept the haymakers out of the fields and the earl and his countess from their morning drive. Katherine and Rudley were sitting together in the morning room discussing the merits and demerits of a new breed of sheep he wanted to introduce on the home farm when Reeves entered with a silver salver and offered a visiting card to Rudley. He lifted it from the tray casually, then regarded it with interest. "Show the gentleman in here, Reeves, and send down for some refreshments."

As the butler left, Katherine asked, "Who is it, Ned?"

He noted her reaction carefully as he replied, "Sir Humphrey Corey—a gentleman with whom I believe you are acquainted."

She rose to her feet, paling noticeably as she took a step toward her husband. "Ned, I—"

She got no further as the door opened again and Reeves preceded Sir Humphrey into the room, then announced him. Finding her knees suddenly wobbly and untrustworthy, Katherine took a step back to the chair she had occupied a moment before and sank down onto it.

Rudley waited in vain for Katherine to offer an introduction. All color had drained from her face and she sat as if turned to stone. Sir Humphrey genially filled the void with good-natured chatter.

"Well, now, Katy, it's a fine, beautiful home you have here, that's for certain." Turning his gaze to Rudley, he extended a hand in greeting. "And you must be the Earl of Rudley. Pleased to make your acquaintance. I'm Sir Humphrey Corey, you know, Katy's stepfather."

Rudley accepted the offered hand and shook it briefly, managing through his surprise to say, "How do you do, sir. Won't you sit down?"

Gordon entered at that moment with refreshments, which gave Rudley a moment to collect his scattered wits. He cast an accusative glance at Katherine, but she refused to look at him.

Accepting a cool drink from the footman, Sir Humphrey continued, "I can see I have surprised you, but I had to deliver a horse down this way and since I was so close, I decided to stop and see how my little girl went on in her new life."

This comment brought a response from Katherine, who now raised her eyes to stare at him with contempt. His little girl, indeed! How dare he come here? Gordon offered her lemonade, which she took gratefully, for her mouth was suddenly dry.

"You're awfully quiet, girl," Sir Humphrey noted as Katherine still had not spoken. "Not feeling quite the thing, I suppose. That's to be expected, considering your condition and all."

Katherine spoke at last. "My condition?"

"You can't expect to keep such a secret in our village. The vicar's wife has been most everywhere telling all who would listen. I suppose she had the news from Lady Harrington. You could have written me, Katy, to tell me yourself. This will be my first grandchild—well, step-grandchild at any rate. But there's not much difference in my eyes."

Katherine was silenced once again. To hear Sir Humphrey prattling on in this way as if he had ever cared for her! As if he would ever care a whit about any child she bore. It was the outside of enough!

Fortunately, Sir Humphrey chose to keep his visit short. After only ten minutes he rose to leave, saying he must not be late delivering his horse. He added that he was putting up at the inn in the village and would perhaps see them again before he left for home.

When Rudley invited him to join them for dinner that evening, Sir Humphrey declined, saying he had a previous engagement.

When he was gone and the door closed, Rudley turned accusing, questioning eyes upon his wife. His face was nearly as pale as hers. Several moments passed in silence until finally he said, "I don't know what to say to you. Can't even think where to begin."

"I should have told you about him," Katherine said simply.

"Oh, really?" he replied scathingly. "And deprive me of perhaps the most uncomfortable ten minutes I have ever spent?" He was angrier than she had ever seen him. He continued, "You told me you had no living relatives. Was that a ghost who visited with us just now?"

"He's not a blood relative."

"Don't mince words with me, Katherine. Blood relative or not, he's your stepfather. He should have been invited to the wedding. He should have been consulted about the engagement. Common courtesy demanded that. Why did you lie to me?"

"I didn't lie to you. I have been my own mistress since I attained my majority. I did not need his consent to wed. I did not want him present at our marriage."

"Ah. Now we are getting somewhere. Why did you not want him there?"

"We don't get on. We never have."

"Not good enough."

"He's normally crude and despicable, nothing like he was today."

He frowned as he asked, "He was acting?"

"No. Not precisely. Sometimes he behaves reasonably, but not often. He is not naturally polite, nor congenial."

"Perhaps you should explain."

As she looked up at her husband, trying to collect her thoughts, tears filled her eyes. "I don't want to explain," she said passionately. "I don't want to talk about him or even think about him. He's a part of my past that I wish to forget."

She raised one hand to her forehead and closed her eyes, looking so pale and shaken that Rudley bit back his next comment.

"I'm feeling rather unwell," Katherine said. "I should like to lie down."

Looking as if he was far from finished with the conversation, Rudley said, "I'll help you upstairs."

He did just that—went with her to her room and pulled the draperies to shut out the light before going downstairs to the estate office. He found Kendall there, busily working.

"Women are prone to emotional upheaval—fits and starts—when they are expecting, Peter, are they not?"

"I believe so, sir. I have heard it said."

"I have discovered who Sir Humphrey Corey is."

"Yes, sir?"

"He is my wife's stepfather."

That same day in the late afternoon Sir Humphrey paid another visit to Rudley Court. This time he found his stepdaughter alone.

She almost refused to see him but decided such an action would be cowardly.

The moment the door was closed she said without preamble or greeting, "You promised. You signed a legal document."

"Now, Katherine, my dear, don't get on your high horse. I was only ten miles away. You really couldn't expect me to ignore such an opportunity to see you."

"You have no reason to see me. Our relationship is over."

Ignoring this remark, he walked to the mantel and fingered the fine Chinese vase that stood there. "I knew Rudley was well-heeled, but I never imagined he enjoyed such wealth. How can you grudge me a little, Katy, when you have so much?"

"You sold a horse today. Didn't he bring you a fat profit?"

"Yes, but not nearly enough to buy a stallion up for auction next week. He is exactly what I need to cross on my heavier mares."

"What happened to the Trojan?"

"Unfortunately, I lost him in a little wager with Sedgewick."

"You gambled away your best breeding stallion?" she asked incredulously. "You show time and time again that you haven't a single ounce of responsibility in your entire being. I will not give you any more money, not one pound, not a single shilling!"

In the estate office Rudley and Kendall finished their work and Rudley went in search of his wife. Usually at this time of day he would find her in the salon. He left the office by its connecting door to the library. He had barely started through the room when he heard angry voices coming from the salon, whose connecting door with the library had been left slightly ajar. Katherine's was one voice; the other he soon recognized as that of their morning visitor. Sir Humphrey had left his genial tone behind on this visit. His voice was harsh.

Rudley's first impulse was to join them immediately, but when he heard Sir Humphrey's next comment he hesitated, wishing to hear how his wife would respond.

Sir Humphrey spoke tauntingly. "Your husband seemed remarkably ill at ease when we met this morning—almost surprised. Could it be that you somehow failed to mention me to him?"

"You're right," Katherine admitted. "I hadn't told him about you. But he knows now. Go away, sir, and leave me in peace. I am asking you to keep the promise you made."

"Don't speak to me of promises," Sir Humphrey fired back. "You who have no intention of honoring the promises so recently made to your husband."

Katherine's voice turned distinctly cold. "And what precisely do you mean by that?"

"Don't play the innocent with me. Your husband may believe that you visited Lincolnshire to collect your sister, but everyone in the village knows it was Parnaby you came to see."

"You are quite mad."

"Am I? You arrived on Tuesday, he arrived on Wednesday. He left for London the same day you did. You went nearly every day to his home. Do you truly think people believe you went there to see his *mother*?"

"Would you like to leave now, sir, or shall I call my butler to show you out?"

"I'll leave on my own—wouldn't want to cause a stir. By the way, whose brat *is* this you're carrying, your husband's or Parnaby's? Or do you even know?"

While Rudley stood rooted on the far side of the door, horrified by what he was hearing, Katherine rose and walked to the bellpull, giving it a vicious tug.

Sir Humphrey rose reluctantly. "I'm going. Tell me, do you still keep a journal where you write all your little secrets? That's how I knew you were in love with Parnaby in the first place. I used to pop into your room and read it from time to time. I daresay your husband would find it entertaining."

As the door opened and the butler appeared, Katherine

said, "Sir Humphrey is leaving, Reeves, please show him out." She hovered inside the salon until she heard the outside door close, then she stepped into the hall to address the butler once more. "If he should ever call here again, I am not at home. Do you understand?"

"Yes, my lady. Perfectly."

Katherine proceeded across the hall and down a corridor to a side door. After the morning's rain the day had turned pleasant. She let herself into the garden and sat there on a bench until her pulse and respiration had returned to normal.

When Katherine had quit the salon, Rudley retraced his steps to the office, where Kendall was studying an estate map.

"Peter?"

"Sir?"

"When you were in Lincolnshire, did Lady Rudley use the coach?"

"Yes, sir, nearly every day to go visiting."

"Whom did she visit?"

"A great number of people. All old friends, I assume."

"And did she ride out?"

"Yes, she did. I saw her myself on several occasions."

"With whom was she riding?"

Unaccustomed to such questioning, particularly about her ladyship, Kendall frowned. "Once she was with Miss Serena and Miss Harrington, once with Lord Harrington, another time she was accompanied by a young lord who lived in the neighborhood. I cannot recall his name, though she introduced us."

"Was it Parnaby? Viscount Parnaby?"

"Yes, sir, I believe it was."

"And how did they seem to you?"

"Seem, sir?"

"What sort of terms were they on?"

"They seemed friendly, my lord. She introduced him as an old friend."

"Were they accompanied by a groom?"

"No, sir, but it was midmorning and they traveled the high road. No one could take exception—"

"Thank you, Peter, you've been most helpful."

Cut short, Kendall watched his employer leave the room. He stared at the closed door for some time after Rudley had gone. Their strange conversation filled him with foreboding.

Chapter 16

RUDLEY ASCENDED THE main staircase and made his way to his wife's apartments. When there was no answer to his knock, he entered, closing the door behind him. The draperies were still drawn from Katherine's nap earlier. He opened them now. All traces of the rain shower had passed, leaving behind a blue sky and soft white clouds. As the light reached the far corners of the room, he turned to regard the furnishings.

Did Katherine keep a journal? She did! He recalled seeing it beside her bed, recalled watching her write in it. It was a slim brown volume. Walking to her bed, he opened the top drawer of the night table. The book lay there in plain view.

He knew a moment's hesitation. Such a violation of privacy was unforgivable, yet the painful questioning of his heart demanded answers. Sitting on the edge of the bed, he picked up the book and opened the cover. There at the top of the first page was the name he had come to loathe: "James Haygarth, Viscount Parnaby." That was all the sheet contained, only the name, written across the top in Katherine's neat script. He turned the page and was astonished to see his brother's name on the top of the second sheet and his own name on the next. As he leafed quickly ahead he saw that each page held a name followed by notes and comments. The back section seemed to be filled with ordinary diary entries.

Turning back to the front, he discovered the listings there were only men. Then, as he read through them with more attention, he realized they were only eligible, single men.

With his heart turning cold, he turned back to the page that flipped held his name and slowly read the notes written there:

Edward Seaton, Earl of Rudley
   early 30s
   widowed several years
   one child-daughter 10?
   excellent memory
   delicate manners
   home in Hampshire
   strong family ties
   first wife-Lady Arabella————?
   interest in Milicent Battle
   often in London
   decisive
   excellent dancer
   unostentatious

He hadn't finished the page when the door opened and Katherine stood on the threshold. At first surprised to find her husband there, she immediately noticed her journal in his hands. She closed the door quietly, wondering vaguely how Sir Humphrey could have worked his evil so quickly.

She crossed the room to stand at the foot of the bed. Rudley neither spoke nor moved, but the bewildered look in his eyes was one she would not soon forget.

"That book is private."

He snapped it shut with one hand. "I've seen enough."

"Did you come here looking for it?"

"Yes."

"Did Sir Humphrey speak with you while he was here?"

"No. I was standing on the other side of the library door for the latter part of your conversation with him."

"Oh, my God," Katherine whispered as she closed her eyes and tried to imagine Rudley listening to the horrible accusations Sir Humphrey had thrown at her. She realized now that she hadn't even denied them—she had long ago discovered how fruitless it was to argue or talk back. "I'm afraid I have much to explain."

"The opportunity for explanation is no longer an option for you, Katherine. I have several questions that you will answer—honestly, if you please."

As he came impatiently to his feet, she moved to a chair and sat down as he fired his first question at her. "What is the nonsense in this book? The names and the notes?"

"It is a list of husband candidates. I started it when I first went to London. I listed all the eligible men I met—their characteristics as well as information about them."

"Why?"

"I had gone to London determined to marry. I think that making the list was one way to convince myself that I would go through with my plan. I also felt it would aid me in making a wise choice."

"Why are some names crossed off? Oliver's and others'?"

"I crossed Oliver off when I realized he was attracted to Charity. The others I deleted for various reasons. Lord Atherford because he drinks too much. Mr. Dale because he gambles to excess. These were traits I did not desire in a husband."

"And you considered marriage with all these men?"

"I was determined to marry one of them."

"How many offered?"

"Four, including yourself."

"Four!" He was pacing the floor now, a disbelieving frown on his handsome face. "Why is there nothing written on Parnaby's page?"

Katherine looked at him, then away, not answering.

"The truth, Katherine, with no delay."

"I didn't need to write about him, I knew everything without writing it down."

"He was your first choice, isn't that so?"

"He never offered for me."

Rudley walked to the window and gazed out with unseeing eyes. He wanted to ask why she had married him. He wanted to ask if she loved Parnaby, but the answer was obvious. She had gone north to meet Parnaby; she had chosen Rudley as her husband because of all the candidates on her "list" he had had the most to offer. He found he could not bring himself to ask these questions, for he knew he could not bear to hear her answers.

The silence in the room dragged on as Rudley continued at the window and Katherine remained in her chair. He threw open one of the casements and allowed the warm breeze to pour over him. The day was as fresh as ever, the sky as blue. White clouds hung soft as feathers above and the surface of the lake sparkled as sunshine bounced off ripples stirred by the breeze.

He saw none of the beauty before him, for he was consumed by only one thought. Katherine was pregnant—possibly with another man's child.

He turned suddenly from the window. His tone was that of a stranger, harsh and unfamiliar. "Did you go to Parnaby's home repeatedly while you were in Lincolnshire?"

"Yes. I went to visit his mother. She—"

"Do you truly expect me to believe that? Even Kendall saw you with him."

"I rode with him. Is that so terrible?"

"You took no groom along. You were alone with a man you once hoped to wed. And you swear nothing inappropriate happened?"

She opened her mouth to deny any wrongdoing, then hesitated as she remembered the indelicate conversation she had shared with James, remembered the kiss to which she had initially responded. The pause lengthened while she tried to form an answer that would be both honest and unhurtful to him.

"Your silence speaks most eloquently, Katherine. I think we have said all there is to say."

He paused for a few moments, and when he continued, his voice was devoid of all feeling. "I will be leaving for London immediately, and I will hope that no pressing business calls me back here in the near future."

She looked up in shock at these words. "Can't we talk? I can explain!"

"You could offer explanations from now until sundown, and not one of them would alter the facts. I knew you were attracted to Parnaby, but I thought that once he was lost to you, you would put it all behind you. I never imagined you would have an *affaire* with him—"

She interrupted him in quick defense. "It was not an *affaire*! I loved him. I kissed him, but we were never together—not in the way you think!"

"So you say. Unfortunately, I find myself unable to believe you. If this is his child, and if it should be a boy, I will be expected to accept Parnaby's bastard as my legitimate heir! Yesterday I would have willingly laid down my life for love of you. Today I cannot forgive you for forcing me into this compromising position and for placing the future of my family in jeopardy."

Then, without waiting for a reply, he tossed the journal into her lap, turned on his heel, and was gone. Katherine knew, as she watched him leave the room, that her only chance for happiness went with him.

Rudley sent orders round to the stables for Navigator, and when he descended the steps twenty minutes later, he found Henderson holding the horse in the drive. "Do not expect him back, Henderson. I'm taking him to London."

"Your lordship would make better time with the curricle."

"I'm not in a hurry, and I wish to have him with me in town."

"But it is forty-five miles, m'lord," the groom objected.

"I'm well aware of the distance, Henderson," he snapped. "If you are concerned for Navigator, rest assured your concern can be no greater than mine. I will not overtax his strength."

"No, of course not, m'lord. I did not mean to imply that you would."

Rudley sprang easily into the saddle, gathered the reins, and moved off down the drive at a brisk trot. When he joined the main road, he did not turn toward London but struck off to the west instead. He followed the high road for a short distance and then turned left-handed onto a narrow bridle path that wound its way slowly downhill until it came to the stream that fed the lake at Rudley.

It was a small stream, perhaps five feet across, and shallow. Years ago, someone had constructed a sturdy footbridge in the event that the path should be used by pedestrians.

Rudley dismounted and, tethering Navigator to a low tree branch, walked onto the bridge and sat down upon its edge. The water was higher than usual with the recent rains, but his boots still cleared the surface by more than a foot.

He stared down into the rushing water and could recall almost word for word the conversation he and Arabella had here nearly eleven years ago. It was on this bridge that she had told him she was increasing and the child was not his. Not content with the initial pain she inflicted, she turned the knife in the wound by adding that the only reason she had married at all was to save herself from disgrace and that she had chosen him simply for his title and his wealth.

Rudley and his wife had been estranged from that day forth. For the next five months until Pamela was born, he suffered agonies, cursing himself for the impatience that prompted his hasty marriage and blaming himself for his stupidity in the choice of a wife.

Until today he had not given much credence to the maxim that history repeats itself, but now he had become an example of it. What evil fate haunted his life that he should be burdened with the support of children, none of them his own? Arabella died without revealing the identity of Pamela's father, and the secret of her birth was now Rudley's alone. He publicly acknowledged her as his own but could never feel close to her, for she was a living testament to her mother's duplicity. Katherine's condition had plunged him back into the same hell from which he had struggled to climb for ten miserable years.

After remounting Navigator, Rudley returned to the high

road and set a steady pace toward London. He stopped for dinner at Woking, having fasted since breakfast, and bespoke a room there for the night. He arrived unexpectedly in Cavendish Square the following day to find that Oliver was not in town but had gone down to Buckinghamshire to spend a long weekend with Lord and Lady Finley.

"I'm going to bathe, Benson. When I come down, I would like some brandy in the library. If anyone should call, I am not at home."

When Rudley announced the plans for his marriage, his aunt Helen had declared her intention to return to her cottage near Greenwich. At the same time Oliver offered to take rooms of his own in town, but Rudley rejected the idea. "Nonsense. Katherine and I plan to spend most of our time in Hampshire and you will oblige me by staying here. You know how much I dislike having the place empty."

So Oliver had stayed on at Rudley House, but the earl was relieved to find him away from home on this occasion. He was not yet prepared to discuss his reasons for leaving the country, and it would be impossible to hide his distress from his intuitive brother.

For three days Rudley stayed alone at home, eating little and sleeping less. As a young man of twenty-two he had been overcome by despair when he learned of Arabella's treachery. To a man in his position, the family, the title, the direct line of descent were paramount. He had carried a heavy burden of guilt for failing those generations of Seatons who had come before him. It had been his responsibility to faithfully protect the line, and he had failed. The family honor had been compromised. He hadn't known what he would do if his wife bore a son. But Arabella had borne a daughter, and disaster had been averted.

Yet now he found himself facing the same impossible situation again. He had lived this nightmare before and knew from past experience that there was no solution to the problem now facing him. Yet he could not bid his mind be still, for this time fate had woven a subtle alteration into the fabric of his dilemma.

When Arabella had admitted her deceit to him, it had been an easy thing for his bitterness and disillusionment to override and destroy any tender feelings he had ever borne her. But with Katherine he was not to be so fortunate. She, like Arabella, had deceived him. Yet, beneath the fury in his mind and the pain in his heart, he could not deny he loved her still.

Oliver arrived in London late in the afternoon on the following Monday, and Benson greeted him at the door with profound relief. "His lordship is here, Mr. Oliver. He arrived Friday, from Hampshire."

Oliver relinquished his hat, gloves, and whip into the man's hands as he answered, "Is he? The Brents are back in town. No doubt he came up to collect Miss Serena."

"Lord Rudley has not been to the Brents', sir. He has not gone out at all since the afternoon he arrived. I am concerned for him. He says very little, and he has eaten almost nothing since he came. He sits hour after hour in the library drinking a bit too much brandy, if you don't mind my saying so. Last night he never went to bed at all but just sat all night by the fire."

"Where is he now, Benson?"

"Still there, sir, in the library, with strict orders that he is not to be disturbed."

"Thank you, Benson. Try not to worry. I'll see what I can do." The butler seemed relieved that the earl's brother could now share his concern, and he turned instinctively toward the library. "You have your orders, Benson, remember? Don't announce me. I'll let myself in." Oliver stepped across the hall and entered the library.

Rudley was standing by the windows that gave onto the square. He turned to face the door as Oliver entered, and Oliver saw at once that the butler was not exaggerating his brother's condition. Rudley had not been shaved and his clothes certainly looked as if they had been slept in. He seemed thinner, and there were dark circles beneath his eyes. The eyes themselves were red-rimmed and bloodshot from a lack of sleep and an excess of alcohol.

Oliver crossed to his brother in a few long strides and held out his hand in greeting. He made no attempt to hide the concern in his voice when he said, "My God, Ned, what have you been doing to yourself? You look awful!"

Rudley took the hand but ignored the question as he replied, "I saw you ride up. Did you find our sister and her husband well?"

"Well enough. What are you doing here? Is there some trouble between you and Katherine?"

The earl gave a short, scornful laugh. "That is certainly one way of putting it. Let's just say I have found it necessary to put some distance between my wife and myself."

"Must we speak in riddles, Ned? Tell me what has happened, and perhaps there will be some way I can help."

Rudley shook his head with finality. "No, dear brother, there is no way you can help this time, any more than you could the last. My wife, you see, has decided to do a repeat performance of Arabella's marvelous pregnancy scene. It is to be my pleasure and privilege to receive, for the second time in my life, the gift of another man's child to raise as my own."

"What madness is this?" Oliver exclaimed in shocked disbelief. "Katherine's child is yours!"

"So I believed. Until last Thursday, when I had the pleasure of meeting Katherine's stepfather and learning from him of Katherine's tryst with Parnaby in Lincolnshire in May."

"Her stepfather? I thought she had no family aside from her sister."

"So did I. It seems that was not true."

"But this is incredible! There must be some explanation. Katherine would not purposely deceive you! She is not at all like . . ." He broke off, unwilling to continue.

"Not at all like Arabella? A week ago I would have agreed with you. But it appears we have both been mistaken."

"What explanation did she offer?"

"She said she was visiting Parnaby's mother."

"Perhaps she was."

Rudley regarded his brother scornfully. "Katherine is not

the forthright person we believed her to be. Do you know she kept a list of husband candidates when she first came to London? We were both on it.''

''What?''

''Truly. Although she told me she generously struck you off when she found her friend, Miss Charity, fancied you. She told me at the time that she needed to establish herself in order to make a home for her sister. As it turns out, she and her sister had a perfectly good home with their stepfather.''

''Then why was she so determined to marry?''

''She is in love with Parnaby, but he needed to marry a fortune. By marrying me she could safely be with him whenever the opportunity presented itself. She won't be the first woman who married one man in order to safely carry on an *affaire* with another. I can tell you something else that will surprise you. Katherine was considering an offer from Arthur Witford.''

''Witford!''

''My exact sentiments when I heard. Fool that I was, I played right into her hands by making an offer ten times as good as Witford's. There is no way Katherine would have refused me, yet she feigned reticence. I remember sitting up half the night, pondering just how to word my proposal in order to gain her acceptance.'' He finished his brandy, then turned the empty glass between his fingers. ''These past weeks, Oliver, I was convinced her love was equal to mine. But I realize now that she has never admitted loving me. Never said the words. Not even once.''

As Oliver sank into a chair, Rudley sat, too. ''My God,'' he said, ''why did I ever sway from my resolve? I had sworn I would never again allow a woman any power over me, but I did. Why? Why did I do it?''

''Because you loved her. Running away doesn't help the situation, Ned.''

''Nothing helps,'' Rudley returned.

There was a pause before Oliver asked, ''Could the child be yours?''

"Yes. But it could also be Parnaby's."

"Did Katherine admit to intimacy with him?"

"No, but I didn't expect her to. When her stepfather accused her, she denied nothing."

"He said such things in your presence?"

"No. I overheard a conversation between them."

"Did you ask her yourself about her relationship with Parnaby?"

"Yes. She answered my question with silence."

"Perhaps you hurt her simply by asking it. If she has been a faithful wife, Ned, such a question would be cruel." As Rudley reached for the brandy decanter once again, Oliver shoved it out of his reach. "Is this your solution?" he asked angrily. "To sit here and drink yourself into a stupor? You should go home and stay there until you have heard every word Katherine has to say."

"I have heard enough. I will not go back. God help us all if this child should be a boy! It is too much to hope for another girl; not even I can expect such luck two times running."

Rudley's face was grim, and Oliver could see that three days and nights of dismal reflections had taken their toll both physically and mentally. If he continued much longer in this state, he was likely to make himself truly ill. Oliver strove for a lighter tone. "Enough of this incarceration of yours," he said. "I am famished. We are going upstairs where you will shave and change and then we are going to dine at Watier's."

To Oliver's surprise, Rudley raised no objection to this proposal and even made a fairly decent meal. Sharing his problem with his brother had seemed to lighten his burden. When they returned home soon after dinner, he went willingly to his bed and slept soundly until morning.

At breakfast Rudley announced his plans to post immediately into Yorkshire, where he had extensive property. "Kendall has been plaguing me for years to look into my holdings there. From what I understand, considerable work needs to be done, and I would like to keep myself occupied.''

"What of Katherine?" Oliver asked.

"She must do without me. I cannot go back, not now."

"The Brents are back in town. That's why I thought you were here—to take Miss Serena home with you."

Rudley sighed. "I had forgotten. Could you take her down?"

"Certainly. Would you object to my taking Charity Harrington as well?"

Rudley considered the suggestion. "Katherine spoke of having her come. It would certainly make my absence appear more natural. Why are we always plotting ways, dear brother, to keep our family wounds from bleeding in public? Surely. Take Miss Harrington if she will go, and fob the world off with the tale that I am detained by business in the north. If you would stay at Rudley yourself, you could do me a great service by helping Kendall to carry on the work we have started. There will be dozens of decisions to be made. I would be easier in my mind if I knew you were there to keep all running smoothly."

"If Katherine is agreeable, I am convinced Miss Harrington's parents will have no objection to her bearing her friend company, especially if they know you are to be absent for some time. You must write the letter though, Ned. To Katherine. I could not invite myself, nor Miss Harrington."

Accordingly, Rudley composed a brief missive and sent it off immediately. He had no plans, however, to wait for a reply. Within a very short space of time he had completed all the arrangements for his trip north and was well on his way when his letter arrived at Rudley Court.

Katherine,

Oliver will be arriving shortly from the city to oversee the management of Rudley in my absence. He will be escorting Serena and has expressed his willingness to bring Miss

Harrington should both you and she wish it. Please inform him as soon as possible of your decision. He will await your answer in London. I have enclosed a letter for Kendall, and you will oblige me by seeing that he receives it.

Rudley

Katherine had broken the seal of this letter with trembling hands, but its contents did nothing to lift her depression. She, like Rudley, had passed through days of emotional turmoil following his sudden departure. Again and again she had relived the horrible scene in her bedroom. She could still see the anger, the pain in his eyes. She had never imagined that keeping her secret about Sir Humphrey would ever escalate into a disaster of such magnitude. One moment her life had been nearly perfect, then Sir Humphrey's visit had brought everything crashing down about her head.

At first she had been shocked to think Rudley would suspect her of infidelity, but after she had time to view it from his perspective, she understood how he could doubt her. She should have told him about Sir Humphrey. She should have refused to ride with James, or at the very least told Ned about their meeting the moment she returned home. She should have denied Sir Humphrey's accusations on the spot instead of retreating into angry silence.

And finally, and not the least of her mistakes, she should have burned the journal the moment she accepted Rudley's proposal. Making such a list was not something she would normally do. She had devised it as a physical prop for an effort she had no stomach for. It had helped her to keep her goal in mind, to steel herself for a task repugnant to her.

She was heartsick to think she had destroyed Ned's faith in her and driven him from his home. By the time his letter arrived, Katherine had had enough solitary misery and welcomed the prospect of Serena's homecoming and a visit from Charity. She prayed her husband would come back, but she knew he had meant his final words to her. He was not the man to speak in exaggeration or idle threat. He had said he could not forgive her, and she didn't know if there was anything she could ever do to restore the trust they had lost.

Chapter 17

RUDLEY'S PRECIPITATE DEPARTURE for town had left Kendall with the entire responsibility for the estate resting on his shoulders. Although he was a competent secretary, he had no power to make many of the decisions that had to be made on a daily basis. He and Rudley had taken on a great many new projects, and he was doing his best—within the limits of his authority—to keep things progressing smoothly. He was, however, greatly relieved to receive the letter the earl had enclosed with his note to Katherine.

Kendall,

I have decided to take your advice and proceed immediately to my Yorkshire property. There can be no doubt my agent there is doing a poor job. I plan to spend a month or so putting things to rights and hiring competent people who I can trust to carry on when I leave. My brother Oliver will be arriving shortly to take over for me in the work we have started at Rudley Court. He stands in my place, by my authority, and all decisions will rest with him. If Lady Rudley should make any request of you, either for money or service, you will oblige me by granting it. I will keep you informed of my progress.

Rudley

Kendall folded the letter carefully and placed it in his desk. All of Lord Rudley's actions recently had been uncharacteristic in the extreme. It was not like him to change his plans suddenly without notice. Whatever Lady Rudley's stepfather had had to say during his visit, it had clearly caused a major crisis in the household. Rudley was gone for the foreseeable future, and Lady Rudley had been transformed from a joyful mistress one day to a preoccupied and cheerless one the next.

Not having the benefit of his employer's confidence, Kendall was determined to follow Lord Rudley's instructions to the letter. He would do everything in his power to support Lady Rudley through her husband's absence.

At the end of the third week in August, Oliver, Charity, and Serena arrived in Hampshire and settled in with the easy familiarity of old friendship.

That same evening Serena cornered her sister in the drawing room after dinner. "Where is Lord Rudley, Katy? I was so looking forward to meeting him."

"He is up north tending to some business matters. He has estates in several parts of the country, Rena."

"Can't you travel with him?"

"I don't think it would be wise. I shouldn't wish to do anything that might endanger my baby." She took her sister's hand and smiled fondly at her. "Just because I'm married now I can't expect my husband to constantly dance attendance on me. He has work to do. And, besides, I have you to keep me company, and for a time Charity and Mr. Seaton, too."

Serena let the subject drop and Katherine was relieved. Tomorrow, when they were alone, Katherine would tell her sister the truth, for she had decided that there could be no half-truths or description between them. Such tactics had destroyed Rudley's trust. She would not make the same mistake twice.

Katherine enjoyed watching Oliver with the children. He had the kind of relationship with them that she had so often wished Rudley could have. He loved them freely and openly, and they returned his affection just as naturally. Sometimes, watching Oliver, there would be a gesture or an expression that would put Katherine strongly in mind of Ned, and she would find herself praying for the hundredth time that he would come home.

Two days after their arrival, when Charity had gone with Mrs. Simpson to gather herbs in the garden, Oliver took the opportunity to speak with Katherine. He found her in the blue drawing room doing some meticulous needlework on what appeared to be a copy of his mother's needlework chair. He had come in silently from the terrace through the open doors and was looking over her shoulder. "Katherine!" he exclaimed. "This is beautiful! How are you managing to do it?"

She smiled with genuine pleasure at the compliment. "Thank you. It was to be a surprise for Ned. It's not difficult, only time consuming. I have a great deal of time on my hands just now."

He moved around to the front of the sofa and sat beside her.

"Ned has told you what happened between us?" she asked.

"Yes."

"I thought as much. Was it your idea or his for you and Charity to come and stay?"

"It was mine, but he approved it."

"Well, I'm glad you came. I was lonely here by myself."

"Do you resent his leaving you?" Oliver asked.

"He can't help the way he feels. He thinks I lied to him and he doesn't trust me anymore. He made it clear why he couldn't stay."

"But he gave you no chance to explain."

"Even if he had heard my explanation, I don't think he would have believed me. That's what frightens me so, Oliver. I don't know if I'll ever be able to regain his trust, and if I can't do that, then our marriage is over."

"You must be patient with him. He has been hurt in the past—he needs time."

"There is something I don't understand, Oliver. If Ned told you why he left—what he believes I have done—why would you offer to come and stay with me?"

187

"I've made some terrible mistakes in my own life," he offered, "and if I've learned anything from them, it's that it's not my place to judge others. Ned and I have a lot in common, but in this one way we are very different. He needs to get away when he confronts a problem. He likes to view it from a distance—that's how he manages to gain perspective. I'm different. I like to confront conflict head-on, get all the facts on the table with no roundaboutation. I'm not saying one way is better than the other. I think both have merits and faults. What I am saying is that Ned's going away is not altogether a bad thing. It's his way. Eventually he'll sort it all out, and if he finds he still has questions that need answers, he'll have to come to you to get them. I can tell you this, though. If you are still in love with someone else, it's unlikely you'll have any answers that will satisfy him."

"I am no longer in love with Lord Parnaby, Oliver. I swear to you I'm not!"

"You should tell Ned that, if you get a chance. It might help."

She shook her head despairingly. "I don't think so. I don't think he would believe me. What's so awful about this whole situation is that I *knew* Ned was unhappy in his first marriage. He told me so. Now I am responsible for hurting him again." There were tears in her eyes and Oliver reached out to take one of her hands in his. "Oliver," she continued, "I need to find a way to talk with him, if only for a short time."

"He will be in London at the end of the month," Oliver suggested. "Write to him and tell him you would speak with him."

"Do you think he would come?"

"If you phrase it properly, I don't see how he could very easily refuse."

Later in the day, with Oliver's suggestion in mind, Katherine drafted several letters to her husband and finally settled on the following:

My lord,

I find it has become necessary for me to speak with you

188

on a matter of some importance. Oliver has told me you will soon be in town. If you could arrange time in your schedule to pay a short visit to Rudley, I would appreciate the courtesy.

Yours, Katherine

She showed the letter to Oliver after dinner and he smiled appreciatively. "There is no way any gentleman could refuse such an appeal. You will have your interview, Katherine."

Oliver had more than one motive in bringing Charity Harrington into Hampshire to stay with Katherine. It was true that he felt Katherine should not be alone. When her condition became apparent, people would think it strange that the earl would leave his new bride in the country while he attended to business two hundred miles away. But it was also true that Oliver was hoping to renew his relationship with Miss Harrington.

He and Charity had enjoyed an acquaintance of only three months before Ned and Katherine's wedding. Oliver had made plans to remove his son from Rudley Court for the first month of his brother's marriage and had spent several weeks with Nicholas and his in-laws in Sussex. When he returned to London in mid-May and called in Berkeley Square, he found that Charity had gone home to Lincolnshire. He had missed her by only two days.

He had no intention of allowing Miss Harrington to depart from his life as suddenly as she had entered it, but he had not been able to hit upon any way to see her again. This, then, was his golden opportunity, and despite his concern over the plight of his brother and sister-in-law, he intended to make the most of it.

After four days of being almost continuously closeted with Kendall, Oliver made a bid for liberty and managed to talk his brother's secretary into giving him a free afternoon. He immediately went in search of Charity, whom he had seen little of except at mealtimes. He found her with Katherine and Serena walking in the shrubbery behind the house.

"That man of Ned's is a slave driver!" he exclaimed as he caught up with them.

"He is certainly hardworking," Katherine agreed. "But he is grateful for your help, Oliver. He has told me so."

"In any case, he has relieved me from duty for the remainder of the day, and I am here to ask any or all of you to come riding."

"I would love to," Charity answered. "Serena, will you come? And you, too, Katy. Henderson could drive you."

"I can't go," Serena answered. "I promised Pamela I would walk to the village with her today."

"I would also rather walk than drive," Katherine added. "But you two go on and enjoy yourselves. There is a little mare, Genevieve, in the stables. I think you might enjoy riding her, Charity. She has a sweet disposition and good paces."

"Excellent," Oliver approved. "We shall try her."

"And you would do me a great favor, Oliver, if you would take Tortuga out," Katherine continued. "He is miserable with Ned away. I have the stable boys turn him out into the paddock for exercise, but it's not the same. He needs to be ridden."

"I will be happy to take him if you are certain Ned would not object."

"You know he would not. We will see you both at dinner."

For the first twenty minutes of their ride Oliver's attention was completely claimed by Tortuga. The big bay was fresh and two grooms were having a difficult time holding him. He was prancing and sidling back and forth across the drive, tossing his head. His antics made little impression on the mare, Genevieve, for she was standing quietly as Katherine had promised. Despite Tortuga's gyrations, Oliver mounted with little difficulty, and he and Charity set off together down the drive.

It quickly became evident that the stallion would not be content with the sedate trot Oliver was demanding of him.

There was nothing for it but to let him blow off some steam. Just ahead was a large open meadow—a flock of sheep grazed contentedly on the far side.

"Will she stand for you, do you think?" Oliver asked Charity.

"I believe so."

"Wait for me here, then. I will let him get some of this foolishness out of his system." He put Tortuga at the stone wall that bordered the lane and gave him his head across the meadow beyond. Genevieve made one move to follow him but immediately yielded to Charity's hold on the rein.

Tortuga galloped with tremendous strength and speed across the field, rapidly eating up the ground with his long stride. Oliver bore left to avoid scattering the sheep. Continuing full circle, he was soon headed back toward Charity.

Watching him, Charity realized she had never before noticed what an exceptional rider Oliver was. Their rides in London had never been a challenge to his ability. As he rode now she was impressed by the harmony between horse and rider. Oliver was instinctively in balance with Tortuga even though, to her knowledge, he had never ridden the horse before.

Charity sighed. As she watched Mr. Seaton, a man she admired more than any other she had ever known, she knew she should be happy, but the situation at Rudley Court did not allow for contentment. Charity had been shocked beyond words when Katherine wrote her of the rift in her marriage and the reason for it. Her natural sympathy brought her swiftly to her friend's side, even though she realized there was little she could do to help. She knew that under any other circumstances she would believe herself living in a fairy tale. Rudley Court was the loveliest place she had ever seen: the house was a masterful tribute to the people who had built and furnished it with loving care; the servants were forthright and friendly; the grounds were breathtaking, a never-ending source of enjoyment.

Then there was the single most important attraction that Rudley Court offered: Oliver Seaton. He was the man Charity had been searching for and had nearly given up hope of finding. He was warm and compassionate, intelligent and sensitive, and he didn't pity her or pamper her because of her lameness. She knew he admired her—she wasn't certain how much.

Tortuga came perfectly in stride and unchecked over the wall again and was pulled up to stand beside Charity's mare. His sides were heaving and Oliver leaned forward to stroke his neck. "You'll behave now, won't you, old man? You only wanted to shake out the wrinkles!"

Oliver was full of praise for the horse as he exclaimed, "What a grand fellow he is! I can't for the life of me discover where Ned finds such animals. He insists the quality comes from the dam's side, but try as I may, I can never find horses to equal his." He turned about as he spoke, then he and Charity set off together to enjoy their ride. Tortuga was a perfect gentleman for the remainder of the afternoon and never once took a step out of line or made further demands to have his own way.

Katherine had just finished discussing the next week's menus with Mrs. Simpson. She made her way up from the kitchen to the blue drawing room—she always seemed to gravitate there when she was left alone. Nicholas and Pamela were busy with their studies. Serena had disappeared into the library with a novel Kendall had borrowed for her at the circulating library in Winchester. Oliver and Charity were riding as they had almost every day for the past week. Oliver had been exercising Karma as well as Tortuga and his own black.

As she entered the drawing room, Katherine paused to gaze at her image in the small gilt mirror above the table by the door. That morning she had chosen a soft white muslin gown, full-skirted and generously embroidered with tiny forget-me-nots. Three rows of perfectly matching blue ribbons surrounded the skirt at the hem while a single row adorned each of the short, puffed sleeves. It was a simple and charming dress, but she was not in a mood to admire it.

In her third month her pregnancy was not yet evident, but she could see in the mirror that it was not her imagination that was making some of her clothes fit more tightly at the waist.

She turned from the mirror with a sigh and noted that the roses in the bowl on the pianoforte were past their prime. She took a pair of gardening shears from the secretaire and made her way around the house to the rose garden to cut fresh ones. There were dozens of late-summer varieties in bloom and for some time she simply strolled about, enjoying their heavy scent and deciding which colors to choose for her new bouquet. She finally elected to cut only pink and red flowers and in no time had collected a large number.

Katherine was not expecting Rudley, so when she heard her name spoken close behind her, she was surprised and turned suddenly, dropping many of the roses.

"I'm sorry," he said. "I didn't mean to startle you, but Reeves said he saw you come this way." He was dressed in riding clothes: a gray whipcord coat and close-fitting buckskin breeches. There was a light layer of dust on his top boots, the only evidence of his having just completed a forty-five-mile trip by curricle. Beyond him, Katherine could see this equipage and a strange team being led to the stables.

Taken by surprise, she said the first thing that came into her head. "Ned! I did not expect you."

"How is this? Did you not send me a letter asking that I attend you here?"

"Yes, I did," she answered haltingly, "but I wasn't certain . . . that you would come." He did not answer her but instead went down on one knee to retrieve the roses she had dropped. Katherine stooped quickly in an effort to forestall him. "Please, it's not necessary. I can collect them myself." She reached about, hurriedly picking up the flowers, but she felt his eyes upon her and looked up to meet his gaze squarely. There was now less than a foot between them and for several seconds their eyes held. His gaze faltered first. Glancing down, he collected the last of the blooms and then stood.

Katherine rose when he did. His close, physical presence

was affecting her profoundly. She had mourned the loss of the intimacy they had shared, and now she had an overwhelming urge to simply reach out and touch him. Knowing she dared not do even that, she turned and moved away.

He seemed completely in control and continued in a cool voice, "You wrote, I believe, that you have a matter of importance to discuss. Perhaps we could speak in the arbor, for although the day is not particularly warm, the sun is strong and I can see you have not brought your sunshade."

Katherine turned to stare at him in astonishment. From where did he draw this abstracted air and cool composure? He had been brought into Hampshire against his will to meet with a woman he despised, yet had such command over himself that he pretended concern about her exposure to the sun! She would prefer that he shout at her again. At least those feelings were honest, and certainly preferable to this pretended solicitude.

It was, however, no part of her plan to argue with him, so she held her peace and walked with him to the shade of the arbor. There was a bench and he motioned her to it. He laid the roses he carried on the seat beside her and stood gazing down at her, a look of mild interest on his face.

Katherine drew a long breath, then raised her eyes to his. She had practiced this speech well and she continued without faltering. "When last we spoke, you asked me a question I did not fully answer. I should like to state plainly that the child I carry is yours. There has never been any question of that, regardless of what Sir Humphrey said or what you may believe. It is true I was once in love with Viscount Parnaby and hoped to wed him, but we were not . . . we never . . . there is no possibility this child could be his."

She watched his expression carefully throughout this speech and saw nothing that would give her hope. His face was set in rigid uncompromising lines, his eyes skeptical, cynical. "If you have brought me here to tell me this, Katherine, you have wasted your time."

"You are very hard," she said, struggling to keep the tears

from her eyes, finding it difficult to believe this was the same man who had held her—loved her—such a short time ago.

"What do you expect, madam?" he asked harshly. "You marry me off a list, choosing me as you would a ripe melon at market. You deceive me about your family, lie about your motives in traveling to Lincolnshire, rendezvous there with your lover, then expect me to believe your child is mine? I am willing to concede it *could* be mine, for I remember well the nights we spent together. . . . But more than that, I cannot believe."

"Then I think it would be best for everyone if Serena and I were to leave Rudley Court."

"Leave? And go where?"

"Anywhere. A small village—a cottage—preferably far away from here."

"And what would you do in this cottage?"

"Live . . . with Serena . . . and my child."

"And what exactly do you think people will have to say when the Countess of Rudley goes off with her sister to live in a little cottage in the middle of nowhere?"

"I don't care what they say. Why should it matter?"

"You may believe *I* care what they say," he responded frostily. "Do you think I wish to broadcast to the world that my wife has been unfaithful? That she is to bear another man's child?"

Coolly, in a carefully expressionless voice, she said, "I want you to divorce me, Ned. I know it's expensive, but I truly think it's the only answer."

"Divorce you? Expensive? Do you think I would count the cost? Shall I divorce you on the grounds of adultery? The fact that this shame shall become public knowledge doesn't concern you? You would be shunned by everyone. Accepted nowhere. Serena's chances of establishing herself would be destroyed."

He turned and walked several paces away. When he spoke again, his voice was softer, more controlled. "Divorce is not an option. There has never been a divorce in this family and there never will be. You will continue to live in this house as befits your station. You will continue to be my wife so long as one or the other of us lives.''

''And you will continue to stay away,'' she returned bitterly. ''Won't people talk about that?''

''I will be here from time to time. But it is a large estate; we need not see much of each other.''

She bit her lip as tears suddenly welled up and spilled down her cheeks. ''Oh, Ned, please let me go. This is your home, not mine. I can't bear to stay where I'm not wanted.''

There was a great deal of pain in her voice and he recognized with regret that during the weeks of his absence she had suffered much. He was discovering he had no wish to hurt her, for in some unfathomable way he felt her pain as keenly as his own.

''You have no choice, Katherine. Nor do I,'' he said. ''I think it would be best if I leave now. Such meetings between us serve no useful purpose.''

Another uneasy silence followed and finally Rudley spoke again. ''Is there any other way I can serve you while I am here?''

Once more she was struck by his solicitude, which this time seemed sincere, but she replied in the negative.

''Then I must go,'' he said. ''Please convey my compliments to Miss Harrington, your sister, and my brother and tell them I was sorry to have missed them. Good-bye, Katherine.''

She managed a half-whispered good-bye before he turned and strode off in the direction of the stables. Katherine stayed where he had left her and twenty minutes later saw his curricle and team of chestnuts come from the stables and disappear from sight as they passed before the house and down the drive.

Rudley's drive back to London was accompanied by considerable confusion of mind. Since he believed Katherine had married him to screen her relationship with Parnaby, he was at a loss to understand why she would suggest that he divorce her. If she had married him for the wealth and security he could offer, why would she now be willing to trade it all for a humble, remote home that she would share with her sister and her child?

He could clearly remember Arabella's comments concerning the disposition of her offspring. "I find the thought of bearing a child disgusting," she had said. "I will get fat and ugly, and then there is the appalling pain of the labor itself. I only hope, my dear Edward, that after all my suffering I can manage at least to produce a boy. That would almost make the whole ordeal worthwhile. The very idea of another man's child as heir to all you possess is diverting in the extreme." He could have willingly strangled her that day, and he did achieve a small victory when she bore a girl and not the boy she had wished for.

The day Rudley had left Katherine he had equated her behavior with Arabella's, and in that he now knew he had wronged her. It was obvious after their interview today that she had no intention of using her child as a weapon against him.

His chestnuts made good time to Woking, and he had them taken out there with instructions for them to be returned to Rudley the following day. He had a new team put to immediately and pushed on, eager to arrive in town before nightfall.

Chapter 18

TWO DAYS AFTER Rudley's visit, in the morning, Oliver offered to take the children fishing at the lake.

"I'm afraid I haven't had much experience with fishing," Charity said doubtfully.

"You need not worry about the worms," Pamela said encouragingly. "Uncle Oliver will put them on for you. He does for me."

"Girls!" Nicholas said with disgust.

"Worms?" Charity asked tentatively.

"Yes, Charity," Katherine said. "Earthworms. They are used for bait. You cannot honestly expect a trout to sacrifice itself on an empty hook just to satisfy your sensibilities."

"Must we go fishing?"

"Honest, Miss Charity," Nicholas chimed in, "it's the greatest fun. You'll like it; I know you will. I can show you how to keep the fish from wiggling while you take it from the hook."

Oliver to this point had said nothing, and at that moment one of the footmen appeared bearing the fishing gear. Oliver took it from him and headed for the door. "You children go with Lady Katherine and Miss Serena and choose a good spot to fish. Miss Charity and I are going to go dig some worms."

He was making every effort to maintain his composure, but the expression of profound horror on Charity's face was too much for him. He and Katherine burst into laughter simultaneously.

"You may both laugh at me all you like," Charity said.

"You have succeeded between you in teaching me to ride, but I promise you there is absolutely nothing either of you can say or do that will prevail upon me to *dig worms*!" With this bold pronouncement she moved off in the wake of the children to choose, as Oliver had put it, a good spot.

As Nicholas had predicted, Charity did enjoy the fishing and even managed to catch one fish big enough to eat. But Oliver noticed that what she enjoyed most was throwing the small fish back. Serena caught a huge trout and promptly apologized to Oliver for making his largest catch look so small.

Katherine glanced up at the sound of hoofbeats across the lake and was surprised to see two mounted, liveried grooms leading a third horse. They were advancing at a steady trot down the drive. She rose to her feet. "I think I had best go back to the house to see who has arrived."

Oliver rose with her as Charity said, "You two go ahead. Serena and I will stay with the children."

As the riders drew closer, Katherine recognized Lord Gilborough's livery. Then to her astonishment she realized the horse being led was Lady Halfmile! Oliver greeted Lord Gilborough's head groom warmly. "Hallo, Wanderman. It's been a long time. What brings you to Rudley?"

"Good day to you, Lady Rudley, Mr. Seaton. Lord Gilborough has sent me to deliver this brood mare, Lady Halfmile."

"Deliver her?" Katherine asked in surprise.

"So this is the famous Lady Halfmile?" Oliver eyed the mare appreciatively. "I have never seen her before, but I can see that Ned did not exaggerate her charms."

"No, sir, she be a fine mare. None better in my book."

"What do you mean, you came to deliver her?" Katherine repeated her question.

"Why, just that, m'lady. Got the papers pertainin' to her here in my pocket, to be given to Mr. Seaton or Mr. Kendall, and a note for you especial."

"Do you mean to say Lord Rudley has actually bought this horse?" Oliver asked.

"Yes, sir, day afore yesterday."

"The day before yesterday!" Katherine exclaimed. Quickly remembering her manners, she continued, "Please, Wanderman, won't you and your companion take your horses down to the stables and then come back to the house and see Mrs. Simpson? I am sure you could use some refreshment after your long ride. You may leave the mare with us."

"Why, thank you kindly, m'lady. It's a bit of a warm day. Best o' luck to you with the mare."

Oliver took the halter shank from Wanderman as the men rode away. "I can see you know more about this than you are saying."

"I know only that Lord Gilborough has always refused to sell her and that once, in jest, I told Ned I would take her as a wedding present."

"That's it then. He has bought her for you. Didn't he say anything about her when he was here the other day?"

"Not a word. But he couldn't have bought her for me. Why should he, especially now?"

"Why don't you read the note Wanderman mentioned? Perhaps it will shed some light." Oliver shuffled through the papers the groom had handed him. There was among them a sealed note bearing Katherine's name and directed in his brother's hand. He passed it to Katherine and she opened it quickly. It contained only a few lines.

Katherine,

I know you will probably consider this bad timing, but I must tell you that this mare has been yours since the day you asked for her. We were waiting only to wean the foal. Please accept her with my compliments.

Rudley

"You are right, Oliver, she is a wedding present. Look. From this it sounds as if he purchased her some time ago." She handed the note back to him.

"I hate to disagree with you, Katherine, but here is the bill of sale. As you can see, it is dated only two days ago. He must have stopped at Gilborough's the same day he visited here. Good God! Look what he gave for her! A handsome present, indeed!"

Katherine declined this invitation to see the price of her present but said, "Your brother is generous to a fault. You must admit she is a very practical gift, however."

"True enough," he agreed. "And she is much more than a gift; she is an excellent investment, for she will easily pay for herself with her produce if her offspring continue to win as they have in the past."

"But none of this explains why Ned should buy her now," Katherine insisted.

"No doubt he had a verbal agreement with Gilborough," Oliver offered, "and the time came to put it in writing."

"No matter how I try, I simply cannot comprehend him," Katherine said.

"I daresay he is having as much trouble understanding you. But you're married, Katherine, and unless you both intend to be miserable indefinitely, sooner or later you must settle your differences."

He saw the glimmer of hope in her eyes as she asked, "Oh, Oliver, do you really think that will ever be possible?"

"I think that as long as you don't give up hope, anything is possible." He gave her a brotherly hug, and turning together, they led Lady Halfmile off to the stables.

Later the same week Charity and Oliver rode to see Weiring, the rambling stone house where Oliver's mother had lived until her marriage. "My mother was an only child, and she and my father were childhood sweethearts. Her family is all gone now. When her father died, the property passed to a cousin two or three times removed. Ned has tried to buy the place from him, but he isn't interested in selling."

As they turned their horses toward home, Oliver spoke of what had been foremost in his mind since breakfast. "Katherine told me this morning that you will be leaving for Lincolnshire at the end of next week.''

''Yes. I hope it will not be inconvenient. My parents are anxious to have me home. But I have promised Katy I will come back to her in February and stay through the lying-in.'' She continued with rare confidence. ''This situation in which Katy finds herself has been hard on her—too hard. It is not right that she should suffer so. I have known Katherine since she was fourteen and in all that time I have never known her to willingly hurt anyone. She is a loving and giving person, and she does not deserve such treatment from your brother.'' She spoke passionately, and Oliver was certain that although she seldom mentioned them, her friend's problems were never far from her mind.

''Charity, Katherine may not have intended any harm, but you cannot deny harm has been done. I am not defending Ned's actions in this matter, but neither can I criticize him. How he deals with it must be left to him. It benefits no one if we choose sides or assign blame. We must help in any way we can, if and when we can, but Ned and Katherine must weather this storm themselves.''

Charity was forced to agree with him. ''I suppose you are right, and I will try to heed your advice. But it's difficult for me to see Katherine so unhappy. And it's not healthy for her or the baby.''

''Then you and Serena and I will have to make it our job to see that she has plenty to occupy her mind and little time to dwell on sad things.'' Then, changing the subject, he asked, ''What would you say to a gallop through the home wood?''

They took off instantly, riding for some distance side by side. When the path narrowed, Oliver checked Tortuga to allow Charity to precede him.

''No, please,'' she objected, ''you take the lead, for I am not sure I know the way.'' He moved ahead and she followed several yards behind as they slowed to a canter. Oliver followed no definite path, for the trees were not thick and the wood had been cleared of all undergrowth and windfall.

They had gone only a few hundred yards when without warning Tortuga stumbled and came down heavily. Oliver was thrown violently forward over the horse's head and shoulders. Charity's mare broke stride and shied away, but she managed to pull her up short of where the stallion had fallen. Tortuga meanwhile had scrambled to his feet and, apparently unhurt, trotted a few paces away and dropped his head to graze.

Charity dismounted quickly and hurried to Oliver. She knelt on the ground beside him. To her dismay he was unconscious. Reaching forward with a trembling hand, she laid her fingers against his neck and breathed a sigh of relief when she felt a strong pulse beating there. She deftly loosened the stock at his throat and undid the top buttons of his shirt, hoping to allow him to breathe easier.

She was undecided as to what she should do next. Should she stay, or should she leave him and go for help? Even as she asked herself these questions, she knew she could not leave him. She took one of his hands in hers and with her fingers on the pulse of his wrist settled to wait for him to regain consciousness. A few moments later, as she reached to brush back the hair that had fallen across his forehead, his eyes fluttered open. She instantly released his hand.

He gazed at her in bewilderment and spoke her name, and she smiled in relief as he asked, "What happened?"

"Tortuga came down with you. Are you in any pain? Do you think you have broken anything?"

He pulled himself into a sitting position. "I'm fine, I think. I don't remember anything. What could have brought us down so suddenly?"

"I think Tortuga may have put his foot in a rabbit hole," Charity suggested. "He—"

"A rabbit hole!" Oliver exclaimed. "Good God! Where is he? Is he all right?"

"He's over there"—she pointed—"and yes, he appears to be fine. He certainly trotted off soundly enough."

"I hope you may prove to be right, for if any harm should

come to that animal at my hands, Ned would most likely shoot me.''

"Come now," Charity argued. "It cannot be considered your fault if your horse has the misfortune to step into a rabbit hole!"

"If not mine, then whose fault should it be?" Oliver demanded.

"Why, the rabbit's, of course," she answered sensibly.

He threw back his head, his rich, warm laugh erupting. "Charity, what am I to do with you? You are forever saying something adorable." Impulsively, he reached forward and, taking her by the shoulders, pulled her to him and kissed her.

Charity found herself in the uncomfortable position of having two equally strong emotions warring within her. She had been secretly hoping for weeks that Oliver would make her an offer, and she had shamefully wondered what it would be like to be held in his arms and kissed by him. She had not, however, expected the kiss to come before the proposal, and she was therefore shocked by the impropriety of the present situation.

After a few moments, summoning all her will, she pushed him away, saying in as dignified a tone as she could manage, "Sir, I cannot think it is proper for us to be sitting here in the woods and for you to be kissing me." She began to rise and he, too, gained his feet, taking her arm to help her. But when she turned to her horse, he kept her arm and made her stay.

"Don't expect an apology. I'm not sorry I kissed you." He took her other arm and turned her to face him. "I'm in love with you, Charity . . . I want you to marry me." She smiled at him then, and he could see her answer in her eyes, but still he asked, "Will you?"

"Yes, Oliver. I will."

"I won't allow Nick to plague you, I promise."

"Don't be silly. I love Nicholas. He's a wonderful child."

"Even when he insists you go fishing?"

"I shall enjoy reading to him, and *you* may take him fishing."

He laughed again, and when he took her in his arms once more, she raised no objection.

It was found that Charity had been right after all—Tortuga had suffered no injury from his fall. They returned home to share their news with Katherine, who seemed pleased but not the least surprised by it. Charity held to her plans to leave at the end of the following week. Oliver, however, now arranged to travel with her to Lincolnshire to make formal application to Lord Harrington for her hand.

By the end of September, having completed his work in Yorkshire, Rudley returned with his servants to London. Katherine heard once from Countess Finley that he had been to see her, but he hadn't stayed long and seemed to have little to say. It was clear from Lady Finley's letter that she had no idea her brother was fixed in London. She had assumed his visit to her was only a short excursion away from home. Those of his acquaintance who remained in town were led to the same conclusion, for he would not leave the house for more than a week at a time. When they didn't see him about town, it was only natural for them to assume he had returned to the country.

Rudley realized that with the Little Season starting, people would begin flocking back to the city and it would become necessary for him to leave. He knew that eventually he would have to return to Rudley Court. If he continued to absent himself during Katherine's confinement, it would give rise to the very sort of gossip and speculation he was most anxious to avoid.

Oliver stayed only two days with the Harringtons. When he stopped overnight in London, he discovered that Rudley had arrived that morning. He found him in his bedchamber dressing for dinner.

"Well met, Ned. Had I been one day sooner I would have missed you."

"Had you been one day later you would have missed me

as well. I leave in the morning for Scotland. Culross has invited me for fishing and shooting.''

Oliver frowned. ''Did you have my letter before you left Yorkshire?''

''None recently. Why? Did you have news?''

''Only news of my engagement. Hold the fifteenth of April open on your busy calendar, will you? I should like you to be my best man.''

Rudley's smile was genuine but showed no surprise as he replied, ''I would be honored. I wish you happy, both of you. You must give Miss Harrington my regards.''

''I shall, when next I see her. I am headed back to Rudley now to deal with the harvest. Needless to say, I could use your help. Must you go to Scotland? I was hoping you might consider coming home.''

''I've already decided I must come for the last two months before the child is born, to silence the gossip as much as possible. Until then I will stay with Culross. I'm his only guest, and he understands that I don't wish to broadcast my presence there.''

''Ned, you have admitted there is a possibility this child could be yours. Have you no concern at all for the well-being of its mother?''

''Has Katherine been ill?''

''No. Serena bullies her into eating and getting enough rest. But she is suffering from a depression of the spirits that none of us can remedy.''

''No more could I. It's Parnaby she pines for, not me.''

''I don't believe that. She told me herself she is no longer in love with him.''

''Nor is she in love with me. I can't come down, Oliver. Just think for a moment what it would be like. During the day Katherine and I would be avoiding each other, always uncomfortable when we happened by accident to meet. Dinner would be a daily trial. Sitting at the same table, practicing civility, exchanging trivialities. That situation would be more painful than my simply staying away.''

"Why painful? It seems to me you have written her off—"

"No. I haven't done that. I haven't been able to. I still love her, Oliver."

"Then go back to her!"

"Loving her is not enough. How can I explain? I have loved her since very early on in our relationship. I knew, also early on, that she was attracted to Parnaby. When he became engaged and eliminated himself from the picture, I began to believe she and I had a chance. But it has been made most clear to me that he is not out of Katherine's life. Regardless of what she may have told you, her actions speak otherwise."

Despite Rudley's stubborn resolve to proceed to Scotland, Oliver returned to Hampshire in excellent spirits, his marriage foremost in his mind.

"We have set the date for the fifteenth of April," he told Katherine. "Lady Harrington insists she cannot be ready a single day sooner. Charity hopes you will be able to be there."

"I will certainly try."

Oliver seated himself beside her. "I saw Ned in London."

"How is he?"

"He's off to Scotland for a few months to stay with a friend, Duncan Culross. He plans to come back here sometime in January."

"For appearance's sake."

"Whatever his reasons, it will put you both under the same roof again. If I am convinced of anything, it is that you two must communicate if you ever hope to mend this rift between you."

Not wishing to toss her into melancholy reflection, Oliver changed the subject. "How is your work progressing on the chair?"

"Very well. I have an appointment next month with the man who is to remove the old fabric and replace it with the new."

Oliver studied her work with admiration. "I had forgotten

how striking it was before the colors faded. This is a true labor of love, Katherine. I hope Ned will appreciate it. I certainly do.''

''Do you? Truly?''

''Yes, of course. My mother would be deeply touched if she could know how Ned cherishes and protects this chair. But you must understand that she was neat as a pin. Had she been alive when the chair started to show signs of shabbiness, I know she would have been the first to have it refurbished. So, in effect, Katherine, you have retained our memories and at the same time satisfied my mother's meticulous nature. And you have done it with an excellence in needlework that rivals her own.''

Katherine had not expected such warm praise for her work and she was touched. She leaned over to kiss him lightly on the cheek. ''Thank you, Oliver. You are a dear brother. I could not create a better husband for Charity if I had all the attributes in the world to choose from.''

''Now that is high praise indeed!'' he said, smiling and rising to his feet. ''But I must be off. Henderson wanted me down at the stables half an hour since to look at a lame horse.''

''Will you take Karma out today?''

''Certainly, if you wish it. I will be going down to Pool's Cove later to see how work is progressing there on the new barn. It should be a good outing for her.''

As he picked up his hat, whip, and gloves and headed out through the doors opening onto the terrace, Katherine called after him, ''Beware of rabbit holes!''

Chapter 19

THE MONTH OF October passed busily. Each day seemed to bring continuous demands on both Katherine's and Oliver's time. Katherine had urged Serena to accept an invitation from Lady Brent to spend a few weeks in London, but Serena refused to leave. When Katherine had informed her of the events leading up to Rudley's departure, Serena was astonished. "He believed Sir Humphrey rather than you? That's incredible! Sir Humphrey is a puffed-up buffoon. Why would Lord Rudley believe him rather than his own wife?"

"His first marriage was not a success. He told me his wife lied to him. He thinks I have lied to him, too."

"Isn't there some way you can convince him you're telling the truth?"

"I don't know, Rena. Once trust has been lost, I'm not sure if it's possible to win it back."

Four days before Christmas Oliver sent servants running about the house to gather the whole family in the great hall. Serena had been playing the pianoforte while Katherine read in the drawing room. Nicholas and Pamela were summoned from their lessons.

When they were all assembled, Oliver demanded that they put on their coats for a walk down to the stables.

"Are we going for a drive, Papa," Nicholas asked, "instead of studying?"

"I don't intend to answer any questions," Oliver replied. "Just put on your coats and come along."

They trooped in a little group down the drive to the main

stables, holding their cloaks tightly against a brisk northerly wind. Oliver stopped inside the main doors where Henderson was holding the lead of a strange horse.

"This mare has just arrived, Pamela," Oliver said. "According to the note that came with her, she is a birthday present for you."

Pamela stared in awe at the coal-black horse with four perfectly matched white stockings and a symmetrical star on her forehead. It was an actual horse—a full-sized horse—not a pony. She walked forward, reaching out a hand to touch her wonderful present and exclaiming, "For me? Oh, Uncle Oliver, what a wonderful, wonderful present! Thank you ever so much!"

Turning her back on the horse, she rushed into Oliver's arms and hugged as much of him as she could.

"Wait a minute, miss," Oliver protested. "This gift is not from me. She has come all the way from Scotland. There is a note. Listen:

"Culkaldy Castle, Fife

"Dear Pamela,

"So impressed was I by your riding last summer that I have decided you need a mount equal to your skill. I found this beautiful little mare at a horse fair in Dunfermline. I took one look at her and knew she was exactly the horse for you. Her former owner called her Black Star, which, though simple, does seem to suit her. I will be home by the end of January and will hope that by then you and she will be great friends.

"With love on your birthday, Your Father"

Nick's voice cut through all of the exclamations of pleasure over Pamela's new horse. "How come Pamela gets a present before Christmas? It isn't Christmas yet, is it, Papa?"

Oliver scooped up his son and set him on the new mare's back. "No, Nick. It's not Christmas yet. And this isn't a Christmas present. Tomorrow is Pamela's birthday, remember? Uncle Ned couldn't wrap this present, so he had to send it along this way. But you know, now that Pamela has a new horse, maybe she would be willing to let you have her pony. You've always liked him. What do you say, Pam?"

Nick's face broke into a pleased grin when Pamela readily acquiesced to this scheme.

While Pamela demanded of Serena if she had ever seen four stockings so evenly matched, Katherine smiled. Less than a year ago when she had asked Ned if Pamela admired horses, he had replied that he couldn't say. Now, far away in the wilds of Scotland, he had remembered his daughter with a special gift. Katherine wondered what other thoughts occupied his mind during this time of solitude he had sentenced himself to.

Christmas passed with as much festivity as the household could manage in the face of Rudley's continued absence. Mrs. Simpson labored for days over tarts and sweets that she knew the children would enjoy. The whole family partook of a sumptuous Christmas Eve dinner, after which Oliver invited all the servants into the dining room to toast the holiday.

Several weeks earlier Serena had received an invitation from Rudley's sister, the Countess Finley, to attend a house party at her home in Buckinghamshire. At first opposed to the idea, Serena had finally yielded to her sister's entreaty.

"I won't need you, Rena. The baby isn't due for more than two months and you plan to be gone two weeks."

"I will only be a few hours away," Serena assured Katherine on the morning of her departure.

"Go. Enjoy yourself. You're young; you deserve to have a good time. And remember, Lady Finley will be your chaperone as well as your hostess. Be certain you attend to her in all things."

"Yes, *Mother*," Serena mocked lightly as she hugged her

sister good-bye and allowed Kendall to assist her into the coach.

"Thank you, Peter, for taking her," Katherine said. "I know I can safely trust her in your hands."

He surprised her considerably when he took her cold fingers in his and said seriously, "We'll be fine, my lady. You just see that *you* take care of yourself. I should be back tomorrow afternoon."

Then, saying nothing further, he climbed into the coach, and it set off down the drive.

That night, as a steady rain fell, the temperature dropped below freezing. Sleet, driven by high wind beat against the windows. By daylight the storm's damage was all too evident. The weight of the ice had stripped countless branches from the trees. In the park several entire trees had been toppled, one of which had fallen directly across the main carriage drive.

Kendall returned as promised in the afternoon. He reported that he had left Serena safely in Lady Finley's hands.

On the following day the men were still hard at work trying to clear the carriage drive. Katherine stood looking out the salon window; she could see that they had pulled the last of the tree to the side of the road but would be busy cutting it up for some days to come.

As Katherine turned from the window, she felt a sharp, sudden twinge. Startled, she stood perfectly still, holding her breath. The sensation went away as quickly as it had come, but a few moments later she felt another, stronger pain. She was only in her seventh month—too early for labor pains. She pulled the bell rope and a footman immediately opened the door.

"Yes, my lady?"

"Will you send Mrs. Windom to me and send someone for Mr. Seaton. Quickly, Gordon, please."

Oliver had left the workers on the drive and was already on his way to the house. He arrived moments later. Entering the salon, he took one look at Katherine's white face and asked, "Is it the child?" She nodded assent as he took two quick steps back to the door. "Gordon, send one of the grooms for Dr. Bailey. Tell him to hurry." He returned to Katherine and asked, "What is it?"

"I'm not sure. Labor pains, I think. But, Oliver, it's too soon!"

"Let's wait to see what the doctor has to say. Come, I'm going to carry you upstairs. Put your arm around my neck. There's a good girl."

He lifted her gently and easily in his arms. They met Mrs. Windom in the hall and she hurried ahead to turn down Katherine's bed.

Katherine was frightened and in pain but trying bravely not to show it. Foremost in her mind was the thought that she *couldn't* lose Ned's baby. It was the part of him that she had clung to during all the months he had been away—the only thing that had cheered her through the darkest, bleakest days. Whether he believed it or not, it was his child, a child already beloved by her.

When the doctor arrived, Oliver retreated to the estate office, where he found Kendall pacing the floor.

"Her ladyship?" he asked.

"The doctor has arrived," Oliver replied, "but Katherine thinks she is in labor."

"We need to send a message to Lord Rudley."

"My God, Kendall, he's in Scotland! Do you know how long that will take?"

"But he's not in Scotland. I had a letter from him yesterday. He arrived in London four days ago. He wanted to be back for the opening of Parliament."

"Then we must write. But what to say?"

The two men waited another twenty minutes, but it seemed like hours before the doctor came to them. They listened carefully to Dr. Bailey's diagnosis, and when the doctor left to return to his patient, Oliver summoned Reeves. "Dr. Bailey wishes us to fetch the midwife. Also, send Henderson to me immediately and have him bring his best rider with him."

As Reeves went to do his bidding, Oliver pulled a piece of writing paper forward and dipping his quill, began a letter to his brother. He had just finished sealing it when Henderson and his companion arrived. He wasted no words. "It is imperative that Lord Rudley receive this letter without delay. Is this your best rider, Henderson?"

"Yes, Mr. Oliver, this is Tom Smithe."

"Very well, Tom. You are to leave immediately on the strongest horse we have, excluding Tortuga. Which would that be, Henderson?"

"That would be your own black, Mr. Oliver."

"Take the black, Tom, and do not spare him. Make the best time you can while there is still daylight and change horses as often as necessary to make all possible speed to London. When you arrive, you will probably find his lordship at Rudley House, but if he is not there, find him wherever he has gone and place this letter into no hand but his. Do you understand?"

"Yes, sir."

"Good. Here, then. Take this money and the letter, and may God speed you." Without another word young Tom hurried from the room and Oliver turned his attention to the head groom. "Henderson, I also have a job for you."

Tom Smithe arrived at Rudley House in London a few minutes after eleven o'clock that evening. He was tired and liberally spattered with mud, but he had made good time considering the condition of the roads. Upon hearing the earl was at home, he requested an immediate audience and was shown without ceremony into the library. "I have an urgent letter, m'lord, from Mr. Seaton." He handed it directly to the earl as he had been instructed and then stood waiting.

Rudley broke the seal and spread the single sheet upon the desk.

Ned,

Katherine has gone into premature labor and there have been some complications. Bailey will not commit himself, but he did admit that if the labor is prolonged Katherine's life could be endangered. The roads are bad and in the dark I think you will come to us fastest if you ride. Henderson will meet you with Tortuga at the Bull's Head in Woking. He is fit and will do all you ask of him.

Oliver

"Run down to the stables, Tom, and saddle Navigator. I am leaving for Hampshire immediately." Tom hurried to do his bidding while Rudley quickly went upstairs to exchange his evening dress for riding clothes.

Within fifteen minutes Rudley was setting off at a smart pace through the London streets. There was three-quarters of a moon, but the sky was cloudy and the moon flitted in and out of cover, allowing for a few moments a good view of the road ahead and then suddenly plunging all into blackness. Rudley held Navigator to a strict trot until he was thoroughly warmed. Then, as they reached the outskirts of town, he allowed him to break into a canter. They galloped on through the night, meeting no one and seeing nothing but the road underfoot.

Within an hour of the doctor's arrival Katherine's condition had improved, but there was no doubt she was in labor and, early or not, the child would probably be born that night. Oliver asked if he could sit with Katherine and the doctor said he had no objection if Lady Rudley had none.

On his way upstairs to Katherine's room Oliver encountered Pamela. Her tearstained face told its own story. "How is Lady Katherine, Uncle Oliver?"

He could see no reason to hedge—Pamela was old enough to understand. "Dr. Bailey feels the child will be born tonight, but it is coming too soon, and it may not live, Pamela."

"And Lady Katherine, will she be all right?"

"We must believe so, and pray for her. She is young and strong; the odds are in her favor."

"Papa should be here."

"I have sent for him. I am sure he will come as quickly as he can. Meanwhile, why don't you go to your room and do some work on the painting of Karma that you are doing for Katherine. The doctor says I may sit with her for a while. I promise to come to you immediately if there is any news, but I must warn you that these things take time and it may be morning before we know anything. Be sure you get to your bed early and rest well; we may need your help tomorrow."

He kissed her then and walked with her as far as Katherine's door. He waited until Pamela disappeared into her own room, then knocked quietly and entered Katherine's room.

"The doctor has said that I may stay with you if you wish it," he said. "It's likely to be a long night, and I doubt the pains will allow you to sleep." He pulled a chair to the side of the bed and took one of her hands in his. "May I stay and help you through this, Katherine?"

She smiled and squeezed his hand lightly. "Yes, please, I should like it if you would stay."

So Oliver sat with her through the long hours of the night and into the early hours of the morning, praying that there would be no further complications and that Ned would arrive quickly.

Mrs. Windom and some of the other servants had not retired, and during the night the housekeeper came several times into the room. After Oliver had noticed her for the third time casting a discountenancing glance in his direction, he rose quietly and motioned her to follow him from the room. "To what do I owe these dagger looks you are giving me, Mrs. Windom?" he asked bluntly.

"It is not proper for you to be in her ladyship's bedchamber, Mr. Oliver, especially with her in childbed. It is not fitting—"

He interrupted her harshly. "Do not preach the proprieties to me, Mrs. Windom. I think I need not remind you that I lost my own wife in childbed. I will not leave my brother's wife alone so long as she derives the smallest degree of comfort from my presence. Please allow me to add that it is not your place to either approve or disapprove my behavior.''

He turned abruptly and reentered Katherine's room, leaving the housekeeper in the hallway with her mouth agape. When she later returned to the room later, he saw no signs of her earlier disapprobation. He knew not whether she had altered her opinion or simply seen the merit in choosing not to show it, but whichever was the case, he found he didn't care.

Rudley judged Woking to be no more than three miles ahead. The road had deteriorated greatly and Navigator was laboring. When Rudley turned into the yard of the Bull's Head, he realized Henderson must have been watching for him, for the groom was at Navigator's head before the horse came to a complete stop. Rudley slipped from the saddle. ''Do you have any news from home, Henderson?''

''No, m'lord,'' the man answered apologetically. ''I left only minutes after Tom, and I can tell you nothing. Will you stop to rest or do you ride on?''

''I ride on.'' Henderson beckoned to a boy standing nearby and he stepped forward leading Tortuga. ''Do your best for Navigator,'' Rudley said as he patted the horse's sweat-covered neck. ''He has galloped his heart out for me tonight.''

''Aye, m'lord. I am sure he has. And this one will do no less.'' He tossed the reins over Tortuga's head and held him while the earl mounted. ''We have had heavy rain, m'lord, and the roads are bad, especially between Stynum and Pool's Cove. Take care how you go on.''

''I will, Henderson. Thank you.'' Rudley gave Tortuga the office to start and within a few hundred feet they had disappeared from sight.

It was a blessing that Rudley's continuous concentration on his horse and his riding gave him little time to dwell on anything else, for the few thoughts that did crowd in were not pleasant ones. A week ago he had been pondering how to arrange his life so as to see as little of his wife as possible.

Now, with her life in danger, he realized that he valued no other person above her.

Beyond Stynum, as Henderson had warned, the road was very bad. He and Tom had both passed through this area in the daylight. Now, in the dark, there was nothing Rudley could do but pull Tortuga to a walk and allow him to pick his own way along the pockmarked and rutted road. By the time they reached Pool's Cove it had begun to rain, but the road was better here and familiar to both horse and rider. One final time Rudley asked his stallion for a canter, and although Tortuga's pace was slower, he still drove steadily on, arriving at Rudley steaming, trembling, and blown.

The earl rode directly to the stables, where there were three grooms waiting, clearly expecting him. With Henderson gone, Rudley realized that young Wilson was now in charge. Dismounting, he handed Tortuga's reins to him. "This horse is to be rubbed down and properly cooled if it takes you the rest of tonight and half of tomorrow to do it. Do you understand?"

"Yes, m'lord," Wilson answered as he immediately began to loosen the saddle girth. Rudley turned without another word and strode off toward the house, but his tone left little doubt in the minds of his servants what their fate would be if they failed to obey him.

The front door was opened for him by Reeves. As he stepped into the lighted hall the butler was startled by his appearance. Rudley had been soaked through by the rain and his boots and breeches were caked with mud. Stripping off his gloves, he demanded the time.

"It is nearly half-past five, my lord."

"So late! I had hoped to do better."

He shoved his dripping hat and gloves into the butler's hands and started up the stairs two at a time. He met Oliver in the upstairs hall. "How is Katherine?"

"The child was born an hour ago." Rudley started past him, but Oliver grasped his arm. "You can't go in now, Ned. The doctor is still with her, and we dare not distract him from his work."

"Tell me what has happened while I get out of these clothes."

They went together to the earl's rooms as Oliver continued. "There was some hemorrhaging after the birth. Katherine's condition is serious; the next few hours are critical. Bailey doesn't hold much hope for the child, being almost two months early." He answered Rudley's unspoken question. "It's a girl, but she's not strong. Kendall has gone to the rectory for his father in the event we should need him."

Rudley was buttoning a clean shirt, but he turned to his brother then and Oliver could clearly hear the pain and guilt in his voice. "I didn't want this! You can't think I would ever wish the child dead."

"I don't think it," Oliver assured him. "Nor will Katherine."

"Is there nothing we can do?"

"No, nothing, only wait . . . and pray."

Outside Katherine's room the earl encountered Nicholas's nurse coming from the room directly opposite. "Lord Rudley, no one told me you had arrived. If they won't let you in to see her ladyship, would you like to see the babe?"

Rudley stared at her uncomprehendingly. Then he realized that she, as well as the other servants, believed this child to be his. Naturally they would expect him to want to see it. He saw that Oliver was about to come to his aid with some excuse or other, but he forestalled him as he decided that he did indeed wish to see Katherine's child. He reminded Oliver to send for him the moment he could see Katherine and then turned to enter the room.

It was a small bedchamber in which a large fire had been lit. Mrs. Windom and two maids hovered near a cradle set to one side of the fireplace. Crossing the room silently on the carpet, Rudley looked down on Katherine's newborn girl. She was closely wrapped to keep her warm, but he could see she was very tiny. He was surprised to see that her eyes were open and if he listened carefully, he could hear her making tiny, whimpering sounds, much like those of a newborn puppy.

For months he had bitterly resented the existence of this

child. Now, as he looked down at her innocent face, he knew how unfair he had been. All his bitterness faded as he realized that this tiny living creature was a small part of the woman he loved. If the doctor proved to be correct and the child did not survive, Rudley knew he would mourn her even as Katherine would. But doctors had been known to be mistaken, and the earl knew that although it was unusual for a baby this premature to survive, it was by no means impossible.

A few minutes after six o'clock Dr. Bailey quit Katherine's room to report that her condition had stabilized. She had slipped into a state of semiconsciousness, but her pulse was steady and he thought the worst was over.

As Rudley entered Katherine's room, the midwife stepped toward him. "She is not conscious, my lord."

"Please leave us alone."

"For a few moments only, my lord."

"I understand." He stood near the door until the midwife had gone; then he walked to the side of the bed. Katherine's appearance shocked him. She was deathly pale and still. She did not even appear to be breathing. The hand he lifted in his own was warm and he was reassured, but it was hard to accept the drastic change in her since their last meeting. That day, in her white dress with the blue ribbons and flowers, he remembered thinking she had never looked lovelier.

Then, kneeling down by the bed and holding her lifeless hand to his cheek, he prayed, not for forgiveness or understanding or the hope of reconciliation but simply that God would be merciful and restore her to health, for if he should be granted that, he would spend whatever time and effort was necessary to make all the rest come right. Never again would he allow his pride to run roughshod over those he loved.

True to his promise, he stayed less than five minutes and then rejoined Oliver in the corridor. "The Reverend Kendall is downstairs, Ned, and the doctor has seen the baby again. He says her breathing has deteriorated and if you wish to have her christened you should not delay."

The rain continued through the morning, and the impenetrable cloud cover held the dawn to a creeping, gradual event, turning the black to gray but allowing not the least ray of sunshine to break through. And in the same slow yet steady progression did the life drain from Katherine's child. She had not been completely prepared for the world she had been thrust into, and she could not now find the strength necessary to survive in it. Rudley was alone with Katherine when Oliver brought the news to him. Sitting there in the gray light, emotionally drained and physically exhausted, he shed tears for that tiny life he had scorned—and then loved—all in the same day.

Chapter 20

OLIVER STOOD BEHIND Pamela, watching her create fallen leaves on the ground with soft touches of her amber-tipped brush. Karma stood in a thin wood. Nearly half the leaves had fallen from the trees about her. She stood poised, her head raised and her ears flexed forward as if someone had called her name.

"Katherine will love this," he said. "You're nearly finished, aren't you?"

"Yes. Mr. Williby will want to see it later."

"How do you like him?"

"He's wonderful. His paintings are lovely. I shall never be able to paint as he does."

"He is not here to teach you to paint as he does. He is here to teach you technique. You must paint in your own way—that is how you can best use your talent. Did you get any sleep last night?"

"A little. Did the baby suffer, Uncle Oliver?"

"No, I don't believe she did. I think she just went to sleep."

Pamela seemed to consider this for a moment, then said, "You look tired, too."

"I am. I've been up all night, but I'm going to bed now. I will look in on Katherine first. I promise to let you know if there is any change."

Oliver had strongly advised his brother to get some rest, but when Oliver's valet awakened him at six o'clock that evening, he learned that Rudley had continued to sit with

Katherine. Outside Katherine's room Oliver nearly collided with Bess, exiting the room with a heavy tray.

"What's this?" he asked, as the tray looked untouched.

"Mrs. Simpson has made some of his lordship's favorite dishes, sir, but he told me carry it away again, for he wants nothing."

"Give it to me," Oliver said, taking the tray from her hands. "I will try to persuade him to eat something."

Rudley looked up as the door opened again and frowned when he saw his dinner returning. "Don't scowl at me, Ned. I'm not as easily put off as your servants. Whatever this is, it smells wonderful, and if you will not have it, then I promise you I shall." He set the tray on a small table as he glanced at Katherine. "Has there been any change?"

"No. Her color is a bit better, but she has not regained consciousness."

"I know you won't appreciate my saying so, Ned, but another twelve hours of this damned vigil of yours and she will most likely be looking better than you. You spent the better part of six grueling hours in the saddle. You haven't slept in over thirty hours nor eaten in the last twenty. You look fagged to death. What service will you be to Katherine if she wakes to find you so?"

Being a reasonable man, Rudley saw the wisdom of his brother's words. Still he hesitated. "I want to be here when she wakes, though I doubt she'll be pleased to see me."

Oliver thought of several things he could say but quickly decided against interfering. Katherine could speak for herself when she was able, and he suspected his brother was ready to listen at last.

"Ned, eat some of this food Mrs. Simpson has sent up and then get some sleep. I will sit with Katherine and I will not leave her for an instant. I will come for you the moment she wakes. You have my word." He poured some wine and held it out to Rudley. He was relieved when his brother reached to take it from him.

Toward midnight the midwife gave it as her opinion that Katherine was no longer unconscious but merely in a heavy, exhausted sleep. She no longer lay motionless but from time to time would turn her head upon the pillow. Several times she murmured soft, unintelligible sounds, but she did not wake, and Oliver made no move to disturb the earl.

Rudley blinked several times and then sat up with a start. Early-morning light was streaming in through the open curtains, and he realized he must have slept the clock around. He leaped from bed and, pulling on a dressing gown as he went, hurried to Katherine's room. Both of the communicating doors stood open and he found his brother standing at the window watching the sunrise. The sky had cleared and from all indications the day would be fine. Oliver spoke quietly. "She has been sleeping normally for some time now, but she has not yet awakened."

"Give me time only to shave and dress and I will come to relieve you." Rudley turned to leave but hesitated at the door. "And thank you, Oliver, for bullying me into getting some rest last night."

Rudley found that twelve hours of uninterrupted sleep had done much to restore his strength. One look at Katherine's face, still pale but no longer ghostly white, brought the return of his appetite. He sent down to the kitchen for some breakfast, a request that so gladdened the heart of Mrs. Simpson that she had two footmen carry up enough food to feed three hungry men.

When Katherine opened her eyes at last, bright noonday sun bathed the room. She focused carefully and then stared unbelievingly at the large armchair by the window. Her husband was sitting there, reading. She couldn't imagine why he should be there, for he was supposed to be in Scotland. Thinking that perhaps she was dreaming still, she spoke his name.

Rudley laid his book aside instantly and came to the bed. He had spent long hours holding her hand while she was unconscious, but now that she was awake, he wasn't sure he had the right, so he simply sat on a chair pulled up close to the bed and smiled at her.

"Hello. You have had a very long sleep. There is a whole

house full of people who will be happy to know you are awake at last.''

"How do you come to be here?"

"Oliver sent for me, the evening you began your labor."

"Oliver was wonderful. He sat with me the whole night. I was frightened, for it was too soon. What of the baby? I can remember the doctor saying it was a girl."

Rudley had expected the question and did not hesitate to answer. "Katherine, I'm so sorry. There is no easy way to tell you—she was not strong enough. She lived only a few hours." He thought he saw resignation rather than surprise mixed with the sorrow in her eyes.

"I feared, all those hours I waited for her to be born, that she might not survive, but I hoped . . . I wish I had seen her, just once."

Rudley wanted to tell her that he had seen the child, but he felt it was too soon. Best let her deal first with the fact that her child was dead. There would be time for the rest when she was stronger. "Katherine, we have much to discuss, but for now you must rest and concentrate on regaining your strength."

"Will you be staying on at Rudley?"

"Yes. I will be staying."

Katherine's eyes drifted closed. When she was asleep again, Rudley went down to the blue drawing room and found Oliver there sorting through the morning post. Oliver looked up with interest, knowing his brother would not leave Katherine without good reason. "Is she awake?"

"She was. She woke a few moments ago and almost immediately drifted off again."

"Thank God! She spoke to you?"

"Yes. She was coherent. She is tired and weak, and distressed at the loss of her child."

"You have also suffered a loss."

"Have I?"

"I truly believe this was your daughter, Ned."

"There is no way I can be certain of that."

"You need not be certain. Whether you mourn her as your

own or mourn her as Katherine's, you must put this business with Parnaby behind you and start building again.''

When Rudley frowned, Oliver decided he had interfered enough. ''Look at this mountain of correspondence,'' he said, ''bills, invitations, letters. I'm worn down. I need a holiday. I have received an invitation from Lord and Lady Harrington for an extended visit in Lincolnshire.''

''By all means accept it,'' Rudley replied. ''Kendall and I can manage here.''

''Kendall is gone, by the way. He went to Meg's to collect Serena. She was invited there for a house party. They should be back anytime now.''

''Oliver,'' Rudley began, ''Katherine has just told me that you stayed with her through her labor.''

''Yes, I did.''

Rudley knew that Oliver had sat with his own wife, Lydia, through the endless hours of a difficult birth and had been sitting with her still when she died. ''I know what it cost you to do that and I am in your debt.''

Oliver shrugged his shoulders. ''If the situation had been reversed, you would have done the same for me, so say no more about it.'' He turned and walked to the fireplace. ''You have had no chance to relax in Mother's chair since you came home.''

''No,'' Rudley replied. ''I haven't even been in this room.''

''Have a seat. I will pour us some wine.''

''What miracle is this?'' Rudley exclaimed as his eyes came to rest on the chair.

''No miracle, only the skillful hands of your wife.''

''Are you telling me that Katherine has duplicated Mother's work? What has become of the original?''

''Katherine has kept it safe in the event you should refuse this one out of hand and demand the other back again.''

''When did she do all this? It must have taken countless hours!''

''I believe she started it shortly after you were married. It was to be a surprise for your birthday.''

Rudley's birthday had come and gone a month earlier. Taking the glass of Madeira Oliver offered him, he dropped into a chair opposite his birthday gift and sat, staring at it. "Why should she do such a thing?" he asked.

"She did it to please you. I daresay she was motivated by a feeling similar to the one that made you buy that mare for her." Rudley raised his eyes to his brother's and they locked and held for some moments, but he made no comment and finally Oliver continued, "I will leave as soon as arrangements can be made, and I will take Nicholas with me."

Nearly an hour later, while Rudley was dealing with the correspondence that Oliver had tossed scornfully aside, the door opened and he looked up to see a young lady in a dark blue dress.

"Excuse me," she said, her hand still on the doorknob, "I didn't mean to disturb . . . I didn't know anyone was in here."

"Serena?" Rudley rose and moved toward her. "Please come in. It's time we met. I'm Rudley." He extended a hand in greeting.

Serena closed the door and came to take his hand, curtsying prettily. "I'm pleased to meet you, Lord Rudley. It's unfortunate we must meet under such circumstances."

"Have you seen Katherine?"

"Briefly. She was sleeping."

"Did Kendall tell you about the baby?"

"Yes. I shouldn't have left Katherine alone. I should have been here."

This comment so perfectly mirrored his own feelings that he felt for a moment as if she were speaking his thoughts.

"There was nothing you could have done," he said mechanically. "But she will need you in the days to come."

She didn't answer but stood regarding him with a curiously guarded expression.

"What is it?" he finally asked. "I can see there is something you wish to say."

"Will *you* be here, Lord Rudley, in the days to come?"

Her words were edged with bitterness. Clearly, in the dispute between himself and Katherine, Serena considered her sister to be the injured party.

"I don't know how much Katherine has told you about . . . our situation," he said evenly, "but it is perhaps useful to remember that it *is* precisely that—*our* situation—and no one else's."

She said nothing, but he admired the way she refused to look away. After a moment he said, "To answer your question, yes, I will be here. I hope there can be harmony between us."

A few minutes later Serena returned to Katherine's room to find her awake. She took one of Katherine's pale hands between her two strong ones and offered her sunniest smile. "I stopped to see you earlier, but you were sound asleep."

Katherine's smile was slight. "I'm so glad you're here, but you've had to leave your house party."

"There will be lots of house parties. I have just met your husband."

When she seemed disinclined to continue, Katherine coaxed, "And?"

"And he is quite handsome, very tall, and extremely daunting."

"Daunting? How so?"

"He asked me to say what I was thinking, and when I did, he advised me, ever so circumspectly, to keep my opinions to myself."

Katherine frowned. "You didn't quarrel?"

"No. Not at all. Nor will we. We have pledged ourselves to harmony."

During the days that followed both Serena and Pamela were committed to helping Katherine pass her waking hours pleasurably. They would sit and chat with her or read to her. When she took one of her frequent naps, they would slip away quietly, only to return with their needlework or a meal on a tray.

Katherine was disappointed when she learned Oliver was leaving them, but she understood that he was anxious to be with Charity again. He told her he would be taking Nicholas to Lincolnshire and asked if she would like him to remove Pamela as well. But Katherine was convinced that Pamela should stay. She was sorry to have been the cause of separating Rudley from his daughter for so many months. Now that he was home again Katherine felt it would be best for Pamela to be there, too.

On the morning set for Oliver's departure Katherine was so much improved that he found her sitting up in bed when he came to say good-bye. "Now if that's not a lovely sight! You're mending so fast you'll be back on that horse of yours in no time."

"How long will you be gone?"

"Nicholas and I have been invited to Harrington Manor for two weeks, and then I will see him back here again before I return to London. I must say I look forward to some relaxation after having slaved away here for months."

"You know you enjoyed it!" she insisted. "But we shall miss you."

"Not for long. Ned has offered to let us set up in the dower house after the wedding, at least until we can find something we would like to buy. Since our mother died, the place has been empty except for the caretaker and his wife who live there. I shall be down from time to time to see to the preparations."

"Oliver, I know you won't like it, but you must allow me to thank you for coming down to stay with me. I don't know how I would have managed if you hadn't been here. You kept me from being lonely and from feeling sorry for myself, and your high spirits more than once cured my depression. For your support on the night I gave birth there are no words adequate to thank you. Let me say only this. If you were the brother I never had but always wished for, I could not love you more."

He smiled and leaned over the bed to kiss her on the cheek. "My brother showed unquestionable good taste in marrying you, Katherine, and if he is wise enough to give you some rein, you may yet succeed in making him a happy man. Good-bye and good luck."

"Good-bye, Oliver."

During the first week of her recovery Katherine saw little of her husband. He came to visit several times each day, but he seldom stayed long. He had been inordinately pleased with Katherine's restoration of the chair. Like Oliver, he believed his mother would have been the first to applaud such a move to eliminate the shabbiness and yet manage to preserve a fragment of the Seaton family heritage.

His conversation during all of his visits was the merest commonplace. He asked how she was feeling, made comments on the weather, and kept her current on who had called and written. But he never brought the conversation around to any more personal topic than these. Katherine wasn't certain why he had come home, and she had been unable to tell if he was still angry. She could see that he was greatly troubled but clearly unwilling to discuss his feelings with her. She finally decided that his reticence stemmed from his consideration for her recent loss and her current state of health.

Pamela, however, was no stranger to Katherine's room and the two passed many enjoyable hours together. Pamela also saw a great deal of her father and would regale Katherine with accounts of a ride they had taken together or a meal they had shared. She flew into the room one day frantic with the news that her father had permitted her to jump her horse.

"You know the great stone wall beyond the wych elm grove?"

"I know the one you mean."

"How high is it, would you say?"

"Two feet at least."

"We jumped it, Black Star and I, with room to spare!"

Katherine could see that Ned was making an effort with the child and that it was bearing fruit. What she didn't know was that Rudley's attitude toward Pamela had done an almost complete turnabout. With his acceptance of the innocence of Katherine's child there had come a similar realization concerning Pamela. When he looked at her now, he saw only the blameless victim of Arabella's wantonness and his own neglect. Pamela was not his child, but circumstances had placed her in his care. He was accountable for both her physical and emotional well-being and he no longer intended to shirk his responsibilities where she was concerned.

Less than three days after Oliver's departure Katherine was permitted to walk about her room and sit up in a chair for a few hours. By the end of the week the doctor said she could go downstairs and sit for a time in the drawing room. Two days later Rudley and Pamela visited her together, Pamela insisting that Katherine accompany them on a stroll to the stables.

After stopping to give an apple to Karma, Pamela went off to visit Black Star while Rudley and Katherine made their way to Lady Halfmile's stall. The horse put her head over the split door to greet them and Rudley took hold of her halter.

"Ah, my beauty. I never thought to see the day you would grace my stables."

"How did you finally convince Lord Gilborough to sell her?" Katherine asked.

"I didn't. You did."

"Me? How?"

"Just by being you. Gil was so pleased with you, I think he would have given you anything you asked for that day."

"Surely not," she said, disbelieving.

"Do you remember the note he gave you?"

"Yes, of course."

"He told me then that I could have her. I was going to surprise you one day by leading her home. But then . . ." He shrugged and stopped in midsentence. As he scratched the mare under the jaw she lowered her head and stretched her neck in appreciation.

Theoretically she was Katherine's horse, but Rudley was plainly so pleased to have her in his stable that there was no end to the praise he showered upon her. He was already making plans for the foal she carried, even though it was not due to be born for another month.

"I wanted to speak to you about something, Katherine,"

he said. "I need to take a trip. Only a short one. Four days, five at the most."

"And?"

"I said I would stay. I don't want you to think I'm going back on my word."

"I don't think it. If you have business, you must attend to it. I have Serena and Pamela. I am well looked after."

He stared at her in silence for a few moments, then said abruptly, "Katherine, I . . ."

When he paused she prompted, "Yes?"

He shook his head. "Nothing . . . It's not important . . . I will keep my trip as short as possible."

Pamela soon rejoined them. When she asked her father a question, Katherine watched him with a troubled frown on her face. What was in his mind? Would he ever share his thoughts with her again? How desperately she wanted to discuss her loss—their loss. But how could she when he didn't even believe the child was his?

Chapter 21

THE MONTHS OF Rudley's self-imposed exile from Rudley Court had been difficult for him, but they were as nothing to the torment of living once again under the same roof as Katherine. He was plagued by conflicting emotions that he could not reconcile. At one moment, sitting with Katherine, listening to her talk, he would feel as he had during the days of their intimacy: warm and content, fulfilled, in love and loved. Moments later, reminded of the lost child and her dubious paternity, he would be cast again into a morass of doubt and insecurity.

At night he was troubled by dreams. In one he saw himself and Katherine. It was summer and they were on the lawn in the park beneath a giant hornbeam tree. Katherine had a child on her lap and its face was the face of the child who had died—the face Rudley saw night after night when he closed his eyes to sleep. In this dream he and his wife and child were happy and content, yet he would wake from the dream in a cold sweat. If the child were indeed his, if his absence was responsible for Katherine's unhappiness and the child's early birth, then he had contributed to the death of his own daughter.

In another dream, equally disturbing, he saw Katherine and Parnaby—they were laughing as they rode together. They did nothing more, nothing improper, yet this simple, innocent behavior chilled his heart as thoroughly as the other dream.

These dreams recurred night after night in almost equal proportions until he finally realized he would never know any peace until he found some answers to the questions that haunted him.

His four-day journey would take him to Lincolnshire, where he sincerely hoped he would find Viscount Parnaby in residence. Traveling by curricle and changing horses often, he arrived at the Parnaby estate early on the afternoon of the second day. He handed the butler his visiting card and stated his desire to speak with Lord Parnaby.

"Lord and Lady Parnaby have gone driving, my lord. His lordship didn't say when he expected to return."

"Would it be possible for me to speak with the dowager viscountess?"

Rudley was shown into a handsome salon while he waited for his visitor's card to be taken to Parnaby's mother.

When the butler carried the card to her ladyship and read it to her, she smiled and cocked her head with interest. "Lord Rudley! How lovely. And his lady is with him, of course."

"No, my lady," the butler corrected. "His lordship is alone."

"How curious. Show him up. I am anxious to see him."

Some minutes later Rudley was ushered into Lady Parnaby's sitting room. As he entered, the lady rose from her chair and extended a hand. He crossed to her and took it in his, noticing that her vacant blue eyes did not meet his but stared past him.

"Lord Rudley!" she exclaimed. "What a pleasant surprise. You are the last person I expected to see today." She smiled slightly. "You will understand that when I say 'see' I do not intend to be taken literally. Please sit down. May I offer you some refreshment?"

When the butler was sent for wine, she continued. "I remember you well from your early days on the town. I need add only a few years, and my mental picture will be quite accurate, I daresay. I must tell you that your wife is one of my favorite people."

"She speaks highly of you, too, Lady Parnaby. Since I had business nearby, I knew she would wish me to call and pay my respects."

"How kind."

"You have known Katherine a long time, I believe."

"Indeed, ever since her mother married Sir Humphrey and came to live nearby. Sir Humphrey was a different man in those days—before the drink and the evil of gambling consumed him. Katherine and Charity Harrington were inseparable from the beginning, and Charity's mother and I go back further than creation. I can't say as I took much note of Katherine, though, until she was about sixteen or so. I was at the lending library, and my eyesight was failing even then. She offered to help me choose a book. Later, when I could no longer read myself, the dear child came and read to me. Sometimes she brought the most inappropriate things. Novels. Can you imagine? But I never objected; I listened with attention to every word."

The butler returned with the wine. After Rudley was served he said, "Katherine told me she found several opportunities to visit with you while she was here in May."

"Bless her heart, the child came nearly every day, and heaven only knows there are dozens more interesting things a young woman can do with her time than sit listening to an old woman chatter. I asked her all about you, sir, and she sang your praises most eloquently."

Rudley frowned, relieved that she couldn't see his reaction.

When he was silent, she asked, "Have I embarrassed you? I did not intend to." She held her hand out into space and Rudley leaned forward to take it. "You have chosen a wonderful woman for your wife, my lord. When she was here with me, I could see that you have made her happy. I can ask for nothing more than that."

Rudley stayed another ten minutes with the viscountess, then took his leave and followed the butler down the stairs to the great hall. As he collected his hat and gloves, the front door opened and Viscount Parnaby and his new wife entered.

"Rudley!" Parnaby exclaimed, trying to sound pleasantly surprised but unable to keep a hint of incredulity from his voice.

Rudley greeted them both before addressing Parnaby. "I have been visiting with your mother and I was hoping to have a word with you. Perhaps you could accompany me to my carriage."

"Certainly." After assuring his wife that he would see her for dinner, Parnaby left the house with the earl. As they walked down the drive toward the stables, Parnaby said, "I must say, you are the last person I ever expected to see here."

"Your mother said exactly the same thing."

"I can't imagine what we could possibly have to talk about."

"Can't you? You saw Katherine when she was here in May."

"Yes. I saw her once. We ran into each other quite by accident here in the stableyard. I escorted her home."

Rudley said nothing but regarded Parnaby steadily with one eyebrow raised.

"Very well," Parnaby continued guiltily. "Obviously she told you I did more than escort her home. But it was months ago. Ancient history, in fact. If you have come here with some belated intention of calling me out, you can forget it. I'm a happily married man now, and I don't intend for my wife to become a widow."

When Rudley persisted in stony silence, Parnaby demanded, "What? What else do you want to know?"

"I want your version of what happened that day."

Parnaby sighed. "I was feeling sorry for myself. I thought I had made the world's greatest mistake in my choice of bride. I kissed Katherine; she pushed me away. As it turns out, I was wrong. My marriage is working out well—quite well."

When he saw that Rudley was still frowning, he insisted, "It was only a kiss! Nothing worth shooting a man for. Besides, she made it perfectly clear she wanted nothing from me."

Rudley stopped walking abruptly, and his hand on Parnaby's arm brought them face-to-face. "I have only one more question and I want an honest answer. Before I ask it, I give you my word that regardless of your answer, I will not call you out or take any other action that would endanger either your life or your happy marriage."

Parnaby looked at his companion as if he had taken leave of his senses. "What's the question?"

"Have you at any time during your relationship with Katherine been intimate with her?"

"What?" Parnaby nearly yelled at him. "Are you out of your mind? What kind of a cur do you take me for?"

Rudley's voice was deadly calm as he said, "You have not answered the question."

"The answer is no. I loved Katherine. I would never have done anything to compromise her."

Henderson had been a groom at Rudley Court since he was fifteen—when the previous earl was still alive. He had ridden beside the present Lord Rudley since the early days when he first mastered the skill of driving a four-in-hand. He had been with him through the years of his estrangement from his first wife and his service in the military. During that time he had often seen his employer quiet and thoughtful, using words sparingly. Never had he known him as reticent as on the return trip from Lincolnshire. For two days Rudley drove in complete silence. He left it to Henderson to deal with the changes of horses; he ordered a room or a meal with the fewest words possible.

When they arrived at Rudley Court in the late afternoon, the earl handed the reins to his groom, then swung down from the carriage. "Thank you, Henderson. I'm sorry I was such poor company this trip."

Startled by this outpouring of words after hours of silence, Henderson mumbled, "You need not apologize, m'lord."

As the curricle rolled away, Rudley paused for a moment to look up at the facade of the house. As each mile passed on the way home, he had become more and more aware of how impossible it would be to confront Katherine. He wanted to go anywhere but back to her, do anything but face her. But he had promised he would come back and he knew he could not add cowardice to the list of his transgressions against her.

Inside the house he went quickly to his rooms and ordered a hot bath. Afterward he dressed carefully for dinner, but when the time came, he found he could not go down. He took off his coat, then undid his neckcloth and tossed it on the bed.

In the salon downstairs Serena and Katherine were waiting for dinner to be announced when the door burst open and Oliver strode in.

"When did you get back?" Katherine asked, moving to greet him with a kiss.

"About an hour ago. Nick has already galloped upstairs to find Pam and no doubt eat a monstrous dinner. I can't believe the amount of food he can stow away."

As the dinner gong sounded, Oliver asked, "Isn't Ned joining us?"

"He's not home. He had to go away on business."

"He may have been away, but he's home now. The lads were stabling his team when I got here."

The three sat down to dinner, Oliver sharing news of the Harringtons and of his two-week visit with his betrothed. His wedding was just over two months away, and he complained of how hard it had been to leave Charity and how he wished the wedding was over so they could be together. Then, in the next breath, he was bemoaning the great amount of work necessary to set the dower house to rights and swearing he could not possibly have everything ready in time. When the ladies retired to the drawing room after dinner, he hurried off in search of Kendall to demand his always efficient assistance.

Serena and Katherine were left feeling as if a small whirlwind had passed over them. "Your brother-in-law is clearly in a lovesick condition," Serena commented.

"I, for one, hope he never recovers," Katherine said. "He has made Charity wonderfully happy."

The sisters spent a quiet evening together and retired early, Katherine carefully following the doctor's orders. She was in bed reading when there came a quiet knock on the door connecting her rooms to Rudley's.

She said, "Come in," and was surprised to see her husband partially dressed for dinner. She wondered briefly why he hadn't joined them. Then he moved into the light of her candles and the expression on his face drove all thought of his apparel from her mind. His face was tired and drawn, his expression grave.

"Ned, what's wrong? Why didn't you come down to dinner?"

"I had to talk to you alone, so I waited for you to come up."

He walked to the open draperies and looked out to where a pale sliver of moon etched a path across the shadowy lake.

"I owe you an apology," he said. "God, how pitiful that sounds! I have behaved in an unforgivable fashion. I am an utter and complete fool."

Shocked to hear such words pouring with great pain from her husband, Katherine said, "Why? . . . What? . . . Please don't say such things. You are not a fool. . . . You have not behaved—"

"Katherine," he interrupted, "I have just come from Lincolnshire. I spoke with Parnaby's mother—his *blind* mother, the one you visited every day. I spoke with Parnaby himself. He told me about the kiss, that you pushed him away."

Some moments passed in silence while Katherine took in this shower of words. Finally she said quietly, "I should have told you about it myself."

"He told me you had never been lovers."

"I told you that, too."

"I didn't believe you."

"No."

He sat despondently in the chair next to the bed, his hands folded between his knees, his voice thick with emotion. "That tiny, perfect child was mine."

"Nurse told me you saw the baby the morning she was born."

"Yes. I did. She was a little over an hour old when I arrived."

"Would you tell me about her?"

"I had planned to when you were stronger. She was born at about four-thirty. I saw her for the first time shortly before six. She was incredibly small, but perfect. Bailey said from the beginning that she was too weak to survive, but she wiggled and squirmed and made tiny, almost inaudible noises. She even had her eyes open whenever she was awake! I remember being amazed by that.

"They wouldn't allow me to sit alone with you in those early hours, so I spent the time with her. Mostly she slept. That night, while I was riding down here, all I could think about was you and your well-being. Then, when Nurse asked me if I wanted to see the baby, I went in to her and I really didn't know what to expect—how I would feel.

"What I did feel is rather hard to explain. When I looked at her, I could suddenly see how much you must have loved her as you nurtured her with your own body, and in that moment I wanted to protect her for your sake and I would have done anything in my power to keep her safe for you. But it was God's will that she be with Him. I held her when she was christened. Sometime around nine o'clock they told me I could sit with you, and shortly afterward she died. The doctor said she did not suffer but only went to sleep and did not wake again."

Katherine listened without interruption. Tears sprang to her eyes almost as soon as he began speaking and occasionally one would overflow and fall onto her folded hands. She looked up as he handed her his handkerchief, and she steadied her voice to say, "You never told me what name she was given."

"I had her christened Rosalind. Rosalind Katherine Seaton."

Rudley had named the child after his own beloved mother! "But you didn't believe she was yours," she said.

"It didn't seem to matter. When the rector asked what

name, I said Rosalind Katherine, I didn't even think about it. She was yours and you loved her. That was enough.''

Katherine stared, unblinking, at her husband and in that moment a great deal of healing took place.

"But I failed her," he said. "I should have been here. I called you a liar. I accused you of infidelity. I read your diary, invaded your privacy. Oliver said you were depressed. That was my fault, too."

Katherine slid from the bed to kneel in front of him. She wrapped her hands around his clasped ones.

"Ned, I may have been depressed; I certainly missed you. But I loved our baby, and I did everything as I should. I ate well, slept a great deal, obeyed the doctor to the letter. But she came early. It's not your fault; it's no one's fault."

He looked up to meet her eyes. "For two solid days I have been asking myself why I couldn't simply believe you. Why did I think the worst of you, assume the worst had happened between you and Parnaby? It's almost as though I look for ways to make myself miserable—to do my best to destroy all that is good and true in my life."

"You told me once that your first wife was not honest with you, that she deceived you. I think perhaps it is difficult for you to trust."

"But you are nothing like Arabella," he said. "She purposely lied to me—planned her deception."

"I think you should tell me about her," Katherine suggested. "Everything. All she did, all she said. If you will do that, then I promise to tell you all the awful things about Sir Humphrey that I have wanted to forget. Then perhaps we could start again, with no secrets."

"All right," he agreed. "I'll tell you—but not tonight." He rose and, taking her hands, pulled her to her feet. "I think you should be in bed. It's cold and the doctor was very clear about the amount of rest you need. Sleep now. We will talk again in the morning."

He waited while she got into bed, then added several logs

to the fire and carefully placed the firescreen before blowing out her candles. He said good night then and left.

Katherine was disappointed. After the intimate conversation they had shared, she had hoped he might offer her a kiss on the cheek or at least take her hand in parting. It was clear from what he had said that he blamed himself not only for doubting her but for the death of the child as well. She knew that simply saying it wasn't so, would not take away the guilt he felt.

The following morning Katherine had Gordon walk with her to the bench in the rose arbor. He settled her there comfortably, carefully tucking a rug over her lap before she dismissed him, asking that he come to fetch her in twenty minutes.

It was early February, but the day was fine. A bright winter sun had warmed the stone bench and the brick wall behind her. From this location behind the house she couldn't see the lake, but she had a wonderful view of the park and the forest to the south—mature trees stripped of their leaves by winter. She realized that in no time at all they would be green again with the promise of another spring. The sun on her face was warm, the fresh air exhilarating after weeks indoors.

Katherine had enjoyed her outing for only a few minutes when she looked up and saw Rudley walking toward her across the lawn. She suddenly remembered the last time they had been there together, the day he said there would be no divorce. He had been so cold, so detached, but as he came to her now there was no indifference in his eyes and only concern in his voice when he spoke. "Gordon told me he brought you here. May I sit with you?"

"Please do."

He sat down beside her, remaining silent for a few moments. When he spoke, he echoed her earlier thoughts. "I am reminded of the last time we met here. My behavior that day was unforgivable."

"Why do you say so? You behaved as you felt. There can be no fault in that."

"No, you're mistaken. I did not say what I felt. Far from it. I went away that day allowing you to think I hated you and, Katherine . . . I have never hated you. I don't believe I ever could."

He rose suddenly and, walking a few paces away, stood with his back to her. "I made a lofty speech on our wedding day about honoring marriage vows, then, hypocrite that I am, I deserted you at the first sign of trouble without even giving you an opportunity to explain."

"You had provocation."

He turned to face her. "Enough provocation to think the worst of you? Oliver didn't! He thought you must have had some logical explanation for your behavior. But I would not even listen when it was offered me!"

"You cannot compare your reaction to Oliver's. I'm not his wife; he wasn't the one who felt betrayed. When you asked me to marry you, Ned, I tried to explain that there were things about me that you didn't know. I had no wish to deceive you or to misrepresent myself.

"I was wrong not to tell you about Sir Humphrey. And I should have told you about meeting James when I went north. I had heard he was in France, otherwise I would never have gone near his house. But his mother is a dear friend and I so wanted to see her."

When she paused, he sat again and after a few moments offered, "After Arabella I swore to myself that if I ever married again I would be so cautious, take my time, choose a wife with utmost care.

"Then I met you, and loved you, and decided to throw caution to the wind. I put my trust in you—and I wasn't disappointed. During those days following our drenching in the rain, I was as certain as any man could be that you loved me. But when I heard what your stepfather had to say, when I saw the list of names you kept to choose a husband, it all seemed so sordid."

Even as she reached out a hand to touch him, he rose

once again from the bench. "Ned, I'm so sorry. I never meant—"

"No, Katherine," he interrupted, turning to face her. "Don't apologize. It's my place to do that. For months I've regretted the words I spoke to you the day I left Rudley. I allowed myself to become angry and permitted my temper full rein. I was wrong and I'm sorry."

"I didn't mind your shouting at me," Katherine insisted. "It was easier for me to accept than your cold indifference the day we spoke here."

"Indifference!" he exclaimed. His eyes softened, remembering. "When I saw you standing there, with the roses in your arms and around your feet, I couldn't believe how sweet it felt just to be close to you again—for despite everything . . . I still loved you . . . as I love you now."

She smiled up at him, a smile threatened by tears. She brushed them away, then laced her fingers in her lap, gripping them tightly together. "When I first met you," she said, "I found you attractive, but I thought you were just being kind because of your friendship with the Brents. Later, when you sought me out, I was flattered. In the midst of my upside-down world you seemed so steady, so secure and sure of yourself. Sir Humphrey had been getting progressively harder to live with. His gambling was out of control; his drinking started earlier each day. He was always begging me for money because he spent his within days of receiving it. When he announced that he intended to marry Serena to a toothless fifty-year-old man, I was forced to act. I resolved to marry. I wanted James, but he couldn't afford to marry me. I told him I wouldn't wait, for as much as I cared for him, my first obligation was to Serena. When you asked me to marry you, the security you represented was the most tempting thing anyone had ever offered me.

"With every day that passed after our engagement and after our marriage, I became more certain I had made the right decision. We got on so well together, and I was positive that I could be a good wife. I went north to strike a bargain with Sir Humphrey. I signed over my income to him in return

244

for guardianship of Serena. Lord Harrington had the papers drawn up. It was all tidy and legal."

When he frowned, she said, "I should have told you about that, too. If you had known my real reason for going north, you might not have believed Sir Humphrey. Then, after you and I . . . after we became close . . . when I could have spoken, I found I no longer wished to. I was so happy—*we* were so happy—I didn't want to spoil it. James and Sir Humphrey and everything to do with them didn't seem important anymore. I wanted never to think of that unhappy time in my life ever again."

"She paused, giving him time to respond. When he said nothing she continued. When I first went to London, I was in love with James. When you asked me to marry you, I was still in love with him, but I knew he was lost to me. When he kissed me in Lincolnshire, I didn't like it. Partly I felt such behavior was a betrayal of you, but even more than that I found that his kiss no longer excited me. In fact, it left me feeling nothing at all.

"On my way home I was so eager to get here; I had missed you so. My trip had gone splendidly. Serena was free of Sir Humphrey's power, and I owed it all to you. You had made it all possible. I know now that I loved you even then, but I didn't realize it until the day you left. When you became so angry and accused me of such awful things, I didn't blame you in the slightest. I was only angry with myself—for not being honest, for not telling you everything, for keeping secrets and in the process losing your trust."

"Katherine, those hours you were unconscious, I prayed I had not stayed away too long, that I had not destroyed the tender feelings you once had for me."

"I don't think it's possible for you to destroy the love I have for you," she said simply.

These were the words he had hoped to hear, but even as she spoke them he was finding it difficult to believe he had heard her correctly. He stared at her for some moments in silence and then held out both hands to her. When she put her own in them, he drew her to her feet and took her into his arms, slowly and gently, as if she were one of the fragile blossoms that would grow there in abundance when the summer came. He did not kiss her but only held her close against his heart, for he knew beyond any doubt that if their love had survived these past months, it would be equal to or stronger than anything the future could hold.

Chapter 22

WHEN KATHERINE DESCENDED the stairway to the great hall in the late afternoon, she found Rudley in conversation with his brother. After Oliver had greeted Katherine then disappeared toward the estate office, Rudley said, "It is a beautiful day. Shall we go for a walk?"

As she took the arm he offered, she said, "We can walk along the stream to the little footbridge in the woods . . ." She stopped and turned to Rudley, for at her mention of the bridge he had halted abruptly. "Once before you refused to take me there, Ned. What is it about the bridge? Why won't you go there?"

"Phantoms again, Katherine," he replied. "Shadows of Arabella—very unpleasant ones."

"I think now is the time for you to tell me about Arabella. In what way did she deceive you, and why did your marriage end?"

They moved back into the blue drawing room and he led her to a sofa and seated himself beside her before he continued. "It was on that bridge, a little over a month into my marriage to Arabella, that she told me she was pregnant with another man's child."

"Oh, no!" Katherine could not keep from exclaiming as she laid her hand on his sleeve.

"She went on to say—and very flattering it was to my ego, let me tell you—that she was already in her fourth month and had married me only to protect her reputation. I should have exposed her then. A public scandal would have been much easier for me than the years of lying and pretense. But I didn't know that then, and I had been raised to think that scandal was to be avoided above all things, whatever the cost. She knew that, of course, so she had little fear of being cast off by me. When I asked her why she accepted *me* instead of marrying the child's father, she explained, with typical brutality, that I held a higher rank than the father and was considerably wealthier.

"Parts of this story you know. From that day forward our marriage was a marriage in name only. We were never reconciled. When the child arrived, people either thought it was premature or believed that Arabella and I had engaged in some premarital familiarity. No one, to my knowledge, ever doubted my paternity.

"So perhaps now you can see why Sir Humphrey's accusations came as such a shock to me. I couldn't credit that such a thing could happen to me twice! In my confused state I compared your behavior to Arabella's. I wasn't willing to await explanations. Like a wounded animal, I wanted only to run and hide, and feel sorry for myself, and allow myself to hate you as I had hated her."

When he paused, she interjected a question she had been anxious to ask. "What became of the child? And if your marriage was over, how did Pamela come to be conceived?"

"Pamela was the child Arabella carried. I have raised her as my own, though admittedly I have done a poor job of it."

"But I don't understand," Katherine insisted. "Pamela *is* your child."

"Legally, yes, but Arabella was already three months pregnant at the time we married."

"*Were* you intimate with Arabella before you married?"

"Katherine! What questions you ask! Certainly not!"

"Then the baby must have been premature, or there has to be some other explanation, for there can be no doubt Pamela is *your* child."

"Katherine, what are you trying to say?"

"I am saying there can be no question that you are Pamela's *real* father. You have only to look at her. Haven't you ever *looked* at her? She is without question a Seaton. She has the same deep-set eyes, and the same color, too, the same sweep of the brow, the same lines in the chin. She is so like you, I cannot believe you would ever doubt she is yours. It is true that she is fair like Oliver, your sister Margaret, and your father, but . . ."

She stopped speaking as a strange look came over her husband's face. He went rigid, the color quickly draining from his cheeks. He looked directly at her but didn't seem to see her. It was as if he were looking through her into something beyond.

Then, suddenly, he startled her by speaking. "My God! My own brother!" The tone of his voice made her blood run cold. He leaped to his feet and, seeming to forget Katherine and not bothering to excuse himself, stormed from the room. Confused and frightened, she followed him.

Rudley quickly crossed the hall to the estate office, where he found Kendall and his brother at work on plans for the dower house. "Kendall, leave us," he said sharply.

Kendall needed only one glance at his employer's face to obey without comment. As he left the room, Katherine entered it and quietly closed the door, setting her back against it. She was most likely not welcome, but she was determined to stay.

Rudley crossed the room to where Oliver had been sitting behind a small desk. Rudley's words to Kendall and his expression had brought Oliver to his feet. "Ned, what's wrong?" he asked.

The question Rudley shot at him was not one he had expected. "Are you Pamela's father?" Rudley's voice was frigid and heavy with undisguised fury. Oliver had spent the last decade wondering when, if ever, the light would finally dawn. He saw no reason to make a denial now that it obviously had. His eyes met Rudley's unwaveringly as he answered.

"Yes."

Oliver's lips had barely formed the word when the earl's hand shot out and caught him a powerful blow on the chin

249

that sent him sprawling backward over the chair behind the desk and crashing into the wall beyond.

"Ned!" Katherine's anguished cry from behind made Rudley spin around.

"Leave us," he commanded her. "You have no business here." Clearly expecting to be immediately obeyed, he wasted no more time on her but turned again to Oliver, who was beginning to rise from the floor. Rudley moved around the desk and assisted his brother by grasping the front of his coat and hauling him roughly to his feet.

Oliver raised no hand to defend himself. "I will not fight you, Ned. It will accomplish nothing."

If Rudley had considered hitting him again, he now changed his mind and, still grasping the cloth of Oliver's coat, contented himself with slamming his brother with all his strength against the wall.

Katherine, who had stood her ground, stifled another exclamation, covering her mouth with her hands.

"I have loved you, trusted you, all our lives," Rudley spit at him. "Tell me what I have done to deserve such treachery from you."

Glancing past his brother's shoulder at Katherine's horrified face, Oliver came close to guessing what must have happened. "I daresay I should have forseen this," he said. "It was inevitable that you would eventually tell Katherine that Pamela was not yours. It was not to be expected the likeness would escape her, although it certainly eluded *you* long enough." This speech was not calculated to be conciliatory, and Rudley once more clenched his fists. "Really, Ned, it will not be necessary for you to hit me again. You have made your feelings quite plain."

"Get out of this house! You are no longer welcome here, nor on any other piece of property that belongs to me."

"That also is plain." Oliver stepped past Rudley and walked without haste to the door. "Good-bye, Katherine." As he passed her, she grasped his arm and held it.

"Oliver, please," she pleaded.

He carefully pried her fingers loose and pushed her gently

aside. "Let it go, Katherine. It's best this way." He stayed only long enough to say good-bye to the children. Then he ordered his black brought around—the only horse in the stables that belonged to him—and within twenty minutes was gone.

In the estate office Rudley and Katherine had remained standing, she by the open door, he still with his back to her, beside the desk. She had disobeyed him by remaining in the room; now she was afraid to speak.

She was bewildered by what had occurred and two things only were clear to her. First, that Oliver had admitted to being Pamela's father, and second, that her carelessly uttered words had been responsible for the bitter confrontation she had witnessed. Never in her life had she seen one man strike another in anger, and never had she thought to see Ned display such impassioned, naked, violent emotion.

Suddenly he turned. He was pale but in command of himself again. Walking to the door, he paused beside her. "I am sorry you had to see that, but I did not invite you to follow me."

As he started to walk away, she found her voice. "Ned, whatever Oliver—"

He cut her short. "I cannot discuss this with you, Katherine." He abruptly crossed the hall and disappeared into the library. Clearly he wished to be alone, and she knew if she tried to join him she would only be rebuffed. She considered going in search of Oliver but decided against it for the same reasons.

Rudley did not put in an appearance at dinner that night, but the next day he went about all his normal activities. He spoke seldom and seemed preoccupied when spoken to.

Katherine heard him tell Kendall to cancel any plans that had been made for the dower house since Oliver would not be using it after all. He said nothing, however, about Nicholas and Pamela, and she was relieved that he would not allow his anger to extend to Oliver's children. She wished he would confide in her, hoping she would be able to help mend the rift between the brothers, a rift she felt partially responsible for.

Three days passed, then four, and still Rudley kept his own counsel. After five days Katherine took matters into her own hands. She retired early after dinner, bathed, and donned her night attire. She then proceeded to her husband's room and settled comfortably into one of the large upholstered armchairs before the fire, determined to stay until he came to bed. Inevitably she fell asleep, but woke when he opened the door. He was about to ring for his valet when she forestalled him.

"Don't ring for Wiggin. Let me help you." He looked around in surprise, for he had not expected to see her there. Even though they had made their peace in the rose arbor several days earlier, they had continued to retire to separate rooms each evening. He waited as she crossed the room to him, her nightgown and wrapper of palest yellow silently brushing the floor. Her attire was nothing short of provocative, but he doubted she realized how tempting she appeared.

"If you have come to seduce me, Katherine, you must know you are not sufficiently recovered to indulge in such a pastime."

"I have not come to seduce you—only to act as your valet." She began deftly to untie his neckcloth, and he stood impassively, gazing down at her in amusement. He had forgotten how much it soothed him to have her close. She helped him out of his tight-fitting coat and then began to unbutton his shirt. When she pulled the shirt from his breeches, she couldn't resist the impulse to run her hands up the smooth, hard chest. She heard the sharp intake of his breath as his languor deserted him. No longer able to resist her, he took her face between his strong hands and kissed her long and hungrily.

"Katherine," he murmured against her lips, "you are beginning something I am not permitted to finish."

"I have missed being close," she said. "These last few days you have been pushing me away. We agreed to share everything." Safe in his arms, she found the courage to introduce the subject she knew was tormenting him. "Please talk to me about Oliver. Tell me what you feel."

He answered without hesitation. "I feel betrayed and deceived. Duped by my own brother, who until a week ago I would have sworn would never lie to me."

"Did he actually lie to you?"

"Don't quibble, Katherine! For ten years he kept the truth from me. It is the same as a lie, make no mistake. At the time I asked Arabella to marry me, she had already been intimate with my brother."

"And what would you have had him do?" she asked sensibly.

"Warn me. Tell me what she was like."

"You were both so young. I doubt very much if he realized then what she was capable of. But if he had, and had told you, would you have believed him?"

He considered the question, remembering how all-consuming his passion for Arabella had been. "No, probably not. I would have been much more likely to call him out for impugning her character."

"Then you have your answer. He did not tell you because he knew you would not believe him."

"At best, that is a weak assumption on your part, Katherine, but I can see you are prepared to give him the benefit of the doubt."

"And so should you be," she insisted.

"No. I cannot agree with you. Whatever his motives for keeping their relationship a secret, he could have no excuse for remaining silent after Arabella and I were estranged. He was in my confidence, he knew how infuriated I was that Arabella would never tell me who the father was. She probably planned to use the information against Oliver someday, but she didn't live long enough."

"You have now answered the question of why he didn't speak after the estrangement."

"Because he feared me, you mean?"

"He apparently had good cause, considering your behavior in the estate office the other day."

He frowned. "I am afraid I must disagree with you again. I saw him display no fear of me then—only defiance. But since you have set yourself up as Oliver's champion, perhaps you would like to explain why he has kept silent all these years since Arabella's death?"

Katherine had wondered this herself, but she said only, "I don't know, but don't you think the best way to discover that would be to ask him yourself?"

"This entire conversation has consisted of the wildest conjecture. If Oliver has not had the decency to explain himself in eleven years, I see no reason why he should trouble to do so now, simply because I have discovered his perfidy. I will not ask for any explanation from him, for anything he could say comes much too late in the day to have any value or meaning for me."

Rudley went into his dressing room to finish changing and Katherine settled herself comfortably in her husband's bed. She could see that trying to reason with him would not serve, for he was being ruled by his emotions. A rational discussion, no matter how calmly approached, would have no power to sway him. She wondered if there would ever be an end to the erosion of faith and the destruction of peace that Arabella was perpetrating, even from beyond the grave.

It was the same old wound, ready to open and bleed again at the slightest provocation. Katherine had unwittingly opened it, and now she could only let time once more do the healing. Rudley had forgiven her, and he would forgive Oliver, too, when the pain died to a dull ache and the reasonable mind of a fair man came once again into its own.

Katherine realized that her husband, like most people, would continue to seek love in his life, even when time and again he had been betrayed and humiliated in the name of it. It seemed to be the nature of love to be a double-edged sword. If it was incapable of hurt, then it would bring no joy. If it could not die, then it would find no victory in survival. If there was no price to pay, then the attainment would hold no allure.

Whatever Oliver's reasons for keeping his terrible secret,

Katherine had no doubt that the primary motivation overriding them all was his love for his brother. And another thing she realized, which her husband did not see, was that Oliver, too, must have suffered. If he and Arabella had been lovers, then he certainly must have cared deeply for her. How had he felt when she turned away from him—in favor of his own brother?

And then there was Pamela. How hard it must have been for Oliver all these years to accept the title of uncle when it was a father's love he bore her. So easy now to see why there had been such rapport between Pamela and Oliver—such distance between Pamela and Rudley. And in the middle, poor Pamela, wanting only to be loved and belong, never realizing how her mother had used her as a pawn in a vicious game.

Now Katherine herself was in the middle and found she did not mind being there. She would stay close to Ned, and she would try to keep in touch with Oliver, if he would allow it. Then, perhaps, when the time was right, she would be the bridge over which the bonds of reconciliation could pass.

When Rudley returned, he extinguished the candles and joined her under the quilts. She nestled like a contented cat against him, her head on his chest, his chin in her hair. The leaping flames of the fire cast eerie shadows across the walls and furnishings.

Rudley let his fingers play up and down the softness of her arm, feeling the warmth of her skin penetrating the thin material. His fingers encountered a stray curl and he absentmindedly twisted it around his finger, then loosed it again. All those weeks he had been separated from Katherine, this, he thought, was what he had missed most. Her physical nearness. Not possessing her physically, but simply having her there, close to him, touching him.

He bent his head and kissed the soft chestnut curls that tickled his face. During all the months he had been away from her, first in Yorkshire and then London, he had never been tempted to find solace with another woman. And it was not only his marriage vows that deterred him. He had found such completeness in Katherine's arms that the memory of those days and nights with her had destroyed his desire for any other woman and had made the pain of the separation just that much harder to bear.

Looking down at her now, he could see only the outline of her face in the dimming firelight, but he knew she was sleeping. He pulled the quilt up closely about her shoulders, and closing his eyes, he, too, was soon asleep. His sleep was sound and dreamless when she slept at his side.

Chapter 23

IMMEDIATELY UPON HIS return to London Oliver removed his possessions from Rudley House and took rooms in St. James's Street. Having settled himself there, he hired a chaise and posted to Lincolnshire. He arrived at Harrington Manor to find that Charity and her mother were away from home. Lord Harrington, however, welcomed his guest warmly. "It is good to see you, Oliver, but we did not expect you back so soon."

"There is something I must discuss with Charity, sir, and it could not wait." That he was impatient to see his betrothed was evident, for he seemed disinclined toward conversation and paced back and forth across the drawing-room carpet, nervous as a cat.

When the women returned, he wasted no time in taking Charity off alone. "You will be happy to know that Ned and Katherine seem to be overcoming their differences. However, I am afraid we now have a new problem. Ned and I have had a set-to. Or perhaps a falling-out would be a better phrase."

"You and your brother? How is this possible? You never quarrel."

"We didn't quarrel precisely, but he did throw me out of his house and made it quite clear that I was not welcome back."

Her amazement showed plainly on her face. "But, Oliver, why?"

"He had good reason, believe me. Come and sit down, Charity. There is something I must tell you. I wanted to tell you long before this, but I was not the only person involved; there were also Ned and Pamela to consider.''

"Pamela?'' She was now totally mystified.

He continued as if she had not spoken. "I pray you will understand. Ned doesn't and I can't blame him. I see now that I have been very unfair to him in keeping my secret so long.''

"Oliver,'' Charity complained, "I must beg you to make yourself clearer, for I do not in the least understand what you are trying to say.''

"There is not an easy way to say this, Charity. Pamela is not Rudley's child. She is mine.''

"Yours?'' Her voice was incredulous. "But I understood she was born to your brother and his wife during their marriage.''

"She was, but she was conceived by Arabella and me several months before their marriage took place.''

"What exactly are you saying, Oliver?'' Her voice was barely above a whisper and her countenance had grown quite pale.

"Arabella and I were lovers. She had agreed to marry me, but when she met Rudley she changed her mind and married him instead.'' Charity was shocked by the bitterness in his voice as he recalled how the woman he had loved had jilted him. "I had only just turned twenty, Charity. It was all such a long time ago, but I have never been able to put it behind me, for Pamela is a living reminder. All these years Ned has known Pamela is not his, but he never knew who her real father was.''

"And now he does, and that is why he is angry with you?''

"Angry! That's putting it mildly! Sickened by the sight of me would be a more accurate description. I will never forget the look of contempt on his face as long as I live.''

When she did not respond and the silence between them lengthened, he finally said, "Please tell me what you're thinking, Charity.''

"I'm wondering how old Pamela's mother was when she . . . when you and she . . .''

258

"She was eighteen."

Charity rose and turned away, but not before he saw the disappointment in her eyes. "I don't understand," she said.

"What?"

"I don't understand how you could take advantage of such a young girl. Surely you knew it was very wrong."

"Of course I knew it was wrong, and I'm not trying to make excuses for myself. But *she* came to me, Charity, and she was as eager as I. I knew it was risky, but we had decided to marry."

She still stood with her back to him, her shoulders rigid with disapproval.

He stood close behind her and spoke quietly, his voice slightly uneven. "If you feel you would like to be released from your commitment to me, I will understand."

She turned. "It's not that, Oliver. I don't love you any less because you once made a mistake in judgment—even though it was a mistake that hurt many people, not the least of which is an innocent child. What worries me is that you didn't tell me about it until you were forced to. If you have any other surprises for me, I would like to hear them now, please."

"There's nothing else, I swear."

"How did Lord Rudley discover the truth?" she asked.

"I'm not certain, but I think he must have finally told Katherine that Pamela was not his. She, of course, would not have believed him, for she would have seen the family resemblance. Evidently, she pointed it out to him, and he guessed the truth. I always thought it strange that he never saw the likeness himself, but I suppose as in so many things we see only what we wish to see. However he came to suspect, he simply asked me outright if I was Pamela's father. I could not deny it, Charity. I have never lied to Ned, and if I had he would have known instantly; and I love Pamela dearly, even though all these years I have been unable to tell her she is mine. Now that Ned knows, I cannot be sure what will happen next. I don't think it likely that he would jeopardize Pamela's happiness by casting her off, but in his present mood I must admit it to be a possibility."

"No," she interjected. "He would never do so. She is, after all, his niece, and I am convinced he could never be so cruel."

"I hope you're right, but regardless of what action he takes, if you marry me, you will become directly involved in it. Whether it turns into an open scandal or remains a private war, it will not be pleasant either way."

He stared out over the room, looking at nothing in particular, seeming to speak to no one in particular. "After all this time, I thought that part of our past was dead. I guess our sins always have a way of coming back to haunt us. Damn! I should have told him . . . he would have taken it better if I had told him myself. But I was afraid that just this sort of thing would happen. All I ever wanted was to keep Arabella from coming between us, but she has managed it at last. She's dead, but she has what she wanted. She always hoped to destroy our friendship; she has finally succeeded."

He seemed to recall himself and turned to face Charity again. "So, you see, I have botched the affair from beginning to end."

"You did what you thought was best at the time. None of us can do more than that. I never thought you were perfect, Oliver. I love you as you are, and I will always love you. Whatever the future holds for us, good or ill, we will face it together."

Since the use of the dower house was now out of the question and the wedding only two months away, Oliver decided to hire a house in London. Once he and Charity were settled in town, they could take their time finding a suitable place, for Oliver did not intend to buy anything that she could not first see and approve.

Upon his return to town Oliver started an active search for an appropriate house to hire, keeping his ears open as well for properties for sale. He was not enormously wealthy, but his father had left him a comfortable income. Much of this had been allowed to compound, for he was not spendthrift, nor did he gamble, and living with his brother he had not the expense of lodging or board. Over the years he had accumulated a respectable fortune. He felt confident that he could provide a comfortable home for Charity and Nicholas.

It was during his search for a house that he heard, quite by chance, that the former Ashley estate, where his mother had been born, might be available. He was talking with his friend, Lord Everett, and mentioned that he was looking for a suitable house to hire. "You know," Everett said, "the property to the west of Rudley's might be offered for sale one of these days."

"Weiring?" Oliver asked, amazed. "What makes you think so?"

"The fellow who owned it lost it to Claremont last week."

"Gambling?" Oliver asked. Everett nodded. "What a fool!"

"I didn't see the game myself," Everett continued, "but word is he had been under the hatches for some time and was making one final attempt to come about. But it didn't work. He lost everything: house, furnishings, land—the lot. I never met the man, but from what I hear he was a real odd one. Used to be a sailor, I think. Anyway, they say he seemed relieved to be out from under the property. Said he never felt he belonged there in the first place."

"What makes you think Claremont will be selling it?"

"Stands to reason, don't it? He already owns one of the largest houses in London and has at least half a dozen country places. What would he be wanting with another?"

Acting on this information, Oliver called on the Duke of Claremont the following morning. The duke admitted he had not given the subject much thought, having had the property in his possession little more than a week. He said, however, that he was not opposed to the idea of selling and would consider the matter and have his man of business contact Oliver within a few days.

Oliver was ecstatic. What incredible luck that the only house he had ever really wanted should be available at exactly the time he needed it! Weiring was not a large estate, but properly administered it could provide a comfortable living.

Oliver suspended all plans to rent and waited impatiently for word from the duke's representatives.

When the news came it was bittersweet. The duke was willing to sell, and the price he asked was fair and reasonable, but Oliver knew that even if he collected all his available assets, he would still fall short of the amount needed. He asked for some time to consider the proposal and review his financial situation, and Claremont's lawyers gave him sole option on the property for six weeks.

Oliver dispatched a letter to Charity immediately. "I am short of the amount needed to finalize the sale," he wrote, "but the property would be so perfect for us that I will beg or borrow what I need to get it." There was no mistaking the determination behind his words.

Oliver cursed the bad luck that made this property available at a time when he was estranged from his brother. Rudley could purchase three estates such as Weiring and hardly notice the expense. Oliver knew that only two weeks earlier Ned would have willingly advanced him anything he needed in the form of a loan. Unfortunately, under the present circumstances, any application to Rudley was impossible.

The following week, still five thousand pounds short of the purchase amount, Oliver rode down to Hampshire to view the property with the eye of a potential owner. Perhaps, seeing it, he would find some inspiration that would show him where to secure the balance of the money he needed.

He did not present himself at the house, which was still inhabited by the luckless gamester who had recklessly thrown it away. Instead he stopped his horse at the edge of the woods and sat staring. He had always loved the place. He had proposed to Charity on the day they rode here. If he could not manage to buy it himself, he was determined to have Claremont contact Rudley, who would, he was sure, not hesitate to buy it. At least then it would be in the family again.

Turning his horse, he started back toward the high road. Now that he was so close to home (somehow he would always think of the place where he had grown up as home) he wondered how Katherine was. He missed her. Had she recovered completely from her ordeal in January? Should he risk running afoul of his brother for a chance to see her, if only for a few moments?

He was not welcome on his brother's property, yet he was at that very moment riding across Rudley acreage. He turned his horse toward the stream above the lake and, crossing it, left the bridle path and made his way through the woods and up the slope. As he crested the hill, he reined in. The carriage drive lay immediately below him, halfway down the hill. Rudley Court lay to his right, and midway between him and the house, standing on the bridge that spanned the stream, was his sister-in-law. She was wrapped in a warm hooded cloak against the chill of the March day, but he could not doubt it was Katherine.

His luck was in. He started his horse down the slope but had only covered a few hundred feet when she heard him and turned. Her smile was warm and spontaneous, and as he stepped down from his horse, she came forward with both hands outstretched. He bent to kiss her. "Hallo, sweet sister! May I say you are much improved since last I saw you? How long has it been?"

"Almost a month. Why didn't you write at least?" she scolded. "I have been worried about you."

"No need to worry, dear Katherine. I go on well, thank you. I saw Serena in town a few days ago."

"Lady Brent invited her for the Season, and since I am recovering so quickly, she agreed to go. But tell me what brings you to Rudley?"

"I have not come to Rudley. I have been to Weiring, and I rode this way on impulse. I never dreamed I should have the good fortune to encounter you."

"You had not planned to stop at the house?"

"How can you ask that, Katherine? You were there when Ned made his wishes known."

"His wishes, however, are not mine, nor those of the children. We all miss you."

"How are Pamela and Nicholas?"

"They are well and happy. But you have still not told me what brings you to Weiring."

"It is for sale, Katherine! The owner lost it gambling, and I have the sole purchase option until the twelfth of April."

"Oliver, how wonderful! But can you afford to buy it?"

"Ah, there you have it! I have scraped together every available penny and I am still five thousand short. But I still have more than a month; perhaps a miracle will happen." He could see from her expression that she was already considering ways to help him. "And please, Katherine, don't embarrass all three of us by mentioning this to Ned. You know I could never ask him for the money, or accept if he offered it. And under the present circumstances we both know he never would."

As ill luck would have it, Rudley himself appeared at that moment, trotting down the drive on Navigator, and Katherine realized how careless they had been to stand there talking. She was expecting him and in fact had walked out purposely to meet him.

They could do nothing now but stand and watch his approach. He was soon upon them and brought Navigator to a standstill. He looked from Katherine to his brother but said nothing, favoring them only with an impersonal stare.

Katherine broke the tense silence. "Oliver stopped to say hello. He is down this way on business."

"Then it would be best not to detain him, my dear," Rudley answered. "I will wait for you across the bridge." With a nod at Katherine, but not so much as a glance at his brother, he rode on. Dismounting at the far side of the bridge, he stood gazing out over the lake.

"Oliver, I'm sorry."

"Don't be. He has good cause for his disgust of me. I can only be thankful that his anger hasn't extended to the children."

"There is no chance of that," she assured him. "He and Pamela are closer than ever."

"That is something to be grateful for, then. Nicholas will, of course, come to us after the wedding. What becomes of

Pam will largely depend on Ned, but whatever he decides, we must not hurt the child. She cannot be held accountable for my mistakes. She has already had more than her share of unhappiness."

"We both love her, Oliver. She will come to no harm here, I promise you."

"I believe you." He turned to his horse then and, gathering the reins, mounted swiftly. "I must go. Give my love to the children. I will see you all at the wedding, I hope."

"Yes, I will bring the children. We would not miss it." She reached her hand up to him and, bending in the saddle, he lightly kissed it. "Good-bye, Oliver, and good luck in your business venture."

"Thank you. I shall need it." He wheeled his horse and cantered off down the drive. Katherine watched until he disappeared beyond a bend in the road and then turned and walked on to join her husband.

"What a tender and touching reunion," he said caustically.

"Ned, please, let's not argue about Oliver. You have declared war upon him, not I! He has rendered me more service than I can ever repay. I will not be unreasonably cross with him."

"Which is to say I am."

"Oliver feels you have just cause to be angry with him, and you feel the same. Since you both seem to be in complete agreement, I fail to see how discussing it further can serve any useful purpose. How was your visit with Lord Gilborough? Did he sell you the mares you wanted?"

Early the following morning, when Rudley had gone to speak with his forester about some timber that was to be cut, Katherine went in search of Kendall. She was hoping she might be able to help Oliver out of his monetary difficulties and Kendall would be the best person to advise her.

She found him where he was most often to be found, in the estate office. "Peter, I need your advice."

"Certainly, my lady. In what way may I serve you?"

"If I needed some money, how would I acquire it?"

"I will be happy to supply your ladyship. How much do you need?"

"What if it was a large sum, Peter?"

"Exactly how large, my lady?"

"Five thousand pounds."

"For so large a sum, it would be best to apply directly to his lordship."

"Is there any way I could acquire such a sum without asking his lordship? Do I have any money of my own?"

"Certainly you do, my lady. It was settled on you at the time of your marriage, but it is invested in the Funds. The interest is at your disposal, but the principal cannot be touched."

This conversation was rapidly taking a direction that Kendall found disconcerting. He was not at all comfortable discussing such matters with the knowledge that the countess planned to keep her activities to herself. On the other hand, the earl had made it clear on more than one occasion that Kendall was to grant *any* request Lady Rudley made of him, without question.

Katherine continued. "You are telling me, then, that there is no way I can obtain such a sum without my husband's knowledge?"

Kendall made his decision. He would obey Lord Rudley's instructions. "No, my lady, actually there is a simple way. When his lordship went to Scotland last fall, he instructed his bankers in London to allow both Mr. Seaton and you to draw upon them. Mr. Seaton's power has since been rescinded, but yours never was."

"What exactly does that mean, Peter?"

"Simply that it would take only a draft with your signature to obtain the funds you seek."

"Is this not unusual power for a wife to have?"

"Unusual, perhaps, but not unheard of. It takes a great deal of capital to run an estate of this size. Lord Rudley wanted to be certain that in his absence there would be no problems arising from any monetary shortage."

"I see. Thank you, Peter. I appreciate your help."

She knew it was unnecessary to ask him not to mention their conversation to her husband. If she had learned anything of Kendall in these last months, it was that a more discreet soul did not exist.

Katherine was elated. She could help Oliver and Charity herself. She experienced some qualms over the fact that it was Ned's money she would be lending, but she would make sure Oliver never knew. She would enlist Lady Finley's help. Surely Oliver would not refuse a loan if he thought it came from his sister. And if it was a deceit, it was only a very small one, and certainly a necessary one if she was to overcome the gargantuan pride of the Seaton family, particularly that of its two eldest sons.

That evening at dinner Katherine introduced a subject she had been considering for several days. "Ned, do you think it would be possible for you to take some time off from your work here to go up to town for a few weeks?"

"Would you like to go?"

"Yes, I thought it might be enjoyable. We could take the children along and show them some of the sights. Then, when it comes time to travel north for the wedding, we would have a shorter journey than if we left from here."

"I'm sorry, Katherine. I haven't even thought that you might be eager for a change. I had forgotten that you have been stuck here in the country for months now."

"Don't be silly." She smiled at him. "You know that I love it here. I thought it would be enjoyable for the children, especially Pamela, who doesn't get away as often as Nick does. And, actually, I do have a few selfish motives: I would like to see how Serena is handling her first Season, and I would love to have a new dress made for the wedding."

"Then it's settled. When would you like to leave?"

She could see that her mention of the wedding irritated him, and she knew it would be useless to discuss it further. He had flatly refused to attend, and no argument she had put forward made the least impression on him.

They settled on the last week of March to remove to London; Katherine knew that would give her plenty of time to arrange Oliver's loan. With her plans made, she wrote to her sister-in-law.

My dear Lady Finley,

I am writing you to beg your assistance in a matter of some delicacy. As you may or may not know, Oliver still needs the sum of five thousand pounds in order to purchase Weiring. I have this sum available and wish to lend it to him, but I know he will not accept it from me. I already feel I owe Oliver more than I can ever repay. For his sake, and for my dear friend Charity's as well, I am determined to do this for them. Would it be possible for you to convince Oliver that this money is a loan from you and Lord Finley? I am hopeful he would accept it upon such terms. If you feel you could help me in this matter, I would be most grateful; but if you prefer not to involve yourself in such an intrigue, I will understand.

Yours sincerely, Katherine, Countess of Rudley

Several days later at her London town house, Lady Finley finished reading Katherine's letter, then set it aside and reached for quill and ink to write an immediate reply. She smiled to herself as she considered her good fortune in having acquired such an insightful and courageous sister-in-law.

During the past several weeks Katherine had developed the habit of sleeping in her husband's bed. This unfashionable behavior delighted the servants, particularly those who had been with Lord Rudley through the years of his unhappy marriage. Katherine was there now, propped up against several pillows, reading poetry by the light of a branched candelabra on the table nearby. Her nightgown was of a pale blue diaphanous material; her hair was brushed out loose and hung down about her shoulders.

This was to be their last night at Rudley Court. Everything

was packed in readiness for tomorrow's journey to town. The children had been in high twig for days pondering the promised treats that awaited them in London, not the least of which was seeing Oliver again. Katherine had retired early, having spent a hectic day organizing and packing.

She noticed that the clock on the mantelpiece showed a quarter past eleven and wondered what was keeping her husband so late. Less than ten minutes later she heard his voice and that of Wiggin in the adjoining dressing room. Rudley entered the room, crossed to the fireplace and snuffed the candles on the mantel, then paused beside the bed. "Would you like to continue reading?"

"Not really," she answered. "I would rather talk."

He left the candles burning on the bedside table and seated himself on the edge of the bed. "That is a very becoming color, Katherine. I don't think I have ever seen you wear it before."

"It's new," she said. "I want to model it for you." In a flash she was out of the bed, twirling before the fireplace. The fabric of her gown was thin enough to see through without the light; with it, nothing was hidden. He could see every line of her trim body—the slender hips, the swell of her breasts as she turned in silhouette. She danced over to him and stopped with her thighs brushing his knees. "Do you like it? Do you remember once you warned me not to stand before firelight?"

"Yes, I like it. And yes, I remember telling you that." He rose to his feet and took her by the waist, pulling her close and holding her against his chest. "You are teasing me, Katherine. Why? You are not normally one to play with fire."

"Is that what I'm doing? Playing with fire?"

"When you parade about half-naked before a man who loves you and has been denied you for months, yes, I would call that playing with fire, or at the very least tempting fate."

His lips took hers then and for long minutes only the ticking of the mantel clock and the crackling of the fire could be heard in the room. When she could speak again, Katherine said, "I saw the doctor today."

269

"And what did he say?"

"He said I am completely recovered and he has no plans to see me again. He said his time would be better spent visiting sick people." Then shyly, with her eyes cast down before his, she added, "He also said we should be able to have as many children as we want—beginning anytime we like."

As she finished he took her chin in his hand, forcing her to look at him. "Can you imagine the torture it's been for me all these weeks?" he asked. "Lying each night beside you, not trusting myself to touch you?"

"I don't have to imagine it, my love," she responded. "It has been the same for me."

He pulled her tightly against him and then rolled her over onto the bed. "My God, Katherine," he said passionately, "your doctor had best be right, for I promise you, I shall not use you lightly."

She smiled to herself at that. "Indeed, my lord, I hope not!"

Chapter 24

THE JOURNEY TO London was totally pleasurable. Rudley, Katherine, and the children all sat together in his lordship's traveling carriage. It was roomy and well-sprung and they passed the time chatting and gazing out the windows at the changing landscape.

A warm wind scuttled in from the southwest, raising the dust on the road and casting about the remains of last year's fallen leaves. The bare elm branches displayed dark pink blossoms; soon they would burst into green. The wild pear trees were already blooming, their flowers thick as snow on the branches. Numerous birds sheltered in the hedgerows where tiny clusters of pale leaves dotted the hawthorn. Robins, blackbirds, and thrushes flitted from tree to tree, preoccupied with nest building. The delightful song of the meadowlark mingled with the raucous call of the jay.

Rudley rarely traveled in a closed carriage, preferring to drive himself or ride whenever possible, but today he was disposed to be with Katherine. They sat close, sometimes holding hands, often smiling at each other for no apparent reason. They were acting much like a love-struck couple on their honeymoon. They looked as if they had a secret, private between the two of them, and indeed they had. They had made love into the early hours of the morning, and now they were remembering it and looking forward to the time when it would happen again. That was their secret, though perhaps not much of a secret, for lovers have always shared it. They were in a mood to be

271

pleased, and found themselves agreeing to almost anything the children suggested.

Pamela looked at Katherine's hand held lovingly in her father's and felt no jealousy of a child of her age in the present situation. She had liked Katherine from the beginning and had been grateful to her for bringing the earl home to live. She had always known her father was unhappy. But now with Katherine he was content, and in loving Katherine his capacity for love had increased to include her. Pamela no longer doubted her father's love for her.

They arrived in Cavendish Square in the afternoon. Katherine had been to Rudley House several times: for her first London party, for several family dinners preceding the wedding, and for the wedding breakfast itself. She had, however, seen little of the house on these occasions and was most anxious to tour it room by room.

When the butler offered to be her guide, Rudley left to call on his brother John. Not finding him at home, he went on to Brooks's, hoping to have better luck there. He encountered many of his acquaintance, but not John. Glancing through one room in the club, he noticed Oliver playing faro, which surprised him considerably, for Oliver never gambled—or at least he never used to.

Two days later, when Rudley announced that he would be occupied with business until after luncheon, Katherine finally found her opportunity to visit the earl's bankers. It was not customary for ladies to call upon bankers in the City, but in her own carriage, accompanied by her own servants, she knew there could be no question of impropriety. She ordered the town coach and was soon on her way.

It had not occurred to Katherine to involve anyone else in her plans. She would withdraw the money herself and then arrange to meet Lady Finley. That way there would be no chance that Rudley would learn of her activities. She had not anticipated, however, the reaction of his lordship's bankers. Kendall, with a good understanding of the earl's character and specific orders to obey, had not mentioned his conversation with Katherine to the earl. Rudley's bankers, however, were made distinctly uneasy by this unusual request for funds. They did not hesitate to honor Katherine's draft, for they did, after all, have Lord Rudley's authorization to do so. They felt no compunction, however, in mentioning the transaction to the earl, for he was a valuable client and one they would not happily lose. Even before Katherine had departed their establishment, a courteous and carefully worded note had been dispatched by hand to the earl's residence in Cavendish Square.

Rudley was in the library when the note arrived and Benson brought it directly to him. "A letter has been brought round, my lord, by hand." Rudley lifted it from the salver Benson presented. Breaking the seal, he quickly read the few lines.

"Her ladyship went out this morning, Benson?"

"Yes, my lord."

"Has she returned?"

"Not yet, my lord."

"When she does, ask her to join me here."

"Very good, my lord."

"That will be all, Benson, thank you." The butler turned to leave and Rudley lowered his eyes again to the note in his hand, as if it could offer him some further explanation. Katherine had withdrawn five thousand pounds! It was incredible! Why would she need such a huge sum of money? And, more to the point, why would she withdraw it without saying anything to him? He was not given much time to ponder these questions, for barely five minutes passed before Katherine returned home and joined him in the library.

"You wished to see me, Ned?" she asked as she entered the room.

"I didn't know you were going out this morning. You said nothing at breakfast."

"I had an errand to attend to," she said simply.

"What sort of errand?"

"Nothing that would interest you," she prevaricated.

"Did you order a new dress for the wedding?"

"I did that yesterday." She didn't want to deliberately lie to him, and she couldn't understand why he was belaboring the point.

"There is no need to dissimulate, Katherine. I know where you went this morning." She didn't see how that was possible, but from his tone she was inclined to believe him. He placed the note on the desk between them. "My bankers value my patronage. They were understandably concerned when you chose to circumvent me in a request for funds. May I have the money, please?"

She stared at him in stunned silence, feeling trapped and guilty. Then, reaching into her reticule, she drew out a neat packet of notes and held it out to him. When he made no effort to take it from her, she dropped it onto the desk.

He had not taken his eyes from her face and now, as she stood stiffly and silently, his voice softened as he continued, "Katherine, please. Sit down." He indicated a chair several feet to her right. Moving to it, she sat rigidly, folding her hands in her lap. He reseated himself behind the desk. "Katherine, I am not angry with you. I have only two questions. Why do you need such a large sum of money? And why could you not simply ask me for it?"

She glanced up briefly and he could see tears beginning in her eyes. She dropped her gaze quickly, without speaking.

"Come now, Katherine, we agreed we would have no more secrets. Is it Sir Humphrey?"

"No," she replied vehemently. "I have not heard from him. Besides, I would never give him a penny."

"Then why? I'm afraid I don't understand."

"I can't tell you why I need the money," she said finally, "and I didn't ask you for it because I knew you would not give it to me."

"Why do you say that?" he asked in surprise.

"Because I know you would disapprove of the use to which it is to be put."

He stared at her in amazement. "And this explanation is expected to satisfy me?"

She leaned forward, gripping the edge of the desk anxiously. "Ned, please, I need this money desperately! You must let me have it!"

"I may yet let you take it," he said, lifting the bank notes from the desktop, "but first you must tell me why you need it."

"I can't do that." She slumped back into her chair. She was defeated. She had failed Oliver and antagonized her husband in the process.

"So this is where the conversation ends," he said curtly. "You admit that I will not approve of your use of this money, yet you stick by your resolve to have it. Undoubtedly one of us is a fool, but at the moment I am unable to decide which." He held the notes out to Katherine. "Here, take your money and keep your secret." His tone was reproachful.

She looked up at him, her eyes wide with astonishment. "You will let me have it?"

"You have just said you need this money desperately. I would prefer to have you confide in me . . . but I will not leave you desperate."

She took the notes with a trembling hand. Then, no longer able to contain her tears, she managed a mumbled "Thank you" and fled.

That evening at dinner Rudley behaved as if nothing untoward had occurred between them. He was polite and solicitous, and his manner increased Katherine's remorse. She believed he had spoken no less than the truth when he said he was not angry with her. Yet when she retired, she knew she could not go to him, nor was she surprised when he did not come to her.

Early the following morning she dispatched a note to Lady Finley and within the hour had a reply. Meg would call that very morning, she said, and Katherine could entrust the money to her. According to schedule, the Countess Finley presented herself at Cavendish Square and conveniently found Katherine alone.

"I have never seen Oliver so keen as he is over this property," she declared, "unless you consider his captivation with your lovely friend." She smiled warmly at Katherine. She had been opposed to Ned's marriage initially, but she had been proven wrong and was more than willing to admit it.

"When I first offered Oliver the five thousand," she told Katherine, "he flatly refused it, saying Finley had no obligation to him. But eventually we convinced him to accept it as a loan. I insisted that Weiring was my mother's home as well, and I would be pleased to see him there. However, from what he tells me, the place is in great need of repair. The house and the land have both been shamefully neglected. I fear the renovations needed will be a great drain on Oliver's income. Don't mistake me, I cannot regret his acquiring the place. Indeed, I would not have helped you if I was not convinced that nothing short of Weiring would satisfy him. But if it proves to be more than he can handle, he will be risking his happiness, and I must admit I hate to see him gambling so."

Rudley entered the room at that moment and Lady Finley deftly turned the conversation, asking Katherine if they planned to attend the Seftons' ball on the following Friday. The final words of her last subject, however, had not escaped him.

"Serena will be there, but I shall be unable to go," Katherine answered. "The children and I are leaving early Saturday morning for Lincolnshire and will stay through the wedding."

"Yes, of course, I had forgotten you were going early," Meg replied, casting a scornful look at her eldest brother. "I take it you will not be gracing Oliver's wedding with your presence, Ned? I have been unable to pry one word from Oliver concerning this feud between the two of you, so I am certain it would be a waste of my time to attempt any explanation from you."

He raised one eyebrow, answering her with perfect civility. "Quite right, Meg."

"Permit me to say," she continued, "that I think you are acting like spoiled children. It is not enough that you are making each other miserable, but you must make life uncomfortable for the rest of us simply because we are unfortunate enough to love you both."

Katherine could have shouted "Bravo," for Lady Finley had the courage to voice what she herself had been thinking for weeks but had been afraid to say.

Rudley made no response to his sister's remark, but taking the poker instead, proceeded to replace a log that had rolled partially onto the hearth.

Lady Finley returned her attention to Katherine. "Well, my dear, I must be going. If I don't see you again before you go north, then I will see you at the wedding. Give my love to Charity." Katherine offered to escort her sister-in-law downstairs, and Rudley was left alone with his reflections.

What was it Meg had said? "I hate to see him gambling so." Was that it? Was Oliver gambling? Rudley could hardly credit it. Yet he himself had seen Oliver at the faro table only a few days ago. Had Oliver acquired debts? Surely he had not lost as much as five thousand pounds. And yet it would be an easy thing for a reckless, inexperienced player to do. Had his argument with his brother driven him to such a destructive pastime? If this were true, it would explain many things. If Katherine were seeking to pay Oliver's gambling debts, she would not apply directly to her husband for the money, for he would have refused her, as she had said he would. And if it were indeed a debt of honor, there was no denying it must be paid, hence Katherine's (or rather Oliver's) desperate need.

Rudley realized he had no facts upon which to base these conjectures, but if any portion of what he was thinking came anywhere close to the truth, then Meg's criticism was just. Katherine was caught in the middle—between her love for him and what she felt was her responsibility to help Oliver.

The thing that puzzled him most was how Katherine had become involved in the first place. Surely if Oliver had accumulated debts he would never have approached Katherine for assistance. She must have discovered his predicament some other way, perhaps through Charity. Rudley sighed. Whatever was happening, it was clear that no one had any plans to share it with him, and it was unlikely he would be able to uncover the facts even if he tried.

Determined, however, to at least make an attempt to come at the truth, Rudley set out for Brooks's. There, during a seemingly casual conversation with his brother's friend, Lord Everett, he learned that Oliver had only been watching the play that day and not himself participating. Having now had his carefully developed explanation for Katherine's strange behavior blown into pieces, Rudley was once again at a loss and admitted to himself that the only way he was likely to discover the whole story would be to wait, however impatiently, for his wife to explain.

Three days after her visit from Lady Finley, Katherine received the following note from Oliver:

Dear Katherine,

I have just finished with the lawyers, and everything is finalized. I am now a landowner! The previous owner has already vacated, so I am going down immediately to look things over. I am afraid Ned will not be best pleased to find we are neighbors, but Charity couldn't be happier.

Oliver

Katherine folded the note and laid it aside. The time had come for her to explain herself to her husband. Now that the sale was final and she was relatively certain there was nothing he could do to interfere, she must tell him how she had used his money and try to make him understand why she had done it. She was determined to speak to him at her first opportunity.

She was not destined to find that opportunity. Rudley was not home for dinner that evening and had still not returned by the time Katherine retired for the night. The following morning she had not yet risen from her bed when he came to her room to inform her that he was departing for Hampshire.

"Now?" she asked, for he was dressed for driving.

"Yes, why not? You are leaving tomorrow, and everything is in readiness for your journey. There is no reason for me to stay on in town. John will be escorting you to Harrington Manor, and you may rely upon him to take excellent care of you and the children. He has also volunteered to see you safely to Rudley Court after the wedding. I'm sorry if my absence will be an embarrassment to you. If anyone should mention it, you may tell them that urgent business has kept me away. They may or may not believe you, but no one would, we must hope, be ill-bred enough to pursue the subject."

"But must you leave immediately? There was something I particularly wished to discuss with you."

"You may have ten minutes, but no more, for Henderson is already walking the team. There is a sharp wind this morning."

Ten minutes! She could never manage to explain in such a short time. She briefly considered asking him to stable the horses but could see he was eager to be on his way. "Ten minutes will not suffice. We had best save it for another time."

She realized it would probably be best not to broach this particular subject just before they were to be separated for several weeks. There was a good chance Ned would be angry with her for her involvement in Oliver's affairs, and it would take time for her to fully explain her motives.

He sensed what he thought was her disappointment and offered generously, "Shall I stay?"

She made her decision. "No, go ahead, it will keep. Just remember I love you."

"I'm not likely to forget it," he said, and then, to her surprise, he leaned over the bed and kissed her long and

279

deeply. Straightening again, he said, "I'm off then. Have a safe journey and hurry home. I shall miss you, Katherine."

In a few moments he was gone, and for the rest of the day she wondered if she had made a mistake in not having him stay until her story was told.

Chapter 25

CHARITY AND OLIVER were married in the same church where Charity had been baptized. The wedding was simple and perfect. The church was full to overflowing with family, friends, and neighbors, and if Oliver was disappointed that his brother Edward had not stood up with him, he took care not to let it show.

Katherine and the children left Harrington Manor on the day following the wedding and took the better part of three days to return home. They spent one night on the road, one night in London, and arrived at Rudley Court early in the afternoon of the third day. Katherine had been away for nearly a month and separated more than two weeks from her husband. Her first view of the lake and the house beyond was a wonderful sight.

Alighting from the carriage, the children stopped briefly for a deferential hello to the earl, then were off, probably to recount their many adventures to whichever of the servants would be willing to listen. John stayed only long enough to partake of some light refreshment, insisting he had promised Fanny he would be home again that evening.

Alone in the blue drawing room, Rudley handed Katherine to a chair near the fire and went to pour her a glass of wine. For several minutes he made polite conversation concerning her journey and then continued in a matter-of-fact tone. "Nurse removed most of Nick's belongings to Weiring yesterday." Katherine looked up quickly and he could see that his news did not surprise her. "You knew Oliver had bought the old Ashley estate?"

"Yes, I knew," she said.

"Why do I get the feeling I helped him?"

"Your sister and I lied to him, Ned. We allowed him to think it was Lord Finley's money because we knew he would not have accepted it otherwise."

"How did he manage it?"

"He used all his accumulated income. He sold his black horse and his curricle team, and with the five thousand from me he had enough."

"You amaze me! But tell me. How does he plan to make improvements there? The place has been neglected for years."

"I suppose he plans to do so slowly, as he is able."

"Then it will take him a lifetime, for there will be numerous and continuous expenses."

"He wanted the property desperately, Ned. I'm sure he knows it will be hard."

"Yes. I distinctly remember your use of the word *desperate* in describing your need for the money."

"Would you have given it to me if I had told you why I wanted it?" she asked.

"Probably not. So, you see, you were right not to tell me."

"Why *did* you give me the money, Ned?"

"I'm not sure, but I suppose it was because I have a difficult time denying you anything."

"And why is that?"

"Because I love you to distraction."

"And can you tell me you don't love your brother?"

After a slight pause he said, "You know very well I can't tell you that."

"Then, please, Ned, ask him to explain. Don't let this estrangement drag on month after month, as it did with us."

His brows drew together sharply. He walked away and stood with his back to her. Several minutes passed before he spoke again. "I'm doing the same thing again, aren't I?" he asked. "Judging without hearing the defense. It seems I cannot learn from my mistakes."

"You have been repeatedly hurt by people you trusted," she said. "It is not remarkable that you react so. You have stopped allowing yourself to trust your heart and will allow only a calculating brain to rule you. It is perhaps the safest way to live, but certainly not the most rewarding. In my case, and in Oliver's too, you reacted impulsively, turning a deaf ear to what your heart was telling you. You said once that you could not bring yourself to hate me as you had hated Arabella. That was because in your heart you knew I truly loved you, as you know Oliver does."

He came across the room to her and took both her hands in his, raising them to his lips. "My clever wife! What did I ever do to deserve you?"

He took her into his arms then and held her close and she knew he had finally overcome his bitterness. She hoped he would see Oliver now and perhaps hear his explanation. If he could bring himself to do that much, she was convinced that the love they bore for each other would do the rest.

Two days later Rudley drove to London. He was gone three days, and when he arrived home again, he found that Katherine and Pamela had gone riding. He had Navigator saddled and rode out toward the footbridge in the woods. He had not been there since the day he had left Katherine, but now as he rode down to the stream, he found there were no memories of Arabella to haunt him. He splashed through the water without stopping and cantered up the far bank through a carpet of bluebells, then on through the woods to the west, to Weiring.

Rudley pulled his horse up at the edge of the trees as Oliver had done not so many weeks before. He had not been in the house since before his mother's death. It looked much the same as it always had from the outside, except that the lawns and garden had been permitted to grow wild. Shrubberies had gone untrimmed, and the ivy that clung to the stone walls had crept over the windows.

He drew a deep, resolute breath. What he was about to do would not be easy for him. He prayed for a portion of Katherine's capacity for understanding as he trotted Navigator up to the house. He dismounted, then tied the horse to the stone balustrade running the length of the veranda. The door was opened by Charity.

"My lord Rudley! How good it is to see you."

He smiled at her, realizing that despite all that had happened, her greeting was sincere. "Please, Charity, we must not be so formal. We are brother and sister now."

"Yes, of course. Won't you come in?"

They walked together to a small salon on the ground floor before he asked, "Is Oliver here? If he is, I would like to speak with him."

"Yes, he is home. If you will wait here, I will go and find him."

He started to say she should not trouble herself and he would find Oliver himself, but she was already gone. So he waited, gazing around the familiar room his grandmother had called the parlor.

He walked to the handsome fireplace, crafted, like the house itself, from local stone. He could remember as a child sitting near the heat of a roaring fire while his grandmother read him fairy tales of dragons, brave princes, and damsels in distress. He had always thought the fireplace enormous; it didn't seem so now. He picked up a curiously wrought gold-enameled snuffbox from the mantel, recognizing it as one his father had given Oliver years before. He still had it in his hand when the door opened behind him and Oliver entered.

Rudley turned and they stood facing each other, the entire width of the room between them. For several moments neither spoke, nor did either look away. Finally Rudley shifted his gaze to the snuffbox in his hand and he was the first to speak. "I have not seen this for years. It belonged to Grandfather, did it not?"

"Yes, I believe so."

"I am pleased that you should be established here, Oliver."

"I had convinced myself that you would be most displeased."

"Oliver, there is something I must say to you. I would like you to listen and when I have finished, I would like to hear your story concerning Arabella—the simple truth, with no holds barred, and no effort to spare my feelings. And when you have finished, regardless of what you tell me, I want to bury the memory of Arabella and her influence over us forever. Do you agree?"

Oliver nodded his assent but did not speak. He went to pour some brandy and brought his brother a glass.

Taking the brandy, Rudley moved to stand by the windows, allowing his gaze to roam over the park. His thoughts, however, were far from the pleasant prospect that presented itself. "All our lives, as you know, there has been a unique bond between us. We are brothers, yes, and I will admit the tie of blood is a strong one; but there was always something more, an inexplicable hold we had upon each other, a sensitivity only we shared. At each time of crisis in our lives, we were there for each other. When we were boys and you would have drowned in the lake, I was there to pull you to safety; and in Spain you searched acres of dead and dying men to find me and keep me from bleeding to death. These things, and dozens of others, are all part of the trust and faith we have shared."

Rudley turned to face his brother as he continued. "These past ten years I have had an unwavering regard for you and nothing but contempt for the man who fathered Pamela. When I learned you were that man, I could not reconcile the two feelings. In my eyes you were not worthy, had never been worthy, of the trust I had placed in you. So I struck back in the way I hoped would hurt you most—by breaking all ties between us. But in my heart I have always known, and Katherine has forced me to admit, that bonds so strong and binding are not so easily severed. I was wrong to strike you that day, and I apologize. I was even more wrong in thinking I could cut you from my life—for I cannot, nor do I wish to. Can you forgive me for treating you as I did?" He held out his hand to his brother and Oliver stepped forward willingly to take it in a firm clasp.

"I forgive you freely, as I hope you will forgive me when you have heard my part in all this." Oliver evidently preferred to tell his story sitting, for he crossed to an armchair by the fire, folded his long body into it, and propped his booted feet upon the footstool before him. He gently swirled the brandy in his glass. "I met Arabella almost four months before you did. I was just turned twenty, as you know, and my head was full of romantic folly. You remember what she was like: men ten deep around her, a face like an angel. I thought her incomparable, utterly adorable. We were in love, or so I thought at the time, and within a few weeks I had asked her to marry me and she had accepted."

Rudley frowned at this, for of all the things he had suspected, this had not been one of them.

Oliver continued. "Now you are thinking, If there was an engagement, why was it not announced? You may recall that Arabella's father was out of the country at the time. We were both under age, and we had to wait until the duke returned in order to make proper application for his permission.

"We were spending the weekend as guests of Lord and Lady Grafton when Arabella showed up in my bedchamber in the middle of the night. I should have sent her away immediately, but I was not so wise in those days, and I let her stay. We found a few similar opportunities during the next several weeks to be together.

"Then enter my brother, the dashing Earl of Rudley. I barely had time to be jealous of the way you looked at her when she told me she would have to break her engagement to me, for she planned to marry you instead. I don't know whether you had already asked for her hand, but in any case she must have been very certain of you. I was, of course, flabbergasted, and I asked her how she could marry you if she loved me. She said she had misunderstood her feelings for me and although she was fond of me, it was you she loved. That was the only time in my life, Ned, that I truly hated you! You, and your damned title, and your damned wealth! For even though she said it was not so, I knew those things had influenced her."

"Why didn't you tell me?" Rudley broke in. "If I had known the two of you had had an understanding, I would never have interfered."

"By the time I realized what was happening it was already too late. When I had overcome my anger for you, and for her as well, you had already announced your engagement. Her vacillating feelings filled me with foreboding, but I knew if I spoke against her I would only sound like a bitter, rejected suitor. Somewhere, in the back of my mind, I thought that if you truly loved her and could bring out the best in her, the two of you would be happy together. Of course, at that time I had no idea how spoiled she was, how selfish and deceitful she could be. I thought her only young and fickle. I knew you so well, Ned. I could see you loved her beyond anything, and I thought that if she loved you as she said she did there would be no point in my standing in your way. So, I said nothing, a decision I tried to make in your best interest, and that I have regretted ever since."

Oliver dropped his feet from the stool and leaned forward, setting his brandy aside.

"When you told me shortly after your marriage that Arabella was increasing, I knew I had failed you, but I didn't see what purpose would be served by telling you that she and I had been intimate. For the first time it occurred to me that I may not have been the only man she had been with. So I decided to await developments.

"When I saw Pamela shortly after her birth, I could tell nothing. The next time I saw her she was nearly three. Lydia and I had been married more than a year. When I saw Pamela, I was shocked by her appearance. She looked so much like Father. I couldn't believe you did not see the resemblance. I wanted to tell you then, because there was no longer the slightest doubt in my mind that she was mine, but Arabella was a bit too clever for me. She guessed my intention and practiced a little blackmail—only one of her many talents. For some reason she preferred to keep you in the dark about Pamela's paternity."

"She knew I was determined to know the man's identity,"

Rudly said, "and she did everything possible in those days to thwart me."

"That would certainly be consistent with her other behavior. She warned me that if I made any move to tell you about Pamela, she would go straight to Lydia and fill her ears with stories of how I had conducted myself as her lover. I could not doubt she would do it, Ned, and I could not take the chance. Lydia's happiness was more important to me than making a confession to you that could, after all, change nothing. I must admit, however, to wondering why Arabella never told you herself. Certainly if she wanted to wound you, causing a rift between us would have served her purpose admirably."

"She probably guessed we would unite against her eventually," Rudley answered. "She undoubtedly felt she had more to gain by keeping me in the dark and using her secret as a lever against you whenever the opportunity arose."

"She certainly did that—and the best is yet to come! When Lydia died, Arabella had the gall to tell me that I need not even consider going to you with my story or she would tell *Pamela* that you were not her father and I was!"

"Good God!" Rudley exclaimed. "Was nothing sacred to her?"

"It seems not. So you and I took off for Spain and Arabella was left at home with Pamela. Still I could say nothing. During those next two years we learned a great deal—particularly how fragile life could be. We both changed a lot, I think, but me most of all.

"By the time Arabella died, I found I had changed my own mind about telling you. We had come home from the war in one piece, even though it had almost killed you. The wife I had loved and the wife you had despised were both gone. I'd had enough of death and pain and desolation. I knew if I told you I was Pamela's father there would be new wounds and new pain and more remembrances of a time best forgotten. I also felt that if you had not seen the resemblance in six years, you would probably never see it. So the secret was mine alone, and I chose to keep it.

"For myself, I wanted to tell the world that Pamela was mine, but I knew there was no way I could acknowledge her without ruining her life. I thought if I could keep the peace with you, even if it meant keeping such a painful secret, then I could stay close to her, if not as a father, then as a loving uncle. Until you knocked me down that day, I hadn't realized the wound was still so fresh for you. I should have told you sooner; I regret now that I didn't. But you're right about the influence Arabella still holds over us, Ned. She's been dead more than five years and still she manipulates our lives—yours, mine, Pamela's, even Katherine's."

"No! No longer," Rudley replied. "Katherine and I have removed Arabella from our lives, and you and I are doing the same today. We are placing the last shovel of dirt upon the grave, and she and her wickedness will be gone forever. Pamela will always be welcome and loved in my home, and when we feel she is old enough to understand, we will tell her who her true father is. Now, enough of these maudlin thoughts. Let us speak of more pleasant things, shall we?"

"Then you are declaring a truce between us, Ned?"

"Yes, indeed. A truce that will, we hope, last a lifetime. I have, however, one more apology to make. I am more sorry than I can say that I missed your wedding. As some slight reparation, I have brought you a gift." He drew a small packet of papers from the inner pocket of his coat and handed it to his brother.

"What is this?" Oliver asked, puzzled.

"The one on top you should certainly recognize. It is the note you gave Finley against his loan of five thousand pounds, which was really a loan from Katherine, disguised to make you accept it. The second is, I believe, the bill of sale for your curricle team. When I recall how painstakingly we searched to find four horses so closely matched, I don't know how you even considered selling them. The third is for your black. That one was by far the hardest to come by, for the new owner was more than happy with his purchase. He could not hold out against me, however, when I told him that I had bred the horse myself, that he had been a present from me to you, and that only dire necessity had made you part with him.''

Oliver, too startled by his brother's words to say anything, stared at him incredulously as Rudley continued, ''The last is a draft on my bankers for an additional ten thousand, to be used at your discretion to put this house to rights and improve the estate. It can be a profitable property if handled wisely.''

Finding his voice at last, Oliver stammered, ''But . . . Ned . . . I—I don't know what to say to you.''

'' 'Thank you' will be sufficient.''

''But you don't understand. I could not possibly accept all this as a gift from you! It's too much! You must allow me to pay you back—''

''Pay me back? Don't you realize, Oliver, if you had not risked your own life to drag me off that rotting battlefield, everything I now have would be yours? I will not listen to any nonsense about repayment. Being the head of the family does not mean sitting upon a pedestal, hoarding the wealth, and allowing those you love to struggle when you have the means to help them. You will accept this gift as it is offered you, or I very much fear we shall be at loggerheads again.''

Oliver knew his brother well enough to know when he would not be moved. He recognized that stubbornness now, so he smiled and admitted defeat.

''Very well, then, I will say thank you from both Charity and myself, and from our children, who will grow up calling this house their home.''

''And don't forget Mother. How pleased she would be if she knew her home was in the family again!''

''I'm not forgetting her. It was she who taught me to love this place. And I won't soon forget your generosity, Ned. You are the best brother any man could have—and the truest friend.''

A light breeze played through the open casements of Pamela's sitting room, setting the curtains billowing. Bright summer sunlight splashed across the polished wooden floor.

Katherine and Rudley stood before an easel, studying Pamela's most recent painting.

"She has captured it exactly, don't you think?" Katherine asked.

"Yes. It's excellent—and not a particularly easy subject."

The setting of the oil was a large loose box in the stable. The floor was deeply bedded with yellow straw. The central figures were Lady Halfmile and her new filly, born on the Ides of March and nicknamed, appropriately, Ides. The mare stood with her head craned around and her nose just a fraction from her foal, checking to be sure all was well. The foal stood, too, but not expertly. Seemingly too-long legs were spread at random, seeking the proper balance points.

"Pamela has shown that one aspect of a newborn foal that makes it unique."

"The wobbliness," Rudley supplied.

"Yes. A motion, a way of moving. And she has put that motion onto this still medium. It is quite remarkable."

"I have sent several of her pieces out for framing," he said. "I thought we would hang them in the picture gallery."

"What a wonderful idea! Was she pleased?"

"I haven't told her yet. I thought we could surprise her."

"There was something else about Pamela I wanted to discuss with you, Ned. I have been thinking that she has long outgrown these rooms. Do you suppose she might like to move into the suite next to ours? The rooms are larger than these and have a lovely view of the lake. She could take a hand in redecorating them; she would enjoy that, I think."

"I have no objection. If she wants the rooms, she is welcome to them."

"Good. Then, once she moves out of here, would you mind if I spent some time redecorating these rooms?"

"Why should you want to redecorate these?"

"They were a nursery once. I thought they would serve well again in that capacity."

"Why should . . ." He took her shoulders and turned her to face him. "Why should we need a redecorated nursery?"

"Why does anyone need a nursery, my love?"

Rudley drew his wife into his arms and kissed her long and passionately. He didn't hear the door open behind them, nor did he see Pamela's blushing face as she quickly turned and left the room again, quietly closing the door behind her.

More Romance from Regency